Operation Grouse

A Political Thriller

Robert FHC Turner

Pen Press Publishers
London

First published in Great Britain by
Pen Press Publishers Ltd
39-41 North Road
Islington
London N7 9DP

ISBN 1-900796-04-X

A catalogue record for this book is available from
the British Library

Cover design by Bridget Tyldsley

I dedicate this book to my wife Daphne, whose faith never wavered. Also to my twin brother, who would be David John. He never quite touched this earthly plane.

To my friend Patrick Barnard, the Basildon based medium. He predicted everything but the timing of this publication.

My heartfelt thanks to Michael and Hazel for their kindness to my wife and myself.

We also extend our thanks to Brian Woods for his unstinting kindness.

And last but not least, our intrepid aviator, John Studd. Thank you John.

Robert FHC Turner

CONTENTS

CHAPTER ONE
THE LETTER

The right honourable Henry Beddows PM processed the last document concerning affairs of the state, pressed the button on his intercom and spoke into it. 'John, a nice cup of tea please, and bring in my morning mail.'

'On my way, Prime Minister,' was the crisp reply. A click and the intercom went dead.

A few minutes later, John Deeman, private secretary and close confidant to the PM for many years, entered the room with a silver tray complete with matching teapot, sugar bowl and milk jug. He laid these on the table especially cleared by his friend to accommodate them. The PM immediately reached for the pot to do the honours.

'What have we this morning, John?' Beddows murmured with just a passing glance at the thick bundle of mail in Deeman's hand; his mind was concentrating more on the teapot.

'The usual stuff, Henry,' John replied, 'although there is one letter here that doesn't fit the usual pattern.'

'Let me see it.' Beddows took the letter from Deeman's hand and turned it over. 'No return address.' He sounded bemused. Then he looked at the front of the envelope and noted the posted postmark: August 9th 4pm. 'Strange, this letter is addressed to *The Prime Minister, 10 Downing Street*, and nothing else.' He looked up sharply. 'Has it been scanned?'

'I presume it has, all your letters have been since that bomb scare a few weeks ago, Henry,' John replied somewhat cautiously.

Beddows studied the letter intently for another minute, back and front, before picking up the paper-knife. 'Better open it, I suppose.' He gingerly inserted the sharp edge under the folded flap of the envelope. His lips tightened involuntarily as he very, very gently slit open the letter, closing his eyes as he did so ...

There was no explosion.

He realised that he had been holding his breath and exhaled slowly, hoping his friend had not noticed the tension in him. He inserted two fingers inside the envelope and pulled out a single folded piece of paper. He opened it, read it, frowned and read it again.

'Is this some sort of a joke, John?' he asked without lifting his eyes from the letter.

Sensing the change in Beddow's tone and general attitude, Deeman once more replied cautiously, 'A joke, Prime Minister?'

Beddows studied his secretary for a few seconds. 'Your face tells me that if it is, it's none of your doing.' His eyes dropped once more to the paper. 'Listen to this:

My Dear Prime Minister,

Forgive me for remaining anonymous for the time being at least, but I have a simple demand that I hope you will experience little difficulty in complying with at this time. It is my intention to kidnap the Lady Alison, Countess of Westminster.

You can, however, forestall this act of abduction by having delivered to me the sum of one million pounds sterling, in a manner made known to you by my good self in due course.

Please, do not treat this demand as a hoax because it is not, I can assure you. In truth, fact can be stranger than fiction, so please believe me when I tell you that the abduction of the Lady Alison will be simplicity itself, in spite of any preventative measures you may introduce to thwart such an act.

Act wisely, Prime Minister, after all, by the time you have read this epistle, she could be gone.

You will hear from me in due course.'

Beddows looked up at John and offering the letter to his friend said, 'What do you make of that?'

Deeman took the proffered letter and read it through two, three times, not knowing quite what to make of it. He frowned and quietly replied, 'If this is for real, we have problems, Henry.'

'Yes, I can see that,' Henry replied, 'more problems than you can envisage, my friend.'

'How so?'

'Well now, let's just imagine that she *has* been kidnapped; you can also picture us permanently incarcerated in the tower for allowing it to happen in the first place.'

He studied his desk top, deep in thought, and after a while he spoke quietly. 'John, we'd better treat this thing carefully, just in case this fellow is serious. We may or may not look like prize jackasses eventually, but better to be safe than sorry, I suppose.' And with the air of a man who had made up his mind, he got to his feet briskly. 'Get me Donald Matlock on the phone.' He paused, then added, 'Top priority' Sir Donald Matlock was Chief of the Metropolitan Police.

John went to the phone, dialled a number and waited. He didn't have to wait very long; this was a direct line to Matlock's office. 'Hello, Sir Donald, I have the Prime Minister for you.'

Beddows took the phone, 'Donald, we may or may not have ourselves a little problem. I can't really discuss it over the phone, can you come over as quick as you can? Yes, I'll be in my private office ... Within the hour then.'

He replaced the phone, walked over to the window and looked out. Absently, he reached into his jacket pocket for his tobacco pouch and pipe, filled the latter automatically and lit it with care.

'John,' he said quietly over his shoulder, 'I have a bad feeling over this and I wouldn't mind betting the crown jewels that things will get worse.'

CHAPTER TWO
SEND FOR MACDONALD

Sir Donald Matlock was ushered into the Prime Minister's office and was greeted with a handshake.

'Glad you could make it so quickly, Donald. Would you like some tea, or something a little stronger?' was the PM's welcome.

'Tea will be fine, Prime Minister,' Sir Donald grinned, 'but first, what's this little problem you want me to solve?'

Beddows handed him the letter with the envelope. Sir Donald caught the seriousness of the moment and the grin faded from his face. He read the letter through and through, then looked up slowly, his face reflecting mixed feelings.

'When did this arrive, Sir?'

'In this morning's post bag, through the normal channels,' the PM replied.

'I see,' mused Sir Donald. 'So what do you think, Sir? A joke or a crank maybe?' He paused and furrowed his brow in thought. 'It just might be the IRA or some extremist group.'

'Why do you think that?'

'Because whoever wrote this letter is either off his or her rocker or they really think it can be done, security or no security. I think we had better treat this thing seriously.' Sir Donald sounded worried.

'There's something else too, Donald,' said the PM. 'Hoax or not this has got to be handled very very quietly, with kid gloves, so to speak. After all, the Countess hasn't been kidnapped yet, although she will have to be told.' He shook his head slowly and added, 'How do you tell someone they are about to be abducted at some future date, yet to be given?' He threw his arms into the air in a despairing gesture. 'This whole thing is bloody ludicrous!'

He sat down at his desk searching his mind for inspiration, but none came. Finally he spoke. 'Can you picture it, Donald, can you really picture this whole silly situation? Here we are with a demand for one million pounds just to avert an abduction that we don't even know is going to happen, yet we dare not ignore it. I feel as if I'm sitting on a bomb, blindfold, with a fuse I know not how long and what's more, I don't know if the fuse has been lit!'

Sir Donald sighed. 'I think I will have that drink after all, Sir, I'm beginning to get the same picture as you.'

He poured them both a double scotch and water, handed one to the PM and said: 'You know, Sir, there are not many people in this country, the whole world even, who can put the wind up the Government's top gun *and* the Chief of Police, but I think this fellow has managed to do just that.' He raised his glass. 'A toast to the double-dyed twit, whoever he is. May he turn somersaults and disappear up his own exhaust pipe.'

The PM grinned ruefully, 'Hear hear, say I, because if he doesn't, you and I had better do the same thing.'

'A sobering thought, Sir,' agreed Sir Donald. 'I think we had better inform the Home Secretary. Between the three of us we should kick about a few ideas, then maybe we can stifle this little idea before it can get airborne. Oh, and while we're about it, I think we had better send for Macdonald.'

'Yes, I agree,' said the Prime Minister.

CHAPTER THREE
JOHN MACDONALD MEETS JANET STEWERT

Detective Inspector John Macdonald stood six feet one and a half inches tall in his socks and weighed thirteen and a half stone. He had brown hair which tended to curl slightly and his eyes were blue. The damage done to them by powder burns from a revolver could not be detected, but this close encounter with death had resulted in his need to wear spectacles for small print. None of his other faculties had been affected, however, and his approach to his job, coupled with successful 'results', ensured his continuing presence in the police force.

He had started his career in Aberdeen and done his stint as a wooden top before getting transferred to the Gorbals in Glasgow. It was there, in the police canteen, that he had literally bumped into one Sergeant Janet Mary Stewert, spilling his tea down her smart uniform.

Startled, he began a most profuse apology. Their eyes met and he never finished it (at least, to this day, he cannot remember whether he did or not). The chemical composition that attracts people to each other surpassed its own formula on this particular occasion because suddenly for both of them nothing else existed except for that very special magic moment.

They became almost inseparable from then on and within three months of meeting, they were married with the blessing of the Chief Constable.

That was all of twelve years ago. They had their first child, a girl, within a year and named her Jennifer, Jenny for short. Eighteen months later Jan produced a little boy, Ian.

Jan had resigned from the Force when her pregnancy made work a burden and thus Glasgow Police lost the best data analyst they had ever had, although she did it strictly unofficially at home for her husband.

John and Jan still adored each other and their children.

Contentment was the keynote of their home, though their lives were far from humdrum. Because of the nature of her husband's job, Jan could never tie down mealtimes unless he phoned home; the result was often a race to see which got to the table first, John or his meal. Sometimes she won, sometimes she lost. This time she lost.

She heard his key in the lock of the front door first, then the familiar 'thunk' as the lock pall retreated from its tight seclusion in the door jamb. She sensed rather than heard the front door opening as the outside sounds increased for a few moments and then receded, accompanied by that familiar voice.

'Darling, I'm home.'

Jan sighed and smiled wryly. Once again she had managed to come second.

They met halfway down the hall and kissed each other lovingly. 'Hello sweetheart,' he said.

'Hello yourself,' she replied, smiling up at him. 'You've caught me on the hop, you great lump ...'

She got no further as he grabbed her round the waist and pulled her towards him. 'You'll do for now,' he growled and made a dive for her neck with his teeth.

She squealed in mock horror, both hands pushing at his chest as she cottoned on to his carnal motive. She glanced quickly at the clock.

'Oh no you don't,' she said, disappointment in her voice. 'The bairns will be home from school any moment now.'

He sighed. 'Pity.'

She hugged him close to her, nuzzled his nose with her own and gave him a coy, seductive look. 'If you've been a good boy all day and be a good boy now and help me do some vegetables for dinner, I'll put you on a promise for tonight, sweetie.'

His eyes twinkled. 'OK, you're on, just let me get my coat off and I'll be right with you.'

'Away with you and sit down, love,' she laughed. 'Dinner won't be more than twenty minutes. Go on, sit.'

He grinned, kissed her and obeyed. They played this game more often than not and more often than not, dinner came second. But not this time.

The children rolled in from school at ten past four and

pandemonium reigned for about five minutes as they argued which programme was going to grace the television screen, eventually plumping for Blue Peter.

The meal over, the family had just settled down in comfort in front of the telly when the phone rang. John sighed as he got up from his seat.

'It's probably for me, HQ or Smithy.' Sergeant Tom Smith had been John's personal assistant for four years.

He picked up the receiver and spoke. 'Macdonald ... Oh, hello, Sir.' He looked at Jan and mouthed: 'The chief.' He listened intently for a couple of minutes, then said, 'Right, Sir, I'm on my way ... that's OK, Sir, all part of the job. I'll be as quick as I can.'

As he replaced the receiver he turned to Jan. 'Sorry love, there's a bit of a flap on at the Yard.'

Jan sighed and thought, 'Here we go again.' But aloud she said, 'Never mind, darling, it must be important to recall you so soon. Have you any idea what the flap is about?'

'You mean what time will I be home?' he grinned at her.

'Something like that,' she smiled coyly.

John got the message rapidly. 'ASAP and I do mean as soon as soon as possible, but erm ... well, the Chief seems to be in a right old state, judging from the tone of his voice. He wouldn't tell me what it was over the phone, only that it was urgent. So don't bank on me being back too soon, love.'

Jan just nodded. 'I'll get your hat and coat, sweetie. You'd better say goodnight to Jenny and Ian now ...'

She fetched his coat and helped him on with it. John turned to the children, 'OK, you two, give us a kiss in case you're in bed when I get back.'

Jenny and Ian tore themselves away from the telly just long enough to give their dad a kiss, then practically forgot all about him as the programme reclaimed their interest. John and Jan smiled affectionately at their children, then at each other. At the front door, John opened it, kissed his wife and said, 'See you later love' as he walked to his car.

Jan watched him drive away. 'At least he has a hot meal inside him,' she thought, then she frowned. 'It must be something big to call him out so soon after his shift ended.' She shrugged her shoulders, went inside and shut the door.

CHAPTER FOUR
GETTING A TEAM TOGETHER

August 10th, noon. In the private office at No 10 Downing Street, four men were in earnest conference: the Chief Constable, Sir Donald Matlock; the Home Secretary, the Honourable David Hurst; the Right Honourable Henry Beddows, Prime Minister; and Detective Inspector John (Mac) Macdonald. CID (Met).

They had dissected and studied the demand note at great length and were about to embark on a course of action.

'Right, gentlemen,' began the PM, 'we've been kicking this thing about long enough and we're no nearer a solution.' He stopped to fill his pipe. 'Any suggestions, anyone?' His enquiring glance scanned their faces one after the other.

'Yes, Prime Minister, I have one.' It was the Chief Constable who spoke.

'Yes, Chief, and what would that be?'

'I'd like a certain Professor Hasketh to examine the letter, Sir,' said the chief.

'Professor Hasketh?'

'He's a graphologist, a handwriting expert,' the Chief continued. 'A handwriting expert with a difference.'

'Oh! How do you mean, Donald?' The PM was curious.

'Professor Hasketh can read a person's character from their handwriting better than anyone I know; he's helped us enormously in the past.'

'Sounds good to me,' the PM nodded. 'Everyone in agreement?'

They all nodded acquiescence.

'Right then, first things first. I'll get in touch with Hamilcourt House - quietly, of course - and see that the Countess is forewarned. And get hold of her list of engagements for the next few weeks.'

'Good idea, Sir,' said the chief. 'If we can get her to cancel all her engagements the kidnapper will have to abduct her from her residence and that should make our surveillance a dam sight simpler.'

9

'That's what worries me,' said the Home Secretary. 'Her engagements, I mean.'

'How's that, Sir?' Mac asked respectfully.

'She's headstrong, stubborn, I don't think she'll cancel. If I know the Countess, she'll look upon it as her duty to attend, threat or no threat.'

'What about the Earl, Sir, surely ...' Mac began.

'He's in Scotland for the Glorious Twelfth which, I may add, he wouldn't miss for all the tea in China. What's more, he'll stay to the end, he always does,' said the PM. 'Lady Alison hates blood sports or killing of any kind and they clash frequently over his 'lust for blood', as she calls it. And that information, gentlemen, is strictly confidential and must go no further than these four walls, clear?'

The three men nodded.

The PM turned his attention to Macdonald. 'I want you to form a team, just in case, Macdonald, just three or four men plus yourself. Swear them to secrecy, threaten them with the Official Secrets Act if need be, but they must understand that Mum's officially the word, understand?'

'Yes, Sir, what do you want us to do?'

'Keep an around-the-clock watch on the Countess and don't let her know that you're about,' replied the PM.

'How do we keep out of sight if we're on the inside, Sir?' Mac was puzzled.

'You won't be on the inside for a start,' said the PM, 'because she won't allow her personal bodyguard inside the front door. She only tolerates them for the sake of the Royal Family, and her husband of course, but once inside that front door ... that's it.'

'Forgive me, Sir,' said Mac, 'but that's just Jim Dandy. We shall have to rewrite the police manual on undercover surveillance in the open air.'

'Come, come, Mac, it can be done, you know,' the Chief said scornfully. 'Have you seen the grounds of Hamilcourt House? It's surrounded by walls eight feet high *and* the grounds are thick with trees and shrubs. I think you'll find a few old huts as well as a groundsman's lodge. I'm sure you'll find a way to keep an eye on her.'

Mac groaned inwardly as he envisaged long lonely hours hiding in bushes and sheds full of spiders, compared to the comfort of his own home ... He sighed, resigned now to his lot, then said with an enthusiasm he did not feel, 'We'll damn well give it a try, Sir.'

'Good man.'

'Well, I don't think anything will happen for the next few days,' said the Home Secretary. 'This madman, whoever he is, is bound to give us time to organise our thoughts on this, if only to scrape the money together. His letter did mention time and place so we do have a bit of leeway to get things going.'

'Quite so, quite so, yes I agree.' The PM nodded his head rapidly. 'I think we should sleep on it tonight and get things moving in the morning.' He rose to his feet and everybody followed suit.

The police Chief turned to Mac. 'Contact me first thing in the morning and we'll get a plan together. We'll need a code word, of course.'

'Ah yes, of course,' the PM butted in. 'Any ideas, anyone?'

Mac grinned ruefully. 'How about Operation Lame Duck, 'cause that's how I feel right at this moment, Sir.'

The PM chortled. 'That's a good one, Mac, but it's been used recently on another job and, considering the secrecy of this operation, if we use it again over the airwaves, there may be some confusion.'

'Could well be, Sir,' Mac had to agree.

The Home Secretary suddenly snapped his fingers and said, 'By George, I think I have it!' He sat up, warming to the theme now. 'How does Operation Grouse sound to you? You know, royal implications and all that, yes?'

'Brilliant,' said the Chief after a few moments' thought.

'Oh absolutely,' agreed the PM.

'That sounds about right to me,' said Mac. 'Yes, spot on.'

The Home Secretary beamed at his own brilliance and basked in what he took to be admiring looks from the other three men.

'Pompous ass,' thought the PM.

Bloody clot,' thought the chief.

'What a twit,' thought Mac.

'That's settled then,' said the Home Secretary with a self-congratulatory sigh.

'Right, that's it then,' the PM confirmed, 'Operation Grouse it shall be.'

'All that leaves now is communication with each other,' said Mac.

'Yes, yes there is that small detail to attend to,' put in the Chief hurriedly, just as the Home Secretary was about to put in his two pennyworth. 'Hand sets, the pocket size ones, set on a tight wavelength.'

'That's more or less what I had in mind,' said the Home Secretary with a slightly injured air.

'I'll lay it on,' said the Chief. 'We're also going to need video cameras fitted with special zoom lenses, infra red light etc.'

'Cameras, infra red?' queried the Home Secretary. 'Why do you ...?'

'For the darkness, Sir,' Mac broke in. 'If the Countess is got at, Heaven forbid, we shall want faces to look at, see who got close and such. Of course, we mustn't let anything happen, but if it did ...'

Ah yes, of course,' the Home Secretary nodded, now fully aware of his obviously stupid gaff and kicking himself inwardly.

The PM smoothly polished over the Home Secretary's embarrassment. 'That's what policemen are for, David, they are trained for situations like this and they have to be clued up on all the latest technology. I think you and I would need a cape and a phone box each to change our clothes in if we had their jobs.' He smiled at the now placated Home Secretary, then gave his attention to the others.

'Anything else, any more questions ... no? Right then, off you go, gentlemen, get a good night's sleep and we'll get a good nights sleep, then we'll get the show on the road first thing.'

CHAPTER FIVE
THE EARL AND COUNTESS OF WESTMINSTER

August 10th was an important day in the lives of the Earl and Countess of Westminster. It heralded a blazing row between them, as it had every year of their married life.

Blood sports was the bone of contention that could never be resolved. The Earl, whose ancestry could be traced back to the Norman Conquest, was steeped in tradition. He had grown up in a world of fox-hunting, deer-shooting, badger-baiting and pheasant-shooting.

Today, he was due to drive up to Scotland for the grouse shoot as he did every year. From a sense of duty, he always asked his wife to join him, knowing full well that she would flatly refuse and rebuke him.

In what was now a yearly ritual, she would at first plead with him not to go. He would bluntly refuse and for the next half hour or so, the argument would rage back and forth with no ground gained on either side.

The Earl knew the form inside out and backwards, so he always timed his approach close to his intended departure for the north, usually at ten o'clock in the morning. After the feud, Alison would always walk in the spacious grounds of Hamilcourt House to calm her nerves. She hated, abhorred blood sports of any kind. The thought of killing anything made her physically ill. Yet she loved her husband very much and he loved her equally.

'Oh, my darling!' she sighed to herself, sadly shaking her head. 'I don't think for one moment you realise what you're doing.'

Walking among the tall trees and shrubs always made her feel better. Four huge horse chestnut trees drew her attention as she spotted a red squirrel shoot up the trunk of one of them at breakneck speed. She laughed delightedly at the sight and the squirrel, recognising a friend, came down the trunk just as rapidly.

Alison sat on an old wooden bench and watched the bushy tail flicking occasionally as the little rodent sorted through windfalls. Soon it was joined by others as they sensed no danger from the person sitting on the wooden bench. Just sitting watching them made Alison feel at peace with the world once more.

She was calmer now, resigned to her husband's trip and soothed by the knowledge that she had at least tried. *Que sera sera ...*

Alison stayed with the squirrels for a short while, thinking of the lonely existence she always led when her husband chose to be away. A day or two, even three she could bear, but fourteen days ...

It was at times like this that Alison would champ at the bit to get out and about, anything to stave off the sheer boredom which was part and parcel of life for a woman of her status. Her diary had produced only two engagements for the fortnight of the Glorious Twelfth. The first fell on the eighteenth, eight days away, and Alison was looking forward to it.

Ramsdean hospital was a very modern, up-to-date place of healing, boasting some of the world's most up-to-date surgical techniques and equipment. Although it was a privately run institution, Alison was assured, as always, of a rapturous welcome by the local populace.

She rose from her seat and made her way back to the huge building that was her home. Her staff would be going about their various duties as usual, like the proverbial ants - never ending, always beginning. The footman would let her in; it was his job to see that Alison never had to ring or knock to gain admittance and she smiled inwardly as she imagined an eye permanently glued to a side window, strategically placed for just that purpose.

The door opened at exactly the right moment and Alison entered.

'Thank you, Jenkins.'

The footman bowed slightly. 'Your Grace,' he murmured, then disappeared to she never knew where.

Alison made her way to her stately bedroom and sat in front of the huge mirror at her elegant dressing-table. She gazed at her face for some minutes and her mind went back, way back, to her childhood. She often did this when she felt depressed. Memories flooded back, happy memories of times long gone, never to return.

She thought of Andrew, dear Andrew, picturing him in her mind:

a fair-haired bundle of fun and energy, her knight in shining armour. Andrew, who always took the blame for the broken window when they played cricket, tennis or football, even though she was guilty sometimes. And who comforted her when she was hurt, who 'kissed it better', whether it was a bump or a graze.

They were idyllic days, happy days that they'd hoped would go on forever. But all good things come to an end and as they grew older their tastes began to differ. They gradually drifted further apart, though remaining firm friends.

In their teens, Andrew's eyes began to rove towards 'the ladies', as he chose to call them, especially when they were required to attend young ladies' coming-out balls, or 'debbie bashes', as they were generally known. Andy was a gifted mimic, Alison recalled, and was often coaxed onto the stage or even a table to 'do' somebody or other, male or female.

It was at one of the bashes that she met Robin, eldest son and heir to the Earldom of Westminster. Though it wasn't love at first sight, they liked each other immediately and love soon blossomed. Their wedding at Westminster Cathedral eighteen months later was a splendid spectacle, attended by royalty. The Earl and his brand new Countess chose the Bahamas for their honeymoon, and sailed there in their own luxury yacht.

Alison and Andrew had lost touch with each other over the years since her marriage. She now moved in different circles, a higher society that was more privileged than that of her single days. Her hectic social and personal life left her little time for old friends, even though she often thought of Andrew.

As she pondered the past, Alison recalled her and Robin's attempts to start a family and the agony of three premature births - the mental agony of learning that her baby was stillborn, not once, not twice, but three times. She relived the crushing despair she'd felt on learning that her last baby was in fact her last. Robin was understandably devastated too, but he had comforted her with his love and compassion, even though he knew that she could not provide him with a son and heir.

Alison came back to earth then, not wishing to dwell on tragic memories. She glanced at the electric clock built into the top of the dressing-table mirror, wondering where her husband would be on his journey to Scotland.

The phone rang so suddenly it startled her. Composing herself, she picked up the handset. There were many phone extensions in strategic places to lessen any delay in answering, and no member of the staff was allowed to lift a receiver if the Earl or Countess was in residence.

Alison never referred to herself by her title on the phone. 'Alison speaking,' she said.

The voice that answered was still as familiar to her as her own and her face glowed with delight as she listened, impatient to reply.

'Andrew, Andy, what a lovely surprise!' she bubbled, overcome with joy. 'I've just been thinking about you. Where are you? Oh it's good to hear your voice again, it's been ages.'

'Alison, my dear, dear cousin, it's good to hear you too. How are you and how is dear old Robin?'

'Oh he's fine, Andy, thanks, and so am I now.'

'Now? Did you say now, Alison, have you been ill?' Andrew sounded concerned.

'No, I haven't been ill,' she laughed gently, 'it's just that I'm on my own, Robin's gone to Scotland you see and ...'

Oh yes, of course, my dear, the grouse season and you don't like bl—'

'No I do not,' she broke in, 'and I wish Robin would give it up.'

'Ah! I'm beginning to see now, you feel better because I called, is that it?'

'Yes, Doctor,' Alison replied happily.

'Alison?'

'Yes, Andrew?'

'Would you like me to stop by and see you? We could chew the fat over old times.'

'Oh please do, I'd love you to,' said Alison gratefully.

'Right then, my dear, I have a few engagements in London over the next few days so I have to find myself accommodation, you know, theatrical digs, as we call them.'

'That won't be necessary, Andy, I insist you be my guest here at the house and I won't take no for an answer, do you hear me?'

'But I—'

'No buts Andrew! You will come, won't you?' she pleaded.

Andy chuckled down the phone. 'All right, my dear, if you insist, I shall deem it an honour.'

'Oh bless you, Andrew!'

'My pleasure, my dear, but what about my theatrical equipment? I need to have it all at hand.'

'Oh, bring it with you.'

'Bless you, my angel.' He sounded pleased.

'When can I expect to see you? Tonight, tomorrow, when?' Alison was impatient.

'Whoa, slow down, Alison, I have to leave here first,' he laughed.

'Where's here?'

'Lincolnshire, I've been here for five years now.'

'Have you indeed? Time certainly flies.'

'That's the truth. I tell you what Alison, love, if I start out just after breakfast tomorrow, I can be there, say, noon or just after, will that suit you?'

'Oh Andy, that'll be lovely, just in time for dinner.'

'Right then, that's settled, noon tomorrow it is, m'dear.'

'I'll be expecting you then, don't let me down, Andy, please.'

'I won't. Until tomorrow then, bye for now.'

'Goodbye, Andrew, I'll be waiting.'

There was a click in Alison's ear as the line went dead and she put the phone down, smiling to herself. She walked over to her bed, lay down and closed her eyes. Her mind full of happy thoughts, she soon drifted off to sleep.

Andrew had drifted into the theatre as a result of his skill as a mimic and his love of an audience. He travelled extensively at first, but acting jobs became fewer and fewer because his huge ego irritated his fellow thespians and quite simply, no one wanted to work with him. So he found himself doing more of the nightclub circuits.

The old Victorian house that was now his home had been a snip when Andrew bought it. His nightclub work tended to drain him mentally and the house in Lincolnshire was his haven, with no landladies to creep past in the early hours after a hard audience, especially in the north. It was a place to take his ladies when the mood took him.

The following morning, Andrew ate an early breakfast, cooked by his fellow thespian and companion, William Brent.

He checked his equipment in detail, especially the wigs and the latex pads, which included false breasts. He carried these in a special container lined with thick cotton wool, damped in a special oil to keep the contents in their original tip-top condition. The last two things to be packed were hair remover for his legs and a skin hugging, roll-on corset.

Andrew double-checked everything until he was completely satisfied that nothing had been overlooked. With Brent's help, he loaded everything into the car and set off for Westminster. By driving at breakneck speed, he arrived at 10.30 am.

CHAPTER SIX
THE SECOND LETTER ARRIVES

Mac had picked his team well, though his choice wasn't difficult. Bearing in mind the type of operation they were undertaking, he had decided on four men.

Sergeant Tom Smith, one-time boxer for the Metropolitan Police (he retired undefeated) was a good man to have on your side in a pinch.

Detective Constable Terry Sanderson had had a choice of careers, photography or the police force. He had wisely chosen both; his expertise with a camera was legendary and he was called in many times to do specialist work.

Detective Constable James (Jimmy) Finch had the ability to be inconspicuous in a crowd. The story went: 'Where's Jimmy?'

'Behind that street lamp.'

'Which street lamp?'

Detective Constable Robert (Bob) Saunders, expert mechanic, possessed the ability to fix anything from an engine to a watch.

The day after the would-be kidnapper's letter arrived, Mac had quickly got his team organised. They decided on six-hour shifts within the mansion grounds and, dressed as gardeners during the day, they laid trip wires and various other devices under the walls and denser bushes. These were connected to the main lodge so that the night shift could monitor any intrusion in comparative comfort.

The stately home was fairly central within the spacious grounds and the lodge was so positioned as to enable the front and rear (north and south) to be covered from the west by the vigilant policemen. The shifts were so arranged that although they were six hours long, they overlapped each other by three hours. Thus, the first man would arrive at 6 am. The second would arrive at 9 am, then the third man would start at noon while the first man would go off duty. The fourth man would arrive at 3 pm and so on, thus ensuring that two men were on duty at all times. This arrangement relieved the boredom somewhat.

Mac included himself in this arrangement, although he need not have done. His ability to muck in as well as command made him well liked. He was off duty and at home enjoying Jan's excellent cooking when his handset beeped.

He frowned, 'Now what?' and pressed the button on the side of his handset.

'Macdonald.' He listened for a few seconds and his eyebrows lifted. 'Yes ... yes, Sir ... yes, I'm on my way.' He lowered the beeper slowly.

Jan saw the look on his face. 'Trouble, sweetie?'

'Oh er, yes love, 'fraid so. That was the chief, number two has arrived.'

'Number two, what number two?'

'Sorry, love, can't tell you that, top secret.'

Jan was silent for a few moments then she pursed her lips and nodded. 'I'll get your coat, the weather doesn't look too rosy.'

Mac gazed lovingly after his wife, longing to tell her but he dared not. He knew she was dying to ask but would not; he was also confident that she would never breathe a word if he did tell her. He sighed. Jan came back with his top coat and helped him into it. He turned round and held her tight, kissing her gently.

'Keep it warm for me, love,' he grinned.

'Keep what warm?'

'My dinner,' he said, straight-faced , but his eyes were smiling.

She slanted her eyes at him. 'Liar,' she said softly, pushing him away. He grinned and made a sudden grab at her; she squealed, trying half-heartedly to escape.

'Unhand me, you villain,' she whimpered in mock horror, 'for I am still pure and untouched.'

He laughed out loud. 'Now who's telling lies, and to a copper too!' He hugged her again. 'Must go, love, the chief's waiting.'

'Away wi' ye then, sweetie, or he'll have your hide.'

Mac arrived at number Ten Downing Street and was let in without delay. He was ushered straight into a private room. His Chief was already there with the PM, who came straight to the point.

'The very thing we were hoping never to see has arrived,' he said, handing Mac a sheet of paper.

20

Mac took it, opened it and read:

'Remember me, Prime Minister? I thought I had better drop you a line, just in case you had forgotten me. Now, regarding the million pounds you owe me.'

Mac growled, 'Cheeky sod, the nerve of this bloke!' He stabbed his finger at the letter. 'A million quid we owe him!' He read on:

'As you know by now, presuming you read my first demand correctly, I requested one million pounds in old notes of five and ten pound denomination. However, I did not tell you where or when. I will tell you now.

'Tomorrow, August 18th, Alison, Countess of Westminster, will be opening a new hospital at Ramsdean - a private hospital, I might add, the most advanced of its kind in the world. I would like to point out that it is exclusively for the rich; the poor must suffer or try elsewhere. What a decadent, two-tiered society we live in, run by people like you. You, masters of the double standard; you, pampered upper-crust parasites, privileged from birth to death, who banquet on money enough to feed the hungry in this country, not to mention the Third World.

'You people with the limousines and extravagant lifestyles, for the love of money, would construct such a building for the sole purpose of milking your fellow rich. Maybe not you personally, but you do see my point. However, I digress, so back to business.

'I do not have to tell you that one million pounds can be rather bulky and somewhat cumbersome to carry without some form of transport, so I will arrange for a small van to be parked just inside the hospital grounds with the rear doors open. The van will be marked 'Oxfam'. Please place the money in the back of the van, shut the doors and clear the area of all police, dogs, cars etc. It is imperative that you believe I am in deadly earnest. If, for any reason, the money is not placed in the van, or I sense any sort of trap and have to leave empty-handed, the Countess will be abducted and the price will be doubled to ensure her safe return.

'Read this 'request' and read it well. I do not make idle boasts.'

Mac let out a long low whistle. 'This bloke certainly means business. What's our next move, Sir?'

'This is the same handwriting as the first letter,' the Chief replied. 'I've had our handwriting expert go over it with a fine toothcomb.'

'Is he on file, anyone we know?'

'No, Mac, I had some of the wording photostated out of context and had it checked out. He's not known to us - yet.'

'Tell him the interesting bit, Donald,' said the PM.

The Chief cleared his throat. 'According to Professor Hasketh of Birmingham University, the person who wrote this letter has a single-mindedness of purpose; he's ruthless and will ride roughshod over anyone who gets in his way. He is also very bold and will take chances to within the blink of an eyelid. He also has a caring nature of sorts, which ties in with his comments in the letter about the rich and poor. He has an artistic side to him too - likes to play to a crowd, you know, like an actor.'

'He can tell all this, just from a few words?' Mac whistled, not a little impressed.

'He most certainly can,' said the chief. 'Professor Hasketh is probably the foremost handwriting expert in the world, with over thirty years' experience. His expertise has helped to solve a few crimes over the years.' Well into his stride now, he took a deep breath. 'You may or may not recall a case a few years ago, the Midwest Bank job in the west end. Three men walked into the bank, one quietly closed the doors and slipped the bolts, then stood guard while the other two walked up to the counter and slipped a note to each of the tellers.'

The Chief paused for breath and smiled at his now captive audience. 'The interesting thing is, they were not wearing stocking masks or carnival masks but they were in disguise. You see, they were wearing a special kind of make-up, not just greasepaint: I mean a kind of restructuring of the whole face, nose, cheeks and so on, probably using latex. And they were well dressed into the bargain.

'Anyway, the whole point is, they would have got away with it, they could have remained free men with six hundred thousand pounds pocket money each.' He paused for effect. 'Except for those two notes.'

Mac and the others were drinking it in now and the Chief was really enjoying himself. It was Mac who asked:

'Don't leave us dangling, Sir, what was in the notes?'

'I can't recall word for word, but they both read more or less something like this:

'Please keep that pleasant smile on your face. Do not sound the alarm if you value the life of your husband, father or mother, or whatever, because they are now being held at gunpoint until our men hear from us. Now, still smiling, go and show this note to your manager and he will invite us through the security door. Go now, please.

'That's more or less the gist of it. The tellers, both girls in their late twenties, did exactly as they were told and the whole scam was over in about five minutes.'

Mac whistled out loud. 'Cool customers,' he chortled. 'Did I say customers?'

The Chief smiled at the joke. 'The girls had the presence of mind to hang onto the notes and we called in Professor Hasketh. It was his expert analysis of the handwriting that narrowed the suspects down from thousands to fifty or so. He told us to look for a man of some breeding, probably university educated; and we actually caught the big man in less than a week. Mind you, we had to be sure, so we obtained handwriting specimens from half a dozen suspects before we pounced,' he chuckled at the memory. 'You should have seen the surprised look on his face when we fingered his collar. We got his sidekicks too.'

Mac shook his head in admiration. 'I'm impressed, Sir, very impressed, which gives me an idea. Can we show the professor the second letter? All of it, I mean. Then not only can he study the crossed Ts, he can also get a better overall impression from the whole contents.' He hurried on before his Chief could get a word in. 'He sounds like he could put Sigmund Freud in the shade on the strength of what you have just told us.'

The PM intervened. 'I'm inclined to agree with Macdonald. We want this man and we want him quickly.'

The Chief stroked his chin thoughtfully. 'Yes, I think you may be right, Sir. Just think of the damage to police morale if he pulls it off, it would be an open invitation to any budding kidnapper to have a go.'

'That's not all,' said the PM soberly. 'If he did pull it off, Heaven forbid, every police force in the country would be looking for him. Try keeping that quiet,' he ended grimly.

Mac thought for a moment before asking his chief. 'Can I pull my men out of the grounds, Sir? I mean, this maniac isn't going to try anything, at least until the official opening of the hospital.'

The Chief looked at the PM. 'What do you think, Sir?'

The PM thoughtfully filled his pipe and applied a match until the pleasant smelling tobacco was glowing to his satisfaction. 'It does make sense when you think about it, doesn't it.' He looked at Mac. 'No comings or goings at all?'

'Apart from the Countess's guest, no, Sir.'

'Guest? What guest?' The PM sounded alarmed.

'Don't worry, Sir, they go way back apparently,' said Mac reassuringly. 'They are practically inseparable.'

'You have checked him out, haven't you?' queried the chief.

'We're trying to do that now, Sir, without causing the Countess any undue alarm,' Mac replied.

'If you asked her outright, you'd get a flea in your ear,' said the PM. 'When did he show up?'

'The day after the Earl left for Scotland, as a matter of fact, Sir. She went and picked him up herself in the car,' Mac replied.

'Sounds safe enough to me,' said the PM.

'We're keeping an eye on him, Sir, have done since he arrived.'

'What about the hospital, Mac, what precautions are you taking there?'

'Well, Sir, from what we've deduced, this chap isn't going to make a move until the Countess has officially opened the hospital and gone, so if you pull us out of the house now, Sir, we'll give Ramsdean a good going over before she arrives.'

The PM pursed his lips and stroked his chin for a few seconds before he spoke. Finally, he made up his mind. 'Pull your lads out, Mac, size up the situation at the hospital, work out a plan of action and—' He stopped in mid flow. 'Sorry, Donald, I appear to be doing your job, got carried away I'm afraid.'

The Chief smiled broadly. 'Don't worry, Sir, you were doing just fine, and don't worry about Mac either, he knows his job.'

'Steady on, Sir,' Mac smiled self-consciously, 'you make me feel like Sexton Blake.'

'Precisely why you were picked, Mac,' said the PM, smiling at his embarrassment.

The Chief grinned broadly too, and Mac smiled in return, shaking his head slightly.

'Right,' said the chief, 'I'll see to it that Hasketh gets this letter while you get yourselves organised.' Then he added with some feeling, 'It is of paramount importance that this man, whoever he is, is stopped - dead.'

'Amen to that, but let's see what our pet graphologist comes up with shall we?' And with a wave of his pipe he murmured, 'Away you go gentlemen.'

CHAPTER SEVEN
RAMSDEAN HOSPITAL

Mac and his team arrived at the hospital in ones and twos in unmarked cars to remain as inconspicuous as possible to any watching eyes, one pair in particular.

As arranged with the head of the hospital management, they duly appeared everywhere as porters, and gave the hospital an expert going over. Hours later, they all met at a prearranged venue and proceeded to formulate a feasible plan of action.

'I for one am glad that you picked this place for a chin wag, Guv,' said Sergeant Smithy, a pint of best bitter in his hand. 'After that little stake-out at the mansion, this' - he held up his pint - 'is barely going to touch the sides.' And without further ado, he quaffed a good half of it in one go.

'Watch him, he'll be pie-eyed in no time,' said Jimmy, ducking as the big sergeant took a playful swing at him.

Mac grinned at the horseplay in the bar of the Tilted Jug and motioned everyone through to the back room. He was a great friend of the landlord, an ex-policeman invalided out of the force many years ago. He had been 'kneecapped' in a gangland bust but, thanks to the miracle of modern surgery, his leg was saved. He walked with a pronounced limp, but bore his burden cheerfully.

When they were all seated around a huge oak table, Mac said, 'All right, lads, let's get down to it, shall we. Who's first?'

Smithy cleared his throat, unfolded and spread out a huge plan of the hospital. 'I've been all over the grounds and the inside, checking doors, windows and various hidey holes, Guv.'

'And?'

'We can lock quite a few of these doors and windows.' He stabbed his finger at the plan, 'such as here, here and here, without endangering too many avenues of escape in case of fire or whatever. This way we can control which way this bloke can come and go - that is, if he shows.'

'Sounds good so far. What about the cameras?' Mac looked at DC Sanderson. 'Terry?'

Terry leaned forward and pointed out various locations on the map. 'There aren't many places we can conceal them, Guv, but I've picked out a few likely spots.'

'What about outside, anywhere we can put a couple more?'

'Doubtful, Guv, the building's brand new as you know and the outside is bare of anything substantial as yet, such as shrubs and trees.' He shrugged his shoulders. 'The only place we can set up any sort of equipment is across the way.'

'You mean the block of flats?' Sanderson nodded.

Mac groaned. 'All we'll get from there is the back of their heads. Still, who knows, we may just get lucky and she'll call it off, though I very much doubt it. Lady Alison is a stickler for duty and no mistake.' He turned and pressed a button on the wall and within half a minute, the landlord appeared.

'Ah, Harry,' Mac greeted him, 'could you do us some sandwiches, anything, and another round of your most excellent bitter. We may be here for some time.'

Harry chuckled. 'I'm way ahead of you there, Mr Macdonald. When I clocked this lot you dragged in, I guessed it might be a long old session, so the wife prepared something just in case.' He poked his head through the serving hatch, OK, Rene, we were right, bring 'em out.'

'Righty oh, lovey.'

Harry's head appeared again, grinning. 'Good gal, my Rene. I'll just get your ale then you can slip the bolt on the door when I'm gone and if anybody asks why, I'll tell them it's being fumigated,' he added, cocking his thumb in the general direction of his old buddies, hurriedly ducking out of the door as he was threatened with pint pots.

An hour or so later, a reasonable sort of plan had been worked out and Mac sighed with relief. His head ached slightly and he was weary, as was his team.

'OK lads, that's it more or less so let's get it laid on and keep our fingers crossed that all we have to worry about now is this van.'

'We're not going to give this bloke the money are we, Guv?' queried Bob Saunders.

'Now that,' Mac answered flatly, 'is the sixty four thousand dollar question. The Chief and the PM are waiting to see what we come up with before they decide how to move on it.'

'Guv, even if we put the money in the van, I for one can't picture this bloke being allowed to drive off with it,' said Smithy, 'can you?'

'That's a capital N-O, but it hasn't happened yet. Let's wait and see what the top brass come up with.' He leaned back in his chair and stretched luxuriously. 'Is that it then?'

Chairs scraped as everyone began to move, the signal for Mac to gather up his map and notes and put them in his briefcase. As he stood up, a though struck him. 'By the way, make sure your batteries are up to scratch in your handsets. Carry a couple of spares, OK?'

'OK, Guv.'

Mac nodded his head in satisfaction. 'Right, let's do what we have to do. Let's justify the faith the powers that be have in us unsung heroes.'

That last bit of banter brought a laugh, even though many a true word is spoken in jest.

Jimmy Finch spoke thoughtfully. 'You know, my mother should have been a nun.'

'If she had have been,' grinned Bob Saunders, poking his little mate in the chest, 'you wouldn't be here now.'

'That's what I mean,' said Jimmy.

Terry Sanderson slipped the door bolt and grinned wickedly. 'Unless your father was a randy old monk!' He shot out of the door before Jimmy could get at him.

Mac joined in the good humoured laughter. 'OK, you lot, let's split before someone gets killed.'

They departed in good spirits and returned to Hamilcourt House, leaving Mac to get in touch with the Chief Constable to set up a meeting. This business with the van needed sorting out, rapidly.

CHAPTER EIGHT
RED HERRING

Mac, having met up with his Chief at HQ and gained approval for the hospital surveillance, broached the subject of the van.

'This business about the van is bugging me, Sir, I can't for the life of me imagine anyone just calmly getting into it and driving it away, can you?'

'No, I cannot, I most certainly cannot.'

'It's got to be a red herring, a ploy of some sort to put us off.' Mac was emphatic.

'I couldn't agree more, but put us off what?'

'It could be ...' Mac stroked his chin thoughtfully.

'Could be what?'

'He's cocking a snook, Sir, showing off.'

'How do you mean?'

'Well try this, Sir,' said Mac, warming up now. 'Supposing I were this chap and I wanted you to know that I meant business. Don't forget, Sir, I haven't kidnapped anyone yet. You see, the Countess cuts the tape, opens the hospital, everything goes off without a hitch. Off she goes home safely and no one knows whether or not the demand note was the work of a hoaxer or not.' Mac spread his hands out palm upwards. 'So I leave the van in the place I said I would.'

The chief, who had been listening intently to Mac's theory, snapped his fingers. 'You're right, by George, I'm certain of it.' He smacked his fist into the palm of his hand, turned on his heel, walked a couple of steps and spun round. He pointed a finger at Mac. 'It isn't a red herring,' he said with conviction, 'it's his bloody signature, or as good as. It would be like saying, 'Now do you believe me?' '

'It all fits, doesn't it, Sir.?

'It certainly does, and something else too, Mac. He's not going to be there, is he? He's just telling us that he intends to kidnap the Countess at some later date and not at the hospital.'

'Too many people about anyway, Sir. If and when he does do it, you can bet your life he will surprise us and grab her when we least expect it.'

The intercom sounded on the chief's desk. He leaned across and pressed the button. 'Yes, Sarah?'

'Professor Hasketh has arrived, Sir.'

'Send him in please, Sarah.'

'Right away, Sir.' The intercom went dead.

He went to the door to welcome the professor. The door opened just as he reached it and Sarah ushered the great man in, shutting the door behind him.

'Ah Professor, come in come in,' beamed the chief, waving him towards a comfortable armchair. 'May I introduce you to Detective Inspector John Macdonald. Mac, Professor Gordon Hasketh.'

'My pleasure, Sir,' said Mac as they shook hands politely.

'I've been hearing some good things about you, Inspector,' smiled Hasketh.

Mac had the grace to blush slightly and managed a lopsided grin. 'Thank you, Sir, it's probably exaggerated ...' he tailed off somewhat lamely.

The Chief smiled at Mac's discomfort and stepped in. 'Let's get comfortable, gentlemen. Coffee or tea, anyone?'

'Oh tea please, my mouth tastes like a Sumo wrestler's jockstrap.'

Mac's eyebrows shot up in surprise, 'Er, tea will be fine with me, Sir.' He had half expected a stuffed shirt, a pompous, self-important know-all. He couldn't have been more wrong.

Professor Hasketh was a dapper little man, sporting a pair of half moon spectacles which he frequently removed and waved about to emphasise a point. He was absolutely devoid of arrogance, and was a first class orator as well as a good listener. One soon forgot that one was in the presence of a genius.

The tea arrived and the Chief began to pour. 'Well, Professor, what did you come up with?'

Hasketh sipped his tea contentedly, put his cup and saucer back on the tray and reached for his briefcase, from which he extracted a large black book. He leaned back in his chair and opened it, glancing at each man in turn and tapping the book with his forefinger. It had the desired effect and both men leaned forward expectantly.

'Gentlemen, we have here a veritable enigma, at least he would be to anyone not trained in graphology, that is.' He coughed self-consciously. 'Not that I'm looking for medals, of course, this is my bread and butter.'

'Of course, Sir,' said Mac.

'Can you give us a line on this chap?' the Chief asked. 'We've come to the conclusion that he means what he says and is going ahead regardless.'

'Oh, you never spoke a truer word, my friend.' Hasketh tapped his notebook. 'It's all here' - he paused for effect and tapped again - 'in his own handwriting.'

They waited expectantly.

'Firstly,' the professor began, 'as I have already said, this person is very single-minded and once he has made up his mind, that's it, he won't change it. He also thinks things through carefully until he's one hundred per cent certain that the end result will be as he wants it; even then he'll prune all the way around the edges to be certain. Are you with me so far?' They nodded. 'In other words, if this chap said he was going over the Niagara Falls in a barrel just for the hell of it, and coming up smiling, he would, believe me.'

'Phew,' Mac whistled, 'who the devil are we up against, Houdini?

'Sounds very much like it,' said the chief.

Hasketh chuckled. 'There's more,' he went on. 'This man has had a certain type of education, I mean apart from Oxford or Cambridge.'

'How do you mean, Sir?' Mac asked, puzzled.

'I mean a theatrical education.' Hasketh was most emphatic, 'He's an actor of sorts, I can see it in his style.' He tapped his book again.

'An actor!' Mac breathed. 'Well that should narrow the field down a wee bit, or will it?'

'He's left-handed,' said the professor, 'so that helps too.'

The Chief scratched his head and sighed, 'Who is he? I'd give a year's salary to be fingering his collar right now.'

Hasketh's eyes twinkled. 'It's really very simple, chief, all you have to do is look for a left-handed actor quoting Shakespeare from an Oxfam van.' That raised a chuckle. 'Joking apart,' he went on, 'basically, that's more or less just what you are looking for, you know.'

'If only it were that simple,' said Mac.

'What else did you find?' asked the chief.

'Well, as I said before, he likes an audience - on his terms, mind you - and we, gentlemen, or rather you, are that audience. He has set the first act, so to speak, to get you on the edge of your seats and wondering what's going to happen next.'

'Yes, I see what you mean,' said the chief, nodding.

'You can see now that he intends to carry out his threat, can't you?'

'Yes I do,' the Chief agreed soberly.

'Precisely his intention,' Hasketh continued. 'As I told you, this man has planned well to achieve his aims and ...' He left the sentence unfinished.

'Do you mean that we're doing more or less what he is telling us to, Sir?' said Mac.

'I do.'

'Including the fact that we think that van is a red herring - or not a red herring, as we finally decided, but proof that he really means it and it's not a hoax?'

'Precisely.'

'Do you think we can get on this bloke's wavelength, you know, so that we can outwit him?'

Hasketh shook his head. 'That I very much doubt. You are going to need a lot of good fortune to catch this fellow, believe me. After all, he's done nothing yet except send you two demand notes. All I can do is give you a character breakdown of the fellow from the demand notes themselves.'

'You have told us quite a lot already, Sir,' said Mac, 'and I have a better picture of him from your analysis.'

'Oh, there's a little more yet,' Hasketh went on. 'I get the distinct impression that he thinks the whole world owes him something, as if he's been suppressed, held back, you know. He feels someone's got something that is rightfully his, that kind of thing.'

32

'An angry young man type, a rebel?' said Mac.

'Yes, more or less,' Hasketh agreed. 'He can't get what he believes to be his by right, so he's out for revenge of a sort.' He tapped his book again. 'It's here, it's all here.'

'You sound very sure, Sir.'

'Inspector, take it from me, this man will carry out his threat without thinking for one moment that it cannot be done. He tells himself that he cannot be caught. He is not the eternal optimist, his mind just works that way.'

Mac shook his head in disbelief. 'Holy smoke,' he groaned.

'Holy smoke indeed,' Hasketh said quietly. 'There's something else that you're up against.'

'And what is that Sir?' Mac half expected the answer and he and the Chief sat looking at the dapper little man who was now sitting back, removing his half moons.

'He's quite mad,' Hasketh replied quietly.

'Good lord!' the Chief said, quite aghast.

'Oh, he's not the raving lunatic type. His is the sort of madness that doesn't manifest itself obviously, it's the sort of madness bordering on genius - a controlled madness, if you like, characterised by extreme intelligence. This man has a perfect mixture of both, you see, and ninety-nine times out of a hundred, nobody would spot it,' he concluded.

'Unless he wrote you a letter, Sir,' Mac said smiling.

'Oh! Well, ermm, thank you,' Hasketh smiled modestly.

Mac grinned at him with affection and admiration. 'You're welcome, Sir.'

CHAPTER NINE
KEEP YOUR EYES PEELED

The day finally arrived for the official opening of the hospital. The red carpet had been rolled out and the good citizens of Ramsdean lined the pavement, waving little union flags.

A piece of tape had been positioned across the main casualty reception area inside and, in a prominent position, a plaque bearing a suitable inscription was covered with twin curtains ready for Alison, Countess of Westminster, to unveil.

All the local dignitaries were present, from the Lord Mayor downwards. Nurses were talking in excited little groups, waiting for the command to form a double line through which the Countess would pass. Any patient requiring so much as a bed pan would have to wait, or resort to their own devices.

'First things first' was the order of the day and today, the Countess came first, naturally. After the introductions, the nurses would go quietly but with all speed back to their charges just in case anyone had had an 'accident'. If such was the case, a rapid clean-up would get under way or the patient would be removed, whichever was more expedient.

Outside the hospital but within the boundary walls, TV vans packed with equipment manoeuvred into position. These were to be used for live coverage. Teams of cameramen with shoulder-slung videos checked out their gear with their sound men and boom microphone carriers. There was the usual friendly bickering with rival crews as to who was going to stand where. Gradually, the chaos settled into some semblance of organisation and good order as zero hour approached.

Nobody questioned the presence of the two stetson-wearing tourists carrying battery-driven video recorders and smoking green Havanas - alias Sergeant Tommy Smith and DC Terry Sanderson.

'Gawd, Sarge, I feel a right pillock in this bleedin' hat.'

'You *look* a right pillock,' Smithy whispered back. 'Nah, you look

OK, just don't open your mouth. Look, if you have to talk, don't take your cigar out of your cake hole, it'll help you sound like a Yank if you clamp your teeth over it.'

'OK, but don't blame me if I'm sick all over the Countess. I hate the bloody things,' Terry complained.

'Well, don't light the sodding thing then,' sighed Smith as he shook his head and muttered to himself, 'More trouble to me than a house full of bleedin' kids.' He looked at his watch. 'We'd better get into position now, things are beginning to happen over there.' He nodded towards the reception area.

'Right, Sarge.'

'You know what to do, you take that side and make out that you're taking pictures of the Countess, OK? And—'

'Yeah, I ain't forgot, Sarge, get as many of the crowd as I can, right?'

'Right, and I'll do the same from my side. Now off you go and don't let anyone try to flog you the Tower Bridge,' Smithy grinned.

'Ha flippin' ha, how do I know somebody ain't flogged it to you already?' quipped Sanderson.

Smithy beetled his brows and started his foot back and Terry departed rapidly.

Meanwhile inside the hospital building, Mac was dressed in a doctor's white housecoat with a stethoscope in his hand. DCs Finch and Saunders were similarly dressed. Mac had arranged this with the hospital governors, who were under the impression that they were bodyguards, undercover of course, to Lady Alison.

The governors, of course, could not see how anyone could be a threat but reluctantly agreed, as long as the men 'kept a low profile'.

'Pompous lot,' Mac thought. 'I wonder what they're like at home?'

A faint cheer broke his train of thought as it signalled the approaching Countess and her entourage. Mac put his hand in his pocket and pressed the button twice on his beeper, this being the prearranged signal to his men to be ready. He received two lots of beeps in return from outside and a nod each from his lads inside, who were within sight but out of earshot. He nodded back.

The beeps had been heard by some of the nurses and he received a couple of curious looks from people close by. He moved to a wall phone as if to answer his pager. He lifted the phone, turned his back to the nurses, pressed the phone cut-off with his finger and spoke into the dead mouthpiece. The nurses lost interest in him then and after a few moments of imaginary conversation, he resumed his position.

'False alarm,' was his disarming mime to a questioning glance from one nurse who looked at him as he approached. She smiled and turned away.

Two police motor cycles, blue lights flashing, drove through the main gate, turning left and right respectively, parking on the newly-laid turf on either side of the Tarmac drive.

Then a large saloon car full of security men swished through the gate, doors opening long before it stopped. Four big men stepped out and made their way to the beginning of the red carpet as the saloon was driven away to a prearranged parking spot.

The driver got out with another man and they lost themselves in the crowd.

The clapping and cheering, now growing in volume by the main gate, heralded the arrival of the purpose-built limousine that literally floated along on the Tarmac before coming to a halt exactly where it was supposed to, bang on the edge of the red carpet. The rear offside door was opened by an elegantly dressed man who had rapidly vacated the limousine via the nearside door as soon as it had stopped.

A pair of nylon-clad legs swung out and the Countess stepped on to the carpet, smiled serenely to the crowd as she waved her 'royal' wave. The Lord Mayor stepped forward, took her hand and, bowing stiffly from the waist, murmured his well-rehearsed greeting. He then introduced all the other chosen ones in pecking order.

Either side in the crowd, Smith and Terry were doing there stuff.

The Countess, flanked on either side by the Lord Mayor and the hospital governor, walked regally to the purpose-built platform, climbed the two steps and stood in front of the microphone. She retrieved her prepared speech from her handbag and with a dazzling smile, faced her audience.

Smithy and Terry were panning like mad; nobody was to be missed if they could possibly help it, these were Mac's specific orders. Mac and his 'doctors' could hear Alison's opening speech as they waited impatiently inside the reception area, hoping against hope that everything would go off without a hitch.

'This is stupid,' Mac thought to himself. 'Who on earth would try an abduction in broad daylight, in a crowd this size and with all these gorillas for bodyguards? But then again, according to the professor ...' he sighed. 'Better safe than sorry I suppose.'

He turned his thoughts to the Oxfam van. Where was it, when was it going to show, if at all?' He sighed again. What a ludicrous situation this was, to be sure. If the van showed, he could take it as proof of intention, if it didn't ... a hoax? He sighed again.

With the tape cut and the hospital officially opened, the Countess entered the reception area. She spent some time shaking hands with the doctors and nursing staff, Mac included. He was somewhat surprised at the size of her hand but then again she was a very tall lady, a good five feet eleven inches in her elegant high heels.

The hidden cameras inside the hospital had been running from the moment the Countess had entered the main gate. Anyone lurking inside would be on tape unless something went wrong with the equipment, though Mac doubted that. Terry Sanderson had installed them and he was the best.

The tour lasted about an hour-and-a-half and finally, the Countess took her leave, disappearing the way she had come. She arrived back home safely, not knowing that the six men in the leading car had been specially hand-picked by Mac. He had told them a cock and bull story about a suspected demonstration by an animal rights group against the Earl's love of blood sports.

Mac's handset beeped. He removed it from his pocket and listened. A voice on the other end said, 'All clear, Sir' and he grunted an acknowledgement.

The team, after searching for any trace of the van, turned in negative reports. Mac was annoyed at what appeared to be a waste of time and manpower. 'Gutless bloody wonder, he's made right idiots out of all of us, but still, we couldn't take chances, after all, we don't know whether he was here or not.'

'Ten to one he's one of your old collars, Guv,' said Smith.

'He didn't send me the ransom note,' Mac reminded him, 'he sent it to the PM.'

'I'm not trying to flatter you, Guv but, you are one of HQ's top men, if not the best, if you don't mind me saying so. And this bloke knew that if he threw a big enough scare into the PM, you're the man he would call in.'

Mac grinned at his big sergeant. 'You have a way with words, Smithy, remind me to have you demoted.'

Smithy grinned sheepishly at his boss then glared at his colleagues, daring them to add to his discomfort. They all gazed cheekily at the ceiling or their boots as if they hadn't heard a thing.

Mac smiled at all this and cut in. 'OK, you lot, collect all the gear and we'll slope off back to the Yard and run through what we have, just in case, that is.'

With all the gear duly collected, labelled and stowed carefully in the police van, they started down the Tarmac drive in convoy. As they approached the main gate, Smithy, who happened to be driving, slowed the car down then stopped about twenty feet inside the gate.

'Something wrong, Smithy? Why have you stopped?'

Smithy pointed over to his left. 'Over there, Guv, he said quietly, 'about ten o'clock.'

Mac's eyes followed his big sergeant's pointing finger and his jaw dropped. 'I see it, but I don't believe it,' he breathed, obviously shocked at what he saw. He stared at it for a good half a minute. 'This bloke certainly takes the biscuit for downright cheek.'

Mac and Smithy could not take their eyes off the little object perched proudly, mockingly, on the newly-laid turf. It stood about eight inches high with the legend 'Oxfam' painted on the side in red.

It was a little toy van.

Andrew arrived in Westminster around 10.30 am. He had no intention of going directly to Hamilcourt House; he had things to do first.

First he drove around looking for a safe place to garage his car within a few minutes' drive from the Countess' home. This was of the utmost importance. He had to find a place that was well away from prying eyes and safe from vandals. He passed quite a few public car parks and dismissed them as quite unsuitable, too open, too prone to the public gaze for his liking. He drove around the back streets for quite a while searching, searching.

Suddenly his eyes gleamed as he spotted a sign on a row of what looked like garages. He drew closer. 'Garages for rent, reasonable rates,' the sign read. There was an address and a telephone number at the bottom of the notice board and he made a note of them. He drove directly to the address, parking his ostentatious car just around the corner; he deemed it prudent not to let the garage owner see the car just in case the sight of it suddenly doubled the rent.

As it turned out, the rent was exorbitant anyway. Andrew would have refused to pay on the spot but for the importance of keeping the car hidden. He was also required to pay one month in advance although he emphasised that he only needed the garage for one week only.

'Can't 'elp vat, mate, me terms is monfly only and no refunds.'

Andrew managed to hold his temper in check, but only just nodded his agreement, promising to make a bonfire of the place when he vacated. He grinned maliciously to himself at the prospect. Still seething, he drove back to the garages and found his allotted number. He inserted the key the owner had given him into a huge padlock and the double doors opened with a creak of rusty hinges. He looked inside. There was a small hole in the roof near the back but not big enough to worry about. Andrew nodded his approval. 'Perfect, just perfect.' Driving the car inside, he then closed the double doors and replaced the huge padlock.

He walked to the nearest phone box and called a mini cab, telling the driver to come to the garage. By the time the cab arrived, he had retrieved his theatrical trunk from his car and was sitting on it outside the garage. The driver took one look at the offending trunk and said, 'Sorry Guv, but that won't fit in me taxi.'

Andrew groaned inwardly. 'But I have to get to the railway station in a hurry.' His temper was just below boiling point.

'Sorry, Guv, but you can see for yourself, I ain't got no room for it.' The driver was adamant.

Andrew cooled down a bit at that. Suddenly he had an idea. 'Have you any estate cars on your fleet?'

'Sure we have, Guv. But what about my time? I have to book ...'

'Will a fiver cover it?' said Andrew, reaching for his wallet.

'Cor! Suits me, Guv, thanks,' said the cabbie, 'hold on a bit.' He reached through the cab window for his two-way radio handpiece.

'Control, this is twenty-eight, come in, over.'

'Control, what's the problem? Over.'

'No problem, the fare has a big basket to transport and I can't manage it, we need an estate. Over.'

'Where are you, twenty-eight? Over.'

The cabbie told him.

'Give me a minute, twenty-eight. Out.'

It was a good five minutes before the controller came back on the air.

'Twenty-eight, this is control. Over.'

'Go ahead, control.'

'There's an estate on its way, be there in a few minutes. Over.'

'OK control, thanks. Over and out.' The cabbie replaced the handset. 'Laid on, Guv,' he said with a triumphant smile.

'Thank you very much indeed, that's fine,' said Andrew and he handed the cabbie a five pound note.

'Cor, thanks, Guv, you're a toff,' said the driver happily accepting the money.

'That's all right, my friend, you've earned it.'

The cabbie smiled ruefully. 'It makes a pleasant change, Guv.'

'What does?'

'Well, usually when we pick up or drop a fare around here, they argue like buggery over the fare. And here's you giving me a fiver for sod all practically.'

Andrew smiled inwardly and congratulated himself on his preparation for this journey. The cabbie was looking at a man wearing horn-rimmed glasses, perched on a slightly larger nose than Andrew normally sported, and he had a scar all of two inches long on his left cheek. The cabbie would remember him as he looked now, Andrew had just made sure of that.

The estate duly arrived and the cabbie helped to load Andrew's trunk into it. The driver strapped his load in safely and shut the back doors. He then climbed into the driving seat, inviting Andrew to sit beside him.

'Where to, Guv?'

'The railway station please.'

Ten minutes later, they pulled into the taxi rank at Bedlington Cross Station. Andrew helped the driver off-load his trunk onto the pavement and paid him, tipping him a fifty pence piece and thanking him for his trouble.

'Shall I get a porter, Sir?' asked the driver helpfully.

'No, that's OK, my train isn't due for an hour yet, I'm waiting for some friends anyway. Thanks anyway.'

'Sure, Guv?'

'Quite sure thanks.'

'Have a nice journey then, Guv,' the cabbie said cheerfully and climbed back into his cab. He picked up the handset and pressed the button.

'Hello control.'

'Car four free.'

'Stand by four.'

Andrew grinned as he listened to the two-way flow of conversation. It reminded him of a fighter pilot calling into base He could almost imagine the cab driver wearing a flying helmet and goggles, tearing down the runway, trying to get airborne without the benefit of wings.

The cabbie eventually received instructions and drove off, giving Andrew a quick farewell nod. When he had gone, Andrew swiftly searched for a timetable on the numerous notice boards outside the station. He spotted one and quickly checked the times of trains arriving from Lincolnshire, grunting with satisfaction when he found what he was looking for.

There were quite a few trains from that general direction and one of them suited his purpose admirably because it was due to arrive about now. All he had to do was wait.

He made his way into the station with the intention of asking a porter when the public address system burst into life. In between garbled words he managed to hear that the train now arriving at platform three was indeed the train that he was supposed to have arrived on.

He found a public telephone with a hood over the top, dialled a number and waited.

Suddenly a voice said, 'Alison.'

'Alison, darling, it's me Andrew, can you pick me up?'

'Andy!' Alison cried out in sheer delight. 'Of course I can, where are you?'

'I'm at the station, my dear, my car broke down so I caught the train instead,' he said cheerfully.

'Oh you poor dear!'

'Not to worry, my sweet, just a minor repair. Trouble is, I have my equipment with me, namely a very large theatrical trunk.'

'That won't be a problem, I'll pick you up myself. I'll bring the estate car, your trunk should fit into that quite easily,' Alison cried out happily.

'Bless you, m'dear, that's solved that little problem then.'

'I'll be there in ten minutes or so, Andrew. Where are you exactly?'

'By the taxi rank, my love, just look for a big pile of luggage with me sitting on top looking like Sherpa Tensing,' he laughed.

Alison's voice tinkled with happy laughter over the phone. 'I'm on my way now Andy, don't go away, I'll see you in ten minutes.'

'I won't.'

He hung up and made his way to the gents' toilet. He found a vacant cubicle, went in and shut the door. With the aid of a small hand mirror, he removed the false nose and two inch scar. He carefully placed them in a small plastic bag he had brought along for the purpose and put the bag into his pocket. Using cotton wool

42

and a small bottle of solvent taken from another pocket, he carefully cleansed his face of any spirit gum and make-up. He left the cubicle and washed his hands and face at the hand-basins, dried himself on the roller towel, then combed his hair in front of the mirror. Satisfied with the finished result, he grinned at his reflection.

Andrew Grant, actor, performer, grinned back at him.

True to her word, Alison arrived in ten minutes flat. She spotted him in seconds and without more ado, pulled onto the taxi rank. A couple of the drivers began to object until they realised who she was, then their tune changed rather quickly and they gave her a respectful nod.

She barely noticed them as she literally jumped into Andrew's arms. He lifted her off her feet and swung her round in a circle and Alison laughed with delight, much to the amusement of the cabbies. To any watching eyes, they were greeting each other as only kin or lovers can.

'Oh Andrew, it's so good to see you again!' said Alison, her eyes moist with tears of joy.

'It's good to see you again, my long lost playmate,' replied Andrew as he kissed her cheeks tenderly.

'Please don't leave it so long next time, Andrew,' Alison pleaded.

'I'll try not to, but I don't get a lot of free time in my profession,' he sighed. 'Besides, you have a husband to think of now.'

'Yes, but it's not the same thing. I mean, I love him very much but ...'

'Yes, my love, I think I know what you mean,' he laughed gently, understandingly.

Alison brightened again. She stepped back to look at his luggage. 'My my, you don't do things by halves, do you, Andy? But then, you never did.' She opened the back of the estate car and a couple of the cabbies helped to load Andrew's luggage.

'Thank you, gentlemen,' said Alison, 'you're very kind.'

'Our pleasure, M'Lady.'

Andrew tipped them for their trouble and they thanked him.

'Come on then Andrew, let's get you home,' Alison said eagerly, moving to the car door.

'Coming, my love. By the way, what's for dinner?'

Alison laughed as she selected first gear and answered him as she used to when they were children. 'Boiled wellingtons and custard.'

He wrinkled his nose and said, 'Pshaw!' just as he had all those long years ago.

They both laughed out loud, and chatted animatedly as they drove to Hamilcourt House. They drove through the big gates at exactly noon and followed the long Tarmac drive up to the mansion.

Jenkins the butler was waiting on the forecourt flanked by two footmen to greet his mistress and her guest. As the car came to a halt, he moved forward to open the door for Alison and the two footmen went to unload the luggage.

'I have had the guest room prepared, M'Lady,' said Jenkins as Alison alighted from the car.

'Thank you Jenkins, please have the luggage taken up.'

'M'Lady.'

Alison caught hold of Andrew's arm to propel him inside the house. 'Come along, my lad, you and I have a lot to talk about,' she bubbled happily.

He allowed himself to be manhandled, and they disappeared through the big oak doors. Apart from Andrew's late night club cabaret acts, the two cousins were practically inseparable from that moment onwards.

The following morning, Alison was up bright and early and she rang a very sleepy Andrew in his bedroom. 'Come along, Rip Van Winkle,' she chirped, 'you're taking me shopping today, remember?'

'Oh yer - 'ats right,' he yawned, 'I almost forgot, you're opening that new hospital tomorrow.'

Dead right I am and I need to pick my new outfit this morning so chop chop, my boy,' Alison chuckled happily.

'Give me ten minutes to find out where exactly I've hidden my carcass,' he groaned.

She laughed loudly at that remark. 'Take more water with it, you naughty boy.'

An hour later, with Andrew at the wheel of the big silent limousine, they rolled out through the gate heading for the 'top people's' shops, out of the reach of the ordinary pocket. As they approached the elite quarter, Andrew said casually, 'I'm sure you don't need me in there, do you, my love? I'll probably feel like a duck out of water so, as I have pressing business to attend to, I'll slope off and I promise I'll see you in an hour.' He smiled broadly. 'That's showbiz my love.'

They arrived at the classy complex Garrats. Alison opened the door and swung her legs gracefully onto the pavement, attracting a few wolf whistles from some workmen who could not recognise her from their scaffolding.

Alison pretended not to notice and, barely hiding a tiny smile, she turned to Andrew. 'No more than an hour then, promise?'

'I promise, my love, but I really do have to take care of some business first.'

Andrew was telling the truth. For one thing, the nightclub he was due to perform at would not accept phone calls as confirmation, due to some prankster who had once imitated another artist and cancelled an engagement for a prank or spite; when the real artist had turned up, he'd found his spot filled.

And Andrew had even more important business to attend to.

Firstly, he parked the limousine in a public car park, just a few minutes' walk from where he had parked his roadster. He made his way to the lock-up and let himself in. After a few minutes, fully satisfied, he locked the doors.

In his pocket was a letter, written two days earlier. He went and bought a booklet of stamps and stuck one firmly on the top right-hand corner, making quite sure it was firmly stuck down. Taking one last look at the address, he nodded in satisfaction at the bold print:

'THE PRIME MINISTER, TEN DOWNING STREET'

The very brevity of the address would ensure delivery, the GPO would see to that.

Andrew Grant, actor extraordinaire, smiled to himself and pushed the letter into the slot.

As promised, he collected Alison, who came complete with an armful of boxes. She was followed out to the limousine by a handful of striped-suited undermanagers, also carrying boxes. The manager himself hovered in attendance like a broody hen with chicks. The cardboard boxes were carefully stowed away in the spacious boot and after much bowing and scraping by the servile managers, Andrew and Alison finally set off back to Hamilcourt House.

'Phew! do you know something, Andrew? Sometimes I wish just once that I could walk into a shop without being recognised.'

Andrew did not reply immediately; he was biting his bottom lip as if deep in thought.

'Alison, love?'

'Yes, my dear cousin?'

'How would you like to watch one of my performances, say erm, tonight?'

'I'd love to, but what about my engagement tomorrow? I must look my best and a late night most certainly won't help.'

'Ah, but you won't have a late night, my love, I only have a half hour spot tonight, 8.30 till 9 o'clock and what's more, you can go incognito.'

'But how? I'm too well known,' Alison protested mildly, but clearly beginning to like the idea, 'I'll need a disguise of some sort, I—'

'When I've finished with you,' he cut in, 'you won't recognise yourself, my love. As a matter of fact, you wont know what hit you.'

It dawned on Alison that with Andrew's expertise, she could get away with it, and it would be fun at that.

'Why not,' she breathed in excitement at the prospect.

'Why not indeed? Andrew egged her on. 'It'll be simplicity itself.'

She laughed out loud. 'You, my dear cousin, have just got yourself an audience of at least one.'

Andrew Grant laughed with her, but his eyes lacked sparkle. If Alison could have read his mind at that moment, she would have been transfixed with fear, probably the most frightened woman in Westminster.

Later that evening at 7.45, the limousine, with Andrew at the wheel and Alison seated quite happily in the passenger seat, swished past the 'gardeners' and out of the main gate. Grant smiled to himself: 'gardeners' indeed. He was hard pressed to stop himself from laughing out loud. If they only knew ...

Alison was really excited at the prospect of sitting in a crowded room, totally unrecognisable as the Countess of Westminster. Andrew had altered her appearance with nothing more than plain glass spectacles, a black wig, and different make-up.

Much earlier in the evening, he had taken Jenkins into his confidence.

'Jenkins?'

'Sir?'

'The Lady Alison is travelling incognito tonight.'

'Yes, Sir, I understand.' But he did not.

'She'll be wearing a black wig and spectacles, all in fun of course, but it would not do for the staff to know, understood?'

'Oh! I see, Sir.' He was still at a loss.

'And erm, we shall enter by the tradesmen's entrance when we return and what the eye doesn't see ...' He placed his index finger along the right side of his nose and winked.

'I fully understand, Sir.'

'Oh, and please keep the staff out of the way, with discretion of course, when we leave.'

'Certainly, Sir, you may rely me.'

'I certainly hope so.'

And now the limousine with the tinted windows was speeding towards the place where Andrew's roadster was garaged. Alison was puzzled when Andrew left the main thoroughfare for the back streets. 'Where are you going, Andrew? This isn't the—'

'Don't worry your pretty little head my love,' Grant laughed, 'I just want to show you something first.'

'What is it?'

'A surprise,' he replied mysteriously. 'I've been saving it all the week, just for you.'

'A surprise? How lovely, Andrew, please tell me.'

'Wait and see, don't be so impatient, my darling.'

A few minutes later, he turned into the street where his car was garaged and stopped outside the garage doors. He pointed through the car window. 'Look there my sweet, isn't that lovely?'

'Where?'

'There, my dear, over there!'

Alison leaned forward in her seat to see just what it was that Andrew was pointing at. As she did so, the man pretending to lock his garage doors turned swiftly and rapidly made for the limousine. He reached it in two strides, opened the passenger door and climbed in before she could turn round. He reached forward quickly and clamped a pad over her mouth before she could utter a sound. She also felt her wrists being held as if in a vice by ... Realisation dawned as her senses slowly drifted away and she screamed his name in her brain. The person gripping her wrists so tightly was ...

'Andrew.' She tried to shout his name out loud as the sickly smell, that all too familiar hospital smell, began to overcome her every resistance. 'Chloroform, oh Andrew why-y-y...?'

She managed to look into his eyes as the man behind her, feeling her resistance weaken, relaxed slightly and Grant read the question in her eyes before she slumped into oblivion.

Brent, his accomplice, sitting in the back seat, felt sick at what he had just done and Andrew Grant spoke sharply to him. 'Pull yourself together, man, what's done is done!'

'Yes, Andrew, I know but—'

'Do not fail me now Brent.' There was quiet menace in Grant's voice.

'I won't, I promise Andrew, it's just that—'

'You've never done this before, I know, and neither have I, so that makes two of us, right?'

'I suppose so, I ... I n-never thought of it like that.' Brent's voice trembled slightly.

'All right, all right, now let's get moving shall we?' Grant was now brisk and businesslike. 'Did you bring blankets and a mattress?'

'They're all inside the hired van, just like you said.'

'Good, now get it over here quickly, time is very short and I still have lots to do. Quickly man, quickly!'

Stung into action, Brent ran to the van and quickly drove it alongside the limo, positioning it as close as possible.

'Help me move her,' Grant grunted as he struggled to drag Alison through the passenger door. Brent moved quickly to grab her feet and Grant took a swift look up and down the street; there was no one in sight. They transferred Alison to the back of the van and laid her on the mattress, covered her with blankets and locked the van doors.

'Hear me well now, Brent: keep an eagle eye on her on the way home. Do not, repeat, *do not* allow her to regain consciousness, I cannot stress this strongly enough. Do not let her wake up, if she as much as stirs, stop the van and give her the pad again. Are you taking all this in, my friend?'

Again Brent nodded.

'Good, she hasn't seen your face so she can't implicate you if anything goes wrong, which it won't. So wear you ski mask when you take her out of the van.'

'Ski mask,' Brent repeated.

'Ski mask, and wear it every time you have to attend to her, right?'

'Right,' Brent nodded, licking his lips nervously.

Grant sighed and continued, 'Shackle her to the bed by the wrists the way I showed you, remember? And when she has to pay a visit, shackle her ankles before you undo her wrists, got it?'

'Yes, I have got it, I'm not all that stupid!' Brent attempted a little show of indignation which made about as much impression as a damp squib.

Oh, are you not? Grant thought to himself but he spoke soothingly, patronisingly to Brent. 'Now *that* I know full well which is why I've chosen you and trust you. Now, please, hit the road, go go go!'

Gratified, Brent climbed behind the van wheel and started the engine. Grant placed his hand on the door handle. 'Brent,' he said softly.

'Yes, Andrew?'

'Two hundred and fifty thousand pounds - think about it, my friend.' He shut the van door and motioned his accomplice to go.

Brent thought about it and kept thinking about it all the way to Lincolnshire; it was the only thing that kept up his very weak resolve.

Grant in the meantime moved fast. He opened the garage doors, went inside and pulled them to behind him. Opening the car door, he got into the seat, switched on the interior light and opened the glove compartment. He reached inside, took out a folded plastic bag and opened it out on the seat, then wound down the passenger window. He got out of the car and went round the back to the boot. Out of it he lifted a dressed female dummy, which he propped up on its feet by the passenger door. Then he set to work.

Half an hour later, the dummy was sitting in the limousine. Andrew had worked well and to the world at large, the dummy was Alison looking out through the tinted glass.

With the garage safely locked, he climbed into the limousine and moved 'Alison' into a more natural pose. He looked at his watch: 8.45. It was nearly dusk now and Grant reckoned that by the time he arrived at Hamilcourt House, it would be dark enough to fool anyone with the dummy 'Alison'. He spotted one of the 'gardeners' reporting in on his handset; although he had tried to

49

conceal the move with a handkerchief, Andrew had spotted it. He chuckled in satisfaction because he knew that someone 'on high' had just been informed of the safe return of the Countess and her guest.

He tooled the limo around to the tradesmen's entrance, stopping as close as he dared. He walked around the car and opened the passenger door wide. He then opened the tradesmen's door so that it overlapped the car door, speaking in a loud voice as he did so.

'Come on Alison, love, you won't be in a fit state for opening tomorrow.'

Then in Alison's voice he replied, 'Oh Andy love, I'm sorry, I shouldn't have had that last one ... hic ... oooh!'

'Never mind, my dear cousin, you're home now, safe and sound, so come on, out you get ... ooh, steady now!'

The pair of watching eyes from the shrubbery could just about make out a man helping a very tipsy woman from the car, although his view was greatly obscured. The eyes belonged to Jimmy Finch and he was talking into his handset.

'Blimey, Guv, she's in a right old state, she's half cut, she'll have a right old head come morning.'

Mac at the other end, smiled at Jimmy's remarks. 'She doesn't open the hospital until 2 o'clock, plenty of time to get rid of the hangover.'

'Can I go and get a cup of cocoa or something, Guv? Nobody's going to have a go at her tonight, I shouldn't think.'

'No, don't relax yet, Jimmy, not yet anyway ... not yet.'

'OK, Guv, sorry. Stupid of me to ask really, considerin'.'

Mac smiled to himself again. 'Stick at it Jimmy, over and out.'

Jimmy watched the man come out of the tradesmen's entrance five minutes later and drive the limousine off to the garage. Very soon, he saw the same figure return and enter the house by the same entrance, closing the door behind him.

Once inside with the dummy, Grant had quickly but carefully dismantled it into six pieces: head, legs, arms and torso. He had placed them into a large canvas kit bag, previously hidden for that purpose in a broom closet, buried under a load of cleaning materials. After folding up the dummy's clothes, he quickly went upstairs with them.

CHAPTER ELEVEN
'IT DIDN'T GROW THERE, DID IT?'

Mac placed the toy van on the Chief Constable's desk and waited for the explosion. He didn't have to wait very long.

'How the hell did he get by you?' the Chief erupted. 'Why didn't you spot it earlier?'

Mac opened his mouth to speak but his Chief was in full flow. 'This man could have emptied the gas meters and nicked them as well and you wouldn't have noticed!' He paced back and forth. 'My God man, he could have reached out and touched her!'

'Sir, that's hardly fair,' Mac protested. 'There were just five of us and we were fairly well spread out.'

'Well it didn't grow there, did it?' He looked at Mac and suddenly his face softened. He grinned ruefully. 'Sorry Mac, I didn't mean to lose my temper. I think it was the sight of that toy that upset me, I wasn't expecting anything like that at all. I naturally assumed it would be the genuine article.'

'So did I, Sir, so did I.' Mac breathed a little more easily. 'It just proves Professor Hasketh right, Sir, about how this chap's mind works.'

'Too bloody true, Mac. It has been dusted for prints, I presume?'

'Oh yes, rapidly, nothing at all though.'

The Chief pondered for a moment. 'Well now, if this toy van wasn't put there during the ceremony, we must assume it was placed there afterwards. Did you put a camera in the flats opposite?'

'Two actually, but one failed for some reason, the other worked perfectly. The one that failed was focused on the spot where 'chappie' parked the van.'

'Who operated it?'

'No one, Sir, it was on automatic.'

The Chief groaned out loud. 'Then we have only straight line shots at the reception area?'

'Oh no, Sir, the other one was set up on one of Sanderson's automatically cranked tables.'

The Chief furrowed his brow and cocked his head inquiringly. 'Cranked tables? Please explain.'

'As you know Sir,' Mac began, 'we didn't put a man in there, being short-handed, so we used one of Sanderson's little patented inventions. It's a tripod arrangement with adjustable legs that lock in any set position.'

'Go on.'

'He has an arrangement of adjustable cranks, driven by a small lead screened motor, er, that's to stop interference on the tapes, and these can be set to pan the camera through any set range of vision that's required. He set it to requirements and switched it on by remote control when the time came, Sir.'

'Brilliant, absolutely brilliant!' the Chief laughed out loud. Then a thought struck him. 'When was it switched off?'

'It wasn't, Sanderson left it running until he went to collect it later, about an hour after the Countess had gone home.'

'Did you pan as far as the gates, where the toy was left, I mean?'

'Yes, Sir,' said Mac 'but I think we may have hit a snag.'

'Oh no! How?'

'The lens was focused on the Countess and the crowd around her so the area around the van may be a bit blurred, I think, but I can't be sure of that,' he added.

'So if anyone put that bloody toy there within the hour, it should be on the video tape.'

Mac was cautious. 'I most certainly hope so, Sir.'

'Right, let's get to it then, we'll run the tapes and with a bit of luck, we may well hit the jackpot.' The Chief rubbed his hands in anticipation. 'Heaven knows, we could do with a bit of luck.'

'I'll get it laid on right now,' said Mac, 'we can only live in hope. We have about eight or nine collective hours to run through, but I'll run the one taken from the flat first if you like, Sir.'

'Yes, we can run it through at a trotting speed until the van appears, or something ... anything. Meanwhile I'll get on to the PM about this' - he gestured towards the van - 'latest blasted development.'

'Ahem, if I were you, Sir,' Mac advised, 'I'd phone him from a safe distance, give him time to come back out of orbit. He's bound to give birth over this little lot.'

'I'm well aware of that, Mac,' the Chief sighed, with the air of a man who has the whole world's troubles on his broad shoulders. 'Better get on with it, I suppose. Get things set up, I'll see you later.'

'Right Sir,' Mac nodded and left the room.

The Chief Constable was not looking forward to the next few minutes. He sighed, took a deep breath and picked up the phone.

CHAPTER TWELVE
'FREEZE THAT FRAME'

Three television sets with video-playing equipment had been rigged up in the 'back room', as it was called at HQ. When a top secret operation was 'going down', no unauthorised entry was allowed. All food and drink for the team was left outside and one of the occupants fetched it inside.

Seven pairs of eyes were glued to one screen as the 'flats' tape was being run. As the screen showed, Terry Sanderson's mechanical marvel worked a treat. The camera had panned from side to side beautifully, capturing the Countess and the crowd on either side, just as Mac had said it would.

'Lovely!' enthused the chief, beaming at Terry. 'Congratulations on a fine job, Sanderson, an excellent piece of ingenuity.'

'Thank you, Sir.'

'Right,' said the chief, turning back to the screen. 'Let's have a look at the tail end of this tape,' and he crossed his fingers as Mac operated the controls, gradually increasing the speed to save time.

They watched the Countess being driven in, the ceremony that followed, the speech, the cutting of the tape, all in fast-motion, and afterwards her departure. The film panned faithfully from side to side, stopping alternately on both the left and then the right of the Countess, without actually omitting her from the picture.

Included in the film was the spot where the toy van was found. As the film rolled on, the team watched as the crowd dispersed rapidly from the hospital reception area and workmen dismantled the temporary staging. After a while, all that could be seen was the occasional ambulance or private car coming or going along the Tarmac.

Everyone waited with bated breath to see if the toy van would be in the frame when the camera panned in that direction.

'By the way, Sir,' Terry addressed Sir Donald, 'this camera is fitted with a special focus, but it only works in special conditions using the long range that we were using.'

'How's that?'

'Well, Sir, on this particular type ...' Terry paused to try to find a simple way to explain a very complex piece of Swiss technological magic. He found one. 'Let me put it this way. There are a couple of ways to set the zoom mechanism. You can set it with emphasis on pull ... erm ... that's zoom out, Sir, and middle distance focus, that's using the one type of lens, or simply far focus and near focus, clear both ends and blurred in the middle.'

'Which one did you use, Terry?'

'Oh, the last one, Sir, we wanted good clear pictures of the Countess and the van, if any of course, and not the middle. After all, Sir, who's going to try anything from the middle?'

'Quite, who indeed?' the Chief smiled. 'By the way, is this your own equipment or does it belong to the firm?

'Mine Sir,' said Terry, 'and it cost me an arm and a leg - not that I mind, Sir, it's my hobby.'

The Chief nodded his appreciation. 'What about crowds, I mean, how does the lens react to, say, a football crowd?'

'Well what happens then, Sir, is the lens settles on middle focus the same way as an ordinary lens, which is precisely what we don't want really.' Terry coughed self-consciously. 'I, erm, also set the crank on delayed return ... both ends ... so that the camera lingered for a couple of seconds longer than it normally would.'

The Chief looked incredulous. 'How on earth did you manage that?'

Mac laughed out loud at that. 'Don't ask, Sir, he just uses a crafty arrangement of slot holes and very light springs. That of course is putting it mildly ...'

The Chief held up his hands, palms outwards. 'Whoa, I don't think I want to know any more thanks, Mac,' he grinned at Terry, 'I think I've had enough surprises for today. Please, let's get on.'

'Erm, Sir?'

'Yes, Terry?' sighed the Chief.

'There's just one more thing about this lens, apart from it costing me two hundred and eighty quid, that is.'

'Oh, and what's that?'

'Well, Sir, when it focuses on the Countess, we shall get an ordinary zoom out that will take in the surrounding crowds, but when it cranks back to this end it should react a little bit, well, different.'

'How do you mean?' The Chief was intrigued.

Terry took a deep breath. 'Well, the lens is designed to do a special job, Sir. What I mean is, well, if there's a crowd, it will accommodate as many as is comfortable, you know, not too many or too few but ...'

'But if there's only one?'

'If there's only one, Sir,' Terry took another deep breath, 'I'll give you my personal guarantee that that person will fill the screen ... rapidly, in full resolution.'

The Chief opened his mouth to speak and closed it again, shaking his head in wonderment.

Mac grinned at him. 'Well, you did ask me to pick a good team, Sir.'

The Chief grinned wryly. 'Yes, I did, did I not? However,' he thumbed towards the screen, 'the proof of the pudding ...'

Everyone looked at the screen automatically. Mac, who was at the controls, looked at the number counter on the video panel. 'We're getting close to the end of the tape now,' he said, speaking to no one in particular, 'still got a vacant space where th—' He stopped speaking suddenly and hit the stop button.

'Something there, Mac?'

'Yes, Sir, there most certainly is. Hang on, I'll run it back a bit.'

The atmosphere was electric and everyone crowded in closer as Mac operated the controls. He reversed the tape rapidly and stopped it. He then reset the forward play to normal speed and with a 'Here goes', pushed the play button.

He tensed as he stared at the screen, waiting for the camera to pan round again. A blurred head came into view just as the camera panned away and the Chief looked questioningly at Terry.

'Don't worry Sir, that wasn't a full picture. If that person fills the frame next time around ... bingo!'

You could have heard a pin drop as seven pairs of eyes, hardly daring to blink, willed the camera on its return journey - and at last, there it was, large as life.

At first, a blurred figure, upright, came into the middle of the frame. The figure stopped and leaned forward with its back to the camera. The blur suddenly became a clear picture and, as Terry had promised, it enlarged to fill the whole frame.

The camera lingered for a few seconds and then began to pan away just as the person in the frame began to turn around - a fraction of a second too late to get a good view of the person's face. Any identification was impossible, but everyone had spotted one thing.

'Blimey!' Jimmy Finch exploded. 'It's a woman, a ruddy female.'

Bob Saunders shook his head in disbelief. 'I see it, but I don't believe it. All this time we've been looking for a bloke and it's a bloody woman!'

'Hold on a bit, Bob,' said Mac, 'let me freeze that frame.'

He ran the film backwards until he found the beginning of that particular sequence, then he ran it forward slowly until he reached the full blown-up shot of the woman.

The Chief nodded. 'It's a female all right.'

The frame showed, in full focus, a female figure in the act of turning, with only a small part of her face showing.

Mac leaned back in his chair. 'Now there's a turn-up for the book. I think our pet professor may just have got it wrong; he said male, not female.'

'I think not, Mac,' said Jimmy Finch. 'If you run the film back a little, you'll see why.' Mac inched the tape back slowly until ... 'There, stop there ... no, forward just a touch ... touch more... There, you see!' he cried triumphantly.

Mac was puzzled at first, then the penny dropped.

The picture he was looking at was blurred, but no so blurred he could not see what 'she' was carrying. It was in her left hand .

The mood changed rapidly from tension to jubilation as the significance of what they had all witnessed went home: Hasketh had been right about the person being left handed.

The Chief spoke quietly. 'OK, lads, something to go on at last, slim I'll grant you, but a start nevertheless.'

'It looks like I spoke too soon, about the professor I mean,' said Mac ruefully. 'He said our man was left-handed.' He pointed to the screen, 'that could be our man in drag.'

'Well look at Danny Street, Guv,' said Bob Saunders. 'When he dresses up, it's for real and if I didn't know he was a bloke to start with, I'd be took in good and proper. Come to think of it, I *was* the very first time, until he opened his mouth, that is.'

'What about that pair on the telly then,' Terry chipped in, 'Locke and Keye. They not only look like women, they walk and talk like them. As near as dammit is to swearing, they *are* females.'

The Chief raised his eyes skywards and shook his head. 'OK, lads,' he sighed, 'let's go through the rest of the films just in case we can spot anything else.'

Hour after hour, they pored over the tapes, coming up with precisely nothing. After a while, Mac took his Chief aside.

'Look, Sir, these lads have been at it hour after hour, on top of which they've been slogging away at surveillance for days on end with hardly any rest.'

'Make your point, Mac.'

'Send them home for a rest, if only for eight hours, and they'll come back with a fresher outlook to the job in hand.'

'Yes, I quite agree. I'm feeling the pinch myself and so are you by the look of it. We could all do with a small break, yes, why not?'

He turned to issue the order and Mac touched his arm. 'Excuse my familiarity, Sir, but there is something else.'

'Oh, what's that?'

'I would very much like your permission for Jan to look at the tapes, Sir.'

'The devil you would! It's out of the qu—'

'Hold hard, Sir,' soothed Mac. 'Jan used to work for us as a data analyst. She's as much at home on a computer as a fish is in water, and if there's anything on those tapes, anything at all, you can bet your best boots she'll find it.' Mac hurried on before his Chief could say no. 'It was her first love before we met, Sir. Besides, she'd give her eye teeth to have a go at this one.'

The Chief cupped his right elbow in his left hand and stroked his chin, deep in thought.

'If I said yes,' he said finally, 'she would most certainly have to know what it was all about.'

'I know that, Sir, but she knows the form. If I say mum's the word, wild horses wouldn't move her.'

The Chief studied Mac for a few seconds. 'OK Mac, it will be my head that will roll, so I hold you fully responsible for the tapes and Jan's silence, do you understand?'

'Loud and clear. Don't worry about Jan, Sir, she practically invented the lip zip.'

The Chief, now committed to the idea, realised he had no real qualms about Jan. He turned around to face the team. 'OK, lads, that's it for tonight, go home to your wives or whoever and be back here in twelve hours.'

'Or in Jimmy's case, somebody else's missus!' Terry chortled.

Jimmy made a menacing move towards his friend and colleague, who backed off rapidly.

'All right, you lot,' chuckled the chief, 'wait until you get outside if you want to knock each other's heads off. Oh, and Sanderson!'

'Sir?'

'Congratulations and my heartfelt thanks for a brilliant piece of camera work. Thanks to you, we now have a lead - a small one, but a lead just the same.'

'My pleasure, Sir.' Then he grinned broadly. 'Fame at last!'

'Right, off you go, all of you, you too Mac. Get some rest and be back here in twelve hours.

Once outside in the corridor, Smithy spoke quietly to Mac from behind. 'Guvnor?'

Mac stopped and turned. 'Yes, Smithy?'

'Look, Guv,' said Smithy hesitantly, 'my missus is away for the weekend looking after her mother.'

'Oh yes, she broke her hip didn't she?'

'That's right Guv,' Smithy nodded, 'and so I was wondering if I could take some of the tapes home with me. We haven't any kids, as you know, mind you, it's not for the want of trying.' He looked sad. 'My Helen adores children .' He stopped. 'Sorry Guv, I didn't mean to go on, what I mean is, it can get a bit lonely at times.'

Mac looked at the big man, a dear friend as well as a trusted colleague, who could take any amount of punishment as well as dish it out but who would be putty in the hands of any walking disaster area that came in the shape of a child.

'I don't see why not, mate, we really could do with some extra help on this, but what about your rest?'

'Guv, when I'm in my favourite armchair in front of my telly, I know I'm home, see what I mean? It don't feel the same without Helen about the house, you know, pottering about, so I wouldn't sleep anyway.'

'I see what you mean Smi—'

Jimmy cleared his throat as he interrupted Mac. 'Pardon the interruption, Guv, but we couldn't help overhearing and erm, we three could quite easily take offence if we were left out, er, if we couldn't help out I mean, Guv.'

Mac chuckled. 'OK, OK, I've got the message.' He furrowed his brow. 'You, er, wouldn't have been eavesdropping on the Chief Constable and me by any chance?'

'Who me, Sir? No, Sir,' lied Jimmy. 'I didn't hear you talking about taking the tapes ho—' He nose-dived.

'Dopey bugger,' Bob grunted.

With three sheepish grins in front of him, Mac roared with mirth. 'All right, all right.' He held his hands up in surrender. 'You shall go to the ball, you creeps, though why I should have to ... Oh never mind. Look, there are five tapes so we'll take one each or better still, we'll make some copies just in case of unforeseen accidents.'

'I'll do that right now, Guv,' said Terry, 'on the new Rapide duplicator.'

'Where is it?'

'In the laboratory at Scotland Yard.'

'Will they let you use it?'

'I'm about the only bloke who can - properly, that is,' Terry said, not quite telling the truth. 'Honestly Guv, I'm in and out of there like a blue-arsed fly doing various jobs, all in the line of duty o'course.'

'Yea,' said Jimmy, 'developing his dirty photos, more like.' He ducked as Terry took a playful swing at him.

Mac laughed. 'How long will it take?'

'Oh! let me see now, five tapes at ten minutes each equals five tens is fifty ... Give me an hour, Guv, they'll be ready by then.'

Mac phoned Jan to tell her what time he would be home and they spent a good ten minutes threatening each other with all sorts of wonderful things. He just loved the sound of her voice; that delightful Scottish burr of hers did funny things to his left-handed flibberty bobble.

At home, Jan was having the same kind of trouble with her grumbly flutees. It was only by using the utmost concentration that she managed to get Mac's kippers on a plate and his slippers in front of the fire.

CHAPTER THIRTEEN
JAN STUDIES THE TAPES

Jan listened for the familiar sound of Mac's car. It always gave her a warm glow, knowing that her man was home, safe and sound, if only for a little while. At last she heard it and a few seconds later ...

'Darling, I'm home.'

She met him by the door as he came in and kissed him passionately, wantonly. He broke free just long enough to ask, 'Where are the bairns?'

'In bed.'

He reached behind her and drew the heavy curtains across, then they spent the next ten minutes locked together, oblivious of everything but each other.

A little while later, Mac was sitting comfortably in his favourite armchair. Jan called from the kitchen.

'Come and get it!'

'I though I just did,' Mac chuckled cheekily.

With a twinkle in her eye, Jan put her head round the door. 'I'm talking about something to eat, you stupid policeman.'

Mac leaped out of his chair and shot towards the kitchen. Jan squealed and retreated rapidly.

'Right, you've had it,' he growled menacingly.

Jan grabbed a large carving knife from the draining board. They stopped and faced each other across the kitchen table.

'You cannot escape me, wench!' he grated in a fair imitation of a villainous landlord.

'Oh, spare me!' cried Jan, now in damsel-in-distress mode.

'No,' Mac cried, 'there will be no mercy for you, my girl. Har, har!'

'But I'm only thirteen, Sir,' wailed Jan, fluttering her eyelashes, 'and completely unsullied.'

'What do I care for your virtue, you little—' Then Mac began to crumble and they both ended up in fits of laughter.

He finally sat down to his meal and she fussed around until he was good and properly fed.

The meal finished, Mac stretched luxuriously and beckoned to Jan. 'Got a job for you, luv.'

'Have you, sweetie, something special?' Jan was intrigued.

'Oh yes, it's a corker, right up your street.'

Jan glowed inwardly at the thought of using her talents again. Mac told her the full story to date as he helped her wash the dishes, relating how his team had insisted on helping out with 'homework'.

'They really are a great bunch of lads, I couldn't ask for better,' he added proudly. 'They do anything I ask of them without question.'

Jan smiled at her husband because she knew why.

The dishes finished, they made their way to the comfortable living room and relaxed on the settee. As Mac reached for his briefcase, Jan was tempted to pinch his bottom but had second thoughts. She was more than eager to get on with the problem at hand and further horseplay would only delay things. Mac opened his case and pulled out a video tape; tapping it with his finger, he said, 'The answer's in here, Jan, I know it, I can feel it in my bones.'

'And you want me to find it for you, Sweetie, if whatever you're looking for is in there.'

'That's about the size of it, luv.' He loaded the tape into the video player.

'OK, big fellow, go to bed, get yourself some well-earned shut-eye and I'll give it a going over.'

Mac started to protest but Jan was having none of it. 'You know I work better on my own,' she chided him gently, 'if I get stuck, I'll whistle, OK?'

Mac gave in reluctantly, realising at last just how tired he was.

'OK, you win, I really could do with some sleep and - oh!' He reached into his pocket, pulled out a long brown envelope and handed it to Jan. 'These are photostats of both demand notes, plus Professor Hasketh's rundown on our dear 'friend's' character.'

Jan took the envelope. 'Right sweetie, leave it with me, now go! And I mean scram.'

Mac smiled, blew her a kiss and went. She watched him until he had shut the stairway door and only when she was satisfied that he had climbed into bed did she set to work.

Jan knew that what she had to do would take all her ingenuity. First, she read everything through many times until she had built up a picture in her mind of this would-be kidnapper. She then ran the video tape through at a slightly faster speed than normal, her eyes racing over the crowd. She spotted nothing out of the ordinary until she came to the part that Mac had asked her to pay specific attention to - the placing of the toy van. She studied the woman on the tape intently, running the sequence backwards and forwards many times, working on it for an hour or so. She then began going a little further back and then a little further forward until she was satisfied with what she had found.

The sequence she finally settled on was a good deal longer than Mac and his team had been studying. She ran it over and over and eventually smiled at her discovery. Happy now, she glanced casually at the clock and sat up with a start.

'My God, it's three o'clock in the morning! How time flies when you're having fun,' Jan mused.

She switched off the tape and removed it from the video machine, placed the tapes and papers in a large envelope and put them in an open roll top desk, pulling down the slatted front and locking it securely. 'Mustn't let the bairns get hold of those, especially the tape.' She shuddered at the thought of it ending up showing an episode of The Pepsi Chart.

Jan was dying to wake Mac and tell him of her little discovery, but she decided against it. 'Poor old sweetie.' she thought fondly, 'it'll keep until morning.'

Upstairs, she undressed in the dark, not bothering with her nightdress, and crept naked into bed. She was careful not to disturb her husband, who was in a deep sleep.

She lay on her back with her hands behind her head, thinking of the day's events. Although she was satisfied with her findings, Jan had a feeling that there was more. She decided to use one of the police consoles; they were more sophisticated and could enlarge things many thousand times. She would get Mac to borrow one in the morning.

She was still mulling things over in her mind as she drifted off to sleep.

After a while, Mac stirred and, remembering where he was,

rolled over. Jan stirred but she did not wake up. He gently eased her arms under the covers and kissed her lovingly on the forehead before closing his eyes and drifting off to sleep again. In his dreams, he was chasing a woman who kept throwing toy vans over her shoulder but, try as he might, he just could not catch her. On a little platform, holding a pair of scissors, was the Countess with her entourage, urging him on, trying to trip him up at the same time with yards and yards of pink ribbon.

Next, morning, Jan woke him with a cup of tea.

'Mac,' she cried, 'the house is on fire!' There was a gleam in her eye as she awaited the predictable result. It took all of ten seconds for Jan's warning to sink in, then he shot bolt upright.

'What th—!' he began. Then he saw Jan grinning impishly. He made a grab for her and she stepped back hastily.

'Swine!' he growled.

'Pig,' she retorted and grinned at him. He grinned back and took the tea.

'Morning, luvvy.'

'Morning, sweetie,' she replied and sat on the edge of the bed just watching him.

He took a good swig of tea and felt better.

'Find anything, luv?' he asked hopefully.

'Yes, I did. It doesn't seem to be much, not at first but ... look, get dressed and I'll show you.'

'Be down in a minute,' he yawned and stretched luxuriously before climbing out of bed.

'My mouth tastes like a Sumo wrestler's jockstrap,' said Mac as he made his way to the bathroom. 'Be down in a few minutes.'

'I've got breakfast going, bacon and eggs do?'

'Can't I have you on toast instead?' his muffled voice sounded hopeful from the bathroom.

'Sorry, out of bread, handsome,' Jan shouted back, chuckling quietly to herself.

'Curses, foiled again,' said Mac, and Jan heard the sound of running water.

Mac appeared in the kitchen some ten minutes later. He gave Jan a hug and a kiss. 'Hell of a nightmare last night,' he said and told her all about it.

'This little lot's getting to you, isn't it love, I mean, for you to have nightmares ...'

'I must admit, it is,' Mac agreed. 'Can you imagine the furore, the panic if he pulls it off, if he does manage to kidnap Alison, I mean ...' Mac's face was filled with consternation. 'My God, Jan, with only a few of us, where would we begin to look for her before it became general knowledge?'

'The Press would have a field day,' Jan mused.

'Now that would never do!' Mac was most emphatic. 'We have to catch this bloke luv ... rapidly.' He punched his fist into his palm for emphasis.

'Come on, sweetie.' Jan made for the roll top desk. 'Let me show you what I found.'

'Something good, I hope.'

She loaded the tape as he looked on. He looked apprehensive as she set the controls.

'Ready?' she said quietly over her shoulder.

He nodded.

'Here we go then.' She pressed play. 'Now here's the bit that interested you.' She went on to show the very short sequence that the team had studied the night before, then stopped the tape suddenly. 'And this is the extra bit that interests me.'

Mac's own interest sharpened somewhat as Jan wound the tape back quite a few feet. She spoke over her shoulder again. 'Now listen as well as watch,' she said earnestly.

Mac nodded. 'OK.'

'I'll lift my finger about a second before the sound I want you to hear, OK?'

Mac nodded. 'A second before the sound.'

'I'll do the same after the woman has left the picture, follow?'

Again Mac nodded.

'Here we go then.' She pressed 'play'.

As the film began to run, Jan raised her closed hand in readiness. Suddenly, her index finger straightened and she breathed, 'Now!'

Mac listened, not quite knowing what to listen for. Jan saw the puzzlement written all over his face and cried, 'The car engine, Mac, listen!'

Realization dawned then as he heard the sound of a car come to a halt off-camera. He heard the car door slam and half a minute later (Jan raised her finger again), he heard the same car door slam again. He looked at Jan but she pointed to her ear.

'Listen!' came her urgent whisper.

Mac did. He heard an engine start or rather roar into life and head off he knew not where.

Jan stopped the tape and looked at Mac with a twinkle in her eye. 'How about that, kind Sir?'

The implication of what he had just heard was not lost on Mac.

'Jan, luv, I think you've cracked it! Let me hear that engine again, from beginning to end, that same sequence.'

He was excited now because he knew that sound, he was almost certain ... They played it over and over until he was certain. Mac kissed Jan gratefully.

'Let's get hold of Bob Saunders.'

'I though you'd do that somehow, sweetie, best engine man in the business.'

'You're not wrong there, luv, if anyone can pick out the make of that car, he can.'

He went to the phone and dialled. 'I hope he's at home.'

The phone rang for some time before a sleepy voice answered. It was Bob Saunders and Mac had roused him from his bed.

'Bob, this is Mac ... Oh, I'm sorry, mate, but I have something for you, it's right up your street ... Yes, I'm at home ... In half an hour ... Hang on a sec.' He turned to Jan. 'Can you lay him on a bit of breakfast luv, save a bit of time.' She nodded. 'Don't worry about breakfast, it's laid on.'

He put the handset down and rubbed his hands together in anticipation. 'Now we're beginning to get somewhere.'

'What if Bob can't recognise it, what then?' asked Jan.

'Voice print.'

Jan looked puzzled. 'Voice print? What on earth ...?'

Mac laughed and began to explain. 'Every voice is different in some way and it shows on a special screen after being passed through a series of, erm, sensors if you like. Look, even if you heard two voices that sounded exactly the same and one belonged to a mimic, this gadget would show them to be two different people.

Even two identical car engines would sound different, or rather look different on the screen.'

Jan was beginning to understand now. 'You mean in peaks and troughs, yes, I've seen those gadgets on the telly.'

'Oh!'

'On Tomorrow's World.'

'I think you may have been watching too many sci-fi programmes and anyway, if I'm correct, there aren't too many engines of that type on the road so let's wait for Bob, eh?'

She nodded and looked at the clock. 'I think I'd better get the bairns up for school.'

'I'll get them out of it, luv, you fix breakfast.'

'OK.'

He bounded up the stairs in five giant strides. Jan heard his footsteps across the children's room and smiled broadly at the happy squeals and giggles as he tickled his children awake.

'Don't eat me, daddy!' yelled Jenny, squealing with both delight and fright.

'I'm a troll, and I love children for breakfast.'

Jan could picture Mac doing a fair imitation of Quasimodo as Ian galloped down the stairs.

'He's not going to eat me, Mum!' Ian was trembling excitedly and hopping from foot to foot and Jan lifted her tousle-haired offspring off the floor into a protective embrace.

'He won't get you,' she said, hugging him tightly and getting hugged in return. 'I'll pull his teeth out and nail his feet to the floor.'

Another squeal came from the direction of the stairs, the door burst open and Jenny hared across the room to hide behind her Mummy's skirt. 'Don't let him get me, Mummy, he's going to eat me all up!' She squealed and laughed at the same time as the 'troll' came through the door, his face all screwed up, his shoulders hunched, and dragging one leg.

'Fee fi fo fum!' he roared as the children laughed hysterically, thoroughly enjoying every moment of it.

Jan laughed out loud. 'Why is it,' she choked, 'you can never find a copper when you want one?'

Grinning broadly, Mac collapsed onto the settee and held his arms wide open. With the 'troll' gone, they ran over to him and he hugged them close, kissing the tops of their heads.

Jan was seeing the children onto the school bus when Bob Saunders finally arrived.

'Morning, Mrs Macdonald,' he greeted her with a rueful smile. 'Sorry I'm late, somebody slashed one of me tyres.

Jan was shocked. 'What on earth is the world coming to? And you a policeman too!'

'Probably why, Mrs M.'

'Go on in, Bob, Mac's waiting for you. I'll be in shortly, just as soon as this bus has gone.'

Bob went inside. 'It's me, Guv, Saunders.'

'Come in, Bob.' Mac's voice came from the direction of the living room. 'I'm in here.'

'Sorry I'm late, Guv, somebody slashed me ruddy tyre.'

'Bastards!' Mac was angry. 'Bloody stanley knife brigade.'

'You know, Guv, just once, I'd like to be behind them with a dirty great club as they were doing it and bugger the consequences.'

'You and me both, son, the temptation would be hard to resist,' he sighed. 'But then ...' He shrugged his shoulders.

'Yea. But it'd be great giving 'em what for just before they slapped us in Pentonville.'

Mac grinned and changed the subject. 'Come and get an earful of this and tell me what you think it is.' He turned to the video just as Jan came in.

'Do him some brekky luv, please, he looks as if he could do with some.'

Bob smiled. 'That's the truth Mrs M, I could eat a horse between two bread vans, spit the tyres out and wash it down with an old brewer's bath water.'

Jan wrinkled her nose. 'Disgusting!'

Mac grinned. 'I didn't teach him that, he must be keeping the wrong company, luv. Erm, would you do me a bacon sarnie, you know, just to keep the first lot down. Please?'

Jan disappeared into the kitchen, shaking her head, and as she rustled up a tasty snack, Mac outlined everything to date. While he ran the tapes, Bob cocked his head to one side in intense concentration. He listened a few times before he was absolutely satisfied that he could name the engine ... and the car. Before he could speak, Mac pulled a folded piece of paper from his pocket.

'I'll stake my job that what I've written here and what you are about to say are one and the same, so ... go on!'

'It's an Ashdown Marsden DB or I'm not DC Robert Saunders.'

Mac exhaled slowly, opened his slip of paper triumphantly and turned it towards Bob. His eyes were shining as he almost shouted, 'Bingo!' He slowly collapsed onto the settee and shut his eyes. He was smiling.

Bob Saunders looked concerned. 'You OK, Guv?'

'Just a little anti-climax. Do you know how many Ashdown Marsdens there are in this country?'

'Oh, 'bout four, five hundred I suppose, probably less.'

'I'd say a lot less. That's a purpose built car, very, very expensive. There's a hell of a waiting list, if I believe correctly.'

'How many would you think then, Guv?'

'Very thin on the ground I'd say,' Mac mused thoughtfully, 'and only where the money is.'

'Well, we're off the starting blocks, Guv, but we've a hell of a long way to go.'

'Yeah, don't I know it.'

'So what's the form the—?'

Jan interrupted from the kitchen. 'Come and get it, before it gets cold.'

'Lovely, let's eat and kick it about a bit at the same time, I can always think better on a full stomach.'

They sat down at the kitchen table and Bob tucked into a good old English breakfast of bacon, eggs, sausage and tomatoes with a steaming mug of tea. Mac munched his sandwich with obvious relish and, speaking in between mouthfuls, he began to count on his fingers.

'Number one,' he pointed at his little finger, 'we'll take it for granted that this fellow means business, OK?'

'Right.'

'Number two' - another finger - 'he's going to pick his own time.'

'And place.'

'Not if I have anything to do with it,' Mac said vehemently.

'Er, no, course not Guv.'

'Number three' - middle finger - 'he's a drag artist.'

'Right, Guv.'

'Number four' - index finger - 'he's left handed.'

'That's what the professor said he was.'

'Number five,' said Mac, holding his thumb, 'we're ninety-nine per cent certain that he drives an Ashdown Marsden.'

'Which is a very expensive piece of merchandise.'

'And that is exactly my point.' Mac spread his hands. 'Just how many people can get hold of one, let alone afford one, eh?'

'Good point, Guv.'

'Also, if he's rich, that narrows down the areas he would live in, wouldn't it?'

'Mmm, I suppose so Guv, yeah, course it would.'

'I hate clever-clogged, big-headed inspectors,' said Jan in a lilting voice as she disappeared through the kitchen doorway, 'he can't find his socks half the time.'

Jan enjoyed her little joke at her husband's expense but she was really very proud of his capabilities, even though she did help him out on the odd occasion.

Mac grinned at Bob. 'Don't worry your head, old son, I've bought her a road map and hiking boots for Christmas.'

He ducked as a rolled-up sock whizzed past his head and all three roared with laughter. When it subsided, Mac said soberly, 'Let's run a trace on all Ashdown Marsden owners, Bob and if we get no joy, we'll widen the circle.'

CHAPTER FOURTEEN
TIME IS OF THE ESSENCE

In the 'back room' at the Yard, Mac and his assembled team had given the Chief Constable an up-to-date report on events so far. He was satisfied with their progress even though they had little to go on.

'So now we're waiting for Swansea, said the Chief.

'Yes, Sir,' said Mac, 'I stressed the urgency because of a threat to national security. I didn't tell them any more than that. I got in direct contact with the head man at Swansea in your name, Sir, I didn't think you'd mind, given the situation, and it seems to have worked wonders. The big man himself has taken charge.'

The Chief smiled modestly. 'Yes, yes of course, you were quite right Mac. Time is of the essence, after all.'

Mac smiled back and nodded before turning his attention to his men. 'Anyone find anything on the tapes? No? I didn't think you would somehow. Thank you anyway, lads, for taking the time out to have a look.'

'That's OK, Guv.'

'Right, let's get on. I'll go through everything we have so far. Yes I know that you already know, but we'll do it again anyway, because while we're waiting for Swansea to come up with the goods, I want any fresh ideas that you might come up with.'

'What puzzles me, Guv,' said Jimmy, 'is how did this woman, I mean man, or maybe it was a woman, how did he or she know when it was safe to bring that van in?'

'Good point, Jimmy, anyone got any ideas?'

'Could be he thought we'd gone away,' Terry ventured.

. 'Mmm, maybe maybe maybe,' Mac mused.

Bob cleared his throat. 'Try this for size. This bloke would think that we would think that he would come as a bloke, not as a woman, with a big van and not a little one.' He shook his head and grinned. 'I dunno what I just said but I know what I meant.'

Mac laughed. 'I think I do too, what you're saying is, nobody would suspect a woman walking through the hospital gates carrying a toy for one of the patients, right?'

'Er, that's what I meant, more or less,' Bob agreed ruefully.

'Did you sue her, Bob?' Terry asked innocently.

'Who?'

'Your English teacher,' Terry grinned wickedly.

'Ha bloody ha!'

'All right, you lot, the question was, how did he know when it was safe?'

'Anti-climax,' said the Chief simply.

'How's that, Sir?' Mac was puzzled.

The Chief held his temples between his right thumb and forefingers and extended his left hand. 'Look, this man is nigh on a genius according to Professor Hasketh, and so, given his brain power, he would assume, rightly, that we would be at the hospital as a matter of course. He would also assume that we would be pumping a lot of adrenaline, uptight, stressed out, do you follow me so far?'

Mac nodded. 'Erm mmm yes, I think I do.'

'Well you see,' the Chief resumed, 'everything works in pairs: nadir and zenith, up and down, night and day. Push is the opposite of pull, hot and cold, high and low.'

'Bless me soul, yes I do see, Sir, quite clearly. This man relied on us being on our toes, on edge, knowing full well that just as soon as the good lady had got safely home, we would relax.'

'Precisely, Mac, the clever bugger read the situation just as if he'd planned it himself.' He shook his head and smiled ruefully.

'Well he did, didn't he? Plan it, I mean,' Mac said quietly.

'Jesus wept,' said Jimmy, 'how do you catch a bloke who's more or less planning *our* every move?'

Terry shook his head. 'It don't bear thinking about.' He turned the corners of his mouth down and shook his head

'Steady on, you lot,' said Mac, 'knowing about it makes the job easier.'

'How, Guv?'

'Well, he's anticipating us, so it follows that we've got to anticipate him, try to out think him.'

'How, Guv?'

'Try to put ourselves in his place.'

'Now, that's easier said than done,' said Bob Saunders, 'this bloke's playing chess with us and he knows all the moves in front.'

'Nicely put, me old son,' said Mac. 'I couldn't have put it better myself.'

Just then, someone knocked on the door and the Chief motioned Mac to open it. A station clerk stood there.

'Excuse me, Sir, but Swansea is on the phone and they're asking for you.'

'Thank you, Constable, hang on a moment.' He turned to the Chief. 'I'll be back shortly, Sir, keep you fingers crossed.' He turned back to the clerk. 'Have it put through to my office.'

'Yes, Sir,' said the clerk as he walked away.

Mac strode rapidly to his private office and closed the door behind him. He sat behind his desk and picked up the phone. He listened until he heard a click and a voice said, 'You're through, Sir.'

'Thank you, now please close this line off.'

'Sir?'

'Put your phone down, Constable.'

'Er, yes, Sir.'

Mac heard the faint click that told him his order had been obeyed. Another voice came on the line. 'Detective Inspector Macdonald?'

'Speaking.'

'Davies here, Swansea. I have what you require, Mr Macdonald.'

'Splendid,' Mac said gratefully, 'well done, Mr Davies. How many are there?'

'Well now, our computer kicked out no less than six hundred and fifteen nationwide and I've split these into areas as you requested.'

'How many in the London area?'

'Twenty-one altogether.'

Suddenly Mac had an idea. 'Can you tell me just how many there are within a thirty-mile radius of Westminster?' He did not mention the Countess's residence.

'Erm, not right off, Inspector, I'm a local man, you see, and not at all familiar with your territory.'

'I see your point,' said Mac, 'it would take hours over the phone.'

'Erm, can you link your computer through the grid if I give you an entry code?'

'That's a bit risky, isn't it?' said Mac. 'What if someone gets hold of it with a crossed line, they could make a fortune punching in non-existent road tax fees that hadn't been paid but the computer would swear blind that they had.'

Davies chortled. 'I'm well aware of that, Inspector, that's why the entry code is changed every so often. As a matter of fact, it's due to be changed this very day.'

Mac thought for a moment. 'How long will it take to transmit the complete list?'

'It'll take about twenty seconds to feed in the code and wait for the "access granted" to appear on your screen. Then you have to ask the computer to put you on to our special transmit relay - I'll give you another code for that. I'll key this one myself, specially for this transmission. Our computer will then tell me the job is done, then all I have to do is wipe that transmission clean and feed in a new code. You with me?'

'I am indeed. Can you hold while I set this up with our computer department?'

Mac held the phone to his chest and picked up the internal phone. 'Get me the computer room please, this is Inspector Macdonald.' He waited a few seconds. 'Taylor, this is Macdonald, I'll be putting a Mr Davies of Swansea over to you in a moment. Do exactly as he tells you and have the end result sent over to my office as soon as you have them. Many many thanks to you.'

'You're welcome,' was the cheerful reply.

Mac pressed a button on the phone stand and a voice said, 'Switchboard'

'Put this caller directly through to Taylor in Computers and isolate it.'

'Will do, Sir,' and the phone went dead.

Mac leaned back in his chair and took a deep breath. The light at the end of the tunnel was not in sight yet, though he thought he could detect the faintest of glows. This much he knew: someone, somewhere owned or had access to a rare and highly-prized car. But who?

Fifteen minutes later, Mac was still deep in thought when a

knock came on his door. He came back down to earth with a start. He shouted, 'Come in!' and a constable entered with a large buff envelope in his hand.

'Urgent from Computers, Sir.' He handed the envelope to Mac. 'For your eyes only.'

Mac took the proffered envelope. Thanking the constable, he followed him out of the office and made his way to the back room, where he knocked and was admitted. He held the envelope out to his chief.

'Six copies to save time, Sir.'

'Good, hand them round and let's get to it.'

'Will you do the briefing, Sir, or shall I?'

'Carry on, Mac.'

Mac nodded. 'Right lads, you each have a list of names and addresses of Ashdown Marsden owners from all over the United Kingdom and what I want you to do is isolate the ones to within, say, thirty or forty miles of Westminster Palace, OK?'

'Why thirty or forty miles, Guv?' Bob Saunders was curious.

'Just a hunch, a feeling. I can't imagine anyone travelling all the way from Scotland or Cornwall and back for this little caper, can you?'

'Don't get me wrong, Guv, but the Royal Family do have Scottish connections as well as German and Greek, don't they?'

'Very true,' Mac conceded, 'but that's not what I meant...'

'If I were a Scot,' Jimmy interrupted, 'and I wanted to pull a caper like this, I'd get me some digs close by.'

'Thank you, that's precisely what I was driving at.'

Mac had pinned a large-scale street map of Westminster and the home counties on a blackboard. As various locations were read out from the Swansea list, a red knobbed pin was stuck into the appropriate location. When the final pin was in position, Mac and the Chief Constable took up position in front of the blackboard.

'Well, there it is, lads, all we have to do is make sense of it.'

The Chief was already drawing large circles on the map, having first set them to the 'miles per inch' grid at the bottom, carefully removing and replacing any pin that impeded the compass. When he had finished, he pointed to the map.

'Right lads, these circles represent ten, twenty, thirty and forty miles from Ramsdean Hospital.' He turned to face his captive audience. 'There are twenty Ashdowns inside a forty mile radius, twenty-one if you count this one just on the perimeter. Nine of these are in the thirty mile circle, four are in the twenty mile circle.' He paused for effect. 'But there's only one within ten miles of the hospital.'

The silence was immediately broken by general speculation.

'Quiet lads,' commanded the chief. 'Mac!'

'Sir?'

'Trace every owner. Get a run-down on every last one of them. Check for any criminal activities, political or otherwise - you know the form. Turn up every stone, log everything, no matter how small or unimportant it may seem, and we'll feed it all into a computer. You never know, maybe, just maybe, it'll come up with some answers.'

Mac nodded. 'Right, lads, first of all, we must find out the colour of that car if at all possible. Obviously the registration number would sew up this little puzzle in next to no time.' He paused. 'Now I know that the two policemen on the main gate went off duty, or rather were recalled as soon as the Countess' car left the grounds for duties elsewhere. Now, it's within the bounds of possibility that they could have seen the car stop outside the hospital wall, seen it depart or both, and what's more, because it's a special type of car, they might even have noted the number.' He sighed and shook his head. 'Then again, it may be that the make of car could have distracted them and they didn't even notice the plates. Hopefully, they can tell us which way it was heading.'

'If I believe right, Guv,' said Bob Saunders, 'all these cars were painted a metallic silver; if you wanted any other colour, you asked for it.'

'Yes, I was aware of that but we may get lucky. There may be other distinguishing marks such as dents, nodding doggies, that kind of thing.'

'What do you want us to do, Guv?'

'Pair off and two of you can check the hospital patients for visitors' names and addresses. Two more can check out the nearby houses - some of the occupants may have been at the opening and stayed to chin wag about it, you know how some women like to rabbit on a bit. Also, there may have been one or two of the local youngsters hanging about and they can have very keen eyes some of them, especially if this rare car is in the vicinity.'

'It's going to be mean a lot of leg work, Guv, can't we enlist some of the uniformed branch?' Bob ventured. 'I mean, they needn't be told why they're looking for it and it'll leave us free to run down these addresses.'

Mac eyed his chief. 'What do you think, Sir? It can't do any harm and it would speed things up a wee bit.'

'Why not indeed? Good thinking, Saunders.'

Bob just nodded.

'There are quite a few wards to cover, Sir, so we'll need quite a few of the uniformed branch.'

'You let me worry about that. Run those addresses down as soon as possible.'

'OK, Sir, if there's anything to be found, we'll find it.'

Subsequently, every suspect was cleared in the Westminster area. Every Ashdown Marsden owner had a watertight alibi and the files turned up nothing of any significance.

CHAPTER FIFTEEN
THE PHONE CALL

Robin Devereaux, Earl of Westminster, had completed another day's shooting, bagging many a plump grouse in the process which were now safely stowed in one of the Landrovers. He made his way to the huge marquee for the customary after-shoot refreshment, accompanied by his entourage.

A flunky approached with a silver tray laden with cocktails, and offered them around the little group. 'Your mineral water is in the centre of the tray, your Lordship.'

'Ah good, you remembered, thank you.'

'My pleasure, your Lordship.' The flunky bowed slightly before retreating.

Robin drank mineral water on most occasions and only drank alcohol in modest quantities, usually one small glass, at very special gatherings such as weddings or birthdays.

As he was enjoying sandwiches from the buffet table, a man entered the marquee and looked around until he spotted his quarry. His eyes alighted on Robin and he quickly approached him.

'Your Lordship,' he bowed slightly, 'may I have a private word? It's rather important.' The man spoke quietly yet urgently, his voice was for Robin's ears only.

Robin caught the urgency in the man's voice and, excusing himself from the company, he motioned the man outside.

The man spoke deferentially. 'Begging you Lordship's pardon, but I was instructed to come immediately.'

Robin's interest quickened. 'Oh, what's wrong?'

'I don't know, Sir, the person on the phone didn't say.'

'Person on the phone.' The Earl wore a puzzled look, 'What was the message?'

'You are to stand by to take a very important message at six o'clock at the Lodge.'

'At the Lodge. I see,' said Robin tilting his head slightly and closing one eye. 'Is this some sort of joke?'

'I think not, Sir, the person said that you must be by the phone at 6pm and entirely alone.' The man was adamant.

'You keep saying "person", was it a man or a woman?'

'I don't rightly know, your Lordship, the voice sounded, erm, well, it could have been either male or female.'

Robin studied the man for a few long seconds and he stroked his chin in deep thought. Then, his mind made up, he said, 'I want you to say nothing about this conversation or the phone call to any living soul, do you understand me?'

Something in the Earl's tone made the man stiffen slightly. 'I understand perfectly, Sir.'

'If this is some sort of a joke, I may be able to turn the tables because I have no wish to look an idiot.' He smiled and tapped the side of his nose. 'We shall see.'

'Yes, I see your Lordship, I shall be the very soul of discretion.'

The Earl smiled. 'Thank you, now off you go.'

'My pleasure your Lordship.' The man bowed slight and took his leave.

Robin was deep in thought as he watched him go. What on earth was going on? He tried for some minutes to unravel this little mystery without success. Finally he shrugged his shoulders, looked at his watch, then strode back into the marquee.

Hours later, he was sitting by the phone at the Lodge, awaiting the call he somehow knew would be on time. It was 5.55pm.

When he was grouse shooting in Scotland, Robin always resided at his Scottish seat, Stirling Lodge, usually alone except for a manservant and his wife, who did the cooking. The Lodge was only used three or four times a year by the Earl and Countess during official visits to Scotland or holidays. The only time Robin was the sole occupant was during the Grouse Shoot.

The phone rang suddenly, startling Robin from his reverie. He picked up the handpiece slowly, not knowing what to expect, and put it to his ear. He took a deep breath and spoke into the mouthpiece.

'Robin Devereaux.'

'Ah, your Lordship! Right on time, I see,' said a voice that Robin did not recognise.

'Who are you, what do you want?'

The voice laughed softly. 'Who am I indeed? That is precisely the question I have often asked myself, your Lordship,' the voice answered sarcastically.

'Please state your business or get off the phone, you are beginning to annoy me.' Robin was getting angry.

'Oh! I cannot do that, you see, and it would be very imprudent of you to hang up, Robin my dear, dear friend.' The voice was mocking now.

Robin nearly exploded at the familiarity but curiosity overrode the impulse to give the culprit a piece of his mind. He took a deep breath and composed himself.

'Please, get on with it, state your business or at least let me in on this joke.'

'Joke! This is no joke, my dear Robin, quite the contrary in point of fact.' The voice sounded smug. 'You see, my dear boy, you are going to make me very rich.'

'Rich?'

'Yes rich. You, my dear friend - are you sitting comfortably? - are going to swell my miserable coffers and you will do it gladly, I may add, by the splendid sum of two million pounds.'

Robin sat bolt upright in his chair. 'What!' he roared. 'Don't be absurd! Tell me, pray, why should I do that?'

'Because, my dear Sir, you are now "missing" one Countess, do you follow me?'

Robin's mouth opened as the significance of what the caller was saying slowly sank into his brain. Alison...?

Robin began to speak and his voice trembled slightly. 'Are you trying to tell me that you have kidnapped my wife?'

'My dear boy, how clever of you to have deduced that little fact so quickly. Well done, old chap, I really have kidnapped your good lady.' The owner of the voice was obviously enjoying himself. 'And all you have to do to get her back, is pay the money into my numbered account in Switzerland.'

Robin was torn between disbelief and fear. 'I do not for one moment believe you. My wife is too well guarded,' he said.

'Look, my friend,' the voice interrupted, 'you can always phone Hamilcourt House afterwards, which of course I would not advise, or alternatively - and I would recommend this - you can go home and see for yourself.'

'And why would you advise against me phoning Hamilcourt House?'

'Because if you do, my dear Robin, and find out that she really is missing, then so will your staff. You do see what I am driving at, don't you, Robin?'

'No, I'm afraid I do not, I fail to see—'

'Then let me endeavour to enlighten you, my friend,' the menacing voice continued. 'If your staff find out - and, I might add, they know nothing as yet - then it will become common knowledge in next to no time at all and that, I'm afraid, will be the end of it.'

'End of it, end of what?' A little alarm bell was jangling now inside Robin's head. The tone of the man's voice demanded respect.

'Quite simple, old chap. If everyone knows of your good lady's abduction, then it must follow that every policeman in the country will be looking for me, so I cannot run the risk of trying to keep her hidden, you see.' He paused for a few seconds. 'And so I will have no alternative.'

'You will let her go, you have no other alternative.'

'Oh, but I cannot do that, you see, because she knows me,' said the voice menacingly.

As the implication of that statement hit him, Robin shot to his feet. 'You don't mean ...?' His voice trembled as the dreaded word formed on his lips but he could not bring himself to speak it.

'Of course I do.' The voice chuckled evilly. 'I shall have to kill her and then she won't be able to give me away, will she, Robin? And please remember that she is just 30 minutes from where I am standing - just 30 minutes from ... death.'

Now all Robin's doubts had left him. He didn't know how he knew, but he knew the man's threats were real. 'No, no, please, give me time to think, I'm so confused,' Robin pleaded, his mind in a turmoil.

'You haven't time to think, you must act now, before it's too late.' Again that malicious laugh.

Robin was beaten now. 'All right, how much time do I have before my staff find out?'

'Until eight tomorrow morning, my friend, and not a minute longer.' There was a click as the phone went dead and Robin replaced the handset.

81

He sat down and tried to sort out his bewildered brain. My God, he thought, tomorrow morning! How do I cover the distance with so little time? He had to get himself under control again, he had to think ...

Suddenly, he snapped his fingers and reached for the phone. He dialled a number and drummed his fingers impatiently on the table as he waited for the dialling tone to cease. Suddenly a voice answered at the other end.

'Cuncliffe residence!'

'May I speak to Roger please, tell him it's Robin.'

He had used his forename deliberately, it would not do to broadcast his title at this stage. Roger would understand at once because this was their standard practice when anonymity was necessary.

Another voice came on the line. 'Robin? It's Roger, what's the problem old boy?'

'Roger, are you alone?'

Roger sensed the urgency in his old friend's voice. 'I'm out of everyone's earshot. What's the problem, are you in trouble?'

'Roger, I need one of your helicopters right now, within the hour, sooner if possible. I must get back home now!'

'That's impossible. I have to file a flight plan first before anything can leave the ground and chopper flights have to be well planned so that we can make use of rivers and so on for safety, especially over that sort of distance.'

Robin groaned out loud, he had completely forgotten about flight plans.

'Are you all right, Robin?'

'Listen, Roger, and listen carefully the first time because I dare not repeat what I am about to say to you over the phone. Are you listening?'

'Shoot, old boy.'

'I have to get back to Hamilcourt House before, repeat, *before* eight o'clock tomorrow morning or the balloon goes up, do you hear me?'

'Listening.'

'Alison has been kidnapped,' Robin said slowly.

There was a deathly silence for about ten seconds. 'Are you at the Lodge, old son?'

'Yes.'

'Stay put, I'll be there as soon as possible. Oh, and Robin.'

'Yes, Roger?'

'Forget the flight plan, this is an errand of mercy, understood?'

The phone went dead before Robin could answer. He replaced the handset, sat down and wept unashamedly.

Within half an hour, he heard the sound of a helicopter approaching. He dashed outside, still dressed in his hunting clothes, and watched as it landed some fifty yards away. He ran towards it, ducking instinctively as he approached the whirling blades. He opened the door and shook hands with an anxious-looking Roger. He shut the door and the helicopter was already beginning to lift off before he could fasten his seat belt.

Roger handed him a set of headphones, indicating to him to put them on. He did so and Roger, pointing to the rotors, said, 'Now you can hear me above this racket. You can speak freely now, we're on internal only.' He held his hand up for a moment. 'Hang on a second while we get on course. OK, fuel tanks full, oil pressure normal, no drift to speak of and air speed, just on one hundred and forty knots ... Right, now give it to me straight, old son, because I'm not sure that I heard you right over the blower.'

'It's true, Roger, at least I think it is, and if it is, I have to keep Alison alive by arriving at Hamilcourt before the staff find out.' He went on to explain everything in detail and when he had finished, Roger whistled into the mouthpiece.

'Just what has this rotten bastard got against you?'

'Heaven only knows, I certainly don't,' Robin replied forlornly.

'Listen, old boy, this crate's only good for two hundred and fifty miles fuelwise so we'll have to go down and tank up. Now be a good chap, keep quiet while I lay it all on.'

Robin nodded that he understood and Roger switched his radio 'air to ground'. For the next five minutes, he held an animated conversation with someone on the ground. Then there was a click in Robin's earphones and Rogers' cheerful voice sounded in his ears. 'All laid on, old boy, now all we have to do is fool the air traffic wallahs that we're indeed on a mercy mission.'

'How on earth do we, er, you do that?'

'Wait and see, old sport, wait and see,' was all his friend would volunteer.

Some time later, the engine note changed as the helicopter began to descend. Roger looked forward and down, as did Robin.

'There we are,' Roger pointed triumphantly, 'bang on the button and bang on time too.'

Robin spotted him then. In a small field, miles from anywhere, a man stood waving a piece of bright orange cloth in one hand and a light of some sort in the other. Roger landed a few yards from him and the man ran towards what appeared to be an ambulance just outside a large gate. He opened the back and reached inside, retrieving a large white box marked with a red cross. Quickly, he ran across to the parked helicopter and handed the box to Robin, who silently took it. The man winked and ran back to his vehicle, waving to them just before he disappeared into his cab.

The helicopter climbed into the air once more and Roger set course for his next destination. Robin was bemused as he examined the box. Roger's chuckle came to his ears and he glanced at his good friend with a quizzical expression.

'Sorry, old boy, under the circumstances, but your face is a picture.

Robin looked the box and read the label out loud. 'Vital organs for transplant, urgent, packed in ice.'

'Sorry, old boy, it was the only thing I could think of at such short notice - no offence to our splendid ambulance service, of course, bless every mother's son of 'em.'

Robin smiled gratefully at his friend. 'You must have pulled a few strings to achieve this and you have my heartfelt thanks.'

'Don't mention it. Alison is as dear a friend to me as you are so don't give it a second thought,' Roger replied gently.

Roger made two more landings to take on fuel at small air fields. He also took on various Air Traffic Control Towers in heated exchanges and won through after explaining his 'mercy mission'.

It was dark when they reached Hamilcourt House and, using his own floodlights to guide him down, Roger landed smack in the middle of the huge flat lawn. As soon as he was down, he urged Robin to disembark by using hand signals and shouting: 'Shoot off old boy. I'll be along in a few minutes, got to make it look like an emergency landing, just in case the law rolls up to investigate. Oh, and let the staff know who I am.'

Robin nodded and raced towards the huge residence, dreading what he was about to discover.

Jenkins had heard the helicopter, as had the rest of the servants. He had also seen the figure of his master racing across the lawn and, pulling a dressing gown over his pyjamas, he rushed down the main staircase to admit him. His brow was furrowed as he tried to think what was important enough to warrant such a dangerous landing by helicopter with his master as passenger.

Robin reached the big oak doors just as Jenkins opened them. 'Your Lordship?'

'No time to explain, Jenkins,' he said breathlessly as he rushed past the servant to the great staircase. As he started up the stairs, he paused just long enough to shout over his shoulder. 'Let the pilot in and see that he's well looked after.' He did not wait for a reply as he resumed his stride up the stairs, two or three steps at a time, reaching the top rapidly. He raced along the corridor until he reached Alison's bedroom, passing startled staff in various night attire.

He did not follow his usual practice of knocking before entering; with bated breath, he flung the door open, eyes searching out the bed. The room was in darkness. He fumbled for the switch by the door jamb, pressed it and gasped out loud. His heart sank at the sight of the empty bed. With rapid strides he crossed the room, stopping outside the bathroom door.

'Alison, are you in there, Alison?' Robin shouted through the closed door. There was no response as he shouted again and again. Sweating now and filled with fear, he flung open the door, knowing full well that he would find ... nothing.

Suddenly, he felt emotionally drained as the truth of the situation hit him. This was the final confirmation he needed that the voice on the phone had been telling the truth.

Alison was gone.

Robin stood staring at the empty bed for long minutes, his eyes filled with tears as he realised that he may have seen his beloved Alison for the very last time. He finally made his way downstairs slowly, his legs moving automatically. Roger, standing at the bottom of the stairs, asked the question with his eyes.

Robin nodded dumbly and Roger stepped forward and took his friend's arm. 'Come on, old son,' he said gently, 'come and sit down.'

Automatically, Robin allowed himself to be led into the library and Roger, gently but firmly, sat him down in an armchair. Roger quickly poured out a large brandy and handed it to his friend who, without thinking, gulped down a large draught of the fiery liquid, choking on its potency.

'My God, Roger, I don't—'

'You just did, old boy, and now you're thinking straight again, right?'

'Right, I mean yes.'

'Very well then, first things first. We've got to sew the house staff up tight and I do mean watertight so call them all in here, Robin, every last one of them.'

Robin nodded and pointed to the bell rope. 'Pull that twice for Jenkins.'

Roger pulled twice and within seconds, Jenkins had made an appearance. 'You rang your Lordship?'

'Yes, Jenkins, please assemble all the household staff in here at once, I have something very important to say to you all.'

Chapter Sixteen
The Grouse Has Flown

Mac was giving his Chief a progress report when the phone rang. It was the direct line to the Prime Minister's office.

The Chief frowned. 'The last time that phone rang it was trouble,' he growled. 'This doesn't look good!'

Mac said nothing. He felt edgy suddenly.

The Chief slowly and deliberately picked up the handset and put it to his ear. 'Matlock.'

'She's gone, Donald.' The PM's voice was flat, lifeless, drained of all emotion. 'The grouse has flown!'

It took a few seconds for the Chief to comprehend what he had just heard, then his jaw dropped and the blood drained from his face. 'What?' he gasped.

'Get over here now,' said the tired voice and the phone went dead.

He held the phone to his ear for a few seconds as if he couldn't believe what he had just heard. 'The bastard's done it,' he whispered, 'he's got the Countess.'

'What?' Mac exploded. 'He's what, Sir?'

The Chief did not answer. His top lip suddenly glistened with sweat and his thoughts were in turmoil. Then he pulled himself together and shot to his feet. 'Come on!'

Mac needed no second bidding and was on his feet almost before the Chief had finished talking. He knew where they were heading as they went out of the door, and only half heard Matlock shouting an order to someone: 'My car, now! Jump to it, man!' and the rapid 'Yes, Sir'.

Mac's mind was in a turmoil with all sorts of questions going through his brain as they sped across town. He opened his mouth to speak to his superior but Sir Donald was looking at the back of his driver's head, his mind obviously elsewhere. Mac decided against it and sat in silence for the rest of the journey to 10 Downing Street.

When they entered the PM's private office, he was in a state of agitation, as was the Home Secretary.

'Lock the door please.' The order was directed at Mac, and he obeyed.

Without wasting another moment, the PM burst out, 'He's done it! He's actually kept his promise. He's kidnapped the Countess. How in God's name did you miss him?' The question was directed at Mac with some venom.

Mac was immediately on the defensive. 'Now hold on a minute, Sir, we didn't miss him. Security was sown up so tight he couldn't possibly have slipped the net.'

'But he must have slipped the net. The Countess has gone, just vanished from under your very noses, all of your very noses!'

Sir Donald intervened at that point. 'This may sound like a stupid question, Prime Minister, but how do you know she's missing? I mean, who informed you?'

'The Earl himself phoned me from Hamilcourt House.'

'But I thought he was in Scotland, Sir?' said Mac, surprised.

'He was, until the kidnapper phoned him at Stirling Lodge. He actually made an illegal flight back, and some of it in the dark, to see for himself.'

Mac groaned. 'So it's true then.'

'It is,' the PM thundered. 'And when I told him about the demand notes, he asked for copies to be sent by special messenger to the mansion with all possible speed, and that's not all. He blew his top when he realised that we'd known all about this threat for a week or so.' The PM threw his hands into the air. 'And you can take an educated guess to whom he is apportioning the blame. Me!'

'Now that's hardly fair, Sir,' said Mac, 'considering the circumstances. I mean, the demand notes asked for money before anyone was kidnapped...'

'Yes yes, I know all about that and I also think it's a little unfair, but ... ' He left the sentence unfinished.

I think, Sir, under the circumstances, it would be expedient to go to Hamilcourt House and begin our investigations,' Mac suggested, 'before the whole thing blows up in our faces.'

'The press *must not* get hold of this at any cost, she's got to be found and quickly,' said the PM.

'If you'll excuse me, Sir, I'll get over there as soon as possible,' said Mac, making for the door.

'Find her, Inspector, and soon or ... ' He seemed to visibly shudder. 'I hate to think of the consequences if you don't.'

'I understand perfectly, Sir.'

Mac got hold of Tom Smith on the car radio and arranged to pick him up en route. He spotted him long before he got to him and manoeuvred the car so that, as he braked gently, Smithy was able to open the door and jump in without Mac losing his place in the traffic. As he drove, he filled his big sergeant in on the latest developments. When he'd finished, Smithy exploded, 'Jesus wept, Guv, how?'

Mac did not answer as he raced across town towards Hamilcourt House, the police siren on the unmarked car clearing a path through the traffic. Half a mile from the mansion Mac turned the siren off, not wishing to attract any attention as they approached their objective. A few minutes later, they came to a halt outside the huge oak doors.

Mac introduced himself and his sergeant to Jenkins, who opened the door to admit them, saying 'His Lordship is expecting you in the library, Sir, please follow me.'

He led them in an unhurried walk, then halted outside what appeared to be a smaller version of the outer doors. He knocked and a voice said, 'Enter.'

Jenkins opened the doors wide and stepped forward a pace.

'Detective Inspector Macdonald and Detective Sergeant Smith m'Lord.'

Robin James Edward Devereaux, the eleventh Earl of Westminster, was in his late thirties, close to six feet in height and solidly built. He was a handsome man with light brown hair that was just beginning to recede. He dismissed Jenkins with a 'thank you'.

'Come in, gentlemen, please sit down.' His voice was a pleasant baritone.

'Thank you, your Lordship,' Mac replied.

The Earl walked over to the window and stood gazing out over a beautiful square lawn with a water fountain playing gently into a goldfish pond. He stood there for a full minute before speaking, his voice filled with emotion. 'Find her, Mr Macdonald, please, find my Alison.'

Mac, who had been expecting a verbal blast, squirmed uncomfortably on his seat, not quite knowing how to reply to this heartfelt plea. 'That's just what we intend to ,do just as soon as we possibly can, Sir.'

Suddenly, the Earl spun round, his distress turning into anger. 'Inspector, I have read both demand notes that were delivered to Downing Street. The threat was clearly there for all to see, so why was nothing done to prevent this man carrying out his threat there and then?'

'With respect, Sir, we took what precautions we could in the circumstances,' Mac replied calmly.

'Precautions? What precautions? She's gone, my wife has gone, disappeared, abducted from under your very noses,' the Earl gestured wildly.

Mac was not going to be browbeaten by rank. 'With respect, Sir, nobody disappears and that's why we're here.'

'Please explain, Inspector.'

Mac took a deep breath. 'If you'll pardon me, Sir, we think the Lady Alison was abducted from here, from Hamilcourt, and it's imperative that we question the household staff as soon as possible.'

'How do you know that, Inspector, how could you possibly deduce that?'

'Because, Sir, when the Countess finished her official duties at the hospital, she was escorted back here by a squad of plain-clothed policemen, unknown to her of course, plus she was under constant surveillance by two of my hand-picked squad, stationed inside the mansion grounds.'

'But I don't understand, Inspector.' The Earl was clearly puzzled. 'If what you say is true then how ...?'

'That is precisely what we intend to find out, Sir, so with your kind permission, we would like to get started as soon as possible.'

The Earl nodded. 'I agree. Please forgive my rudeness, it's entirely out of character, I can assure you, it's just that ...' He left the sentence unfinished.

'Perfectly understandable, Sir, under the circumstances, no offence taken.'

The Earl smiled wanly and just nodded. He walked up to Mac, and as both policemen rose to their feet, he spoke with a gentle, emotional voice. 'Please, I beg you, find my wife.'

As their eyes met, Mac saw the deep hurt in the Earl's eyes. He saw the love, the deep anguish, the hopelessness, the hope and in that moment, he felt a stab of fear as he imagined Jan as the victim of a kidnapper. Heaven forbid. He shuddered at the thought. Right then, he knew precisely how the Earl must feel.

'We'll find her, Sir, by God we will,' Mac said vehemently.

Again, the Earl smiled wanly and nodded. 'You may use the library as an interview room, Jenkins will assist you with the staff. Oh, and Inspector, have you any objection to my remaining here? I promise I won't interfere with your enquiries in any way.'

Mac hesitated as he thought of the 'state' Alison was in when she and her guest returned late the night before the official function, according to Jimmy's report.

'You may be distressed by some of the things you will hear, Sir.'

'I'm fully aware of that, nevertheless, I would like to remain.' The Earl was adamant.

'As you wish, Sir.'

'Thank you.'

He moved to the heavily embroidered bell cord and tugged twice. A few seconds elapsed before the doors opened and Jenkins put in an appearance. 'Yes, M'Lord?'

'Ah, Jenkins, the inspector will be interviewing the staff in here, please follow his instructions to the letter.'

'As your Lordship pleases.'

The Earl selected an armchair and made himself comfortable. He clasped his hands together and placed the tips of both forefingers to his lips, ready to watch the proceedings.

'I'll start with Jenkins if I may, Sir,' said Mac and turned to the servant. 'Please, come in and shut the door.'

Jenkins complied and then sat in the chair indicated to him.

'Take notes, Sergeant.'

'Right, Sir.'

Mac stood in front of the butler. 'When was the last time you saw Lady Alison?'

'When she came back from the hospital, Sir.'

'Tell me about it. Exactly what happened, what did she do?'

'Well, Sir, the car arrived at the steps as usually happens and I opened the door to greet her Ladyship, as is my duty.'

'I see, and?'

'Then, as is the usual custom, I escorted her Ladyship through the outer doors and into the main reception.'

'Did you notice anything strange or unusual, anything out of the ordinary,' Mac pressed on.

'Her Ladyship did mention ... er ...' Jenkins looked uncomfortable and he cast a swift glance at his master.

The Earl nodded almost imperceptibly.

'Go on,' Mac prodded gently but firmly, 'mentioned what?'

'I, erm, don't remember the exact words, Sir, but it was something like, erm, a trying night last night and a trying day today. Oh, and erm, she said she was retiring to her room until morning, and she did mention a terrible headache, Sir.'

'I see, go on.'

'I was very concerned and I asked if it would be prudent to call in the doctor, but her Ladyship refused, saying that she would be perfectly all right in the morning, Sir.'

'And that's it, that's all?'

'Yes, Sir, Her Ladyship didn't even want her personal maid to attend her, Sir, and I got—' Jenkins stopped short.

'And you got what?' said Mac, somewhat impatiently. 'Come on, man, your mistress is missing so leave nothing out.'

'Well, Sir, I got the distinct impression that she was not at all pleased with her guest.' Jenkins was positively uncomfortable now, aware that the Earl was listening to every word.

'Oh, and why?'

'Because,' Jenkins searched for words to put it kindly, 'she was under the, um, erm, influence Sir, you know, slightly tipsy I believe you might call it.' He was really squirming now.

'Do you mean drunk, Jenkins?'

Mac opened his mouth to protest but the Earl hadn't finished and he silenced Mac with a gesture of his finger. 'Do I have to repeat myself? Answer me.'

'The last thing I wish to do is offend your Lordship but, forgive me, that is the impression I got at the time. I'm sorry.'

'And that, Sir,' Mac interceded, 'is exactly the impression my watching constable passed on to me by radio.'

The Earl just nodded then turned his attention to his butler once more. 'Jenkins?'

'Your Lordship?' He bit his lower lip, fearing the worst.

'How long have you known your mistress?'

'Since your marriage, your Lordship.' Jenkins was puzzled by the question.

'And when was the last time you saw her drink alcohol?'

The butler thought for a few seconds and his eyes began to widen. 'Well, er, begging your Lordship's pardon, I cannot remember, I cannot for the life of me recall her Ladyship ever partaking of strong drink of any kind.'

'Exactly my point, Inspector. My wife never touched a drop of alcohol in her life, hence my intervention.'

Jenkins furrowed his brow as he seemed to recall something else.

Mac spotted it. 'Something else, something you've missed?'

'As a matter of fact, I did see something that I thought rather odd at the time.'

'Go on,' Mac prompted.

'Her shoes, Sir.'

'Shoes?'

'Yes, Sir, the buckle holes.'

'Buckle holes?' Mac was puzzled. 'Please go on.'

'Yes, Sir. Well, I didn't think too much of it at the time but later, it struck me as being exceedingly odd.'

'How odd?'

'The strap fastening seemed to have been altered by two holes, Sir.'

Mac was suddenly alert. 'Go on.'

'Well, Sir, either M'Lady had on shoes that were too small, or,' he searched for words, 'her feet had grown larger.' He made an apologetic gesture.

Mac stroked his chin in thought and Jenkins spoke again. 'I'm afraid I'm guilty of a mistake, Sir, although it wasn't intentional.'

'Oh!'

'Yes, Sir, it was the second time M'Lady came back that I saw the slingbacks.'

'The second time, you mean she went out again, after she came back from the hospital?'

'Yes Sir, she said she was going out again, she ordered me to leave the car where it was and said she would be back in about an hour.'

'Are you sure about all this?'

'Yes, Sir, and I recall something else too. When M'Lady left for the official hospital engagement, I noticed that the shoes she was wearing appeared to be tight, very tight - too tight, if I may be so bold your Lordship.'

'Never mind that, do go on, we're wasting time.' The Earl waved his hand impatiently.

'Go on, man,' Mac motioned to the butler.

'Yes, Sir, well I was puzzled when I first noticed, and when her Ladyship returned, I looked again, just to be sure,' he hurried on. 'It was so out of character, you see, her Ladyship is so fastidious in her dressing habits, specially her footwear, that I just could not understand why she would, well, cripple herself.'

A very tiny alarm bell sounded at the back of Mac's head.

'Where was her guest all this time, didn't he welcome her Ladyship back?'

'No, Sir, not the first time or the second, which I thought rather odd.'

'Odd?'

'Yes, Sir, you see, Sir, all the time Mr Grant was a guest at the residence, M'Lady and he were almost inseparable.'

'Now that is odd,' Mac agreed. 'When did he put in an appearance?'

'About an hour after her Ladyship went upstairs, Sir, he, er, looked rather the worse for wear, erm, I think it was what you might term a hangover, Sir.' Jenkins coughed nervously.

'What happened then, did he say anything?'

'He informed me that her Ladyship had retired for the rest of the day, to which I replied that she already informed me, Sir.'

'And?'

'Mr Grant said something like, erm, that she had already torn him off a strip not five minutes ago, and then he said he was leaving shortly, having said his goodbyes upstairs, Sir.'

'Curiouser and curiouser,' said Mac thoughtfully. 'He said he was leaving shortly, how did he intend to travel, by car?'

'Well, Sir, he asked me to call him an estate car, one that would accommodate his luggage.'

'Why an estate, why not an ordinary taxi? Did he have that much luggage?'

'He had a large theatrical trunk, Sir, it required a lot of room. Mr Grant is an actor.'

Mac half turned and smacked his forehead with the palm of his hand. 'My godfathers, an actor,' he breathed. 'Can it be ...?'

'Are you thinking what I'm thinking, Guv?' Smithy spoke quietly.

'I think maybe I ... Who carried the luggage downstairs for Mr Grant, Jenkins?' Mac asked urgently.

'Three footmen, Sir. One carried the smaller cases and two carried the large trunk.'

'Call them in here, quickly now please.'

Jenkins walked quickly over to the house phone and put the receiver to his ear, waiting for a response at the other end. At last a voice said, 'Tomkins.'

'Tomkins, I want you, Edwards and May in the library at once please ... Yes, I do mean now.'

Less than a minute later, a knock came on the doors and Jenkins admitted the three menservants. Tomkins spotted the Earl and, turning towards him, bowed slightly, as did the other two men. 'Begging your pardon your lordship, but we thought ...'

The Earl stopped him with a raised finger and indicated the two policemen.

'Thank you, Sir,' said Mac. He turned to the footmen. 'Which of you three carried Mr Grant's trunk downstairs?'

'We did, Sir,' replied a very puzzled Edwards, indicating May. 'Mr May and me, Sir.'

'How heavy was it, can you remember? It's very very important.'

Edwards and May looked at each other as they tried to remember. 'Not too heavy, Sir, quite manageable for two of us really.'

'That doesn't really answer my question,' said Mac. 'Look, can you be a bit more specific. Would you say a hundred and seventy pounds or so?'

'Oh, I wouldn't say that heavy, Sir,' said Edwards, 'more like say a hundred and forty, hundred and fifty pounds at the outside.'

Mac looked directly at the Earl. 'Forgive me, Sir, but I have to ask this next question.'

The Earl nodded, he knew what the next question was going to be. Mac took a deep breath and turned back to the two footmen.

'Would you say that the weight corresponded to that of a ...' Mac hesitated.

'A woman?' The Earl finished the sentence for him.

Mac just bit his lip and nodded confirmation.

Edwards lowered his head and spoke quietly. 'If you're asking, was there a body in the trunk Sir, the answer is no.'

'How can you be sure?'

Edwards opened his mouth to reply and closed it again. Both he and May shuffled in embarrassment and seemed uninclined to answer.

'Answer the inspector's question please,' the Earl ordered quietly.

'Yes, your Lordship, but it will probably mean our dismissal.'

'Just answer the question please.'

'Because we looked, Sir.'

'Why?'

'Just curious, Sir, no more, no less,' said Edwards.

'We just wanted to see what an actor carried around with him, Sir, we didn't mean any harm, honestly we didn't.'

'And just what did you find?'

'Clothes, just women's clothes and wigs, Sir.'

'We didn't mean any harm, Sir, or mean to steal anything, we were just curious, that's all.'

'All right, all right, no harm done I suppose,' said Mac as he paced up and down thoughtfully with his right forefinger across his lips. He stopped suddenly. 'Sergeant, let's recap here.' He began to tick the items off on his fingers. 'One, her Ladyship travels to and from Ramsdean hospital wearing tight shoes. Why?

'Two, she changes her shoes to more comfortable slingbacks and, according to Jenkins, alters the strap fastenings by two holes - again, why? Is there a medical reason? There could be because, three, she takes to her bed for the rest of the day, not because she was tipsy, but because she may have been having, erm, pardon me, your Lordship, ladies' problems, which can manifest themselves in all sorts of ways, erm, according to my wife, anyway.

'Four, Grant puts in an appearance after she has retired, which of course would make sense if the good lady was, as I have just said, incapacitated.

'Five, Grant leaves in an estate after having said his goodbyes privately, which again makes good sense if—'

'Mr Grant did mention that M'Lady was too upset to wish him goodbye in public,' said Jenkins.

'Yes, that may be, Jenkins, but it doesn't explain how to get a lady drunk when she never touches the stuff, and more to the point, why?'

'That's a good point, Guv, especially if she has to be on top form the very next day. Even an experienced tippler would use moderation, bearing in mind the importance of the occasion.'

'Exactly my point, Sergeant,' Mac said thoughtfully, 'there's something here that doesn't quite—'

Mac's thoughts were interrupted by the cultured voice of the Earl. 'Inspector, there's something that I omitted to tell you earlier. It's been at the back of my mind, nagging at me, and I thought it unimportant - until now, of course.'

'Sir?'

'Yes, you see, the voice on the phone said that it was imperative I arrived back here before 8am because the staff didn't know that my wife was missing.'

'I'm sorry, Sir, but I don't quite see the point—' Mac stopped in mid-sentence as the truth dawned. 'My God, I do! The only way the kidnapper could know that would either be through inside information or—'

'—he was here all the time,' Smithy finished the sentence for him.

Mac snapped his fingers. 'Hell's bells, that's it, er, begging your pardon your Lordship, but if what I'm thinking is correct ... Oh dear sweet Jesus, I wonder, I wonder.' He closed his eyes in deep thought for a few moments and when he opened them again, protocol was forgotten.

'Smithy, we've got things to do.'

The Earl was quite baffled. 'What on earth have you found, Inspector? For the life of me, I can't see—'

97

'Sir,' Mac cut in, 'we showed the demand notes to a graphologist, a specialist in this field. He said that, amongst other things, this man was an actor and—'

'—Mr Grant was, is an actor,' the Earl finished for him. 'But what exactly are you getting at, Inspector?'

'I'm not quite sure yet, Sir, but I have an idea in my head that won't go away and before I commit myself, I'd like to check out a few things first. I have no desire to build up your hopes, Sir, only to disappoint you if I'm wrong.'

'When will you know for sure?'

'In the next few hours, I hope, Sir, and if I'm right, and I think I am, we shall be well on the way to recovering, or should I say rescuing, the Lady Alison. Sir, so with your permission ...' He indicated that he wanted to leave.

The Earl nodded. 'Time is of the essence, Mr Macdonald, God speed to you both.'

Mac paused in the doorway and spoke to Jenkins. 'What you and the rest of the staff have seen and heard tonight must not go beyond these four walls.'

'I'll deal with that after you've gone, Inspector,' the Earl cut in, 'There will be no leak, I give you my personal assurance. Now please, do what you have to do without further delay.'

Mac nodded and they took their leave.

Smithy was at the wheel so Mac took the opportunity to phone Jan on his mobile. He dialled his home number and within seconds, Jan answered. 'Jan, luv, it's me, the grouse has flown.'

'What?' Jan's startled voice made Mac jump.

'She's gone, luv, she's been lifted.'

'Funny thing that, but I knew he'd get her somehow, it was just a question of when.'

'I had the same feeling myself but it's still come as a shock,' Mac sighed. 'Look, luv, I think I may be on to something so will you run the tapes again, the close-ups of the Countess and—'

'I'm way ahead of you there, copper,' Jan cut in with her beautiful Scottish burr. 'I already have.'

'Oh, and er, what did you manage to find this time, bighead?' Mac grinned to himself.

'Come and see for yourself, pea brain,' Jan chortled.

'Mmm, sounds interesting, tell me more.'

'Nope, come and take a looksee for yourself, handsome. Bye.'

Mac had just enough time to say bye before Jan hung up on him. He knew she had found something else, something too important to air over the phone. She had probably reached the same conclusion as himself, only by a different route. He would just have to wait and see ...

Mac was grateful for the mug of hot sweet tea that was waiting for him when he arrived home. He took a few good swigs before he brought Jan up to date.

'... and when the Earl mentioned that eight o'clock was the deadline, things began to fall into place very quickly and I don't mind telling you, the old ticker began to race a little bit because I realised then that our chappie must have been based at Hamilcourt all along.' Mac took another long pull at his tea. 'And when his Lordship mentioned that Mr Grant was an actor, well, you could have knocked me down with a feather. The thing that puzzles me though is—'

Jan cut in with a chuckle. 'Come and have a look at what I've found.'

'What is it?'

'Come and see,' she said brightly, taking his arm and leading him firmly over to the video. She sat down and motioned him to sit down beside her.

'Ready?'

'Ready.'

'OK, listen up. I went over the tape again and, bearing in mind the time lapse between Alison's departure from the hospital and the moment when our mystery person appeared in the picture, there had to be a reason if our mystery person was based where I thought he was.'

Mac furrowed his brow in concentration. 'That's double Dutch.'

Jan chuckled. 'OK, let me put it this way, pea brain. Instinct told me that he was close by or close to Alison - only instinct, mind. Anyway, to cut a long story short, I decided to have a closer look through the tapes. I had a feeling, you see.'

'And?'

She pointed to the screen. 'Watch that carefully and tell me what you see, OK?

Mac nodded as she leaned forward and pressed 'play', watching the digit counter on the console. Suddenly, Jan stabbed the pause button and began to play the tape a frame at a time until the view of the Countess's face was the one she wanted. She held the frame and said, 'Watch' then, using the 'magnify' control, she gradually enlarged the picture until the screen was filled with a close-up of Alison's ear.

'There, what do you see, sweetie?'

Mac studied the picture for some time before shrugging his shoulders. 'All I can see is an ear with an earring on it.'

'Not on it, in it.'

'In it?'

'In it,' said Jan, 'look for yourself.' She handed him some photographs cut from various magazines.

Mac studied the pictures, but still couldn't see a thing.

Jan smiled and handed him a magnifying glass. 'Look closely at the earrings.'

Mac did just that and still saw nothing.

Jan smiled. 'How could you men possibly know anything about us women. Look at me.' She dug her thumbs into the hair above her ears and pushed backwards, 'What do you see?'

'Earrings,' Mac replied simply.

'Yes, but what kind?'

It began to dawn on him then as he studied both the photographs and the video, and he smiled at Jan in admiration.

'To pierce, or not to pierce, that is the question,' Jan grinned at him.

'Big-head!' Mac grinned back.

'Pin-head,' was the rejoinder, 'and there's more.'

'More? You mean there's more on the tape?'

'Come and see for yourself.' She turned back to the console and operated the controls until she had the Countess in profile. 'I'm going to blow this one up as far as the grain will allow, OK?'

She expanded the picture as far as possible to the point of blur, then she went back one magnification for full clarity.

'Can you see what I can see, sweetie?'

Mac studied the blow-up carefully, very carefully indeed, and after a few moments, he saw what Jan had hoped he would see.

'Jan,' he said slowly, 'if what I'm looking at is what I think it is—'

'—she'll be the first Countess who shaves daily,' Jan finished for him.

Mac turned back to the screen and looked at the little black shadows that were unmistakeably bristle, shaved very close to the skin and only visible through the expert make-up because of the magnification.

Without taking his eyes off the screen Mac said, 'If that isn't Alison, who is it? As if I didn't know ...'

'That's right, copper, the Alison we're looking at is in fact the kidnapper.'

'That's painfully obvious,' he growled, 'so where on earth is Alison?'

'Now that, my dear flatfoot, is for out kidnapper to know, and for you to find out.'

Mac just grimaced and nodded. 'That's also painfully obvious!'

CHAPTER SEVENTEEN
THE TAILOR'S DUMMY

On the strength of the evidence that was now beginning to build up, Mac assembled his team in the 'back room' for a briefing. He filled them all in with events to date and then gave a recap.

'Right, lads, here's what we have so far. I can tell you now that I'm almost certain that I can name the kidnapper, so listen up.' He began to tick the items off on his fingers. 'Firstly, Jenkins the butler spotted the tight shoes the Countess was wearing. Secondly, the Earl was told by the kidnapper to get back before 8am, before the staff discovered that the good lady was missing. Thirdly, and this is the important bit, that sort of vital information could only be known to someone inside Hamilcourt House.'

He paused to let that sink in. 'Number four, when we magnified a frame of the Countess' face, it showed what can only described as very closely shaved bristle. In other words, a man's face.'

A murmur ran round the room and Mac silenced it with a raised hand. 'There's more, lads. Fifthly, the Countess appears to be wearing pierced earrings, but we know for sure that she's never had her ears pierced - unusual, I know, but there you are.'

Again he stopped a murmur of speculation. 'Number six, Andrew Grant was noticeably absent when the Countess returned, not once but twice, to Hamilcourt. Not only that, the Countess was also noticeably absent when Grant left for pastures new and that's point number seven.'

He paused for breath. 'Now point number eight is just a little bit puzzling. Jenkins reported seeing the good lady, or someone like her, in what appeared to be a drunken state, yet she never touched alcohol. Point number nine, Professor Hasketh has said that this man is, or has trained as, an actor, and point number ten: Andrew Grant is an actor.'

He paused for a moment and pursed his lips. 'Now let's examine the other side of the page. The Countess and Grant were bosom pals, that was there for all to see, yourselves included. Then there's the fact that she actually picked him up from the station because she couldn't wait to see him again. According to Jenkins, Grant and the Countess go way back. The question is, how far back?'

'We never paid him much attention, Guv, him being so close to her,' said Smithy.

'That was before she disappeared, now he's very much the prime suspect.'

'It's all circumstantial, Guv,' said Jimmy, 'it doesn't matter how you look at it. I mean, maybe it was a bloke in drag who opened the hospital but Grant was back here at the mansion with the Countess.'

'Before, Jimmy, before and after the Countess, not *with* her...'

The penny dropped suddenly for Jimmy and his mouth dropped open. 'Gawd, I'm with you all of a sudden, Guv.'

'It's all clever stuff, Jimmy. Look, here's how I see it. If I wanted to replace Alison with myself, how would I set about doing a swap with no one any the wiser? First, I'd have to incapacitate the lady, but how?'

'Get her Brahms and Liszt the night before, Guv, which she was. I know, because I saw her myself,' said Jimmy.

'Ah, but was she?' mused Mac. 'The Earl has already made it clear that she didn't drink alcohol, so try this for size. Supposing I took her out the night before in the limo, knowing that the windows were tinted. I drive somewhere, then I subdue her, or drug her whatever, and drop her off at a place of safety, then drive back in the dark or near dark, which is precisely what I'm sure Grant did.'

'But he had the Countess with him,' Jimmy insisted, 'I saw her myself, I saw the two of them together.'

'But did you?' Mac smiled mysteriously. 'Did you, old son?'

'How do you mean, Guv?'

'Look, describe exactly what you saw and think carefully before you answer. I want it exactly as you saw it, not how you think you saw it.'

Jimmy thought for a moment. 'Well, I saw the limo come up the drive ... I saw it stop close to the tradesmen's entrance and the driver got out on the side facing me ...'

'Go on.'

'He walked round to the nearside, staggering a bit, and opened the passenger door, then he helped the ... no, no, I tell a lie, Guv, he opened the tradesmen's door before he helped her out of the car and half carried her inside.'

'Was the car door close to the tradesmen's door?'

'Come to think of it, they looked as though they were overlapping, although it was fairly dark so I couldn't be sure. I heard her talk to him though, Guv.'

'Ah! But did you, old son, did you?'

'How do you mean, Guv, I don't quite see ...?'

'Look, we know that this chap's an actor. Well, actors have to play all sorts of parts and do all sorts of things, so he could also be a good mimic. Now, if he has Alison stowed away somewhere, who on earth did he bring back or, more to the point,' Mac said slowly, '*what* did he bring back?'

The puzzled frowns of his team brought a smile to Mac's face. He gave them a clue. 'Tinted windows?' No response. 'Getting dark?' Still no hint of understanding. 'Tinted windows, dark night, overlapping doors?' Mac grinned at the blank faces. 'Try a tailor's dummy for size then.'

He was met by disbelieving looks from at least two members of the team. 'Aw c'mon, Guv, that's like horse manure from China, a bit far fetched i'nnit?' said Terry.

'Is it? Think about it, don't forget what Hasketh said about this chappie. He's brilliant, dedicated and bloody cocksure, not forgetting cheeky, right?'

'Right.'

'Well, if I were him, that's exactly what I'd do,' said Mac.

'Yeah, that's right, Guv. What about that big trunk then, that would be ideal for carrying a dummy, wouldn't it?' said Smithy.

'Exactly, Smithy, and what's more the footmen never mentioned a tailor's dummy when they poked their noses inside the trunk,' said Mac.

'OK, so if he did use a dummy and it wasn't in the trunk, where is it now?' Jimmy queried.

'Let's go and find out. And we have to tie down this Ashdown Marsden, I'm almost certain that it's part of this little caper.'

'It could belong to Grant, Guv, hidden away in town somewhere,' said Smithy.

'Mmmm, true, but why use it? I mean, he could have used the limo or escorts to carry his gear about.'

Jimmy snapped his fingers. 'Speed, Guv, speed. That car can do over a ton with ease and still have plenty of gee-gee's to spare.'

'I'm not quite with you,' said Mac, frowning.

'Look, Guv, if what you say is true about Grant changing places with Alison - I mean, he'd have to get to the hospital and back within an hour, plus change clothes, do the make-up, get the car from where it's hidden, as well as taking it back - he'd need something nearly as fast as Concorde, wouldn't he?'

Mac pursed his lips as he gave that idea some thought. He marched up and down, liking the idea more and more. 'You know, Jimmy old son, I think you've hit it right on the button because if he did own an Ashdown Marsden he couldn't possibly park it at Hamilcourt House, it would be a dead giveaway. And he did have to plant the toy van at the hospital to prove his intention. You're right, he would need some speed.'

'What gets me, Guv,' said Bob Saunders, 'is why go through all this rigmarole of sending a couple of ransom notes beforehand? Why didn't he just kidnap the Countess and be done with it?'

'That, my lad, has been puzzling me too, but I'll put it down to ego for now, although I suspect there's some reason we have yet to find out. By the way, has the uniformed branch come up with anything on this car yet?'

'The chief's handling that, Guv, he's got people legging it in and around the hospital area, just in case,' said Smithy.

'OK, let's go to Hamilcourt and see what we can find. I have a feeling that, well ... we'll see.'

Some time later, they arrived at the big double doors at Hamilcourt House and as usual, Jenkins admitted them.

'Would you please inform his Lordship that we're here and would he kindly allow us to make a search of part of the mansion,' said Mac.

'Thank you, Jenkins,' said the Earl from halfway up the huge staircase.

'Your Grace.' Mac greeted him with a small bow.

The Earl nodded his own greeting. 'Did you say search, Inspector?'

'Yes, Sir.' Mac explained his theory at length and the Earl readily agreed. 'Intriguing to say the least, but please do what you think is necessary, by all means. Jenkins will assist in whatever way he can.'

'Thank you, Sir, now with your kind permission ...'

The Earl merely nodded and retreated up the stairs.

'Right, Mr Jenkins,' Mac smiled, 'please escort us to the bedroom used by Mr Grant.'

'Certainly, Sir.' Jenkins let them to the massive staircase. 'It's quite a climb, but Mr Grant's room isn't far down the corridor.'

As they reached Grant's bedroom, Mac asked, 'Which is the Lady Alison's bedroom?'

Jenkins raised an eyebrow slightly and pointed to the next door along the corridor. 'Why, it's that one, Sir, right next to Mr Grant's.'

'Thank you, Jenkins, we'd like to examine in there too. Jimmy, Terry, go and look in the Countess' room - look, but don't touch, surface stuff only, OK?'

'Right, Guv.'

OK, Smithy, you and I will do the same in here,' said Mac as they entered Grant's bedroom. They took everything in with experienced eyes, looking for anything that looked out of place or unusual, but spotted nothing. They used handkerchiefs to open doors and drawers: still nothing.

'Smithy, we're doing this all wrong you know,' said Mac quietly.

'Wrong, how do you mean, Guv?'

'Well now, if I were Grant, I'd sleep in here, wouldn't I?'

'Well, yes I suppose so.'

'And if I were Alison, I'd sleep next door, right?'

'Course you would, yeah.'

'So it automatically follows that if Grant took Alison's place and *became* her, he'd sleep next door too, wouldn't he?'

Smithy smiled ruefully as it dawned on him, then he laughed out loud. ''Scuse me French, Guv, but what a pair of twerps we are.'

Mac smiled and shook his head. 'Remind me to have a brain transplant when this is over, Smithy.'

They moved out together, still chuckling, and went into Alison's bedroom. Jimmy and Terry looked up in surprise. 'That was quick, Guv.'

Mac laughingly explained what had just occurred to him, then quickly got down to business. 'Listen up, lads, if anyone dresses up as a woman and means to fool everyone a hundred per cent that he's all female, there's one thing he has to do to achieve this. I mean, apart from wigs and make-up of course.'

'He's got to have a shave, Guv, and a good one at that,' said Jimmy.

'You're so right, old son, and what's more, it's got to last some time. So his last shave has got to be as close as possible to show time - it's no good having one the night before, is it?'

'Too right, Guv,' said Terry, 'fancy kissing a girl with a ten o'clock shadow.'

'I thought you had already,' Bob's eyes twinkled in merriment.

'Naw, I ain't been out with your missus yet,' Terry chortled, then added hastily, 'Only joking mate.'

'All right if I take him to a taxidermist, Guv?' laughed Bob.

'He'd not dead yet,' Mac grinned.

'Yet,' said Bob, holding his hands out in strangulation mode.

'OK, let's get on. Now if Grant was Alison, he'd not only sleep in here, he'd shave in here or rather, there' - he pointed to the bathroom. 'So here's what we do. Firstly, you go and get the fingerprint kit from the car, dust and sticky tape every conceivable place that you might find a print. Do the sink and surrounds first, OK?'

'Right, Guv.'

'Oh, and while you're down there, look for a wrench for the sink U-bend.'

'You'll find one in the boot of my car, Bob!"' Jimmy shouted.

'Good,' said Mac, 'let's get cracking, we've got lots to do.'

Soon after, Mac, Smithy, Terry and Jimmy waited patiently as Bob fastidiously powdered and sticky taped all the smooth faces he could find, carefully bagging and tagging as he went along. Finally, he stood up and stretched his aching back. 'Finished here, Guv, you can take it to pieces now.'

'Thanks Bob, you can do the bedroom now while we're busy in here.'

Then Mac turned to Jimmy, 'Right, old son, take the U-bend to pieces but put a bowl or something underneath first. I want everything that comes out of that bend and I mean every last little drop, understood?'

'Understood, Guv,'

'If you get your hands wet, which you're bound to, use a brand new tissue to dry them, then bag it and tag it. I can't emphasise the importance of this enough.

An hour later, Mac was satisfied. They had collected prints from both bedrooms as well as collected all residue from the U-bend and around the plug-hole joint in Alison's room. They collected all the gear together and, along with Jenkins, they all trooped down to the tradesman's entrance for the next stage in their search. Once there, Jenkins opened the door and they stepped outside.

Mac turned to face the door, his brow slightly furrowed, deep in thought. After a while, he gave voice to his thoughts. 'Now, if I were Grant and I did bring a dummy here instead of Alison, I'm sure I wouldn't risk taking it upstairs, so what would I do with it?'

'Pardon, Guv, you talking to yourself or ...?' said Jimmy.

'What? No, look, are you *positive* that he went inside with the Countess or whatever it was?'

'I'm dead certain.'

Mac nodded in satisfaction and waved everyone back inside. 'OK that's good enough for me, let's get inside and have a look.'

Once inside, the team stood looking around at nothing in particular, waiting for Mac's next move.

'OK, I've got this far with the dummy. I'm not going to take it upstairs because I don't want to risk bumping into any of the staff. I've got to stow it somewhere close by, so let's see what we have.' Mac began to look around, counting the doors. 'One, two, three, yes, that's a door, four altogether. Now, if you look closely, they show all the signs of frequent use, not a bit of good to Mr Grant if any member of the staff were to show up at any moment. So there has—'

'Five, Guv,' interrupted Jimmy.

'What?'

'Sorry, Guv, but there's five doors, not four - there's one in the alcove behind this curtain.'

Mac hurried over, expectancy written all over his face. He snatched the curtain all the way back. 'It looks like some sort of a closet and if it is ...' His eyes gleamed. 'Let's take a look.'

He opened the door, to be confronted with a jumble of mops,

plastic buckets, wet vacuum cleaners, dry vacuum cleaners and piles of cleaning materials. Enough to hide a dozen tailors' dummies. Mac took a deep breath. 'The moment of truth has arrived, lads. Now, very carefully, move all this stuff out into the hall if you have to, and if you do find a dummy, don't try to move it, just uncover it, OK?'

They painstakingly removed everything from the broom cupboard, examining each item carefully, trying to miss nothing. Five minutes later, the cupboard was empty but no sign of the dummy. Mac tried to hide his disappointment but couldn't. 'I was so damn sure I was right,' he muttered. 'I was certain.'

'Er, Guv, this looks out of place.'

'What's that, Jimmy, what does?'

'This kitbag. Shall I open it?'

Mac stared at the bag and the adrenaline began to pump. A couple of seconds elapsed before he could nod his head. Jimmy saw the look on his boss' face and said a little prayer. Slowly, he slackened the drawstring as everyone held their breath, and gently opened the kitbag. He looked inside and then slowly raised his head, poker-faced.

Mac's heart was about to sink even further when Jimmy, unable to contain himself any longer, let rip with a western style 'Yeeaa hooo!' and began to jump up and down like a two-year-old with a new toy.

Mac's own expression was a picture to behold as relief and exhilaration flooded through him.

Smithy slapped his arm. 'Well done, Guv, nice one.'

'An excellent piece of deduction, Inspector, my congratulations on a fine piece of work.' The Earl's voice sounded behind them. He had overheard everything about the tailors dummy.

'Thank you, Sir, but you may be premature.'

'Oh, how so, Mr Macdonald?'

'Well for one thing, Sir, the dummy may belong here, or it may be devoid of any fingerprints.'

'The dummy doesn't belong here, of that I'm certain, and that applies to the kitbag too. We have no need of such things. The staff are too young to have seen military service so ...' The Earl spread his hands; he was quite adamant.

'In that case, with your permission, Sir, I think we'd better get on with it.'

'With alacrity, Inspector.'

Mac nodded his thanks. 'Right lads, spread some of these clothes flat out on the floor to lay the dummy on and when you've done that, lift the dummy out, using pencils, string or any holes you can find.'

Jimmy was about to make a rude remark but remembered who was present and thought better of it. He glanced at the Earl guiltily and could have sworn there was a twinkle in his eye, not to mention the ghost of a smile.

They finally laid the dummy, which was in pieces, on the cloth and Bob Saunders got to work. As it was being checked for prints, the Earl led Mac to one side and told him the story of the helicopter trip and Roger Cuncliffe. He laughed as the Earl related a blow by blow account of the flight from beginning to end.

'Mr Cuncliffe sounds like one hell of a man, Sir, if you'll pardon the expression.'

'No apology needed, Inspector. No man could ask for a better friend, indeed, he may lose his license over this.'

'Sir, under the circumstances, I think not.'

'I most sincerely hope not for his sake, it's part of his livelihood, you know.'

'Oh, how so, Sir?'

'Well, for one thing, he's a stunt pilot for films. He also runs a flight of crop sprayers but his forte is, would you believe it, air sea rescue.'

'You mean he's an Air Force or Navy pilot, Sir?'

'No, no,' the Earl replied, smiling, 'he's wavy navy, volunteer reserve, but this is quite apart from his air sea rescue activities. He lives quite near the coast and operates from there most of the time, although he does have another residence quite close to Stirling Lodge.'

'Well, I must say, Sir, I'm really impressed.'

'A truly remarkable man, Inspector, he uses his own choppers, as he prefers to call them, and pays the crewmen out of his own pocket. He also follows that progress of anyone who has been rescued, without their knowledge, of course. He just feels that it's something he has to do. Wonderful man. I deem it an honour and a privilege to be his friend.'

Mac just shook his head in admiration.

'Oh, er, Mr Macdonald, it would be imprudent to talk about our conversation to anyone, he doesn't do it for "gongs", as he calls them.'

'Understood, Sir, and please, don't worry unduly over his operator's licence.'

'Thank you,' the Earl said simply.

'Right, Sir, it looks as if we're ready here, so with your permission, I'd like to get all this stuff back for forensic examination.'

'Please, carry on. I only wish I could be of more help.'

'You already have been, Sir, it was you who gave us the vital clue that started us off really, when you said that you had to be back here by 8am.'

After loading the evidence carefully into the transport, Mac and his team sped swiftly back to Scotland Yard. Smithy was driving Mac's car so Mac took the opportunity to phone Jan at home on the mobile.

'Things are moving, luv,' he said when she answered, 'I'll fill you in when I get home.'

'I bet you will!' she replied teasingly.

'You know full well what I mean,' Mac chuckled, casting a sidelong glance at Smithy, who couldn't hear anyway. But it didn't stop him from putting two and two together and trying not to smile.

'Yes, sweetie, I know full well what you mean.' Jan chuckled and his phone went dead.

'You've got a way with words, Guv.' Smithy tried to keep a straight face and, failing, eventually broke into peals of laughter, joined by Mac. When the laughter subsided, each man lapsed into his own thoughts.

'Old big-head,' Mac thought fondly of Jan..

'He's a lucky man ,' thought Smithy.

Back home, Jan was nursing her own thoughts. 'Pea-brain,' she smiled lovingly, and couldn't wait for her husband to get home.

CHAPTER EIGHTEEN
THE CRIPPLE AND THE CAR BADGE

When Mac arrived back at the Yard, he was greeted by the desk sergeant. 'Ah, Mr Macdonald, Sir, there's a constable waiting to see you with a young cripple lad in a wheelchair.'

Mac frowned. 'Cripple, where is he?'

'We couldn't get the chair into the interview room, Sir, so we carried the lad in.'

'Thanks, I'll go and see him now.'

He found the crippled boy sitting in an armchair that looked suspiciously like the one in his office. He was drinking a large mug of tea, eating chocolate biscuits, and was obviously enjoying himself.

Mac's unasked question was answered by the young constable who was sitting with the boy. 'It's his spine, Sir, er, at the bottom, Sir, he has to sit on something soft, Sir ...' The constable apologetically indicated Mac's chair.

'Say no more.' Mac dismissed the matter and addressed the youngster. 'What's your name, son?'

'Benjy, that is, Benjamin Cartwright. I'm from the orphanage in Squires Lane.'

Mac nodded his head slowly. Squires Lane Orphanage was run by a charitable organisation and catered without complaint for every waif and stray that came their way, some literally left on the doorstep. Benjy Cartwright was one such child, named after the man who found him.

'Now then, Benjy, what's all this about then, eh?' Mac smiled at him.

'Excuse me, Sir, but can I put you in the picture quickly, Sir? It's a bit complicated to start from the beginning,' the constable cut in.

Mac raised his eyebrows at that bit of 'Irish'. 'Go ahead.'

The constable reached into his pocket and pulled out what appeared to be a badge of some sort. He held it out to Mac, who took it and caught his breath as he read the legend embossed on the highly polished surface. 'Ashdown Marsden!' he whispered excitedly. 'Where did you find this?'

'This youngster, erm, borrowed it from a, er, parked car, Sir,' said the constable.

'Oh, I see,' Mac nodded as he gazed at the young cripple, 'and er, just where was this car parked?'

'Outside Ramsdean Hospital gates or rather, by the grass verge, just before the gates,' replied the constable.

Mac's heart skipped a beat. 'What colour was it and did you get the registration number?'

'Dark grey silver metallic and no, he didn't get the number, Sir.'

'Blast,' thought Mac, 'no special colour.'

'Sir, if you look on the reverse side there's a number.'

Mac did so. 'So there is, Constable, so there is.'

'It's put on at the factory, Sir, so as to be able to identify it if it's stolen. They put the same number on various other parts of the car for the same reason.'

'Course they do, stupid me, course they do!' said Mac, feeling excited. He turned and shot out of the room, then shot back in again and stood in front of the boy. 'Don't worry, sonny Jim, if it fell off the back of a car and you found it, you can't get nicked for it, can you?' he said gently, grinning at the youngster.

'But, it didn't fall off, Sir!'

'I didn't hear that, did you, Constable?'

'Hear what, Sir?' said the constable with a deadpan expression.

Mac looked at his watch. '4.15, Constable, you'd better get your watch fixed,' he grinned.

The constable shook his wrist and held his watch to his ear.

'You're probably right, Sir, it's just turned septic.'

Mac left the room, smiling broadly and the youngster said, '4.15, watch, septic? What was all that about, mate?'

'Nothing that you would understand,' sighed the constable as he ruffled the young lad's hair.

Meanwhile, Mac was on his way to the forensic department to make sure that Smithy had safely deposited all the evidence collected at Hamilcourt House into the hands of Roland Summerville and his little band of experts. He explained in detail what he was looking, for with emphasis on face bristle. 'Rollie, I'm looking for a match with any prints from this little lot marked "A", but more importantly, I hope you can find human bristle in this lot marked "AS".'

Rollie was not in on Operation Grouse, so he did not know that 'A' stood for Alison, and 'AS' stood for 'Alison's sink'. No matter, he would do a first-class job as ever.

Satisfied that forensics was fully briefed, Mac made for his own office. He sat down and removed the Ashdown Marsden logo from his pocket, reached for the phone and dialled the switchboard.

'Inspector Macdonald here, can you get me the number of the Ashdown Marsden factory, and when you find it, get hold of their marketing manager please.'

'Give me a few minutes, Sir and I'll get back to you,' the voice replied.

'Right, as quick as you can please.'

He replaced the handset and drummed his desk impatiently as the minutes ticked by. He was reasonably pleased the way things were going and was hoping that forensics and Ashdowns would tie things up nicely. The phone rang then and he snatched it up. 'Macdonald.'

'I have Ashdown Marsdens on the line, Sir, a Mr Marriot, their marketing manager.'

'Thanks, put him through.'

There was a click and a voice said, 'Ashdown Marsden, David Marriot speaking. Whom do I have the pleasure of addressing?'

Mac smiled at that. 'Ah, Mr Marriot, I'm Detective Inspector Macdonald of New Scotland Yard and I need your help, Sir, very badly.'

'Certainly, if I can Inspector, what's your problem?'

'I have a badge, an emblem, the type usually fitted to the boot of your cars. There's a number on it and I was wondering if you could tell me the owner of the vehicle?' Mac enquired hopefully.

'I'm afraid not, Inspector, not the owner.'

Mac groaned inwardly. 'Blast!'

'I can tell you the distributer though. You just give me the number and I'll soon look it up for you,' said Marriot cheerfully.

Mac breathed an audible sigh of relief at that good news. 'Would you please? You're a treasure.'

Marriot chortled down the phone. 'I say, steady on, the wife'll get suspicious.'

Mac laughed as he turned the badge to the light for a better look at the numbers. 'Sorry, here are the numbers. Ready?'

'Shoot!'

'The first four are letters: AMDB followed by the numbers 7,4,4,8, then M for Michael, G for George, T for Thomas, C for Charlie and lastly 1,3,8,7. Did you get that, Mr Marriot?'

'Loud and clear, Inspector,' replied Marriot, 'just hang on while I look through our 1974 file.'

Mac could hear someone talking in the background. '74 file ... at the back. Ah, here it is.' The phone suddenly erupted in his ear. 'Still there, Inspector?'

'Still here, Mr Marriot.'

'Right, here we go then, got your pencil handy?'

'Ready.'

'Right, seven four stands for 1974 and four was the fourth month. Eight means that it was a batch of eight, MG means manual gearbox. TC means twin carbs and lastly, one, three, eight, seven is a consignment number to a distributor.'

'So you can tell me who sold that car?' Mac asked hopefully.

'Certainly, Inspector, this one went to, er, let me see now ... Ah yes, here we are, it was Spencer and Berryman in Bristol, er, 219 to 224, The Broadway, Bristol.'

'I see Sir, so—'

Marriot interrupted. 'Sorry, I meant to add that the consignment number is also in the dockets and the service manual of each individual vehicle.'

'Does that mean the dealer can tell me who bought that particular car then?' Mac could feel the excitement mount in him.

'I would most certainly expect him to be able to, Inspector,' replied Marriot.

'Mr Marriot, you're a blessing in disguise, I can't thank you enough for your help,' said Mac gratefully.

'Don't mention it, Inspector, glad to help at any time,' chuckled Marriot, and as an afterthought added, 'By the way, you don't want to place an order do you?'

'On my pay, Sir, you must be joking,' said Mac with a laugh.

'You're right, Inspector, I'm joking. Bye for now,' Marriot chuckled.

'Bye, and thanks again,' Mac replied and the line went dead. Then he contacted the switchboard again. 'Get me Spencer and Berryman at 219 to 224, The Broadway in Bristol, got that? And ring me back, quick as you can.'

It took less than two minutes for the phone to ring and Mac picked it up.

'Spencer and Berryman for you, Sir, putting you through,' said the voice. There was a click and a different voice said: 'Spencer and Berryman, specialist cars, Spencer speaking.'

'Ah, Mr Spencer, thank you for being so prompt. I'm Inspector Macdonald of New Scotland Yard and I'm trying to trace the owner of an Ashdown Marsden. Ashdown's manager put me on to you.'

'I see, or rather, I don't see ...'

'Allow me to explain, Sir,' said Mac reassuringly. 'I have a badge from the boot of a certain car that I urgently need to track down, and the badge has a consignment number, you see.'

'Yes, I'm beginning to now, Inspector, do continue.'

'Well, it appears that your consignment for this particular batch was one three eight.'

'One three eight!' the man sounded astonished. 'That was way back in the seventies.'

'1974 to be precise,' said Mac, 'and my badge says one three eight seven, so I'm looking for the man who purchased car number seven.'

'Mmm, that's a tall order, Inspector, can I call you back on this?'

'Most certainly you can,' said Mac and he gave Spencer the station number plus his own extension number. 'Will it take long?'

'I've got to dig for this one, Inspector, so give me, say, half an hour.'

'Do your best, Mr Spencer, it really is rather important.'

Spencer caught the urgency in Mac's voice. 'Leave it to me, I'll take care of this one myself so don't stray too far from the phone, Inspector.' The line went dead.

Mac chafed at the bit as he waited for the phone to ring, wondering whose name and address he would be jotting down. It had to be Grant's, it just had to be ... But what if it wasn't?

Mac's mind thought back to the last few weeks. The press had recently run some stories about a series of burglaries at the homes of wealthy aristocrats. They had all had jewellery stolen during the late evening or early hours of the morning, usually while they were attending parties or the theatre. The spate of robberies had coincided with Grant's arrival; they had stopped when he left. Was it just coincidence, or the work of an accomplice?

Mac shook his head. He couldn't come up with any ideas; it was not his case. This one was headache enough without adding to it. For ten long minutes, he sifted through the facts again as he waited for the phone to ring. Everything fitted except three pieces of the jigsaw. Two of these were in forensics, and the third was at the other end of this phone, he hoped.

It rang. 'Switchboard, Bristol again, Sir, putting you through now,' said the voice.

The familiar click and Spencer came on. 'Inspector Macdonald?'

'Speaking.'

'I've traced your car owner for you.'

Mac held his breath, pencil poised at the ready.

'We sold the car on April 12 1974 to one Robert Andrew Penton-Fairfax ...'

'What!' Mac exploded down the phone, startling the poor man at the other end.

'I beg your pardon,' Spencer retorted indignantly, 'did I say something wrong, Inspector?'

'I'm sorry, Sir,' Mac apologised, 'but that wasn't the name I was hoping to hear. I'm sorry if I startled you.'

'Think nothing of it, Inspector,' Spencer chuckled. 'Anyway, I can't imagine a man like Mr Penton-Fairfax getting into any sort of trouble with the law.'

Mac's interest quickened at this remark. 'Oh, and why do you say that?'

'Because of his connections.'

'His connections?'

'Yes, my dear fellow, he's the first cousin of Alison Penton-Fairfax.'

A little alarm bell began to ring in the back of Mac's head.

'Did you say Alison Penton-Fairfax?'

'That's right, she married the Earl of—'

'—Westminster.' Mac concluded triumphantly.

'Right first time, Inspector,' Spencer affirmed.

'My Godfathers,' Mac whispered. 'Holy Mother Macrea.'

'Pardon, Inspector?'

'Er, I was just thinking out loud,' Mac excused himself. 'Mr Spencer, I must thank you for all your trouble, you have just saved us from hours of wasted leg work,' he ended gratefully.

'No trouble at all, Inspector, pleased to be of some assistance,' said Spencer.

'Thanks again, goodbye, Sir.' Mac sat back in his chair, two unanswered questions in his mind: Were Andrew Grant and Robert Andrew Penton-Fairfax one and the same person; and if so, why hadn't the Earl mentioned it, or the butler Jenkins, come to that?

Mac mulled it over in his mind for a couple of minutes and came up with precisely nothing. He decided that there must be a perfectly simple explanation and he would follow it up at the first opportunity. One thing was certain, though: no one had needed to know until after the abduction. He was to find out why much later ...

Suddenly, Mac got up and called to one of the constables sitting at a desk, 'Find Sergeant Smith for me, George, quick as you can.' He returned to his desk and waited. A few minutes elapsed before Smithy appeared, a plastic cup in each hand.

'Coffee, Guv?'

'You must have read my mind,' said Mac as he gratefully accepted the steaming cup. He sat back in his chair and took a couple of appreciative sips before he spoke.

'I've got a job for you, old son, but first, pin back your lugs and listen.'

He related the story about the crippled lad and the car badge, the subsequent phone calls to the car manufacturers and distributors. As the connection between Grant and Penton-Fairfax unfolded, Smithy's interest began to intensify.

'Guv, are you saying that Alison was kidnapped by her own cousin?' he asked in amazement.

'I am, old son, or at least, I think I am.'

Smithy let out a long slow whistle and slowly shook his head. 'Well I'll be buggered,' he said at length.

'I thought you might be. Now I'm just waiting for forensics to come up with something positive, so in the meantime, I want you to run a trace on his address. Start with Hamilcourt House, you can get on to Jenkins, or the Earl himself. Someone has to know where he hangs out.'

'I think I know a quicker way, Guv.'

'How?'

'Phone Bristol. They sold him the car so they'll know his registration number - get hold of that and Swansea'll give you the rest,' Smithy replied simply.

'Now why didn't I think of that?' said Mac, giving Smithy a sidelong glance. 'You know, I was just wondering how you'd look in a Bobby's uniform.'

'Or an inspector's,' Smithy grinned.

Mac grinned back and reached for the phone. Half an hour and two phonecalls later, he had the home address of one Robert Andrew Penton-Fairfax. He leaned back in his chair. 'All we're waiting for now, old son,' he indicated the phone, 'is forensics.'

'Give him a bell, Guv ...'

'No no, he knows the form, he'll ring just as soon as he—'

He didn't finish the sentence as the phone rang unexpectedly and he snatched it to his ear. 'Macdonald!'

As he listened to Rollie's voice at the other end, Mac's expression changed and after a few seconds he said, 'Thanks Rollie.' He replaced the handset, triumph written all over his face.

'Bingo Smithy, bristles and fingerprints, and we know who they belong to, don't we, my old son!' Mac's eyes were shining.

'Nice one, Guv, right on the button. What happens now?'

'Let's go over what we have so far,' Mac replied. 'Firstly, we know that Grant took Alison out in the limousine, and he replaced her with a dummy. But where? We haven't a clue as yet.'

'That means,' said Smithy, 'she's either tied up and locked away somewhere, or she could be with Grant's accomplice.'

'True, and if he brought that dummy with him, that could account for the size of the trunk. Don't forget, he's also carrying a lot of other gear too - dresses, wigs. They have to be put onto dummies or get ruined.'

'I agree, Guv, so now we trace the escort that picked Grant up from Hamilcourt, and the driver can show us where he dropped him off, which if I remember rightly was at the railway station.'

'Not necessarily, he might have said that as a blind at the mansion.'

'Jenkins might remember the cab company, Guv, shall I get in touch with him?'

'If the Earl's there, he'll pick up the phone first so tell him what you want,' Mac said.

'Oh gawd, will you do it, Guv? I ain't got me proper talking tackle on,' Smithy muttered.

Mac grinned wickedly at the big sergeant's embarrassment and dialled the mansion himself. A few minutes later, he was armed with some useful information from the butler.

'The cab firm is the Blue and White and Jenkins remembers the number because he phoned them himself,' said Mac, holding up a piece of paper. He handed it to Smithy. 'Phone them and find the cabbie who called at Hamilcourt, and when they find him, have them bring him back to base then ring us straight away and we'll be down directly.'

'Right, Guv,' said Smithy as he reached for the phone.

'Well, it is your turn, after all, I phoned the Earl,' Mac grinned.

'Oh, I hate toffee-nosed twits,' Smithy muttered.

Mac cocked an ear. 'What was that?'

'I said I wish I had your wits,' Smithy replied with a bland smile.

'That's what I thought you said,' said Mac.

A short while later, they arrived at the minicab depot and Mac spoke to the escort driver. 'You picked up a man at Hamilcourt House on the 18th, I believe. Where did you take him?' was Mac's first question.

'To a row of garages in town,' the cabbie replied.

'Garages, not the railway station?'

'S'right Guv, and that's the second time I've been there in a week.'

'The second time?' Mac queried, slightly puzzled.

'Yeah, and with two different blokes as well.'

'I'm sorry, I don't follow you, two different people?'

'Look, let me tell it from the start, Guv.'

'I think you'd better.'

The driver began. 'Well, about a week before, I picked a bloke up at these garages and took him to the railway station and what's more, he'd got a bloody great trunk exactly like the one I picked up a week later at Hamilcourt.'

'Do you mean you picked up two different people with identical trunks?'

'That's right, Guv. The first bloke, if I remember rightly, had glasses and a moustache, oh, and a scar on his face as well.'

'This trunk, would you say it was the same one?'

'Oh, I'm positive, Guv, I asked the second bloke from Hamilcourt about that and he said it was communal like.'

'Communal? What d'you mean?' Mac requested.

'Well after I helped to unload the trunk, I asked him if I could help him with it into the garage, 'cos that's where I assumed he was going to put it, and he said something like erm, "We'll let that four-eyed scar-faced toe rag do it when he arrives", or something like that,' the cabbie smirked. 'Oh, and he gave me a fiver for me trouble.'

'You mean, he was part of a group of actors?'

'That's right, Guv, he said something like they were travelling troubadours, I think. He also said that they stowed all their stuff in this garage and shared the cost 'cos it was cheaper, like.'

'What happened after that?' insisted Mac.

'I had another call-out and had to leave,' the cabbie replied.

'Will you take us there?' Mac requested. 'Or rather we'll follow you in our own car, if you will, please.'

'My pleasure, Guv,' the cabbie replied.

'Put your time through for this when we've finished,' said Mac.

'Thanks Guv, where do I send the bill?'

'Scotland Yard, through me, Detective Inspector Macdonald. I'll sign your chitty when it reaches me.'

'Fair enough, Guv, follow me then,' said the cabbie and he turned towards his cab.

Later, outside the row of garages, the cabbie pointed out the one used by Grant. Mac thanked him and sent him on his way. Mac and Smith surveyed the garages up and down until they spotted the owner's name. They jotted down the location and phone number.

'Let's go and see this chap,' Mac said, making for the car, and minutes later they were talking to the owner, a man to whom Mac took an instant dislike which he managed to conceal as he questioned him.

'When did you let this garage, the most recent, I mean?'

'Hang on, let's get me book out,' wheezed the owner.

Seconds later, he was thumbing through the pages of a filthy looking ledger. 'Ah, here we are. I rented this one out on the 11th of August for a month but he only stayed a week.'

'Can you describe him, I mean, any distinguishing marks of any kind, hair, eyes, height etc?'

'Oh er, let me fink a bit. Oh yer, he had a mistosh 'n' glarses. Oh, an' a scar on one cheek.'

'Moustache, glasses and a scar, are you sure about that?' Mac was slightly puzzled.

'I shan't forget that creep in a rush!' the garage owner replied vehemently. 'He said me garages was on fire, an' he was larfin' like a bleedin' drain when he run orff round the corner.'

Mac stroked his chin thoughtfully. 'You thinking what I'm thinking, Smithy?'

'Yes, Grant leaves you-know-where as himself and turns up here as scarface, eventually.'

'On the nose, old son, one and the same man,' Mac agreed.

He turned back to the garage owner. 'Is the garage still empty?'

'Yer, but not for long, I 'ope.'

'Let me have the key, I want to look the place over,' Mac ordered , holding out his hand. The man opened his mouth to say something but thought better of it.

A little while later, Mac and his big sergeant were back at the garage site. Mac handed Smithy the key. 'Open it up, old son.'

Smithy complied and opened the doors wide. 'Empty, Guv, not a ruddy sausage.'

'Quite frankly, I'm not surprised. I didn't expect to find a thing after recent events, still, let's take a closer look.'

The sunshine was at the back of the garage, making for poor light inside, so Mac fetched a torch from the car. He cast the beam from side to side, stopping at one particular spot. Bending down, he pressed his fingers to the floor, then lifted them to his nose, smiling triumphantly as he detected a certain smell.

'Ah, this is what I'm looking for, at least, I think it is.'

'What is it, Guv?'

'If I'm right, it's face powder, probably the theatrical sort. Get some bagged up for forensics.'

Smith opened the car boot and retrieved from it a small camel hair brush, scoop, plastic bags and a roll of two-inch wide sticky tape. He ripped off a piece of tape about six inches long which he pressed face down on to the spot Mac indicated. He then made it into a circle by sticking one end to the other, brushed powder on the inside and finished by putting the circle of tape inside a cardboard box. He repeated this process twice more, then used the brush to sweep the remainder of the powder into the scoop and put the contents into another box. He finished the task by bagging and tagging the finished articles with a GG - Grant's garage.

Mac discovered what appeared to be fresh oil on the floor. 'Get a sample of this too, we may get a cross match when we find the car.'

'If we catch him red-handed with Alison, Guv, we won't need any evidence, well hardly any.'

'Yes, well that's what worries me, Smithy: assuming he's got Alison and she's in his house, just how do we get her out? Don't forget, we're supposedly dealing with some kind of mad genius here.'

'And just how do we know that she's in his house, Guv?'

'Precisely my point, old son, we don't.'

Smithy sighed. 'Cute, ain't he?'

'Let's get these keys back to that creep and make plans, shall we? Lock up and let's move it.'

As they drove back, Smithy gave voice to the question in his mind. 'Guv, if he *has* got Alison inside 'is place, how are we going in? I mean if we know for sure that she *is* in there?'

'If she is inside, we'll have to use a lot of ingenuity, guile, stealth or whatever. We'll have to have the edge on him, the element of surprise, or else.'

'Or else what, Guv?'

'He'll kill her,' Mac replied simply.

CHAPTER NINETEEN
IN FOR A PENNY

Back at the Yard, Mac addressed his assembled team and filled them in on the details to date, ending with his own conclusions.

'As you can see, lads, it's practically certain that Grant is Alison's cousin. It's also a racing certainty that he's the man who's lifted her and, what's more, I'll lay odds that she's being held prisoner at his pad in Lincolnshire. Now, we have to move very carefully on this, otherwise she's a goner.' He moved a finger across his throat. 'This chap means business.'

'I can believe that,' said Jimmy soberly, 'what do you want us to do next then, Guv?'

'We go to Lincolnshire and here again we have to be very careful, because we're out of our own manor and we can't very well ask for permission without giving the game away, so—'

'—we do a moonlight flit,' Terry finished.

'Moonlight is the operative word,' Mac agreed. 'Look, lads, we really are going to have to work at night and a bit dubiously, according to the police manual, so if any of you lads don't feel up to it, want to back out, there'll be no hard feelings.'

Terry turned to Jimmy. 'Blackout, did he say? Is there a war on then?' he asked innocently.

'Don't be stupid, Terry, he's on about your teeth - he wants to know if you've got any hard fillings,' Jimmy replied, tongue firmly in cheek.

Mac was inwardly delighted, even though he'd known the answer beforehand. Nevertheless, he was going to have a little fun. He leaned forward and placed his knuckles on the desk. 'When was the last time you two directed traffic?'

'When my mother-in-law packed up and left for distant parts, Guv,' replied Jimmy with a lopsided grin. 'Terry here blocked the side streets to give her a clear passage and Bob put a supercharger on her engine.'

'If I don't strike you pair,' Mac muttered to himself, smiling. 'I take it then, nobody wants out.'

'Not bloody likely, Guv - in for a penny, in for a pound,' said Jimmy, voicing everyone's sentiments.

'I should have had more sense than to ask. Thanks, lads,' said Mac. 'OK, here's what we do. We travel in three cars just in case one breaks down and we arrive separately to avert suspicion. We'll sort that out as we get close to the house.' Mac studied a street map which was spread out on his desk. 'There's a park at the back of the house so a couple of people strolling through won't look out of place.'

'Bird-watchers carry binoculars,' Jimmy suggested, 'they wouldn't be noticed if they had bird books and sketch pads.'

'Nice one, Jimmy, that would cover the back, and the sides as well, with any luck,' Mac agreed. He looked at the map again. 'The house, as I expected, fronts onto a fairly straight piece of road, dictated by the size and shape of the park, so I imagine that anyone inside the house would have a clear view in both directions, especially if that person was on the lookout. So great care is going to be needed if we're not to give the game away. Now, having said that, we need to put together as much info as we can, build up a picture of the inside of the house from the outside, which means strolling by singly at the front and counting the floors and windows. We'll also have to do the same somehow at the back, using the park.'

'And if we find out for certain that Alison's inside, Guv, what then?' Jimmy asked. 'Do we go in?'

'Now that, old son, is one that we'll have to play by ear when the time comes.'

'What about the Chief Constable,' Smithy asked, 'you going to tell him first, Guv?'

'Well, look at it like this: if we're wrong about this, which I'm almost certain we're not, there'll be enough eggy faces about without involving the boss man. Don't forget, we're not supposed to be there in the first place, right?'

'Right.'

'OK, beddie byes, you lot and take your transport home with you. Make your own arrangements who picks who up. I'll be with Smithy, so we'll assemble at his place at 3am, prompt, OK? Now scoot.'

They put away their various bits and pieces and Mac folded up his map. They trooped outside and went their various ways and Mac drove Smithy home before setting off for his own, knowing full well what sort of welcome he would get, and relishing every moment.

CHAPTER TWENTY
THE OLD MANSE

The alarm jangled in Mac's ear at 2.15am but before he could switch it off he felt Jan's warm soft body reach over him, silencing the shrill noise.

'Will you take that out of my ear, love, before I go deaf,' Mac murmured from somewhere underneath Jan's chest.

Jan chuckled in the dark. 'Are you complaining, sweetie?' she murmured.

'Nope,' came the reply, 'not for a couple of minutes anyway.'

As Mac spoke, his hand started to creep backwards until he touched Jan's leg, nipping the inside of her thigh before she was quite aware of what he was up to. She yelped with surprise and shot backwards out of bed, laughing.

'Oh no you don't, sweetie, you have a job to do first so out you get,' she chided him.

'Spoilsport,' he growled, 'it's the railway lines for you when I get back, my girl.'

'No, no, not again,' Jan simpered, 'anything but the railway lines per-lease,' she giggled, hamming it up.

Mac sat upright in bed and began twirling an imaginary moustache. 'It's me or the tracks, me gal,' he growled.

'What time's the next train?' giggled Jan, snatching her dressing gown from the foot of the bed and dashing for the bedroom door before he could grab her. 'I'll make some sandwiches and a flask for you,' she shouted back from halfway down the stairs, 'so get your skates on.'

Mac sighed and dragged himself out of bed, not quite knowing when he would be using it again. He headed for the shower. By the time he'd finished, Jan had cooked him a huge breakfast and was busy making him sandwiches and an enormous flask of coffee.

'That was grand my love,' said Mac, when he had finished his breakfast and washed it down with a mug of sweet tea.

'Before you ask, there are no afters,' said Jan with a twinkle in her eye.

'No?' Mac arched an eyebrow in her direction.

Jan walked over and sat on his lap. 'Bring Alison back, my love, then I can have your undivided attention,' she said, kissing her husband gently on the end of his nose. She stood up and pulled Mac after her. 'Time to go, or you'll be late for Smithy.'

She fetched his coat and put his flask and sandwiches into a picnic container, closing the lid securely. She took his arm and steered him towards the door. They kissed each other tenderly, then he was gone.

'Drive carefully, sweetie,' was all she could think of to say as Mac drove off. But inwardly she prayed, 'Safe return, my darling.' She hadn't forgotten for one moment that Grant or Penton-Fairfax, whoever he was, was indeed a madman.

Mac drove swiftly to Smithy's home to find his team all ready and waiting. 'Morning lads,' he greeted them cheerfully.

'Am I on the right planet?' muttered Jimmy.

'Did you turn right at Jupiter?' said Terry.

'Blowed if I know, they all look alike to me,' Jimmy answered wryly.

Mac grinned to himself. This light-hearted banter was a veneer that hid very tough interiors. 'OK, lads, let's hit the road,' he said as he climbed back into his car.

Dawn had already broken as Mac pulled into a lay-by on the outskirts of Lincoln. He climbed out and stretched his legs. The other two cars were not far behind and pulled in behind him.

'So far so good,' said Mac, 'glad to see that nobody broke down.'

'How far is this house, Guv?' Jimmy asked.

'About a mile and a half.'

'What's the form, Guv?' Smithy asked.

'Well, it'll be hours before the park opens so I want you chaps to feed your faces because I've no idea when you'll get the next opportunity. Meanwhile, Smithy and I'll go and locate this house, OK?

'OK, Guv.'

'We'll be back as soon as we can,' said Mac, as he and his big sergeant climbed back into their car. 'Stay put until we get back.'

Seconds later, they were scorching the Tarmac as they headed for the city ... and Grant.

They were back within the hour and Mac spelled out the details to his eager team. 'It's big, Victorian I'd say, with three storeys, maybe eight to ten rooms on the top two floors,' he explained.

'The park gates don't open till 8 o'clock,' said Smithy.

'Yes, I know, so we'll just have to go over the wall,' winked Mac.

'What about the park keeper, Guv, what if he spots us inside the park during closing hours?' Jimmy asked.

'If anyone gets spotted, just show him your warrant card and bundle him back inside his lodge, or whatever it's called, a bit sharpish.'

'What excuse do we give him, Guv?'

'Tell him a prisoner has escaped from an open prison and we've chased him into this park. Tell him we know that for a fact, because he was spotted climbing in, right?'

'Leave it to us, Guv, we'll cope,' said Jimmy.

'Fair enough, now mount up all of you and follow us. As we pass the house, I'll flash my tail-lights off and on, OK?'

'Right, Guv, anywhere we can park up out of sight?'

'Yes, the house is on your left and fifty feet past there. You make a right turn, it's quiet and discreet,' said Mac. 'Now follow me.'

As they approached the house, Smithy slowed and flashed his lights. He was quickly acknowledged by the vehicles behind. Fifty feet past the house, he turned right and drove just far enough down the road to allow space for the others. Mac got out and made a beeline for Jimmy's car.

'Got a job for you old son,' he said through the open window.

'Shoot, Guv.'

'Take a walk round the park, find an easy way in and be as quick as you can.'

'Consider it done, Guv,' was all he said, and within seconds, he had vanished from view. He was back within half an hour, smiling broadly.

'How did it go, Jimmy, how does it look?' Mac asked.

'Fine, Guv, I've been inside already. I've got to laugh, though, they've got this bloody great wall all the way round, or most of it - the rest is chain link fence, except about forty feet which is privet hedging.' He paused for breath. 'And there's a ruddy great gap in it that you can walk through.

129

'Kids, I suppose,' said Smithy.

'Yeah, there's a housing estate over the back and I just can't imagine kids walking a mile just to come in the main gate. I know I wouldn't.

'Good work old son, how much cover is there?'

'More than enough, Guv, there are plenty of shrubs and bushes all over the place, and they're fairly dense at the back of the house.'

'How far from the house?'

'Forty, fifty yards maybe, we can see three sides of the house from cover with binoculars,' said Jimmy.

'Right, fair enough, now here's what I want you to do. First, check out your handsets, make sure they're serviceable and after you've done that, Terry, Jimmy, Bob, you three take the park and get near enough to note the number of windows including size and shape, you know the form. Take a side each and for pete's sake, don't get spotted. Smithy and I will take the street side and between us, we should be able to build up some sort of a picture of what the inside looks like. Now split!'

The three DCs took off rapidly and Mac gave them five minutes to get into position. Meanwhile, he and Smithy made their own plans. They would walk past the house at five-minute intervals and memorise it without being too obvious.

'I'll go first, old son, give me five minutes before you follow and I'll see you fifty yards up the street.'

'Right, good luck, Guv, see you later.'

Mac walked to the bottom of the side street, turned left at the corner and strolled past the old Victorian house on the opposite pavement. To any onlooker, his glance at the house betrayed nothing more than casual interest, but his eyes missed nothing in those few seconds. A few yards past, Mac gave a backward glance as if looking for a friend, and took in the place once more. There was a convenient bus shelter fifty yards up the road and he stood inside as if waiting for a bus. Smithy joined him a few minutes later.

'What did you make of it, Smithy?'

'Nine windows, three on each floor, four balconies, two on the top and two on the second floor,' Smithy replied.

'They could be bedrooms, the balcony ones, and the other two are bathrooms, I reckon, being glazed windows,' Mac mused.

'I agree, Guv, and I should think the downstairs rooms are dining or drawing rooms and a kitchen.'

'If Alison's here, we can discount the ground floor I think,' said Mac.

'If I were the kidnapper, I'd keep her away from this side of the building, Guv, for obvious reasons.'

'Of course, now hang on, let's see if the lads are in position yet.'

Mac shielded himself behind the huge sergeant and took his handset from his pocket, concealing it with his handkerchief. 'This is Mac, speak to me somebody.'

'Sanderson here, Guv, I'm in position now, directly behind the house.'

'What can you see, Terry?'

'I can see the top two floors, Guv, erm, three windows on both floors, erm, two balconies on each with what could be French windows behind them. The top left window on the top floor is small with plain glass. The second floor left window is small glazing and I can't see the ground floor properly because there's a big wooden garage blocking my view,' Terry replied.

'I can see it,' said Jimmy.

'Where are you?' asked Mac.

'Stuck up a bloody great oak tree on the right-hand side, Guv, I can see practically everything,' said Jimmy.

'What can you see, Jimmy?'

'Three doors on the ground floor, one looks like a kitchen door and there's a dustbin nearby, that's on my left. The middle door looks like any rear exit and the third door on the right is a double French window leading to a small lawn. There's also a paved walk that looks as though it leads to the garage.'

'Good work, Terry. Can you hear me, Bob?'

'Loud and clear, Guv, I can't see a lot of the house from here but I can see the garage quite clearly,' Bob replied.

'Is it open? Can you see a car, the Ashdown?' Mac's voice betrayed his tension.

'Sorry, Guv, the doors are closed,' replied Terry regretfully.

Mac looked at his watch: 7.50am. 'Sit tight lads, the gates open in ten minutes so we'll start from there.'

'There's a light just come on, top floor, right window.' Terry's voice was urgent in Mac's ear. Mac and Smithy were suddenly very alert.

'There's a bloke just coming into view now, he's wearing pyjamas I think, now he's stretching and yawning.'

'Can you describe him, Terry?' Mac asked.

'Not properly, Guv, hang on, he seems to be talking to someone over his shoulder!'

'So, there're two of them,' Mac breathed. 'He *does* have an accomplice!'

'Light on ground floor, left.' It was Jimmy this time.

'Could be cooking breakfast if that's the kitchen,' Smithy suggested.

'Yes, that's sure,' Mac agreed, 'and I somehow can't imagine Grant cooking his own breakfast, him being the brains, so to speak, so it must be the accomplice.' He spoke into his handset. 'Keep your eyes peeled, you lot, Smithy and myself will be joining you just as soon as we can find the hole in the privet.'

'Just keep to the house on your left, Guv, and follow the pavement, you'll be here in roughly seven minutes,' said Jimmy.

Seven minutes later, Mac and Smithy were behind the oak tree that hid Jimmy in its ample foliage.

'Kitchen light's gone out, Guv, they're probably sitting down to breakfast,' said Jimmy.

Five minutes passed uneventfully then ... 'Top left window, light on Guv,' said Terry. Suddenly, he let out a loud exclamation. 'Jesus bloody wept!'

Mac began to tingle. 'What's the matter, Terry?'

'Guv, I could have sworn I just saw ... bloody hell, I did, he's there in plain bloody sight, my God!'

'Who is, what is, for heaven's sake?' Mac asked in agitation.

'He's wearing a helmet, one of those ski masks with a slit to look out of,' Terry replied excitedly.

As the implication of Terry's words sank in, Mac closed his eyes and breathed a sigh of relief. 'Bingo, Smithy, she's here and she's still alive or that creep wouldn't be wearing that ski mask, would he?'

'How are you going to get her out?'

'That, old friend, is just what we have to plan out. Jimmy, can you get in there without being spotted?'

'Guv, if you stage some sort of diversion round the front, I reckon we all could,' said Jimmy.

'Mm, good idea, let me think about it.' He looked at his watch; the park gates had been open for about twenty minutes.

'Hang about, Guv, someone's coming out through the French doors.' It was Terry's voice. 'He's heading for the garage, I think. Hang on, he's out of sight for the moment, yep, here he is, he's opening the garage doors now, he's gone inside ...'

Seconds later, the early morning silence was shattered by the sudden roar of a powerful engine as a metallic grey car reversed out of the garage, executed a neat two-point turn and shot forward down the driveway.

It was an Ashdown Marsden DB.

The brakes came on momentarily at the end of the driveway, then the car turned right and sped off at high speed. Mac listened until the sound faded away and then the idea came to him.

Bob, are you listening?'

'Loud and clear, Guv.'

'Get that second bloke to the front door and talk about Ashdown Marsdens, tell him you want to buy it, anything, just keep him talking until we can get in, OK?'

'OK so far, Guv.'

'When he opens the door, beep twice on your handset, right?'

'Right.'

'As soon as we're in, I'll beep you and you grab him fast. And for Christ's sake, hold him tight until we can get to you, OK?'

'Got it, Guv.'

'Right. Off you go, and don't forget, be casual,' Mac reminded him.

'Oscar performance coming up,' said Bob, 'I'm on my way.'

They watched as Bob Saunders came into view, walking leisurely across the grass towards the park gate. He glanced around nonchalantly as if enjoying the view; but in reality he was making sure that he was out of sight of the house before breaking into a sprint. On reaching the front of the house, he took a deep breath before approaching and rapping three times with the heavy lion's head knocker.

A minute passed and he was about to knock again when he heard the sound of footsteps approaching from inside the house. The door was opened by a dark-haired man in his thirties, who gave Bob a disarming smile. 'Good morning, and what can I do for you?'

As soon as the door was starting to open, Bob had pressed the button twice on the beeper in his pocket. 'Ah, good morning.' Bob returned the greeting with a genial smile. 'I'm Dr John Harvey and I was just taking a stroll through the park before going on duty and—'

'Look, I'm rather busy,' the young man interrupted, though still smiling.

'I'm so sorry, but, erm, didn't I hear an Ashdown Marsden just now, in your back garden, I mean? I'm a fan myself and I just wondered if, well, I could have a look at it,' said Bob, apologetically.

'I'm sorry, but there's no Ashdown Marsden here, you must be mistaken,' the young man replied.

'Come on, Guv,' Bob thought desperately, 'I'm running out of things to say. 'But I could have sworn I heard one just now,' he insisted.

''Fraid not, Doctor, no Ashdown Marsden, sorry,' the young man replied as he made a move to shut the door.

Just then the unit in Bob's pocket beeped twice and the young man paused, a suspicious look on his face. 'I'm being paged already,' said Bob, tapping the beeper in his pocket.

The young man's expression changed as understanding dawned, then a sound, not very loud, made him turn his head slightly. He frowned as he tried to place its origin and Bob seized his chance. Leaping forward, he grabbed the young man's left arm, spun him round quickly and applied a half nelson.

'Through here, Guv!' he shouted towards the back of the house as the young man started to protest volubly, struggling to loosen Bob's powerful grip.

'What the hell's going on? Let me go you, bloody idiot, let me go!' he demanded indignantly.

Mac, having got through the unlocked door easily, had quickly despatched Smithy, Terry and Jimmy to various parts of the house for a rapid search. He arrived at a run and helped Bob to subdue the young man. Bob reached backwards with his foot and kicked the front door shut.

'Look, just who the hell are you people, what do you want?' the man protested. 'Are you the police, or are you burglars?'

Mac and Bob led the struggling man through the hallway and into a lounge full of old fashioned furniture. 'If you promise to be a good boy and sit down quietly, I'll let you go,' said Mac.

The man stopped struggling and after a few seconds' thought, nodded. 'All right, all right, I'll do as you ask, but I still want to know why you're doing this.'

Mac had to be careful, he was out of his jurisdiction and was painfully aware of the fact. 'All in good time, Sir, all in good time,' he replied. He was waiting for Smithy, Terry or Jimmy to appear with Alison.

One by one, they joined Mac and Bob in the lounge, shaking their heads as they came into view. Disbelief registered on Mac's face as the last man put in an appearance. He thought fast. 'I'm Detective Inspector Macdonald and we had a tip-off that this house was being burgled,' he bluffed.

'Burgled, tip-off? I don't believe what I'm hearing, may I see your warrant card, Inspector?'

Mac sighed and reached for his warrant card, knowing that his own district would be spotted as soon as it was examined. He held it out to the young man and asked him, 'Now would you mind telling me who *you* are, Sir?'

'Certainly. My name is Brent, William Brent. I'm an actor and I live here,' he replied, taking Mac's card.

As Brent said his name, Jimmy frowned and, detaching himself quietly from the group, went to leave the lounge. Brent spotted the move. 'And where do you think you're going?' he demanded.

'Sorry, Sir, but I have to use your loo if you don't mind, erm, something I ate, I think,' Jimmy replied apologetically.

'Oh, please be my guest,' Brent said sarcastically, 'don't mind me.'

'Thank you, Sir,' Jimmy smiled blandly, 'I know where it is.'

Brent watched him go out of the room in the general direction of the toilet before opening the warrant card. 'So, you really are an inspector after all, Inspector, and not a burglar.' He gave Mac an icy smile.

Mac, for some strange inexplicable reason, could scarcely repress an involuntary shudder. Brent dropped his eyes to the warrant card again for long seconds before finally closing it and handing it back to its owner. Mac could scarcely believe his luck as he took the card and returned it to his pocket.

'He didn't spot it,' he thought triumphantly, 'he blew it!'

'Now, what's all this about a tip-off, Inspector?' Brent asked.

'I'm sorry, Sir, but it appears we've been misinformed,' Mac replied apologetically.

'A hoax, you mean?' Brent's voice was slightly mocking.

'So it would seem, Mr Brent, we're having quite a spate of them just lately, I'm sorry to say, and they leave us with egg on our faces trying to placate irate citizens such as your good self, Sir.'

'Yes, I was rather annoyed, I must say, but under the circumstances ...'

'It's very good of you, Sir, to take it so lightly and I do apologise on behalf of myself and my men for the trouble we've caused, especially the rough handling.'

'Well, you do have a job to do, I suppose, and these things happen from time to time, I imagine,' said Brent.

There was the sound of a toilet being flushed and Jimmy appeared thirty seconds later, buttoning his coat. 'Thank you, Mr Brent, I feel much better now,' Jimmy smiled gratefully.

'You're welcome, Sergeant.'

'Detective Constable, actually, Sir.'

Brent just nodded and turned to Mac. 'If you gentlemen are quite happy now, I do have things to do, so if you wouldn't mind ...' He gestured towards the hallway.

'Er, yes of course, I think we've wasted enough of your time, Sir,' said Mac. 'OK chaps, let's vacate the premises and leave Mr Brent in peace.'

They trooped out of the lounge one by one, down the hallway to the door, followed by Mac, who led them back to the parked cars.

'Why the puzzled look, Guv? As if I didn't know,' said Smithy.

'Do you know something? He never even noticed that I was from out of town and if he did, he never even mentioned it. Funny that.'

'As a matter of fact, I had noticed, Guv,' said Smithy.

Jimmy sidled up and spoke quietly. 'Have a dekko at this, Guv.' He handed Mac a large photograph which had been hidden inside his coat. Mac took it and looked at it; as he did so, his brow creased into a frown. He read aloud the inscription on the bottom, written across the man's chest: 'With best wishes, William Brent.'

The good-looking young man in the classical film star pose, smiling out at him from the photograph, seemed to mock him.

'If this chappie here is William Brent,' Mac indicated the photograph with his forefinger, 'then who the hell is that bloke in there?' said Mac, nodding in the direction of the old Victorian house.

'It could be Grant or hyphen Fairfax, Guv, whatever his name is, said Smithy, 'but we don't know what he looks like do we? We've never set eyes on him, have we?'

'You haven't but I have,' said Jimmy with a mischievous grin as he pulled another photograph from under his coat and handed it to Mac. Mac took the photograph and looked at it. The hair looked lighter and the face was a few years younger, but it was unmistakable. It was the man in the house - William Brent.

The photograph was signed, 'Best Wishes, Andrew Grant'.

'Well well well!' Mac exclaimed, handing the photograph to Smithy. 'Now what do you make of that, old son?'

'So that's what the sod looks like, tricky bugger, isn't he?' said Smithy, shaking his head in mild amazement.

'Oh what a tangled web we weave,' said Mac thoughtfully.

'You know, Guv,' said Terry, 'I'd have staked my life that Alison was in there, I really would have.'

'So would I, especially because of the ski mask,' Mac agreed.

'Guv, I did something else when I pinched the photos,' said Jimmy.

'What was that?'

'Well, when he said he was Brent, I'd already seen the photos in a drawer when we did a search and, me realising then what we all know now, I stuck a bug in his mouthpiece,' said Jimmy grinning.

'All well and good, but we don't have a receiver to pick him up, do we?'

'I beg to differ, Guv,' said Jimmy and stuck his head and shoulders into on of the cars, emerging with what appeared to be a small radio with a circular aerial. 'This'll pick him up a treat but.the range is only about six hundred yards.' Jimmy was grinning like a Cheshire cat.

Mac grinned back at him. 'OK, you win, tune into him and let's see if he gives anyone a bell.'

'It's got a tape recorder built in anyway, Guv, just in case we need to amplify it at any time.'

Mac nodded his thanks and the frown returned to his forehead again. 'Where the devil is she, Smithy, where has he put her? She's obviously not here, if she was here at all that is.'

'I can't be sure, Guv, but I think she was, or some lady or other was, that's for certain.'

'What makes you say that?'

'That room on the top floor, the one with the ski mask, there's a bed in there and the pillow has lipstick stains on it. And that's not all, Guv.'

'Go on then, old son, don't keep me in suspense,' Mac urged.

'The pillow was soaking wet as though somebody had been crying all over it.'

Mac let that sink in for a few seconds. 'So she was here after all,' he breathed.

'Weighing the odds against what we know, I'd say ninety nine per cent certain, Guv,' said Smithy.

Mac put his hands up, palms forward. 'OK, OK, let's assume she was here in the first place, when and how did he move her and more to the point, where is she now?'

''Scuse me saying it, Guv,' said Smithy, 'don't forget what Professor Hasketh said about this bloke being mad and clear with it; he probably knew that we were coming here eventually and he's probably planned to suit.'

'And if he knew that, he'd also know that we'd be out of our own manor—' Mac broke off suddenly as Grant's plan hit him between the eyes.

'Oh my Gawd, move it lads, let's get out of here before the local law shows up, rapid now! The swine's set us up.'

Without more ado, everyone scrambled for their vehicles, started their engines and, with Mac in the lead, roared off. They were not a moment too soon as the sound of police sirens could be heard in the distance, closing the gap to the old house at high speed.

Half a mile away, Mac turned into a side street and stopped, the other cars following suit. As they all spilled out on to the pavement, Mac gave vent to his feelings volubly. 'That creep set us up for the locals, the mad bastard!' he said, shaking his head in disbelief. 'I'm gobsmacked!'

'They wouldn't have held us, Guv, we're the law as well,' said Terry.

'They would, you know, listen to this,' said Jimmy, holding out his receiver and switching it on. The message on the tape was faint and the first half was missing: '—glars, posing as police ... yes, that's what I said, burglars posing as police ... yes yes yes, posing as police ... they're outside now, please hurry.' Click.

'I wasn't switched on for the first bit Guv, as you heard, but I got enough, didn't I?'

Mac was seething. 'He knew we couldn't tell the locals about Alison, the swine, and even if we did, they wouldn't let us go until they'd checked us out.'

'Delaying tactics, Guv?' said Smithy.

'That, and to feed his ego.'

He turned to Jimmy, indicating the receiver. 'We've come about half a mile, maybe less. Can you pick him up on that do you think?'

'Well let's put it like this, Guv, the tape can pick him up at this range and we can amplify it later, but I doubt very much if we can hear him direct.'

'That's no good, we've got to get closer.'

'Tell you what, Guv, I'll walk back to within earshot of his phone bug.' He reached into his car and emerged with a set of headphones. 'I'll wear these and look like Danny with his trannie,' Jimmy grinned, 'that should give the local law time to pack up and go home.'

'OK, old son, give us a call on your handset when they've gone and we'll drive a bit closer.'

'I've gone, Guv,' said Jimmy, as he turned and walked away, donning the headphones at the same time. As he went, snapping his fingers to an imaginary tune, a thought suddenly entered Mac's head.

'Smithy?'

'Yes, Guv?'

'You know how this bloke's clever enough to know just what we're going to do next, or he has been up to now, d'you think he could have sussed the bug in the phone?'

'Cripes, bloody hell Guv, if he don't, we're quids in.'

'Yes, but only if he can lead us to Alison with a phone call, or at least give us something that we can get our teeth into.'

'He's got to make a mistake sometime, after all, if he was perfect, he'd be Pope, wouldn't he?'

'We can always hope, old son,' Mac sighed.

Suddenly, four different beepers sounded simultaneously and Mac dived into his pocket to retrieve his. He put it close to his ear and said, 'Shoot'.

'Guv?'

'Listening.'

'I'm about four hundred yards from the house and I can't see any of the local law about.'

'Where are you, Jimmy, is there a side street or somewhere that we can park in out of sight?'

'I'm standing in one, Guv, if you coast the last hundred yards or so, you can turn in quiet like, it isn't a sharp corner.'

'Thanks and well done, we're on our way,' said Mac.

A few minutes later, Mac saw Jimmy waving from the seclusion of a bend in the road. Mac flashed his lights in recognition and selected neutral. He kept his engine ticking over just in case and, judging his speed well, coasted round the corner into the side road, closely followed by his companions. They got out and joined Jimmy, who was listening intently to something in the headphones. He held up a finger for silence and everyone obeyed as they saw the intense concentration on his face. Finally, he removed his headphones and handed them to Mac.

'Phew, get a load of this, Guv, it'll astonish you, believe me.' He ran the tiny tape back to the desired position, then he switched to 'play'. Through the slight static there came a dialling sound and a few seconds later, an indistinct voice answered.

'Sorry, Guv,' Jimmy whispered, 'only put one bug in, and that was in the mouthpiece.'

'Shh,' Mac motioned him to be quiet as Grant's voice sounded.

'Ah, your Lordship, right on time I see.' There was a pause as the recipient answered. Grant laughed softly. 'Who am I indeed! That is precisely the question I've often asked myself, your Lordship,' he answered sarcastically.

There was a longer pause as the recipient once again answered.

'Oh! I can't do that, you see, and it would be very imprudent of you to hang up too, Robin my dear friend.' Grant's voice was mocking now.

Again there was a long pause as Robin answered Grant.

'Joke! This is no joke, my dear Robin, quite the contrary in point of fact.' Grant's voice sounded smug. 'You see, my dear boy, you are going to make me very rich.'

Another short pause.

'Yes, rich. You, my friend, are going to swell my miserable coffers and you will do it gladly, I may add, by the splendid sum of two million pounds because my dear Sir, you are now missing one Countess, do you follow me?'

There was a pregnant pause of over half a minute and Mac and his team could only guess at the Earl's reply.

'My dear boy,' was Grant's reply, 'how clever of you to have deduced that fact so quickly. Well done, old chap, I really have kidnapped your good lady' - the owner of the voice was obviously enjoying himself - 'and all you have to do to get her back is pay the money into my numbered account in Switzerland.'

There was another short pause.

'Look my friend,' the voice broke in, 'you can always phone home afterwards, which of course I would not advise, or alternatively - and I would advise this course of action - you can go home and see for yourself.'

Again a short pause. 'Because if you do phone the mansion and find that she really is missing, then so will your staff. You do see what I am driving at, don't you, Robin?'

Another gap in the conversation. 'Then let me endeavour to enlighten you, my friend,' the menacing voice continued. 'If your staff find out - and, I might add, they know nothing as yet - then it will become common knowledge in next to no time at all, and that, I'm afraid will be the end of it.'

Again a gap in the conversation.

'Quite simple old chap, if everyone knows of your good lady's abduction, then it must follow that every policeman in the country and elsewhere will be looking for me, so I can't run the risk of trying to keep her hidden, you see.' He paused for a few seconds. 'In which case I'll have to kill her so she won't be able to give me away, will she, Robin? And please remember that she is just 30 minutes from where I am standing - just 30 minutes from ... death.'

Again an exasperating gap in the conversation.

'You haven't time to think, you must act now, before it's too late.' Again the voice chuckled evilly.

Again silence for a few seconds.

'Until 8 tomorrow morning, my friend, and not a minute longer.'

There was a click as the phone went dead as Grant ended the seemingly one-sided conversation.

'Ye gods!' Mac was filled with rage now. 'The mad bastard's got it sewn up tight, hasn't he? He knows full well that we can't pick him up, even though he knows that we know he's kidnapped her. He's the only one, along with his sidekick, who knows that we know he's kidnapped her.

'Tricky sort of swine, ain't he, Guv? And we've got just two days to find her,' Smithy.

'Don't I know it,' said Mac, pacing up and down. 'Let me think for a minute.' Suddenly he stopped and snapped his fingers.

'There's a couple of things we can do, they're long shots but there's a chance we can pull one or the other off.'

'And what's that, Guv?'

'First, he said it would take half an hour to get to within half a mile of the place, wherever it is, so we urgently need to look at our map of this area and that's in my car. Second, if Grant phones Zurich from here, he has to go through the local exchange.' Mac was getting into his stride now. 'So if we can get the Lincoln exchange to work a small miracle for us, we just might save the Earl two million quid, rescue our lady in distress and nail Grant in one fell swoop.'

'Now you're talking, Guv! I'll get the briefcase out of your car,' said Smithy.

A couple of minutes later, they were studying the map that was spread over the bonnet of Mac's car. He had already marked out a 'half-hour's drive' circle, based on an average forty miles an hour.

'Now let me see,' said Mac, 'Grant mentioned machinery and forty-eight hours, so what kind of machinery is allowed to stand idle for that amount of time?'

'What about farm machinery?' Terry suggested.

'No, I don't think so, not at this time of the year at any rate, because it's harvest time.'

'This is going to be sticky, Guv.' Bob Saunders was shading his head. 'We've got five or six thousand square miles to look at.'

'No we haven't, old son: Grant distinctly said half an hour's drive plus half a mile for a certainty, so if we allow half a mile or so either side of the circle, we can narrow it down considerably.' He straightened up from the car bonnet.

'You blokes get stuck into this map, see what you can come up with. Use the local authority survey maps if need be. Try the libraries, local historians, anything at all, but come up with something. I've got a couple of long distance phone calls to make before we can move in any direction.' He addressed Smithy. 'Take charge, Smithy, I've got to find a phone box that hasn't been vandalized.'

Minutes later, Mac parked his car in a lay-by and dialled the Chief Constable at Scotland Yard.

CHAPTER TWENTY-ONE
THE ARREST

Sir Donald Matlock was pacing up and down his office, fuming with impatience. Minutes earlier, he had been talking on the phone to the Earl of Westminster and he was reeling at the text of their conversation. Based on what he had heard, he had put out an urgent call for Macdonald, only to find out that he was nowhere to be found.

'Forty-eight hours!' he fumed. 'Forty-eight hours to find Alison or that bloody madman kills her!'

Suddenly the phone shrilled and the Chief snatched it up. 'Matlock!' he barked.

'Sir Donald, it's me, Sir, Macdonald.'

'Where the hell have you been?' The Chief was white with rage. 'It had better be bloody good, Macdonald, or I'll have your hide!' he spluttered.

'Hold on, Sir, we haven't been idle,' Mac placated his chief. He then went on to explain everything that had happened, starting with his first clue, right up to the recent events at the old Victorian house in Lincolnshire.

'You're telling me that you actually overheard a phone call from the grouse snatcher to the grouse owner?' the Chief asked incredulously.

'Only the snatcher's voice, Sir, but we got more or less what we wanted.'

The Chief had calmed down by now. 'Mac, knowing how cunning this chap is, you don't think he meant you to hear this conversation do you, to lead you off on a false trail, I mean?' he asked anxiously.

'I did think that at first, Sir, but on reflection, I'm inclined to think that he's made his first slip so no, I don't think so.'

'I sincerely hope you're right.'

'Sir, I have a couple of ideas that should help to nail him within the forty-eight hour deadline.'

'Go on, Mac, I'm listening.'

'Firstly, Sir, Mr Grouse must go through the motions of complying with you-know-who's demand. We can trace the Swiss bank through the account number, using Interpol if necessary. They, the bank that is, can hold the money if we don't find our Grouse in the allotted time limit. We can also instruct them to tell our 'friend' that his money has been deposited, unless of course they receive instructions to the contrary from us.'

'Why send the money at all, Mac, why not just go through the motions?'

'His accomplice, Sir. He may already be in Zurich, armed with the access code and a letter of authority from our chap.'

''Struth, Mac, I'd forgotten about him, stupid of me. You're right, of course, well done.'

'Thank you, Sir,' said Mac. 'Now, it's imperative that we tie up the telephone exchange at Lincoln. I haven't exactly got the weight, so we need your rank to swing this one.'

'Right, I'll get in touch with British Telecom and the Lincoln Chief of Police.'

'We also need someone who can speak with a Swiss accent; they'll obviously switch to English when Grant phones, but it has to sound authentic. He or she doesn't have to know what it's all about, they can read from a script or be prompted by me, Sir,' Mac suggested.

'Leave that to me,' said Matlock.

'I've got the lads trying to trace this machinery too, Sir, they're scouring everywhere for information on the subject.'

'I wish them all the luck in the world, Mac, you have a first class bunch of lads there.'

'They're the best, Sir, I'd be hard pressed to find any better,' said Mac proudly, then a thought occurred to him. 'There's one other thing, Sir - communication. The sets we have are only good for about a mile although the beepers on them carry for about eight or nine miles.'

'Mm, I see,' the Chief replied thoughtfully. 'Tell you what, Mac, I'll get hold of half a dozen VHF long-range walkie talkies and get them to you by helicopter. The pilot can land at Lincoln airfield and you can pick them up there. Set them all to the same frequency, if I may suggest, halfway between A and B police emergency frequencies.

'That's a bit tight, Sir.'

'But safe, Mac,'

'OK, Sir, when can I expect them?'

'Should be there by three this afternoon.'

'Right, Sir, will you be staying where you are?'

'Yes, Mac, I may be needed so I won't be leaving the office for the next forty-eight hours.'

'Right, Sir, let's hope it's all over by then.'

'Amen to that. Oh, by the way, give me a hint next time you embark on the adventure trail, eh!'

'Sorry, Sir, but how could I possibly involve you in anything so, erm ...'

'Dicey, I think the word is and no, you couldn't, thanks Mac.'

'Don't mention it, Sir.'

'Don't worry, I won't.'

'Ahem,' Mac cleared his throat, 'glad to see the back of that little problem. Now, I think we've covered everything so far, Sir, so if you don't mind, I'd like to get back to the lads to see what they've dug up.'

'Good luck,' the Chief replied and put the phone down.

By two o'clock in the afternoon, Mac's team had reassembled back in the side street. Mac wasted no time in getting down to brass tacks. 'Anyone come up with anything resembling a bright idea yet?'

'How about mine machinery, or a disused factory maybe? That's all I could come up with in town,' said Terry.

'No, I don't think so, the power is usually off in those places. No, I think it's got to be something else.'

'What other sources of power have we got besides electricity and gas?' said Smithy.

'Oh that's easy,' said Jimmy and he began to tick off the various power sources on his fingers. 'Petrol, diesel, steam, coal, oil, wind and water, if I can remember my last essay at school. I got a merit for that,' he added proudly.

'You left a few out, Jimmy,' Terry was grinning mischievously

'What?'

'Well what about flower power, even nuclear power ...'

'... not forgetting horse power, overpower, Tyrone Power, even,' Bob chortled.

Mac grinned as he interrupted the banter. 'All right, you three, let's get on with it.'

Suddenly, without warning, there was a screech of tyres as a blue and white car hurtled round the corner, followed by three more. They halted fore and aft of the team's parked cars, men spilling out of the doors before their vehicles had come to a complete halt. Before Mac and his men could protest or make a move to defend themselves - with the exception of Smithy, who effectively flattened one big man with a straight right - they were overcome by sheer weight of numbers.

'What the ...?' Mac exploded.

'Police, you're all under arrest.' It was a uniformed inspector who spoke.

'Under arrest, what the hell for?' Mac asked indignantly.

'Loitering with intent to commit burglary,' replied the policeman.

'I'm a copper myself and this is my squad. My warrant card's in my inside pocket, if you care to take a look,' said Mac as patiently as he could.

'I'll bet you are,' said the inspector, still not convinced.

Mac gritted his teeth. 'Take a look, for Gawd's sake, one look won't hurt, will it?'

'I'll take a look but you're still coming down the nick,' said the inspector. Reaching inside Mac's coat, he retrieved the former's warrant card, opened it and studied it for a few seconds. 'Detective Inspector Macdonald John,' he read. 'Scotland Yard?' He looked at Mac in astonishment. 'If you're a copper, and I do say *if*, what are you doing on my patch? You're well out of your own jurisdiction with no authority that I know of and I want to know why. I'm generously assuming, of course, that this' - he waved the warrant card - 'isn't a forgery.'

He turned away from Mac and began to issue orders to his squad. 'OK, lads, bundle 'em down to the nick.'

'Hold on, Inspector,' Mac interrupted desperately, 'may I have a word with you in private? You can 'cuff me if you like.'

The uniformed inspector opened his mouth to reissue the order but he caught the urgency in Mac's voice and hesitated.

'It's a matter of grave urgency,' Mac pressed the point home.

The man looked Mac straight in the eyes and pursed his lips as if trying to make up his mind.

Mac tried another tactic. 'It could mean the difference between promotion or demotion, Inspector,' he said quietly.

It hit the bone. 'All right,' the inspector agreed, 'but it'd better be good.' He signalled his men to stay put and took Mac's arm. 'Stay there and keep an eye on them,' he ordered, 'and pick that poor sod up,' he said, indicating the man that Smithy had flattened.

He led Mac a few yards out of earshot and said, 'OK, shoot, I'm listening.'

'Well, Inspector er ...?'

'Spalding, Roy Spalding.'

'Inspector Spalding, the job we're on is of great importance. It's also top secret and ...' Mac hesitated, 'I'm sorry, that's all I dare tell you at the moment.'

Spalding looked at Mac for a moment and grabbed his arm to lead him back. 'Bullshit!' he said.

'Please believe me, Inspector. If you don't, get in touch with Sir Donald Matlock, Chief Constable at the Yard,' Mac pleaded earnestly.

Again, Spalding hesitated. 'All right,' he agreed, 'I'll link up through the car radio.'

'No, Inspector, too many ears. I did say it was top secret. Please, take me to the phone box on the edge of town.'

Spalding sighed and shrugged shoulders 'All right, "Inspector" - one way or another, we'll get to the truth of the matter.'

'You can handcuff me to be on the safe side because it can only be you and me.' Mac offered his wrists.

Inspector Spalding studied the intense look on Mac's face, then came to a decision. 'Come on,' he said, turning on his heels. Mac followed him.

'Stay put, you men, I'll be back shortly,' Spalding ordered as he strode quickly to a free car. He opened the passenger door for Mac, making sure that he was inside before going round to the driver's door. Within minutes, they'd arrived at a phone box on the edge of town.

'OK, you go in first and dial the operator, ask for the number of your Chief Constable, then give me the phone,' Inspector Spalding ordered.

Mac did as he was ordered, then handed the set to Spalding, who boxed Mac inside the phone box and spoke into the mouthpiece.

'Thank you, operator, will you please get it for me, I've tried but I keep getting the wrong number,' said Spalding pleasantly.

After a few seconds, a voice spoke into Spalding's ear.

'Matlock, Chief Constable, New Scotland Yard.'

'Sir, this is Inspector Spalding of the Lincolnshire Constabulary. I have a gentleman here who claims to be one Inspector John Macdonald from your division,' Spalding spoke respectively.

'What do you mean, claims to be? Did you see his warrant card?'

'I did, Sir, but he and his squad are here without authorisation as far as I can tell,' replied Spalding.

'Are you telling me that they're under arrest?' the Chief thundered.

'Under the circumstances, Sir, yes. We were tipped off by a householder about burglars posing as police so we had to act accordingly.'

'I see,' said the Chief after a pause, 'you had little choice in that case. So what do you want from me?'

'Proof of his identity and the reason for his being here without Home Office authority, Sir.'

There was another pause as the Chief thought for a few seconds. 'Ask him how his eyes got damaged. He should tell you that it was powder burns from a hand gun, although he won't tell you that he was awarded the Queen's medal for tackling a mad gunman while he himself was unarmed. Also, his wife Jan is an ex-police sergeant and his two children are Jenny and Ian.'

'Right, Sir, excuse me for one moment.'

'How did you damage your eyes?' the inspector asked Mac.

'Powder burns.'

Spalding nodded slowly. 'Wife and kids' names?'

'Jan er Janet, that's my wife. My kids are Jenny and Ian.'

Spalding nodded slowly in satisfaction and spoke into the phone. 'Sir?'

'I'm listening.'

'He is who he says he is, but that doesn't answer the question of his being here.'

'And I can't tell you either, Inspector, because how do I know you are who you say you are?' the Chief countered.

'That's true, Sir. Would you like to speak to Inspector Macdonald?'

149

'Put him on please.'

Mac took the receiver. 'Hello, Sir, it's me, Macdonald.'

'Hello, Mac, how on earth did you get yourself into this little mess?'

'It's a long story, Sir, but basically you can put it down to our chap,' Mac replied, giving nothing away to Spalding.

'Look, Mac, we've got to get this matter resolved with Inspector Spalding as soon as possible, so think of something.'

Mac looked at Spalding, mentally weighing the man's character. 'Sir,' he spoke into the phone again.

'Go ahead, Mac.'

'Inspector Spalding looks like a man who can keep a secret and if he agrees to help we could possibly use his knowledge of the outlying district to speed up our objective. Plus his local resources would be invaluable,' Mac suggested tentatively.

'Ye gods, Mac, too many people are in the know already!'

'With the exception of two, our chap and his accomplice, the people in the know are either hand-picked or in a position of authority,' Mac reminded him, 'and Inspector Spalding looks like he'll fill the bill admirably, or I'm no judge of character, Sir.'

There was a long pause during which time Mac looked at Spalding's face, which registered total puzzlement. Mac grinned at him and was delighted when Spalding grinned back, albeit somewhat lopsidedly.

At last the Chief agreed with great reluctance. 'All right, Mac, but him and him only, not his sergeant, not his men, nobody. Do I make myself clear?'

'Thank you, Sir, you won't regret this, I promise,' Mac replied, feeling elated.

'Sound him out first, Mac, make sure eh!'

'Leave it with me, Sir, I won't let you down. I'll be in touch, goodbye, Sir.'

'Bye Mac and good hunting.' The line went dead.

Mac held out his hand. 'I'm not given to a great deal of formality, I find it cramps my style so please, call me Mac.'

Spalding took the proffered hand. 'Well in that case, you'd better use my handle, or rather half of it. The name's Roy.'

'What's the other half then?' Mac grinned, guessing it could be Royston.

150

'I'm not about to divulge that little snippet, my friend,' Roy grinned and wagged his finger from side to side, 'I took enough ribbing at school.'

Mac nodded and, taking Roy by the arm, walked him slowly back to the car, his face a picture of intense concentration. Finally he spoke. 'Look, Roy,' he began slowly, 'what would you say if I told you that your mother had stolen the Crown Jewels, your father had killed a couple of the Tower guards and that we were hunting them here, on your patch.'

'What ...?'

Mac held up his palms for silence. 'And that you were under oath not to breathe a word to anyone?'

Spalding's face went white and he was visibly trembling with suppressed rage. 'How would you like a smack in the snout!' he replied angrily.

'I wouldn't, Roy,' Mac replied evenly, 'but you haven't answered my question yet.'

Spalding's face registered incredulity. 'Are you serious?'

'Very serious,' Mac replied. 'Well?'

Spalding's face went through a series of varying emotions as he tried to make sense of Mac's question.

'Well, well, you certainly know how to start off what may or may not be a beautiful friendship,' he said, bewildered. He removed his hat and stoked his chin for a few seconds before replying. 'If I'd taken an oath of secrecy, I would stick to it, parents or no parents, but I'll be honest with you, Mac, it would probably be the last thing I'd ever do in uniform. But I'd stick to it all right. Does that answer your question?'

'Admirably. Exactly what I would have expected,' Mac replied, smiling broadly.

'Now you're going to tell me that my parents really have snatched the Crown Jewels, right?'

'Wrong,' said Mac, 'but it's vital you give me your word, your solemn oath, that what I'm about to disclose to you will go no further. Do I make myself absolutely clear?'

Spalding pursed his lips and nodded. 'Crystal, Mac, you have my solemn oath as a man and as a copper.'

Mac nodded in satisfaction. 'OK, old son, hang on to your hat.

The Countess of Westminster has been kidnapped and we have every reason to believe that she's in this area, or at least was.'

Spalding's jaw dropped then closed again. He closed one eye and gave a Mac a quizzical look. 'Is this another test Mac?'

'No, Roy, this is for real.'

'Gordon flaming Bennett, you really mean it, don't you? The Countess snatched?' Disbelief was evident in Spalding's voice. 'But how, for God's sake?'

'It's a long story, so if you'll climb into the car, I'll tell you everything from day one.'

Inside the car, Mac spent a full twenty minutes explaining: the demand notes, the stake-outs, the Earl's madcap helicopter trip and the various clues that pointed more or less in the direction of the old Victorian house. He also told Spalding of Professor Hasketh's expert character analysis of Andrew Grant and how he was sure that Grant and Robert Andrew Penton-Fairfax were one and the same person. Mac left out no detail as he briefed Spalding.

Spalding could scarcely believe his ears. 'Bloody hell, Mac, what kind of a madman are we dealing with?'

'A very clever, very cunning and extremely devious madman, I'm afraid,' said Mac.

Spalding shook his head slowly. 'OK, tell me what you want me to do, but first let me get back to my lot before they start a ruddy war.'

He reached for his radio mike. 'Bravo Oscar, come in.'

'Bravo Oscar, Sergeant Withers, is that you, Chief?' came the reply.

'The one and only, Sergeant, everything's above board and we'll be joining you in a couple of minutes ... over.'

They drove back rapidly to the side street, only to be confronted with the sight of two men bristling at each other: Tommy Smith and the man he had floored, who was now in full control, or almost.

'You caught me with a lucky punch,' said the Lincoln man, poking Smithy in the chest.

'Sorry, mate, but you walked straight into it,' Smithy replied, trying his hardest to ignore the poking finger.

'You wouldn't have managed that in the ring,' countered the poking finger vehemently.

'You'd have gone down just as quick,' Smithy replied in an even voice.

'Hold on, you two!' Mac shouted, just as Smithy was about to give a repeat performance.

'Sorry, Guv, but two more pokes and that would have been his lot,' said Smith disappointedly.

'Now, old son, that's no way for an undefeated heavyweight champion to behave in public,' Mac grinned, emphasising the 'undefeated heavyweight' bit.

Poking finger stopped poking and his jaw dropped open and snapped shut again before slowly breaking into a sheepish grin as recognition dawned. 'Bloody hell, I knew I'd seen you somewhere before!' he marvelled. 'You flattened every poor bugger in sight including the poor sod who stood in for me when I went down with the flu!' He held out his hand. 'Smithy, meet the new horizontal heavyweight champion of Lincolnshire.'

Smithy grinned slowly and took the extended hand in his own oversized mitt. 'It was a lucky punch, mate, you ran into it at thirty miles an hour, otherwise I don't think you'd have gone down so easily,' he said generously.

The two men shook hands and thus began a friendship that was to last a lifetime.

'I say, young man!' a woman's voice sounded somewhere behind a neat little gate on the opposite side of the road.

'Yes, madam, can I help you at all?' Spalding asked politely.

'I was the one who called you, you know,' said the little old lady.

'Ah yes, you'll be Mrs Bunce,' said Spalding, comprehending now.

'No wonder you got here so quickly, you were called twice,' Mac muttered.

'Well, aren't you going to arrest them, Inspector, isn't it?' demanded Mrs Bunce.

Spalding looked at Mac and winked before turning back to Mrs Bunce. 'I most certainly am, Madam. Thanks to you, a lot of people will sleep better with this little lot behind bars.' He pretended to be severe and grabbed Mac's arm. 'This one is the ringleader and we've been after him for a long time now. Thanks to you, Madam, we have him and his gang.'

'Bless me, I don't like the look of that one over there,' said Mrs Bunce, pointing to Smithy. 'He looks a proper ruffian.'

'Oh, he is, Mrs Bunce, but don't worry, my man soon had him under control,' said Spalding, indicating Poking finger.

Smithy turned his back on them, his shoulders shaking with mirth, not at Spalding or Mrs Bunce, but at the grin that had appeared on Poking finger's face.

'I'm Abigail Bunce, you know, and I'm ninety-two. My husband Leonard was a Captain in the First World War. He was machine-gunned at Ypres, killed outright too, poor dear,' she said brightly.

'Oh, I'm sorry to hear that, Madam ...' Spalding began.

'No need, young man, he's with me most of the day, sitting in his armchair. He's probably there now waiting for me to go in. He keeps on to me to hurry up and join him, poor dear, but I keep telling him I have too much to do on God's earth so he'll have to wait.' The old lady smiled sadly. 'I can't see him, you know, but I know he's there because I can hear his voice inside my head, you see.'

The two policemen were spellbound by the simple honesty of the little old lady.

'Please don't think I'm silly or anything, Inspector, but he's all I've got you see,' she said simply.

'Mrs Bunce, the thought never crossed my mind,' Spalding replied, just a little ashamedly.

Then the little old lady brightened. 'Would you like to come to tea, Inspector, when you've finished with these nasty people, I mean? You can bring your wife if you like. I do a lovely strawberry and cream flan, you know, when I can get the strawberries, that is. I tell you what, make it one day next week if you like and that will give me time to get some decent fruit. You know, it does get lonely here sometimes,' the little old lady chattered brightly.

Mac could have sworn he saw Spalding's eyes moisten. Spalding swallowed the lump that was rising in his throat and replied gently, 'Mrs Bunce, I would deem it an honour and a pleasure to bring my wife to tea and with your kind permission, I'd like to send you some of my strawberries from my own greenhouse, er, so that you could give me your opinion of them,' he added hastily.

'Oh, that would be lovely, Inspector, I shall look forward to it,' Mrs Bunce said delightedly. 'Leonard will too.'

'Leonard?'

'My husband. Of course, you won't know he's there, but I will,' she twinkled.

'Oh, of course,' Spalding nodded, at loss to say anything else.

And Mrs Bunce turned and walked back to the house with a spring in her step that belied her ninety two years.

For long seconds, no one spoke until Mac broke the silence with a quiet question. 'For Mrs Bunce's sake, are you going to lock me up, or do I have to hit you over the head with this house brick?'

Startled back to reality, Spalding gave Mac a rueful grin before giving the order. 'OK, you lot, for the benefit of a lovely little old lady, bundle 'em into the cars and if anyone resists, give him a big kiss with your size tens.'

Every man complied, putting on an act for the old lady that would have won plaudits for any actor. Mrs Bunce, watching through her window, smiled in satisfaction at a job well done. After the cars had left, she walked through to the spotlessly clean living room and knelt in front of an old armchair. 'There you are, Leonard my dear, didn't I do well, aren't you proud of your Abigail?' she smiled at the empty space. The invisible figure in the Captain's uniform smiled, and his eyes twinkled as he stroked the head of his lovely young wife.

Meanwhile, the convoy of police cars stopped a couple of miles away and the occupants alighted to sort themselves out.

'I think it would be wise to thank your lot, Roy, if you follow me,' Mac suggested.

'Indeed I do,' Spalding agreed. 'Now listen, lads, before you go about your duties, thank you for the sake of the little old lady's peace of mind, and that goes for your squad too, Inspector. I know it was an unusual request, but you took it in your stride, in the tradition of the police force, even if it was a bit tongue-in-cheek. I must admit, it was a nice break from routine and I just hadn't the heart to disappoint her anyway.'

'On behalf of my lot,' said Mac, 'think nothing of it. Now I have something to say to your lads, Roy, if you don't mind.'

'Go ahead, Mac.'

'Listen, lads. I have something very important to say so pin your ears back. My squad and I are here, out of our patch, because an emergency situation dictated it. For reasons of national security, I can't tell you why because for one thing, the job is still on. Now, it's vital that you forget we were here, you haven't even seen us. Don't be tempted to confide in your nearest and dearest because you know as well as I do that that's the best telegraph system known to man. One thing I can promise you, the slightest leak and ...' He drew his finger across his throat. 'I wish I could say more...'

Spalding took charge. 'You heard the man. I happen to know the score so if I say keep quiet, you know damn well I mean it. Off you go, lads.'

After they had gone Spalding turned to Mac. 'OK, sunshine, what now?'

Mac explained about the possibility of Alison being held in a disused factory or windmill within a forty-mile radius. Could Spalding's team investigate every possibility with the resources at their disposal?

'I think we can manage all that, Mac; then what?'

'Then we contact the phone company through my Chief to see what we can set up.'

'You know something, Mac, I don't think this has ever been tried before, on this scale, I mean. Not only have you got to make this fellow think he's in touch with his overseas bank, he has to be fooled with a phony Swiss accent, and that has to be provided by someone who doesn't know what the hell he or she is talking about. So tell me, my friend, how on earth are you going to stage manage that?'

Mac grinned and tapped the side of his nose with his finger. 'Trust me, old son, because you can bet your sweet life that I'll come up with something. As a matter of fact, I have the glimmerings already.'

It was a beautiful August morning. The sun was shining, casting its rays down through a cloudless sky. The trees were in full foliage, basking in the life-giving sunshine, offering refuge and security to the insects and animal life that had managed to escape man's chemical onslaught. The flowers gave out their lovely scent and the bees were busy bumbling from flower to flower. Happy children fed bread to the water birds as their parents looked on lovingly. Lovers strolled and kissed, grandparents sank back into deckchairs to enjoy the wonderful morning air.

Happiness and contentment reigned in this beautiful and picturesque little park, set on the edge of a Lincolnshire City.

All this was lost on the man standing on the balcony of the old Victorian house overlooking this beautiful old recreation ground. His thoughts revolved around the thing that had been a thorn in his side for years. It had festered like a cancer that multiplied at an alarming rate until it filled his brain to bursting point.

As an actor, Andrew Grant (for that was the man's stage name) was mediocre. He had occasionally won lead roles in touring reviews, but lacked the talent to climb to the top of his profession. His forte was female impersonation, a part at which he really excelled. Half an hour in front of a mirror with greasepaint, gum, latex foam and cheek pads could transform him from a caterpillar into a gorgeous butterfly: thus a mediocre man became a beautiful woman, a total stranger unrecognisable even to his closest friends and family.

Good parts had been few and far between for Andrew Grant lately, so he supplemented his income by working in various working men's clubs as a female impersonator, an act which impressed his audience so much he got many return bookings. Away from the boards, however, Grant kept very much to himself.

People tended to shy away from him after only a few minutes' acquaintance. They felt inexplicably uncomfortable in his presence, completely at a loss what to do or say, and would use any pretext to put distance between him and themselves.

But one person felt no such unease in Grant's presence. William Brent (also a stage name) lived in this large Victorian house too, sharing the running expenses of the place. He was also chief cook and general dogsbody, at the beck and call of Grant, whom he practically worshipped.

Many years earlier (when the festering in Grant's mind was still controllable), he had been instrumental in getting Brent a tiny speaking part in a play he himself was starring in. The play was destined for a short run, but by the time it was over, Andrew Grant and William Brent had formed a friendship of sorts. Grant became the predominant partner in this unholy alliance, an alliance he quickly decided was going to prove very very profitable.

For years, he had planned and schemed to get what he termed, 'my just rewards'. He had devised plan after plan, rejecting them all as too risky or impractical. He had spent hour after endless hour scheming, only to hit yet another snag just when he through his latest plan was foolproof. Years of frustration in his acting career, coupled with his inability to formulate a foolproof plan, had done nothing to ease his tortured mind.

But all that was about to change.

Grant spun on his heels and left the balcony via the French windows. Inside, he poured himself a Scotch on the rocks and added a splash of soda. He then placed a cigarette into a long slender holder, lit it and sat down in a luxurious armchair. It was 9.30 in the morning

'Brent!' he called out loudly. 'Oh Bre-ent!'

He heard the sound of approaching footsteps and Brent stood in the doorway. 'Yes, Andrew?'

'Come in and sit down please.' It was more of a command than a request and Brent speedily complied.

'How would you like to earn a quarter of a million pounds?' Grant's voice was quiet, even and emotionless.

'What?' Brent gasped. 'Did you say a—?'

'—quarter of a million pounds.' Grant finished the sentence for him, smiling now.

Brent's jaw was working, trying to say something, but his brain wouldn't function for a few seconds. He collected his wits and coughed before he finally managed to speak.

'Sorry Andrew,' he said at last, 'you hit me with it so suddenly.'

'Have a drink to steady your nerves, old boy,' Grant invited.

Brent went to the cocktail bar. 'Yes, I think I will.'

'Make it a double,' said Grant softly, 'you may need it.'

Something in the tone of his voice sent a shiver down Brent's spine and he gulped a generous mouthful before taking a seat opposite Grant. He hardly dared to breathe. Grant just sat looking at him for some minutes and Brent found himself squirming under the relentless gaze.

Unable to stand the silence any longer, Brent ventured the question: 'What do you want me to do, Andrew, w-what do I have to do to, erm' - he swallowed hard - 'earn this money?'

'It's quite simple really,' Grant replied off-handedly, taking a long leisurely pull on his cigarette. 'You,' he pointed his finger at Brent, 'are going to look after someone for me for a little while.' He smiled genially.

'I don't understand.'

'It's quite simple really.' Grant blew smoke towards the ceiling. 'I kidnap someone, bring her here, and you,' he smiled at Brent, 'look after her for me. Now, that's simple enough, isn't it?'

Brent gulped and sat bolt upright in his chair. 'D-did I hear you right, Andrew, you're going to actually, I mean, kidnap a lady?'

'That's right, old chap.' Grant was full of himself now, jaunty. 'I kidnap her, or rather we do, then you bring her back here and look after her. Don't worry, her incarceration will be short lived.'

'Who is she, some rich industrialist's daughter? She'd have to be for that kind of money, surely.'

'No, it's not some industrialist's daughter,' Grant teased.

'Who then?'   ·

Grant watched Brent's face for the reaction that he knew was forthcoming. 'No less a person than' - he paused for effect - 'Alison, the Countess of Westminster.'

The reaction was rather more violent than Grant had expected. Brent shot to his feet, spilling most of his brandy. 'The Countess of Westminster!' His voice rose to a high pitch. 'You're mad, crazy, you'll never—!'

Grant shot out of his chair and across the room. The fingers of his right hand stiffened and as he reached Brent, his hand moved upwards at deadly speed towards the underside of Brent's jaw. Just in time, he stopped this lethal weapon a fraction from its target. Breathing hard, he fought to control the quivering rage that had consumed his brain at the sound of the words 'mad' and 'crazy'. Brent closed his eyes in silent prayer as he realised just how close to death he had been.

Grant gathered his composure and his breathing began to slow down. For long seconds the two men looked at each other, the fearful and the feared.

'Don't ever use those words to me again, ever,' Grant's voice trembled with emotion.

Brent, who had been holding his breath without realizing it, exhaled tremulously. 'I'm s-sorry, Andrew, I didn't mean to, what I meant was ...' He tailed off lamely.

Grant held up his hands in a placating manner. 'All right, all right, no harm done. Look, just top up the drinks, sit yourself down and let me explain. Come on now, settle down.'

Brent nodded nervously and topped up the drinks like an automaton, handing one tentatively to Grant. They both sat down.

'Still feeling shaken, about our little venture, I mean?'

'Just a bit, Andrew,' Brent replied, a quiver in his voice, 'you're full of surprises but this one is L'Lulu'.

Grant laughed at that observation. 'Come come, now, it's really a fairly simple task for you to perform ... for a quarter of a million pounds.'

Brent's eyes gradually changed from bewilderment to greed as it sunk in finally. 'Two hundred and fifty thousand pounds,' he breathed, his eyes shining brightly now.

'Just for playing nursemaid,' Grant reminded him gently. 'Look, it's all very simple so listen to me, OK.'

Brent just nodded.

'When you bring Alison here, she'll be under heavy sedation and all you have to do is see that she doesn't escape.'

'But what about when she wants to ... has to ...?'

'Yes yes, I have thought about that. She'll have to be fed and use the ladies' room too, but that's been taken care of.'

'How?'

'Leg irons, my friend.'

'Leg irons?' Brent queried. 'And where do we get those from?'

'Props, from the Hippodrome props room.'

'But I don't understand, we finished there a week ago, so how—?'

Grant interrupted him. 'They're in the boot of my car, have been since the day we left,' Grant grinned.

Brent was beginning to accept the situation now. 'How, I mean when do you, er, we intend pulling this off?'

'Quite soon now, but first I have to organise a few gigs in or around Westminster.'

'Gigs?' Brent raised a questioning eyebrow.

'I've got to get myself booked into a few nightclubs, you know, doing cabaret, to make things legitimate.'

'You make this all sound so easy, too easy.'

Grant beamed a condescending smile. 'It will be, don't worry, and if you play your part right, we'll be rich in a very short space of time.' He looked at his wrist watch. 'Get me a decent meal going, will you, I have a very important letter to write.'

An hour later, the meal was finished, the letter written and safely sealed in an envelope.

'This has to be posted miles from here, in another county,' said Grant as he headed for the door. 'I'll be back shortly.'

He disappeared and made his way downstairs, through the huge old-fashioned kitchen, heading towards the garage. Within minutes, Brent heard the roar of a high-powered engine. As he heard the car reverse out of the garage and pick up speed in the forward gears with a powerful roar, he began clearing away the remains of the meal. His actions were purely automatic; his mind was elsewhere.

He trembled as he recalled the closeness of Grant's fingers to his throat, his brush with death. He had suspected for some time but now he was certain.

Andrew Grant was a madman.

An hour or so later, in the county of Norfolk, Grant halted his car at an out-of-the-way postbox. He climbed out, took the letter from his pocket and, just before he slipped it into the slot, he looked once more at the address: THE PRIME MINISTER, 10 DOWNING STREET.

Nothing else. It would get there with no trouble at all.

He climbed back into his custom-built car and, smiling to himself, drove back to Lincolnshire.

Step number one,' he thought to himself. 'That should stir up a hornet's nest.' He hummed to himself as his thoughts focused on his next move. Three days from now, it would be the 'Glorious Twelfth', the start of the grouse shooting season for the filthy rich, as Grant mentally termed them. Plenty of time to put step number two into operation.

He eased his foot down on the throttle and listened as the gentle hum of the engine turned to a snarl as the car ate up the miles. Just the knowledge that he and he alone controlled this gleaming, beautiful monster, gave him a warm glow.

A sense of power.

Today he had set in motion the chain of events that, with careful control and manipulation, would make him a very rich man. Soon, he would make a very important phone call, a very carefully worded phone call, a call that would make a certain person sit up and take notice.

Grant knew of the friction that existed between Alison and Robin Devereaux regarding blood sports. He also knew that she always stayed behind at Hamilcourt House, fretting the lonely hours away while Robin killed grouse for no reason other than pleasure.

He also knew that the Earl drove himself, plus an entourage of three close, upper-crust and equally bloodthirsty friends to Scotland, usually leaving about ten on the morning of the tenth.

Grant would let Alison wallow in her misery for a few hours, after which she would be most receptive to his phone call.

He drove back to Lincolnshire at a rapid pace, arriving at 4pm. He garaged the roadster and made his way into the big house. Brent, who had heard him drive up, began to tremble. He was afraid, afraid of Andrew, afraid of what he was about to undertake with Andrew, afraid of what Andrew would do if he, Brent, backed out.

And if he did fall in with Andrew's plans? He was afraid of what might happen afterwards, after it was all over.

Grant had came into the room and Brent forced a smile.

'How did it go, Andrew?' There was a hint of a quaver in his voice.

'Fine, fine, I only went to post a letter, Brent.'

'My God,' thought Brent, 'only went to post a letter!' A letter that could put them both away for twenty years.

He attempted a show of outward calm as he tried to converse with his 'friend', trying to conceal the fear that just would not go away. 'Well, that's the first step Andrew, the first link in the chain to a fortune.'

Although outwardly Brent was in control, Grant sensed his fear and walked slowly over to him. He stopped, his own face inches from Brent's. 'You're afraid, aren't you, Brent? I can see it, I can smell it on you.' Contempt was in his voice.

'No, no, not really Andrew, I can do it, really I can.'

Grant looked at him for what seemed an eternity. He raised his right hand slowly and poked a finger at his friend's face. There was menace in his voice. 'Hear me, Brent. The success of this whole operation demands a high degree of concentration on my part, and a very simple little job on your part.' Grant punctuated every word with a stabbing motion at Brent's chest. 'All you have to do at first is hold her here under lock and key. Are you listening to me, am I getting through to you?'

Brent nodded fearfully.

'Don't let me down, my friend, because if you do ...' Grant left the sentence unfinished.

Brent got the message and understood every unfinished word of the unfinished sentence. His mouth was dry and he wished the floor would open up and swallow him.

When Grant spoke again, it was with some levity. 'Don't worry, Brent, there really is nothing to it, honestly, it's simplicity itself. All you have to do is keep her under lock and key, oh, and you can wear your ski mask every time you have to attend to her, no more, no less.'

'Yes, Andrew, I can do it, I won't let you down. I promise you.'

'Very good, dear boy. I know you can do it otherwise I wouldn't have asked you in the first place.'

'Thank you, Andrew,' was all Brent could think of to say.

Abruptly, Grant became more businesslike. 'Right, let's get to it then, shall we? Today is the seventh and in three days' time, old boy, the Earl takes off for Scotland. He leaves on the tenth at about 10am with his upper-crust cronies, leaving Alison behind, and that, my dear Brent, is when she is at her most vulnerable. It's also the time to play my ace,' Grant laughed maliciously.

'H-how do you mean, what do you intend to do, Andrew?' The question was tentative.

'Oh, didn't I tell you? I'm going to spend a few days at Hamilcourt House.'

'Y-you are, how, I mean ...?'

'How?' Grant sneered, full of himself. 'Alison is going to invite me, that's how.'

Brent just opened and closed his mouth, completely at a loss for words.

'And now, my dear friend,' said Grant, 'I have another important errand to attend to.'

'Errand?'

'A very important errand, a journey over the water.'

'Water?' Brent was puzzled.

'Switzerland, my dear boy, Switzerland!' Grant beamed.

'I'm sorry, I don't understand, why Switzerland?'

'Because that's where the ransom money is going to end up, my boy, in a numbered account in a Swiss bank,' Grant said smugly.

Brent's brain slowly absorbed this information and in spite of himself, his eyes widened in admiration.

'Switzerland, of course, I would never have thought of that!'

'Of course you would, Brent, I just happened to think of it first,' Grant said condescendingly. 'Right!' he cried so suddenly that Brent jumped involuntarily. 'Passport and suitcase, please Brent, chop, chop. I have to fly there and back in two days and my flight leaves in a hour.'

Chapter Twenty-Three
'Alison' Returns From Ramsdean Hospital

Alison, Countess of Westminster, stepped gracefully from the limousine when it halted outside the doors of the mansion and Jenkins moved swiftly forward to open the car door.

'May I offer my congratulations on an excellent speech, M'Lady, if I may be permitted to say so.'

'Thank you, Jenkins, it did go down rather well I think.'

She alighted gracefully, walked regally up the stone steps and through the oak doors. She hesitated, turned her head and spoke over her shoulder. 'I shall be going out again shortly so don't garage the car. I'll be away for an hour or so.'

Jenkins bowed slightly. 'Very good, M'Lady.'

Alison climbed the stairs to her bedroom, shut the door and, with a huge sigh of relief, collapsed onto the huge bed.

Alison, alias Andrew Grant, was elated.

'You've done it, you've done it! Andrew, my boy, that was the best character part you've ever played in your life and you did it, you fooled everyone, absolutely everyone. Brilliant, brilliant!' Grant closed his eyes and beamed, overjoyed at his own cleverness. 'Every last one,' he repeated.

But Grant was wrong.

There was doubt in Jenkins' mind - Jenkins, who believed in showing good old-fashioned reverence towards his superiors; Jenkins, whose eyes were always looking down as he bowed; Jenkins, who had noticed, without really trying, a difference in the size of Alison's feet.

There was also doubt in the mind of someone else - someone who had only seen 'Alison' on video tapes; someone whose job it had once been to spot little discrepancies and put two and two together; someone, who had spotted not one but two mistakes that Grant had made.

Her name was Janet Mary Macdonald.

Grant came back to earth eventually. He had things to do and no time at all to do them. Swiftly, he shed his clothes and shoes and his feet practically sighed with relief as he eased out of the very tight high heels.

He selected a dress from the ample stock in Alison's wardrobe, and put it on. Sorting through dozens of pairs of shoes, he selected a pair of adjustable, open-toed slingbacks and put them on, adjusting the strap on each shoe two holes further back. He stood up to try them for comfort and was reasonably satisfied. Then he picked up his shoulder bag and checked the contents. Finally, he crossed over to the mirror and cast a critical eye over his reflection, liking what he saw and smiling in satisfaction. He took a deep breath and said to his reflection, 'Andrew, it's now or never, go for it my boy.'

Twelve minutes later, Grant halted the limousine outside his rented lock-up garage. He opened the garage doors and drove his own car out, then drove the limo in. It was a tight squeeze but he managed to close and padlock the doors without too much trouble.

Once in his own car, he opened his bag and took out a black wig streaked with grey, 'a middle-aged' one. He then removed the 'young' looking makeup from his face and replaced it with a greyish powder. He donned a pair of plain glass spectacles and examined himself closely in the mirror.

A fifty-year-old woman stared back at him.

Grant turned the ignition key and the powerful engine roared into life. He selected first gear and roared off in the direction of Ramsdean Hospital, or rather in a roundabout direction. He made for the outer circular bypass which was now more like a motorway . Once on the bypass, he put his foot to the floor, his speed hitting well over a hundred miles an hour when he could get away with it. He left the bypass about five minutes' drive from the hospital. The route he had chosen was relatively quiet and he drove virtually unhindered to his destination.

As he approached the main gate, he slowed down to pick his way through a group of youngsters playing football. A few yards from the entrance, a young crippled boy in a wheelchair, his eyes gleaming, exclaimed, 'Cor, look at that for a car!'

Grant neither saw nor heard the youngster as he reached down on the passenger side floor. He found what he was looking for and, clutching it under his arm, got out of the car, slamming the door after him. Unhurriedly, like any other fifty-year-old lady, Grant walked through the hospital gates and into the grounds.

There were very few people about and no one gave a second glance to the lady taking a gentle stroll on the green turf. Grant glanced casually around as he approached the chosen spot, and swiftly laid the object he was carrying on the grass. Turning swiftly, he made his way back to his car, satisfied that he had not been too closely observed...

But he had, though not by a human eye. In fact he had been caught on a few frames of video tape, many yards away in a room four floors up in a derelict block of flats.

As Grant approached his car, he spotted the youngster in the wheelchair on the road, directly behind his car.

'Get away from there, sonny Jim, or you may get yourself run over!' he said sharply in a female voice.

'Not unless you're gonna drive backwards, Missus,' replied the youngster cheekily.

Grant did not press the point, he hadn't the time. He climbed into his car, slammed the door and started the engine. He selected first gear, checked his rear-view mirror, let in the clutch and roared off - minus a badge from his boot door.

The boy in the wheelchair examined his trophy and chuckled. His dad would drill a hole in it for him and he could wear it round his neck. Maybe then the other lads would forget his disability and allow him to join the gang.

Meanwhile, Grant retraced his route back to his lock-up where he became Alison again, then drove the limousine back to Hamilcourt House and parked outside the huge oak doors.

Jenkins welcomed his mistress back home with his customary bow. He frowned slightly as he noticed the slingbacks she was wearing. To Jenkins' keen eye, the straps seemed to have been moved back by at least two holes.

Her Ladyship addressed the butler as he straightened up. 'I have a terrible headache so I'm going to retire for the rest of the day, Jenkins. Please see that I remain undisturbed until tomorrow morning.'

'M'Lady?' Jenkins was concerned, the slingbacks temporarily forgotten. 'Shall I call Dr Willard?'

'No, that won't be necessary, it's just that I had rather a heavy night last night and a hectic afternoon today,' Alison replied.

'I understand perfectly, M'Lady, and I shall issue the necessary instructions to the staff immediately.' Jenkins bowed again.

Alison nodded, and went straight up the massive stairs to her bedroom.

Jenkins had noticed something else too; Mr Grant was conspicuous by his absence.

An hour later, Grant came down the stairs, looking decidedly the worse for wear. 'Good morning, or should I say, good afternoon, Jenkins.'

'Good afternoon, Sir.' Jenkins was amused at Grant's appearance but tried not to show it.

'What a night that was, too much to drink, I'm afraid,' Grant said confidentially.

'It's all too easily done, Sir, especially when one enjoys the company of a long lost friend.'

'Yes, I'm afraid your mistress overdid it rather,' said Grant, 'not the sort of gossip that you spread around, of course,' he added meaningfully.

'Of course not, Sir.'

'Your Mistress has taken to her bed for the rest of the day to, er, recover.'

'She did inform me to that effect earlier, Sir,' said Jenkins.

'She tore a strip off me five minutes ago,' Grant grinned.

Jenkins once again stifled his amusement.

'I shall be leaving today, Jenkins, so will you have my equipment brought down please, and while you're at it, would you call me an estate car.'

'Certainly Sir, I'll see to it immediately. I do hope you enjoyed your stay with us,' said Jenkins.

'I've had a simply marvellous time, thank you, but my work calls me elsewhere,' Grant sighed regretfully.

'I understand, Sir, and we shall all be sorry to see you go.'

'Never mind, the Earl should be back shortly,' said Grant.

'Not until the 30th, Sir, the master likes to stay until the end.'

'Ah yes, that's right, I'd forgotten,' said Grant, but he had not.

'If you will excuse me, Sir, I'll have your luggage attended to, and arrange your transport.'

'Thank you, Jenkins, I've already said my goodbyes to the Countess, she seems rather upset at my leaving and she's declined to see me off.'

'It seems such a pity that you have to leave so soon, Sir. We all know how fond you and M'Lady are of each other. If I may be so bold, I can understand why she's upset.'

'We go back a long way,' said Grant wistfully for Jenkins' benefit, 'a long, long way.'

'Yes, Sir, excuse me.' Jenkins bowed slightly and went away to issue the necessary orders.

Fifteen minutes later, Grant was on his way back to his lock-up. Earlier, when the escort had drawn up outside Hamilcourt, he had nearly died of shock; it was the same one that had dropped him at the station a week earlier. The driver had not recognised Grant, but he had given the trunk a second look.

They halted outside the lock-up and unloaded the luggage.

'Pardon me, Guv,' said the cabbie, pointing to the trunk, 'this may sound funny to you, but I could have sworn I had that in my car a week ago and what's even more peculiar, I loaded it here, on this very spot and took it to the station.'

After the initial shock at seeing the same cabbie back at Hamilcourt, Grant was prepared fo this question had his answer ready. 'Ha ha ha,' he laughed, pointing his finger at the cabbie, 'you, my friend, are not the first.'

He pointed to the lock-up garage, grinning. 'There's another one in there, it's where we store some of our gear.'

The cabbie still looked perplexed.

'We're all actors cabbie, travelling troubadours, if you like and we keep all our props in here, you see,' said Grant.

Light began to dawn in the cabbie's brain. 'Oh, I see, now it makes sense, Guv.'

'It's good economics because we all chip in for the rent of this place, and we share the props.

'Cor, what a good idea, Guv, sorry if I—'

'Don't worry about it,' Grant interrupted, reaching for his wallet and tipping the driver generously, 'you're not the first to ask and I don't suppose for one moment you'll be the last.

'Cor, thanks Guv, can I give you a lift with that trunk?' The cabbie indicated the garage.

'Er no,' Grant said hastily then, quickly assuming a normal tone, 'I'm waiting for an actor friend of mine, he wants some of this gear for another gig, so we'll let that scar-faced, four-eyed toe rag do the humping.' He winked at the cabbie. 'It won't hurt him to do a bit of hard work for a change.'

The cabbie laughed as his memory stirred. Scar-faced, four-eyed ... Ah, that bloke last week.

Grant was inwardly pleased as his little shot went home. The cabbie was now convinced that he, Grant, and the scar-faced, four-eyed toe rag, were two different people.

The cabbie's radio piped up and he answered it; thirty seconds later, he was on his way to pick up another fare.

Grant worked fast after he had gone. He quickly unlocked the garage and drove his car out, loaded his light equipment into the back seat, then opened the boot door, hooking it onto two chains which allowed it to lie level and parallel with the ground. He then reached inside for a number plate which was attached to a long length of twin flex and placed it carefully on the top of the car.

Heavy though the trunk was, Grant lifted it easily onto the platform, where it fitted into the boot compartment, filling it completely. He then secured it with three elasticated ropes, complete with hooked ends. Finally, he reached for the number plate, clipped it to the trunk and then checked to see if the 'white' light worked from the light switch.

Satisfied that everything was as it should be, he locked the garage doors and climbed into his roadster. He reached for his make-up bag and took out a false nose, scar and spectacles, fitting them once more for the benefit of the garage proprietor, before setting off to return the key. He chuckled as an idea began to form in his mind.

He reached his destination and parked out of sight. The garage owner answered his bell and Grant returned the keys .

'May I have a refund?' he requested after the preliminaries. 'After all, I've paid for one month and I've only used the place for a week.'

'Friggin' 'ard cheese mate, that ain't my friggin' fault.'

'Suit yourself,' said Grant airily and turned to walk away.

Taken aback, the owner said, 'Oi, 'owdya mean, whatcha done?'

'I've set fire to the place.' Grant was laughing fit to burst as he broke into a run.

The owner spluttered, running first one way, then the other, unable to make up his mind whether to call the police, fire brigade or chase Grant.

Grant turned the corner and glanced quickly back at the perplexed owner; the sight made him howl with laughter. He reached the roadster and quickly got underway just in case the man had decided to take up the chase.

In no time at all, he reached the outer circular and headed for Lincolnshire.

CHAPTER TWENTY-FOUR
FATE TAKES A HAND

Andrew Grant lay on the bed with his hands behind his head, a satisfied smile on his face. Everything had gone according to plan so far and he lay there, congratulating himself on his brilliance.

How many people would think of demanding a ransom before kidnapping someone? He was jubilant at the thought of the top brass trying to fathom that one out; it would certainly make them sit up and take notice. If they only knew, they'd have kittens.

He screwed up his eyes in silent mirth as he pictured the scene in the Prime Minister's private office. The PM would first read the letter, not knowing whether to believe or disbelieve. He would then send for the Chief of Police and they would each try to read the other's mind, avoiding making asses of themselves as far as possible, and yet ...

Eventually, with the help of the Home Secretary, they would decide to treat it seriously, just to be on the safe side. But then, they didn't know, did they? How could they? And by the time they'd decide to act, they would be too late.

Andrew Grant could barely contain his mirth as he delivered the silent punchline: because Alison had already been abducted, she was, in the words of the prophet, 'already plucked'.

He lay there for a long time thinking. He cast his mind back to the happy days of long ago. Alison and he had been inseparable as children, more like brother and sister than cousins. He thought of his parents, of Alison's parents. He thought of the trick that fate had played on all of them.

Grant thought of the odds against twin brothers marrying twin sisters: hundreds, thousands, even millions to one. Yet it had happened with their parents, Alison's and his own. Alison's father was the elder twin by some twenty minutes - an insignificant difference, one would think, but in this particular case, it most certainly was not.

There was an Earldom to cloud the issue.

Alison's father, being the elder, had automatic claim to the title on the death of his father, along with all of the estate, which not only included family heirlooms going back countless years, but a fabulous fortune to boot.

Oh, he was generous to a fault with his younger twin, but there were fat cats and thin cats.

Before the elder twin came into his inheritance, chance had taken a hand in the shape of lovely twin sisters. At a charity ball the two sets of twins had met and love had blossomed. Their joint wedding eventually made the dailies and in due course each couple was blessed with a child, one girl and one boy.

Alison and Andrew were born within a day of each other and were as alike as two peas in a pod. They played together as soon as they left the cradle, went to the same school, sat together, learned the same things. People mistook them for twins for years to come.

During puberty, Grant had a difficult time. The transition from childhood to adulthood is hard to come to terms with for everyone, but he was a little more confused than most. He could not understand, for instance, why Alison was treated as somehow more special than him.

It was only when he was older and wiser that it hit him between the eyes: Alison was his social superior or, to put it another way, he was her inferior ... and that really rankled with young Andrew. It felt wrong, very, very wrong.

As he grew up, Grant realised that through a quirk of fate, a mere twenty minutes, he was doomed to play second fiddle to his cousin. To add injury to insult, Alison's family fortune could be counted in millions while his own family were only 'comfortably off'.

The seeds of discontent were sown in those years, seeds that were nurtured until Andrew's discontentment gradually turned to hate, a hate that consumed him with a burning desire to balance the scales. He wanted his dues and he was going to get them, one way or another ...

Hence the elaborate plan.

Grant opened his eyes and sat up. He looked at his watch, swung his legs over the edge of the bed and walked over to the dressing-table. He sat down, looked at himself in the mirror and spoke to his reflection.

173

'So far, Andy, old boy, so good.' The image grinned back at him in triumph.

He sobered slightly at the thought of his next task: tomorrow would be the first real test of his 'master stroke'.

Tomorrow he would walk downstairs and out through the front door, acting the most demanding role he'd ever played. He would be combining, for the first time in public, his talents as a female impersonator and his acting skills. The first test would be when he came face to face with Alison's personal maid. If she detected nothing, suspected nothing, then Andrew Grant, female impersonator, actor, abductor of the aristocracy, would indeed be Alison, Countess of Westminster.

Next day he rose very early; he could leave nothing to chance.

In the past, he had visited Hamilcourt House on numerous occasions as a guest when the Earl was absent and Alison needed company. Unless her routine had changed, he could expect an 8am call from Alison's maid, carrying a breakfast tray.

In Alison's private bathroom he opened a large handbag. He removed his shaving brush, shaving soap and razor, placing them carefully on the shelf above the immaculate gold-tapped wash basin. He placed the plug in the sink and ran the hot water, then quickly lathered his face until he was satisfied that the stubble was soft enough to shave without pulling on the razor edge. He removed the best part of the stubble, then re-lathered generously before shaving in an upward motion against the growth, stretching the skin to expose more of the stubble than normal. He felt around his face and neck for any that had managed to escape. Finally, after making sure that not one tell tale hair remained, he washed his face thoroughly in fresh water, patting himself dry with one of Alison's towels.

He examined himself in the bathroom mirror and was completely satisfied with the result. Quickly cleaning his shaving kit, he replaced them in the bag, then cleaned away any tiny bristles he found in the sink and surroundings, checking and double-checking.

Back in the bedroom sat in front of the dressing-table mirror.

Earlier, he had removed his wig, false eyelashes and various small latex pads, laying them ready on the dressing-table. He reached for the pads and proceeded to clean the contact side of them with a special fluid. He then applied a special latex gum to his right cheekbone, spreading it evenly with his forefinger. He waited for about a minute for it to partially dry before very carefully applying the pad to his cheekbone, carefully pressing down the feathered edge until it magically appeared to blend with his own skin. He then repeated the exercise on the left cheek.

With the cheek pads in place, his appearance had already begun to alter considerably, although he had only just begun his transformation.

He concentrated on the inside of his mouth next, inserting two wafer-thin pads of a more flexible latex to pad his face out just below the cheekbones. Next came the false eyelashes, only slightly longer than his own. Alison, he knew, did not pluck her eyebrows and his were almost identical in shape and colour to hers. All he had to do was trim slightly to suit .

His teeth, however, were very different. He set about fitting specially-made caps, of which he had a collection, onto the upper four front teeth, using a dental glue that hardened in seconds. They would remain there until he used a special solvent to remove them.

As Grant worked, he cast his mind back to when he used to use braced teeth for his act, sometimes with disastrous results. He recalled them sometimes falling out as he tried to articulate difficult words; they made him dribble and tended to alter sounds. These caps, however, fitted so firmly and took up so little space, he could forget he was wearing them. Another advantage was that he could eat and drink as naturally as if they were his own for up to twenty-four hours.

He then applied enough base make-up to make it look as if Alison had just woken up. Lastly, he put on the wig. He examined the finished result in the mirror and nodded. Andrew Grant looked into the mirror and Alison, Countess of Westminster, looked back at him and smiled. The transformation was complete.

He looked at the clock set in the mirror; it said ten minutes to eight, time to climb back into bed before the maid appeared. He cleared away his own bits and pieces - mustn't make any mistakes at this stage of the game. He carefully mussed up his wig to look like it had been slept in before climbing back into bed. He closed his eyes tightly and put his hand over them to shut out all light. This would ensure that his pupils were enlarged when he reopened them to look at the maid.

A sudden stab of alarm made his adrenaline flow as he realised he had overlooked one detail. Alison's regular maid had departed for pastures new, due to an unfortunate encounter with an amorous footman. Alison would know the new girl's name, of course, but he didn't.

Grant calmed himself and decided to play it by ear: no help for it, just wait and see. With baited breath, he waited for the knock on the door.

Even though he was expecting it, the knock made him jump; it also put him on his mettle.

Knock knock. 'Don't answer, you're asleep,' he thought.

The door opened and he heard footsteps approaching the bed. A hand gently shook him and an unfamiliar voice said, 'M'Lady, it's time to wake up, it's eight o'clock, M'Lady.'

Grant groaned inside and swiftly made a decision. He stirred and gently half rolled over, as if disturbed from a deep sleep. 'Thank you, Susan,' he mumbled.

'It's Sarah, M'Lady, Sarah,' the maid repeated. 'Susan's away.'

'Sarah,' Grant mumbled, as if remembering, 'Oh yes, silly of me.'

Grant pretended to gradually awaken and slowly turned over to face the maid - the moment of truth. Though his disguise was brilliant, he was still tense as he waited for an adverse reaction. There was none, only a smile of recognition.

'I really had forgotten about Susan, Sarah, I didn't get to sleep until the early hours,' said Grant, speaking and yawning at the same time.

Sarah automatically started to yawn, quickly stifling it in embarrassment, and Grant seized his chance to consolidate his position. 'Ah, ah! You see, a yawn is infectious after all,' he smiled, showing a beautiful set of teeth.

'Sorry, M'Lady.'.

'No, no, don't apologise for something as old as Adam.' Grant was Alison to a T.

Sarah smiled gratefully. 'Your breakfast, M'Lady.'

Grant sat up in bed as if this was a daily routine for him. The maid laid the tray across his lap and said, 'Will that be all, M'Lady?'

'Yes thank you, Sarah.'

The maid curtsied and turned to leave.

'Oh, Sarah?'

'Yes, M'Lady?'

'Please don't disturb me this morning, I have to go over my speech for the ceremony this afternoon.'

'Very good, M'Lady.'

'I'll ring when I need you.'

'Very good, M'Lady,' said Sarah as she left the room, closing the door behind her.

'Phew!' Grant breathed a sigh of relief, 'So far, so good.'

He tucked into his breakfast, not knowing when he would eat again.

For the next few hours, he prepared everything to perfection. Nothing was left to chance, no little detail overlooked. Even so, something nagged at his brain but try as he might, he could not put his finger on it.

As the time to leave approached, he went over all the details in his mind. Had he missed anything? Nothing that he could think of. Still, better run though everything again, just in case. The next few hours would be crucial, nothing, absolutely nothing must go wrong today of all days. From the moment he walked through that door, he would be, to all intents and purposes, Alison, Countess of Westminster and nobody must suspect otherwise.

All that it would take was one doubting Thomas and the game would be up. That must never happen. He went over the details yet again and still something nagged at his mind.

Ten minutes later, he looked at his watch, sighed, gritted his teeth and stood up. He was breathing irregularly, unsteadily. 'This will not do,' he thought fiercely and walked over to the mirror. The sight of Alison looking back at him shocked him at first because of the reality of the reflection. But it also served to calm him considerably, and with his newly regained composure, he walked to the door and opened it. Taking a deep breath, he stepped through it as Alison, Countess of Westminster.

CHAPTER TWENTY-FIVE
THE RAPE OF ALISON

William Brent furrowed his brow in trepidation as he drove the van back to Lincolnshire with its unconscious cargo. His head was in a whirl, he just could not believe the predicament he had allowed himself to be drawn into, even for a quarter of a million pounds.

Then again, it was a fabulous reward. Licking his lips, he tried to visualise what that amount looked like in five pound notes, fifties even. He would be able to do whatever he fancied: travel abroad, trendy new clothes and all the women he wanted ... All the women his heart could desire and maybe, just maybe, he would finally be able to fulfil his one great wish: to make love fully for the first time in his life. For William Brent, even through he was a mature man of thirty-four, was still a virgin.

He was all at sea, all fingers and thumbs when it came down to the final act. It wasn't for the want of trying, it just never seemed to happen somehow. He'd tried every line of chat in the book, spent a small fortune on gin or whatever, in fact everything he could think of short of paying for a session with a prostitute. He'd never actually fancied that, yet he'd made tentative approaches to them in his younger years. But he always backed off at the last minute.

Alison, in the rear of the van, moaned just then and Brent quickly pulled over to the side of the road. He had to give her another sniff of chloroform before she regained consciousness. It just wouldn't do for her to scream out at this stage of the game.

He quickly ran round to the back of the van and opened just one door. Reaching into his pocket to retrieve a cotton wool pad and a bottle of chloroform, he put a few drops onto the already damp pad and gently placed it over Alison's nose and mouth. In a few seconds she stopped moaning and lapsed once more into a state of unconsciousness. Brent breathed a sigh of relief and held the pad in place for a few more seconds, just to be sure.

As Alison relaxed once again, Brent could not help noticing just how attractive she was. His eyes involuntarily wandered down to the swell of her breasts before being drawn as if by a magnet to her lower regions. His hand slowly moved down to touch her calf and as he did so, he felt a stirring in his loins.

He realised that he was panting now. Licking his dry lips, he allowed the sensation of touching female flesh to consume his imagination. He gradually slid his hand towards Alison's knee and touched the hem of her skirt, where he paused momentarily before pushing it higher and higher until her thigh was partially exposed.

Brent closed his eyes; he was trembling from head to toe. He quickly withdrew his hand and stepped back, slamming and locking the back door. His back to the van, he leaned against it, sweating profusely and wiping his brow with his sleeve. After a few minutes he walked to the front of the van and got in. He started the engine, selected first gear and got underway. Two miles further on he had made up his mind: he was going to do it. He was going to make love to this lady whether she wanted to or not.

He grinned nervously, a twitch at the corner of his mouth, and reached for a cigarette. Once it was lit he took a deep pull at the weed, inhaling long and deep as the tobacco caught and glowed. In a few hours he would know. He would know just what it felt like to lie on top of the female form, to, to ... Brent shuddered in anticipation and almost left the road, blind to everything except his own lust. His adrenaline flowed as he nearly mounted the pavement and came down to earth with a bump.

Hours later he pulled into the driveway of the old Manse and quickly parked nose first in the big garage. He carried the still unconscious Alison indoors, away from prying eyes. Upstairs in the bedroom where she was to be detained, Brent laid the limp form on the bed and quickly snapped on the shackles that were already attached to the old-fashioned bedposts, one on each wrist. Alison's legs were slightly bent and Brent grabbed her ankles and straightened them, uncovering her knees as he did so. The sight of them stirred Brent once again and he practically whimpered in anticipation...

Swallowing hard, he bent forward, his hand reaching for the hem of her dress. Gradually, oh so gradually, he eased it higher and higher, until the tops of her expensive stockings came into view.

He stopped then as he realised he was holding his breath and his heart was pounding away like a trip hammer. Once again he wiped his brow on his sleeve. Sitting on the bed, he tried to regain his composure and it was a full two minutes before he decided to resume.

Filled with resolve, he stood up and faced the bed. His hand reached again for the hem of Alison's skirt and he began to move it higher until an inch of thigh emerged. He moved the hem higher and higher until the first glimpse of undergarment came into view.

Brent trembled as he once more tilted his head forward and opened his eyes. This time, using both hands, he hoisted Alison's skirt to her waist, fully exposing her panties. He was excited now but thinking more rationally. He knew exactly what he was going to do.

Reaching down with trembling fingers, he pulled her panties down until she was fully exposed. Although he knew what to expect - he had read countless porno magazines - Brent was shocked at seeing it in the flesh. But he was also spurred on to remove the underwear entirely.

All movement seemed to be automatic as he bent forward and slowly opened Alison's legs, his eyes widening, marvelling at what he saw. He straightened up and slowly unzipped his trousers, kicking his shoes off at the same time. He let both trousers and pants drop to the floor, stepping out of them and pushing them to one side.

Gently, he climbed onto the bed, first one knee, then the other. He lifted his left knee over her right leg until he was in position. He then leaned forward, extending both arms to support his weight as he lowered himself . Alison did not stir.

After a lot of fumbling, he entered her, marvelling at this first-time sensation. He began to move, experimentally, then naturally, gradually going faster and deeper. For the next fifty-five frenzied seconds, nothing else existed outside this wonderful feeling and he climaxed with a loud cry, his head flung back. He was breathless and his heart was ready to burst as he sank down on Alison's unconscious form, totally exhausted.

As he lay, he began to cry and he hadn't the faintest idea why.

Eventually, he climbed off the bed and clumsily replaced Alison's panties, only pulling her skirt down when he was sure that she was properly attired. He then collected his own clothes before heading for the bathroom, where he sat on the toilet with his head in his hands, feeling totally drained but elated.

He had done it. He'd had his first taste of sex, albeit with a 'corpse', but sex it had been and it was bloody marvellous. Never again would he be afraid to approach a woman, any woman.

He dressed quickly and made his way back to the bedroom, donning his ski mask as he went. Alison was still unconscious and Brent just gazed at her, almost unable to believe that he had made love to her just a few short minutes ago. He stood there for nearly half an hour, just looking and wondering, feeling a kind of warmth and kinship with her now that they had become lovers. The fact that she was a titled lady never entered his head, nor did it occur to him how serious his actions had been or the dire punishment he could receive as a consequence.

He froze as she stirred and moaned softly, her head moving from side to side as she regained consciousness. She moaned again and slowly opened her eyes.

Brent stood stock still and waited. He knew that she would regain full consciousness in a few short minutes. Would she know, would she be able to sense anything, would she be able to feel anything?

Brent sighed. What did it matter? If he had read Grant right, she was scheduled to die anyway because she could identify her kidnapper. What the Countess of Westminster thought or felt would soon be irrelevant.

Chapter Twenty-Six
The Man In The Ski Mask

Alison tried to rise from the bed where she lay, but she was unable to. She felt violently sick and her head throbbed. 'It's a nightmare, I'm having a nightmare,' she mumbled.

Her head began to clear and realization of what had happened hit her.

'Andrew,' she cried out, 'oh Andrew, why?'

She tried to sit up but couldn't use her arms freely to support herself. The shackles on her wrist came as a complete shock and her jaw dropped in horror as she realised that she was chained to the bedposts. She also realised that she was not alone as she looked up slowly at the man in the ski mask standing at the foot of the bed. Alison shuddered.

'Who are you, what am I doing here? Why are you doing this to me?' she demanded defiantly, in spite of her fear.

The man held out his hand towards Alison and stepped slowly round the bed. She cringed and shut her eyes. Then she heard a tinkling sound and opened her eyes again. He was holding a small bell which he thrust into her hand. Puzzled, she took it.

The man did not speak but held up a note pad on which was written in broad felt tip pen the word 'food'. Alison's heart slowed down a little as she realised he was not going to hurt her. 'N-no thank you, I'm not hungry but please, I'd like a drink of water.' Her voice was trembling.

The man looked at Alison for a long time then swiftly disappeared from the room to reappear a few minutes later, carrying a water jug and tumbler. He filled the tumbler and handed it to Alison, who gulped gratefully, eyes closed, until it was empty. She held out the tumbler with a trembling hand and asked, 'Please, may I have some more?'

The man in the mask nodded and refilled it; Alison drained it, more slowly this time.

'Thank you,' she said simply, handing the tumbler back. As the man took it, she ventured the question. 'Where am I, why are you keeping me here?'

The masked man shook his head and wagged his finger vehemently.

'At least tell me what day it is then, please,' Alison begged.

The man hesitated then, using the note pad and felt tip, he wrote, '18th, 9am'.

Alison sat bolt upright in alarm. 'The 18th! I have to open Ramsdean Hospital this afternoon!'

The man shook his head slowly.

'But if I don't, I'll be missed and people will begin looking for me,' she cried.

Again the man shook his head, turned and left the room, locking the door behind him. Alison frowned and tried to make sense of that last head shake. What did he mean? Of course she'd be missed, that was patently obvious.

Alison automatically looked at the time and realised that her watch had stopped. With difficulty, she removed it and reset the time to what she thought it should be: 9.05am.

The day passed slowly and Alison fretted, ate little, and wept frequently throughout the long day. She could hear children playing close by - a school perhaps, or could it be a park? Every hour, on the hour, a bell chimed somewhere not too far away. Town hall, church bell? She could not be sure. After a while, she gave up trying to piece things together and slept fitfully.

The masked man brought her meals at noon and 6pm, and at around nine o'clock, Alison succumbed to a deep sleep, exhausted by the traumatic events. She was plagued by a horrifyingly real nightmare that culminated in a terrifying encounter with a huge, black mad dog, savagely sinking his teeth into her shoulder and shaking her like a rag doll.

She screamed herself awake to find her shoulder being shaken by the man in the ski mask. He motioned her to sit up and she did so fearfully, unable to take her eyes off the mask.

The man deftly covered her mouth with a piece of broad sticky tape, undid one shackle from the bedpost and snapped it on her other wrist, before releasing the other shackle on the opposite bedpost. He motioned Alison to stand up, helping her to her feet and moving quickly behind her to blindfold her with a thick black scarf.

Panic welled up inside Alison as her imagination ran riot at the idea of being unable to see or speak. Then she felt herself being propelled forward, guided by the firm but gentle hands of her captor.

He guided her along a corridor and down two flights of stairs before she finally felt a cold draught of air on the exposed parts of her face and hands. She stumbled down a small step onto what felt like concrete underfoot, and half a dozen or so steps later she was halted by her captor's firm hands. There was the sound of a door being opened.

Suddenly, she felt a hand on each shoulder guiding her backwards until she felt an obstruction at the back of her legs. Without warning, she was suddenly lifted off her feet and, with a sudden stab of alarm, she realised that she was being placed in the boot of a car.

Alison tried to scream but only succeeded in making a muffled noise as she sensed rather than heard the boot door being closed.

For two minutes she lay there, her heart beating rapidly as she tried to cope with the intense fear that was trying to take control of her senses.

She sensed the boot door being opened again and felt the sickly-smelling damp pad being placed over her nose. Her senses swam as the stench of chloroform permeated her nostrils and she lapsed mercifully into unconsciousness within seconds.

CHAPTER TWENTY-SEVEN
JIMMY IS SPOTTED

It was pure chance that Grant was standing by the top floor front centre window just as the three cars passed by and turned right, some fifty yards past the house. He had been making 'certain arrangements' for Alison's 'benefit' in a once famous building, and had arrived home only minutes earlier.

The room in which he was standing was his bedroom and, as was his custom before retiring, he had walked over to the window to open it an inch or so before climbing into bed for a few hours' sleep.

He frowned at the sight of the cars. Although he was almost certain they contained police personnel, he had not banked on them showing up quite so soon.

Making up his mind quickly, he called loudly over his shoulder, 'Brent, Brent, in here quickly, damn you!'

There was noise from the next room, a sound of hurried movement and seconds later, a dishevelled Brent appeared in the doorway.

'Yes Andrew?'

'Don't put the light on Brent, just listen.'

'What - what on earth's the matter, Andrew?'

'The police are here sooner than I thought so do as I say and don't argue, time is short,' Grant said angrily.

'Pol— Oh my God!' Brent was shocked.

'Put Alison in the boot of the car, tape her mouth, blindfold and shackle her, then chloroform her. Do it now, right now, go, go, do it man!' Grant ordered urgently.

Brent scuttled away to do his bidding and Andrew turned his attention to the window once more. Within minutes, he spotted Jimmy Finch making his way across the road at an angle which could only mean that he was going round the back of the park to reconnoitre the rear of the house. A few minutes later, Grant watched as Mac sauntered casually by, followed five minutes later by Smithy.

Grant read the situation exactly and nodded knowingly. 'Well well, my friends,' he murmured to himself, 'you acted as I thought you would, only a lot quicker than I thought. No matter, I'll just have to move a little faster myself.'

He turned on his heels and quickly made his way across the landing to the bedroom on his left. From here, he could see across the park to where he knew there was a gap in the hedge. He didn't have to wait long before he spotted Jimmy sneaking through the shrubbery. It was only a fleeting glimpse, but Grant grunted in satisfaction because nobody would sneak about at this unearthly hour, only a tramp - or a policeman.

Grant looked down and watched Brent huckling Alison off to the garage. He watched him stow her in the boot and close it, grunting in satisfaction as Brent ran back into the house, unseen by Jimmy Finch. He cursed as he saw Brent run back out of the house, open the boot, administer the chloroform to Alison, close the boot and race back in again.

'Brent, what the hell are you playing at!' he roared as Brent raced up the stairs.

'I-I'm s-sorry Andrew, I f-forgot the ch-chloroform,' Brent replied fearfully.

Grant fumed inwardly, but in a calm voice he said, 'Never mind, you did well. Now listen to me and get it right this time. Now, if I'm not mistaken, very soon the park will be full of policemen hiding in the bushes.'

Brent's eyes widened in alarm.

Grant held up his hands, palms forward, in a calming gesture.

'Don't panic, my friend, because we're going to put on a little show, just for their benefit, just to get them thinking a bit.'

Brent looked perplexed.

'When I tell you, I want you to go to the kitchen and turn on the light as if you're cooking breakfast. Stay there for about ten minutes, then come back here, have you got that?'

'Ten minutes then come back, yes, Andrew.'

'Then, I want you to put on the ski mask, go to Alison's room and put on the light.'

Brent gasped and opened his mouth to protest but Grant hurried on.

'Don't worry, trust me. Show yourself at the window for a second or two then leave the room, not forgetting to put out the light. Now have you got that?'

'I-I think so, yes, I've got it,' Brent replied fearfully.

'Good, now stand by the door and wait for my signal,' Grant ordered, pointing to the bedroom door.

Ten minutes passed in silence as Grant stared out of the window. At long last, he grunted in satisfaction and stepped back into the room, out of view. 'Right, Brent, put on the light and make your way to the kitchen.'

Brent complied and as the light came on, Grant ambled into view, stretching and yawning as if he had just vacated his bed. He spoke over his shoulder as if to another person.

'Be back in ten minutes, my friend,' he said, then he moved back out of sight.

Ten minutes later, Brent reappeared. 'Now Andrew?'

'Now, my friend.'

Brent, still nervous, donned the ski mask and went to Alison's bedroom. He switched on the light and showed himself at the window for a few seconds before returning to Grant, sweat glistening on his top lip.

'What do you want me to do now, Andrew?' His voice trembled slightly.

Grant beamed at him. 'Now get dressed quickly, I have a very important job for you to do.' He handed Brent a folded piece of paper.

'I want you to take the car our of the garage and follow these instructions to the letter and, more importantly, to the minute. Now repeat what I've just said,' Grant ordered.

Brent licked his lips and repeated it parrot fashion.

'Perfect, my friend, I knew I'd picked the right man,' Grant smiled patronisingly. 'To the letter, to the minute and destroy the note before you make the phone call to me at 2pm.'

Brent nodded, 'I won't let you down, I can promise you.'

'Good man, now get dressed and read the first part. You can stop the car a couple of miles from here and absorb the rest of the instructions. Hurry my friend, we haven't much time.'

Brent hastily obeyed and a few minutes later, Grant heard the sound of his powerful engine start up and finally diminish as Brent roared off to his destination.

Grant nodded in satisfaction and made himself comfortable in the downstairs living room to await the knock on the front door that he knew was inevitable.

He did not have to wait long, and smiled to himself as the large lion-headed knocker resounded throughout the house. Slowly, deliberately, he made his way to the front door to talk to the policeman he knew would be there, in one guise or another.

CHAPTER TWENTY-EIGHT
THE EMPTY THEATRE

B rent hurried to the garage, feeling rather than seeing the watchful eyes that followed his every move. He climbed hastily into the Ashdown Marsden, starting up the engine with a mighty roar, reversed out of the garage and executed a neat turn to end up facing the driveway. He selected first gear, let in the clutch and in a couple of seconds reached the roadway where he turned right. A few minutes later, he pulled into a lay-by a few miles from the house.

After making sure that he was not being followed, Brent took out the note and studied it very carefully, shuddering as he read the section concerning Alison. He resumed his journey, heading for Norwich city, his final objective being an old abandoned theatre, now closed due to crumbling substructure too costly to repair.

When he arrived at the theatre, he parked in one of the garages, deserted this past month or so. Having made sure the coast was clear, Brent retrieved his unconscious cargo from the boot and carried her inside the theatre through a rear exit, pencil torch in his mouth. He heaved her through a deserted corridor, passing empty dressing rooms on his way to the stage through the wings.

At the edge of the stage, Brent carefully laid his bundle down on the bare boards and reached into his pockets for a larger torch. The power had been switched off when the theatre had closed, but Grant had catered for this with Tilly lamps as an alternative light source, telling Brent in the note where to find them.

Brent found the three lamps where Grant had left them and quickly made use of them. He spaced them out for full effectiveness and returned to the task in hand.

The stage itself was about fifty feet wide from wings to wings, with a dozen trap doors that had been installed to suit the many and varied productions that had pleased or displeased the many and varied audiences over the years.

The object of Brent's interest stood in the centre of the stage -

an ordinary chair by the side of which was a coil of thin nylon cord. It was positioned in the centre of a large trap door and held by right-angled metal brackets fixed with screws, rendering it totally immobile.

The trap door was a platform lift type that could be lowered or raised at various speeds, according to requirements, and was automatically slowed to stop safely before it reached the bottom, some twenty feet below, by a clever electro-magnetic split circle brake band. This band was kept open by magnetic coils which automatically closed when the power was tripped by the descending trap door, about four feet from the floor, thus enabling the lift to slow down rapidly but safely according to the brake settings cum weight ratio, previously worked out by the operator.

Many times in the past, power failures had rendered the trap door (amongst other things) useless, so the management had installed a second manual control to operate this particular trap door. Although it could be dropped at speed, raising it took the combined efforts of four men turning crank handles.

It was to this machinery that Grant had turned his attention. To drop the trap door necessitated the use of a large wooden handle which, when pulled, released the split brake. The brake automatically engaged again when the trap door was four feet from the floor, shooting the handle back to its original position. The handle itself, on being released, shot back with enough force to injure anyone unlucky enough to be in the way, so a wire mesh cage had been built around it for safety. The returning force of this handle was well known to Grant, and he'd included this in his plans for Alison.

Attached to the top of the handle was a piece of strong twine or cord, which led backwards through a pulley, then upwards into the roof of the theatre and over another pulley. From this pulley, the rope hung down for about six feet with a sandbag weighing a hundred pounds or so, attached to the end. The actual weight of the sandbag was being held by another piece of very thin rope, which was suspended from a handrail on a catwalk that had originally been installed for prop handlers and electricians.

Grant had put a small explosive charge on this retaining rope, feeding the wires to a small box a few feet away. Inside the box was a simple clockwork tripping device in the shape of a twenty-four hour clock, rigged to detonate the explosive charge at the pre-set time. Upon detonation, the thin rope would part, allowing the sandbag to fall, thus pulling the main rope which, in turn, would snatch back the big wooden handle to release the trap door.

Grant had tied the sandbag in such a way as to effect a quick release from the rope's end when the wooden lever had travelled back in its full arc, thus allowing the lever to snap back to its original position unhindered when the trap door struck the mechanism.

Grant had also installed two crossbows, clamped firmly in position and fully loaded with their deadly bolts. He had installed the crossbows above the neon lights so they could not easily be seen from twenty feet below. From the release triggers, he had tied thick strong twine which would release their deadly cargo when pulled. The twine was also fed round a series of pulleys and across in front of the lever, actually touching it, and ended at the wire guard, where it was tied securely.

Grant had already tested this method of firing the crossbows without using the bolts or the explosive charge. He had merely cocked the crossbows and dropped the sandbag by hand from the catwalk until he was satisfied that the deadly contraption worked every time as the sandbag parted company with the end of the retaining rope.

Brent picked up his unconscious load and carried her to the chair. He then securely bound her so that it was impossible for her to move more than half an inch or so from the waist upwards.

After checking her sticky tape gag and blindfold, he stepped back to admire his handiwork. Completely satisfied, he collected the Tilly lamps, dowsed them, replaced them where he had found them and left the theatre. Once outside, he took out the note and read the rest of Grant's instructions.

He was to drive to the outskirts of Norwich, where he would find a small grocers-cum-post office. There he would find a telephone box next to a post box. At exactly two o'clock, he was to phone Grant to tell him that he had accomplished his mission and await further instructions. He also had to park the Ashdown Marsden a hundred yards further up the road in a lay-by that was screened from the road by a hedgerow. Grant had made his instructions perfectly clear: park the car first, then phone, in that order.

Brent reversed the car out of the garage and made for the street.

Once there, he pointed the car in the direction he had come from and put his foot down, reaching the designated phone box at one thirty in the afternoon. After making certain that he was at the right place, he drove on until he found the hidden lay-by.

He hardly noticed the blue hire van, so preoccupied was he with the task in hand. He parked and locked the roadster and walked back to the phone box, arriving at 1.55 only to find it occupied by a middle-aged woman. For a couple of minutes he hung about impatiently then at last, the door of the telephone booth opened and the woman stepped out, giving him an apologetic smile.

At precisely two o'clock, Brent picked up the handset and began to dial.

He never felt a thing as a massive explosion flung him and the phone box door backwards for many yards. Miraculously, apart from a head injury, he was still in one piece.

Eighty yards away, the middle-aged woman broke into a trot, finally disappearing into the hidden lay-by.

A few minutes later, Grant, now divested of his female disguise, drove out of the lay-by in the Ashdown Marsden, rapidly putting distance between himself and the explosion, leaving behind the blue van that Brent had hired a few days previously, complete with Brent's fingerprints.

A few miles behind him, the emergency services were already swinging into action.

Chapter Twenty-Nine
Grant's Deadly Mission

Grant had spotted from Mac's warrant card that the inspector was out of his own manor, which was just as he had hoped it would be. This could only mean that very few people knew of Alison's disappearance, and that was exactly what Grant wanted.

As soon as Mac and his men were out of the house, Grant went quickly to a telephone and dialled Lincoln Central Police HQ. It was engaged. He fumed impatiently as he made another attempt. Three times and five minutes later, he finally got through to a desk clerk.

'Lincoln Central, can I help you?' a female voice enquired briskly.

'Yes, I want to report an attempted burglary,' Grant replied impatiently.

'Just a moment, Sir, I'll put you through to Control,' said the voice.

Grant champed at the bit as he waited for the connection.

'Control, how can I help you?' said a cheery voice.

'I want to report an attempted burglary,' Grant replied testily.

'I see Sir, can I have your name and address please?' the voice requested politely.

Grant sighed and was about to protest but changed his mind and complied with the policeman's request.

'Right, Sir, now what's all this about a burglary?'

'I've just had five men burst into my house and they tried to fob me off with a cock and bull story, but I think they are burglars posing as police.'

'Did you say burglars posing as police, Sir?' said the voice.

'Yes, yes, yes, posing as policemen,' Grant replied, striving to keep his patience.

'Where are they now, Sir, have you any idea?' the voice enquired.

'They're outside now, please hurry.'

'Stay put, Sir, we're on our way,' said the voice and rang off.

Within minutes, there was a screech of brakes outside and Grant moved swiftly to the front door, reaching it at the same time as the knocker sounded. He opened the door to a uniformed inspector and after a few preliminaries, explained the previous events in detail.

'Have you any idea which way they went, Sir?' enquired the inspector.

'None at all,' Grant replied.

The inspector sighed resignedly. 'Right, Sir, we'll have a look round the surrounding area, just in case they're casing any other building.'

'They could be miles away by now, but nevertheless, I would appreciate it very much if you did take a look round, Inspector.'

The inspector left, climbed back into his car and drove off, giving instructions over the radio to his squad. Within minutes he received a report that a group of strangers with cars, were parked in a nearby street, and he rapidly swung his team into action.

As soon as the police left, Grant also swung into action. He collected various items of theatrical gear, packed them into his bag and quickly made his way to the garage at the back of the house. He opened the garage doors wide, quickly making his way to the blue van that Brent had hired a few days before. Within minutes, he was taking the same route that Brent had taken earlier that morning.

Some time later, he reached the hidden lay-by that was so important to his plans, and expertly transformed himself into a middle-aged woman. The transformation complete, he looked at his watch. It said one thirty. Grant smiled to himself as he reached into the back of the van for a parcel whose contents he had taken extra special care to assemble.

Grant climbed out of the van, parcel under his arm, and locked the door, dropping the key in his lady's handbag. As sedately as possible, he then made his way to the phone box that Brent would be using in about twenty minutes from now, timing his arrival to give himself about ten minutes before Brent arrived.

Grant was pretending to use the phone as Brent arrived. He could see Brent in the mirror just above the phone, and smiled to himself in deep satisfaction as Brent drove away to park the car as he had been instructed. A few minutes later, he observed Brent approaching the phone box. He had already placed the parcel on the shelf beside the phone. He now placed his left hand on the parcel and felt with his right hand for a small switch concealed beneath the loose brown paper and flicked it to the 'on' position, before placing a directory over the parcel to conceal it.

The phone was in his hand as Brent reached the phone box and Grant pretended to be having an animated conversation until his watch said it was time to go. At 1.58, he replaced the handset and left the phone box, smiling sweetly at Brent, and began to walk towards the concealed lay-by.

Grant had walked about eighty yards before the deadly parcel exploded, at which point, he broke into a trot and reached the blue van, slightly breathless. He quickly became Andrew Grant again and stowed away all the theatrical equipment into his large bag. He then detached the false knob from the steering wheel which he had been using in order to preserve Brent's fingerprints on the steering wheel.

After checking meticulously that he had left nothing behind, Grant left the key in the ignition, climbed out of the van and, after a last look round inside, closed the door with his knee, satisfied in the knowledge that all the incriminating evidence left behind would point to Brent, and not to himself. He then stowed all his equipment in the boot of the Ashdown Marsden and drove off at high speed towards Lincolnshire. As he drove, he cast his mind back over the events of the last week or so, congratulating himself on his own brilliance.

The police would eventually find the van with traces of fibre from Alison's clothing, plus Brent's fingerprints, and would eventually have to blame Brent for the abduction. They would really have no choice; the kidnapping would have to be hushed up, kept away from the public and the press, otherwise it would give other would-be kidnappers big ideas, and that wouldn't do, would it?

Grant drove steadily, enjoying himself, thinking of the fortune that would soon be his, with Brent taking all the blame: Brent, who could not deny it. Brent, who could not now implicate his friend, Andrew Grant, or rather, Robert Andrew Penton-Fairfax, because Brent was dead, blown to smithereens a few miles back.

CHAPTER THIRTY
THE BLOODSTAINED NOTE

The first police car arrived at the scene of the explosion within minutes, to find Brent motionless on the far pavement. A second and third police car soon arrived, followed by an ambulance and a fire tender.

The occupants of the first car, two patrolmen, quickly ran across to Brent, who was lying opposite the devastated phone box. One of them placed his fingers on the main artery to check for signs of life as a matter of course. Suddenly he stiffened in surprise. 'My God, he's still alive!'

'You're joking, Eddie, he can't be, not after that little lot,' said his partner, jerking his thumb in the direction of the wrecked phone box.

'He bloody well is, I tell you, Lord knows how, but he is,' Eddie said vehemently.

As he was speaking, the ambulance crew approached, complete with stretcher, and Eddie stood up as they arrived.

'He's still alive, mate, God knows how, but he is.'

'OK, mate, leave him with us, we can't move him until we check him out for broken bones,' said one of the ambulance crew.

A uniformed inspector came on the scene and looked down at Brent.

'Who is he, Constable, have you checked his pockets?'

'Don't know yet, Sir, can't move him until the medics have checked him over,' Eddie replied.

'Go with him when they take him to hospital, I want everything that he's wearing, shoes, socks, personal belongings, the lot,' the inspector ordered.

'Right, Sir.'

The inspector turned round and scanned the buildings until he found what he was looking for. He walked towards the sub-post office where a grey-haired couple were standing in the doorway.

He smiled gently as he approached them. 'Mr and Mrs Willmot, I presume?'

'That's right, Inspector,' replied the elderly gentleman, 'it was me who phoned the police station.'

'Is he dead, Inspector? The man who was in the phone box, I mean.' Mrs Willmot's voice shook as she spoke.

'Just about, Mrs Willmot, er what I mean is, he's barely alive - why, I don't know, after an explosion of that size,' the inspector replied gently.

'It could just as well have been the lady, she only left a couple of minutes before it went off,' said Mr Willmot.

The inspector frowned. 'Lady? Did you say lady? Which way did she go?' he asked sharply. 'Anyone you know?'

'Er, no,' Mr Willmot replied, startled at the sudden change of tone. 'She came out of the phone box to let the man in and then she walked up to the hidden valley.'

'Hidden valley?' the inspector cocked his head enquiringly.

'The lay-by, a hundred or so yards up the road. Us kids used to use it to play Cowboys and Indians and what not. We called it that and the name sort of stuck, even after the Council tarmacked it and used it as a lay-by.'

'Any houses up that way?'

'Erm no, none, until you come to the next village, and that's four miles from here,' said Mr Willmot.

The bomb squad arrived just at that moment and the inspector thanked them both. 'I shall probably want to speak to you again, oh, and thank you for calling us so promptly.' He turned on his heels and made his way towards the bomb disposal vehicle, arriving just as the crew were disembarking.

The inspector approached a huge man in army uniform, sporting captains' pips. He extended his hand and the big man took it in his massive but surprisingly gentle paw.

'Captain Jerry Raymond at your service, Inspector, Tiny to my friends, although I haven't a clue why,' he added, grinning amiably.

'Mike Graham.'

'All right, Mike me boy, so what's all this about then eh?'

'That's what I'd like you to tell me, Captain.'

'Right, let's have a look then,' said Tiny, making his way to the scene of devastation.

He surveyed it from a short distance at first, his critical but expert eye taking in everything, before moving in for a closer look. 'Phew,' he whistled, 'that was one big bang.'

'Then how come the chap inside is still alive?'

'Perfectly simple really,' Tiny replied. 'He was standing close to it in a confined space, they do it at fairgrounds as a sideshow, you know. Had he been another two feet away, we would have been looking for bits and pieces of him with a magnifying glass.'

'Well I'll be darned,' said Mike, genuinely surprised, 'you learn something new every day.'

'What puzzles me is, who would want to blow up a perfectly harmless phone box, and why?' said Tiny.

'More to the point, if this bloke was the intended victim, why not shoot him or stab him, or even run him down? Why go to all this trouble?' Mike mused quietly.

'Oh that's an easy one to answer, old boy. First you bait your trap, then you lure your victim from a safe distance, thus ensuring anonymity, you hope,' said Tiny.

'Yes, you're right, of course, then blow everything to smithereens to leave no trace,' Mike agreed.

'Don't you believe it, me lad, they usually leave a little something for us to find, and if it's there, we'll find it, have no doubt on that score,' said Tiny confidently.

The ambulance started up at that moment, and so did the first police car with the two patrolmen inside. The nearside window was lowered and one of the patrolmen shouted, 'Leave it to us, Sir, we'll bring everything back to the station.'

'Right, off you go then,' Mike shouted back.

'Right, Mike, now if your men can clear the area, my men can get to work,' said Tiny briskly.

'Will do,' said Mike, and promptly gave the order to a nearby sergeant. 'Clear the area will you, and send a few men up to the concealed lay-by up the way there to see what they can find, if anything.'

'Right Sir,' said the sergeant, and he in turn rapped out a couple of orders. 'Right you lot, clear the area, and any bits and pieces you see lying about, leave them for the bomb squad. Rope off the area and set up diversions both ways for the traffic.' He singled out two men. 'You two, off up to the hidden lay-by, see what you can find, jump to it.'

With the area cleared, Tiny and his men set about the task in hand as Mike looked on from the edge of the roped off area. As they were examining bits and pieces, one of the policemen returned from the concealed lay-by and reported to Mike.

'Sir, we've found a hire van in the lay-by with the key still in the ignition. I've left one of the lads with it just in case.'

'Did you get the registration number?'

'Yes, Sir.'

'Good, get on the radio and run a trace on the ownership.'

'Well actually, Sir, the hire firm's name and phone number are painted on the side of the van,' said the constable, 'I've got them here.'

'OK good, get on to them and find out who hired it, and if the name matches the chap we found here, all well and good - assuming of course, he carries some sort of identification. If he doesn't, we may get lucky with fingerprints.'

'Right, Sir,' said the constable as he turned on his heel.

It did not take long for Tiny and his team of experts to find bits and pieces from the bomb, the biggest being a badly misshapen, barely recognisable clock face, which was embedded in an almost intact telephone directory.

Tiny called out to Mike, 'Come and see what Santa Claus has brought me.'

Mike walked over to Tiny, who was holding what looked like a lidless shoe box. 'Anything interesting?'

'One thing's for certain, my boy, this bloke could have killed himself, or I've read it all wrong,' said Tiny.

'Oh, and how's that?'

'Well, unless I'm very much mistaken, this' - he reached inside the shoe box and extracted the clock face - 'is a common or garden alarm clock, hammer and bell type, and he's probably used the hammer and bell as a trip switch, which, believe me, is positively dangerous, unless you give it a lot of thought when you're setting it,' said Tiny.

'How do you mean?'

'Well first off, you insulate the bell from the clock body, either with insulation tape or a rubber washer, something like that, and fix a wire to it to form one half of the circuit, set the time for your alarm to go off and ... boom.'

'Yes, I think I understand that, but surely any bomb device is dangerous,' said Mike.

'That's as may be, but in this case, the clock he used as far as I can tell from this clock face, is very temperamental. Look, let me explain. The hammer is on a pivot which is just inside the clock and the bottom of the hammer is shaped just like a garden spade. Are you with me so far, Mike me boy?'

'Erm, yes I think so. Go on.'

'Well, this spade bit is used as a strike pad and the bit that strikes it is a cog wheel that whizzes round at high speed, each tooth striking the spade bit in turn, and the only thing that holds the hammer away from the bell is a very weak spring. And that,' he paused for effect, 'is the dangerous bit that could have blown our bomber away to the big bomb factory in the sky.'

'The spring?'

'Yep, old boy, the spring. You see, this clock is a cheap import from the Far East and the springs aren't made from high quality spring steel, just some cheap old rubbish that stretches after being used half a dozen times or so. Consequently, the hammer is free to move itself after a very short while,' said Tiny.

'I see what you mean, so that means this man is an amateur,' said Mike, shaking his head in disbelief.

'On the nose, me boy, on the nose.'

'So it looks as if we can discount the IRA then?' said Mike thoughtfully.

'Could be a gangland killing, or even a lovers' tiff,' said Tiny.

'Lovers' tiff?'

'Well, you know what I mean, Mike, it takes all sorts,' said Tiny with a lopsided grin. 'It wouldn't be the first time that Cedric had it away from Cecil, and Cecil found out.'

Mike grinned. 'No need to go on, Tiny, I've cottoned on. Anyway we won't know until we find out who this bloke is; I'm off to the hospital.'

'OK, Mike, I've still got a bit to do here, so I'll write out my report and drop you a copy at the station, OK?'

The two men shook hands. Mike got into his car and sped off to the hospital.

The Anglican and General Accident Hospital was built on the site of an ancient monastery. Nightly sightings of many a shadowy, hooded figure had been reported there, especially at the bedsides of serious cases. However, they appeared in the main to be benevolent, and seemed to do more good than evil if the miraculous recovery of some of the patients was anything to go by.

One legend in particular was often recounted by the hospital staff and the locals. A middle-aged married couple were involved in a horrific car crash, suffering extensive injuries that put them both into intensive care.

The woman's injuries were severe, but the man's were worse: he had suffered brain damage as well as terrible physical injuries. He remained in a coma for many days and when he finally did wake from his deep sleep for a few minutes, he called out his wife's name. She didn't answer because she wasn't there; she was recovering slowly in the women's ward.

A nurse, on hearing him call out for his wife, gently informed him that she was in a bed in the ladies' ward. The man, being in poor physical and mental condition, misunderstood the word 'bed' for 'dead' and consequently decided to join his lady love on the other side.

That night, as the man lay at death's door (so the story goes) a goggle-eyed night nurse saw a hooded, monk-like figure appear at his bedside. The monk bent over the dying man and whispered in his ear, apparently, that his wife was alive and coming along in leaps and bounds. After the figure had disappeared, the nurse ran to the man to see if he was all right and was astonished to see a smile of contentment on his face.

Needless to say, from that moment on, the man's recovery was rapid, and within a week he was reunited with his wife in a private ward, to the delight of everyone in the hospital.

Mike Graham strode up to the reception desk and a white coated female receptionist smiled at him. 'I'm Inspector Graham. A badly injured man was brought in a short while ago, two of my constables came with him. Can I—?'

'Yes, Inspector, the man in the explosion. Just a moment and I'll put out a call for Mr Wincanton, the surgeon who attended him,' the girl interrupted. She leaned forward and pressed a button on a panel. 'I'm paging him now, Sir,' she said, 'the phone will ring in a few moments.'

Mike smiled his thanks and thirty seconds later, a phone rang on the desk and the girl picked it up. 'Ah, Mr Wincanton, there's an Inspector Graham in reception ... yes, Sir.' She replaced the handset. 'He's on his way, Inspector,' she smiled.

'Thank you,' said Mike.

Ten minutes later, a dark-haired man of about thirty-five, wearing surgeons' green, a face mask pulled down under his chin and a cap in hand, strode purposefully towards Mike, his hand outstretched.

'Inspector Graham?'

Mike took the proffered hand. 'Mr Wincanton?'

'Yes. I'm afraid I have bad news for you, Inspector.

'Oh?'

'Your man died a few minutes ago, before I had a chance to operate on him,' the surgeon said regretfully.

Mike sighed. 'Couldn't be helped, I suppose, especially after a blast of that size.'

'Actually, it wasn't the blast that did it, it was whatever he propelled into that did all the damage. The back of his skull was smashed and his spine was damaged - it was a brain haemorrhage that killed him. He died before I could relieve the pressure in his skull,' said the surgeon.

'That would be the phone box door that he was blown into,' said Mike.

'I'm sorry, Inspector, there just wasn't enough time,' said the surgeon regretfully.

'Where is he now, Mr Wincanton?'

'By now he'll be in the hospital mortuary for an autopsy some time today.'

'With your kind permission, I'd like to have his fingerprints. We may have something on file about him.'

'By all means, you can lay it on right away if you wish, use the desk phone.' He turned to the receptionist. 'Give the good inspector an outside line, my dear please,' he smiled.

The girl smiled back. 'Certainly, Sir' and pressed a button on the phone base before handing the phone to Mike. Mike thanked her and rapidly made all the necessary arrangements before turning back to the surgeon.

'This is probably a silly question, but, erm, did he say anything before he died?'

''Fraid not, old chap, not a word, at least, not while I was with him,' the surgeon said regretfully. 'A couple of your lads are here though, collecting his belongings, why not ask them? You never know your luck.'

'Thank you, Mr Wincanton, I'll do that, just as soon as I can find them,' said Mike. Just then he spotted his men coming along the corridor. The two mobile constables approached Mike, each carrying a plastic bag.

'That was quick, Sir, didn't expect to see you here so soon,' said Eddie.

'Nothing I could do at that end until I get a report from the bomb squad,' said Mike. 'Got everything?'

'Yes, Sir, clothes, pocket contents, blood group, approximate age and height,' said Eddie.

'Good, good, did he say anything, do you know, anything at all?' Mike asked hopefully.

'Not to our knowledge, Sir, nothing at all,' Eddie replied.

Mike sighed. 'Pity, never mind, let's get this little lot back to the station and give it a going over.'

'What about his fingerprints, Sir?'

'That's already laid on,' said Mike as they left the hospital.

Back at the police station, they laid out Brent's belongings on a table in an empty interview room and Mike took stock of what he saw.

'Keys, coins, one handkerchief, still folded.' He turned to Eddie, 'nothing else?'

'Nothing, Sir, as far as we know, Sir.'

Something in the tone of Eddie's voice made Mike round on him suspiciously. 'What do you mean, as far as you know? You searched the man thoroughly did you not, or didn't you want to get blood on your hands? Well?'

'What we meant, Sir, was that we were going to do a thorough search just as soon as we got back here,' Eddie said lamely.

203

'Then get to it, man, this isn't a simple felony we have here. Someone's been blown up for some obscure reason and we need every bit of evidence and stroke or identification that we can get hold of so, gore or no gore, get stuck in!' Mike said angrily.

Injured pride stung both constables into action and without further ado, they began to search every pocket they could find.

Nodding in satisfaction, Mike picked up the handkerchief and, as he did so, caught a faint smell coming from it. Curious, he put it closer to his nose. The smell was sickly and he recognised it immediately.

'Chloroform?'

'Sir?'

'Smell this and tell me what you think it is.'

Eddie took the handkerchief and held it gingerly under his nose. 'Phew, that's chloroform or I'm a Dutchman.' He offered the hanky to his partner. 'What do you think, Dave?'

Dave, his hands still searching through pockets, leaned over and sniffed at the handkerchief in Eddie's hands. 'Strewth, that's the genuine Micky Finn, Sir, that's chloroform all right.'

Just at that moment, Dave felt something in one of the pockets. He slid out what looked like a folded piece of paper. 'I've found something, Sir, it's a bit soggy thought,' he said as he held out the bloodstained article.

Mike took the proffered paper, turning it over in his hands before carefully unfolding it. 'A bit messy, but legible in some parts so let's see what we can see.' He scanned the bloodstained paper, but the blood was already turning brown and the writing made little sense. 'Better get this over to the lab, boys and see what they can come up with.'

The door opened and a constable stepped into the room. 'Excuse me, Sir, that hire van, Sir.'

'Ah yes, what have you got?'

'The van was hired out to one Walter Brentford and he gave his address as The Old Manse, Park Lane, Lincoln - three days ago, as a matter of fact,' said the constable.

Lincoln? So why does he get himself blown up in Norfolk, I wonder? Mike mused. That is, if this bloke was Walter Brentford.

He spoke to the constable in the doorway. 'Take a couple of

fingerprints boys with you back to the van, unless I miss my guess, they'll probably match up with that chap in the hospital mortuary, and get a move on, will you?'

'Right, Sir.'

Mike turned to Eddie. 'Whip this over to forensics and tell them it's top priority. Take this handkerchief to confirm the chloroform.'

Eddie produced two small plastic bags from a pocket, placed the bloodstained paper in one of them and the handkerchief in the other. Mike followed him out of the room. 'Ask them to get a move on, I'm going to wash up. I'll be in my office when they have anything. I'll get on to Lincoln to see if they have anything on this Walter Brentford.'

Mac had collected the long-range walkie talkie transmitters from the airport and was now back in Lincoln Central with Inspector Roy Spalding. Mac's team was there too, having freshened up.

'Right, you lot, we're in business, so let's get the show on the road before our chap can get his second wind.'

He picked up the phone and phoned his Chief at the Yard.

'Sir, it's Macdonald, I've just picked up the merchandise from the airport and we're ready to try them out.'

'Hello, Mac, good, I've had them all preset and a waveband is very tight, so everything's locked just in case they get knocked or anything. Give them out to your team, one to Spalding, and keep one yourself, of course. I shall call out everyone's name in turn and that person shall acknowledge, understood?'

'Right Sir, give me a minute, I'll hand them out.'

'Pick one each,' said Mac. 'You too, Roy, and acknowledge the Chief when he calls you by name. Just press the button to speak and release it to receive, oh, and switch them on first, OK?'

One by one, the walkie talkies were taken and examined and Mac took one for himself. Satisfied that everyone was ready, he spoke into the phone. 'Ready, Sir?'

'Right, Mac, don't cradle your phone yet, just in case.'

'Right Sir, go ahead.'

There was a slight crackling sound as the Chief switched on his set. 'Macdonald?'

Hearing you loud and clear, Sir.'

The Chief checked out everyone with satisfactory results and then addressed Mac. 'Right, Mac, you can cradle your phone and from now on, all dialogue concerning Operation Grouse will be with walkie talkies only.'

'I feel happier now, Sir,' said Mac. 'Have you seen to the phone people?'

'I have, and we're in luck too, one of the switchboard operators is an amateur actress and she's agreed to co-operate, although she doesn't know what it's all about yet.'

'That's good news, Sir, a regular stroke of luck I'd say. What's her name?'

'One Mrs Joan Caldwell, stage name, Janet Calder. You can brief her yourself later. Now, what have you come up with, Mac?'

'Nothing yet, Sir, I'm afraid, we're just about to get ourselves organised as a matter of fact,' said Mac, 'but rest assured, we'll bring home the bacon.'

'We have until noon the day after tomorrow, Mac,' the Chief reminded him. 'We have to find out where he's got Alison, before he can do her any harm - assuming he hasn't already.'

'I don't think he's harmed her, Sir, at least, not yet, not until he's certain he has the money. I'm banking on that.'

'I hope you're right, Mac, I sincerely hope you're right.'

'What about that Swiss bank, Sir? I think that's going to be a bit sticky. I mean, they're not going to be keen to break the tradition of customer confidentiality on the strength of a phone call, are they? After all, they'll be short of two million quid at the end and that's a lot of investment out of the window.'

'Let me worry on that score, Mac, I have a lot of contacts in Interpol and a couple of them have a hell of a lot of pull, believe me. That money will be on temporary loan only, I can guarantee that. You just get things going your end with our actress friend.'

'Right, Sir, leave it to me and I'll keep you informed as we progress,' said Mac. 'Signing off now, Sir, goodbye.'

Mac switched off his walkie talkie and placed it on the table. 'Well lads, you heard the chief, let's get to it. Oh by the way, don't forget that with your sets switched off, you can only receive, you can't transmit, OK?'

The phone rang just then and Roy Spalding picked it up. A voice said, 'Inspector Spalding, switchboard here, Sir, we have an enquiry from Norwich. Putting you through now, Sir.'

There was a click and a voice said, 'Is that you, Roy? Mike Graham here.'

'Mike, how are you, old friend, what can I do for you?'

Mike chuckled. 'We'll have to split a bottle again some time, old son, but seriously, Roy, we've had an incident down here. Some chap got himself blown up in a phone box, name of Walter Brentford, got an address at your end.'

'Walter Brentford, did you say? What did he do to deserve that?'

'Haven't a clue, I'm doing a rundown on him now.'

'OK Mike, let's have his address and any other details and we'll run a check at this end.'

'He rented a blue hire van about three days ago and he gave his address as The Old Manse, Park Lane, Lincoln and—'

Roy shot bolt upright in his seat. 'Did you say The Old Manse, Park Lane?'

'I did, why, something up?'

'Give me a moment, Mike me old son.' Roy covered the mouthpiece with his hand and signalled to Mac to pick up the other phone. 'Mike, sorry old boy, we had a bit of trouble at that address recently and you giving me the same address startled me for a moment,' he chuckled disarmingly. 'What else have you got on this character?'

'We have his clothes and a few personal belongings, not much, but the curious thing is, we found his handkerchief saturated in what smelled like chloroform,' Mike replied, 'oh, and a folded note or letter of some sort. They're both being processed at forensics right now. We also have the blue van, and I'm having that dusted for fingerprints.'

'Just a sec, Mike. He's got a chloroformed handkerchief, a note covered in blood and a hire van?' he spoke out loud as if reminding himself, but it was to see Mac's reaction.

'Make arrangements for us to go down there,' Mac whispered urgently.

Roy spoke into the mouthpiece again. 'Look, we're still trying to tie up a few loose ends here with that address, do you mind if I come over and take a butchers?'

'Why not, I'd be delighted, maybe we can chew the fat over old times. When are you planning to come?'

'If I start now, I can be there in an hour or so, if it's OK with you.'

'Fine with me, old son, I'd like to get this mess cleared up as soon as possible. When someone gets blown up in a damn phone box, there just has to be a very good reason and so far, that reason escapes me.'

'Early days yet, maybe between us we can come up with the answer, so just as soon as I put this phone down, I'll be motoring. See you shortly Mike, OK?' ,Roy put the phone down. 'This could be what you are looking for Mac.'

'That note interests me, it could give us a lead,' said Mac hopefully, 'or the van even. I don't mind admitting it, Roy, I'm living in hope right now.'

Mac spoke to his sergeant. 'Smithy, you organise a watch on the house and keep in touch. Jimmy, you come with me and bring your camera, we may need it. Somewhere along the line, there may be a clue to lead us to Alison because unless I miss my guess, Grant used this bloke to hide her somewhere and he, knowing too much, had to be disposed of. Yes, with luck, it just may be that Grant has slipped up, because, unless I miss my guess again, Brentford, who could be Brent, should have been blown to pieces.'

'You may have something there, Mac,' said Roy, 'so the quicker we get to Norfolk, the sooner we find out.'

Within minutes, they were hammering towards Norwich, Jimmy driving, Mac and Roy earnestly plotting in the back.

An hour and five minutes later, they pulled into the car park at the back of the police station, and a few minutes later came face to face with Inspector Mike Graham, who was coming out to meet them.

'Mike, me old mate,' Roy greeted his old friend warmly, 'good to see you in the flesh again, how long has it been?'

'Lord knows, Roy, too bloody long and it's good to see you again, me old chum,' said Mike, enthusiastically grabbing Roy's hand and pumping it up and down vigorously.

'This is my sergeant, John Macdonald and DC Jimmy Finch,' lied Roy.

'Nice to see you both,' nodded Mike to both men.

'Sir.'

'Show us what you have then, Mike,' said Roy, hating like hell to have to lie to an old friend.

'OK, well, the handkerchief was definitely used for chloroform - what for, I haven't a clue - and the note is stranger still. It looks like a list of instructions, but again I don't know, maybe you can make sense of it,' said Mike.

'Only one way to find out and that's to have a look see,' said Roy.

Mike led the way to his office and once there, opened a desk drawer, taking out the handkerchief and the note along with the keys and coins. 'That's the lot, apart from what he was wearing.'

'Exactly what happened, Sir?' Mac asked respectfully.

'Well, from what we can make out, Sergeant, we think a woman planted the bomb just minutes before this Brentford chap went into the phone box and the thing just blew up - at exactly two o'clock, by all accounts.

At the mention of a woman, Mac and Roy glanced at each other.

'How big was the bomb?' Roy asked.

'Now there's a funny thing. There was enough to blow him to tiny fragments, but according to Captain Raymond, the bomb disposal chap, Brentford was standing too close to it, like they do in fairground stunts,' Mike replied.

'So what are you telling me, is this bloke still in one piece?' Roy sounded incredulous.

'Virtually, old son, the death blow was apparently on the back of the head, thanks to him being slammed against the phone box door. Had he been a bit closer, he would have walked away with nothing more than a slight concussion, possibly damaged eardrums and maybe a bleeding nose, according to the captain.

'I didn't know that,' said Roy, slight bemused. 'I don't think I'd like to try that trick, not for a queen's ransom, how about you, Sergeant?'

'As Sam Goldwyn said, include me out,' Mac grinned. 'How about you, Jimmy?'

'I find I have an allergy to dynamite, I'm afraid,' said Jimmy. 'Ever since me granny put too much curry powder in me grandad's chilli con carne and the outside toilet roof ended up on the next door neighbours' pigeon pen.'

Mike grinned at Roy. 'Is he always like this?'

'Never a dull moment.'

Roy picked up the bloodstained note but Mike said, 'Here's a copy from forensics, see what you make of it.' He handed Roy a sheet of paper and Roy read it out loud:

'My Dear William,

You must follow my instructions to the letter. You are now an integral and irreplaceable part of this, our perfect plan to put us both on Easy Street for the rest of our natural lives. As you know, I have prepared everything for you at the A.R. All you have to do is put 'A' in the chair (it will be the only chair). Now read on carefully and follow my instructions to the letter. It is vital that you do this. Also, make sure you do not - I repeat, do not - exceed the times by too great a margin or you will upset my own arrangements, which are too complicated to explain right now.

'Step One: By the time you read this, you will be well away from the house. Time your arrival at the A.R. for 10am.

'Step Two: Park the car in the garage marked 'One'. It is the biggest and ideal for your purpose.

'Step Three: Remove 'A' from the boot and carry same to designated chair, using the same route that we used in the good old days. You will find three Tilly lamps behind the right-hand curtain; you will need them so please use them. We must not have any mistakes.

'Step Four: 'A's position must be secure as I instructed you previously - no loose ends, William (my little joke). By 10.15am, douse and replace the Tilly lamps and be away from there by 10.30am sharp.

'Step Five: Retrace your route until you reach the hidden lay-by. The car must be hidden from prying eyes. This is important and I cannot stress it enough.

'Step Six: The last and most important step of all, William, is for you to walk back to the phone box directly opposite the sub-post office, and ring me at exactly 2pm. I repeat, 2pm. Any later than 2pm, William, will result, I promise you, in you and me remaining relatively poor. The reasons are far too complicated to explain at this time: suffice to say that your compliance with my instructions, especially the phone call, will dovetail perfectly with my own arrangements and ensure that we both benefit to our mutual financial satisfaction.

'One final thing, William. After you have hidden the car, destroy this list of instructions before - I repeat, before - you make the phone call to me at 2pm.

Good luck, old friend. In two days' time it will all be over, then you and I can set forth for pastures new.'

Roy knew from what he had read that the list would be more meaningful to Mac, who had been in on the whole thing from the beginning. But since Mac was now masquerading as his sergeant for reasons of secrecy, Roy had to play it casually.

'He was up to something, that's obvious. Do you mind if we have a copy, Mike?'

'Certainly, I'll have a copy made.' He walked to the door and called out to a policewoman sitting at one of the desks. 'Liz, xerox a couple or three of these right away will you please.'

He returned to his desk. 'I'm expecting fingerprints from the hospital and from the van, though I have little doubt that they'll be a perfect match. The question is, what do I do with the van? After all, this man got himself blown up in Norfolk, but the van is in Lincolnshire.'

Roy seized his opportunity. 'Tell you what, Mike, you pursue your enquiries this end about Brentford, and we'll whip the van back up to Lincolnshire.'

'Why?'

Mac groaned inwardly but Roy was ready. 'Because we think it could be tied up in an ongoing enquiry, concerning The Old Manse. There was a spate of robberies, big stuff, and the villains always used a stolen vehicle, though why they should hire one and leave an address into the bargain beats me at the moment.'

'Getting cocky, flushed with success, I shouldn't wonder,' said Mac.

'That makes sense of sorts, I suppose,' said Mike, 'but it doesn't explain the hanky and the list of instructions.'

Jimmy piped up at that point. 'Sir, it could be that they got ambitious.'

'How come, Jimmy?' said Roy.

'Well, Sir, they could have kidnapped somebody, that would explain the chloroformed hanky, and the list of instructions could be directions as to where the victim was to be hidden.'

Roy feigned an enthusiasm he most certainly did not feel. 'Brilliant deduction, Jimmy.'

Mac groaned inwardly. He could have kicked Jimmy's arse. He would have taken odds on what was to come next, and he was right.

Mike smacked his forehead with the palm of his hand. 'Of course, silly bugger, of course, what's the matter with me! It's obvious now that you've stuck it under my nose, everything points to it and that means, lads, that we keep the van here.'

'But the van's in Lincolnshire,' said Roy.

''Fraid not, old son. Some time ago, there was a right old wing ding with both councils as to who owned the so-called hidden valley. It was eventually proved beyond a doubt by the location of an old river bed that it was in Norfolk, even though everyone, including me at times, as I just did, still regard the border as just by the blown-up phone box. There's even a border sign there that our lot wouldn't take down in a fit of pique.'

'What about a compromise, Sir? There's no reason why we can't work together on the same case,' Mac suggested.

The phone rang before Mike could answer and he picked up the receiver. 'Inspector Graham.'

It was Mr Wincanton, the surgeon. 'Ah, Inspector, I was hoping to catch you in.'

'Mr Wincanton, how can I be of help, or have you got something for me?'

'Well, Inspector, I really don't know. You remember you asked me if the bomb victim spoke before he died? Well, he did apparently.'

Mike's interest quickened. 'How do you mean, Sir, I mean what did he say, and to whom?'

'Well, Inspector, after you'd gone, I realised that if he'd said anything, it would have been earlier, before he became comatose. So I decided to ask the ambulance crew, just in case, and lo and behold, they said yes, he had spoken.'

'What did he say, Sir?' Mike was all ears now, as were Mac and Jimmy, although they could only guess at the gist of the one-sided conversation.

'I have the man with me now, so why not hear it first-hand?'

Another voice came over the line. ''Allo.'

'Hello, Mr er ...'

'Thompson, George Thompson,' said the voice.

'Hello, Mr Thompson. What did your patient say?' It could be very important.

'I can't be sure exactly, but it sounded like Alabama or something like that, followed by Roy.'

'Alabama Roy, are you sure about this, Mr Thompson?'

'As sure as I can be. The man opened his eyes wide, grabbed my arm and said what I just said, or as near as I could make out. In real earnest he was, then he went under again, you know, uncon—'

'Yes, yes, I understand, you're sure he said Alabama and Roy, nothing else?'

'Yes, but not like that, it was more like "Alabama Roy", together, if you know what I mean.'

'Yes, I think I do, thank you for your invaluable assistance, Sir.' Mike replaced the handset. 'Now, what were you saying about a compromise, Sergeant?

'Well, it doesn't really matter, Sir, we can always have the van when you've finished with it, that is, of it's OK with Guv.'

Roy wasn't sure what was in Mac's mind, so he played along with it.

''Sall right by me, you have a murder to solve, we just have a few robberies. Anyway, we have enquires of our own to follow up and this just adds one more. The van can keep. By the way, what was all this about Alabama Roy, or whatever? If you don't mind me asking, that is.'

'Oh, they're the words that Brentford said just before he died, apparently,' said Mike, 'mean anything to you blokes?'

'Not to me, not at the moment,' said Roy, but a bell was ringing at the back of Mac's mind and he gently touched Roy in the small of the back, unobserved by Mike. 'So if it's OK with you, Mike, we'll be on our way. If we do come up with anything, we'll do a swap - you never know, we may even solve a crime between us!' Roy grinned.

Just then Liz came back from the lab with the xeroxed lists.

'Ah, just in time, thank you, Liz,' said Mike as he took them from her. He selected one and handed it to Roy. 'Here you are, if you can make any sense out of it, give me a shout, and maybe we can wrap this thing up.'

Mac hid a rueful grin and thought to himself, 'You think you've got problems, if only you knew what we were up against.'

Roy took the list. 'Thanks Mike, if we do come up with anything at all, I'll give you a bell. As Jimmy said, it could be a kidnap and if it is, it concerns everybody, so if you come across anything, you give us a bell, right?'

214

They shook hands all round and Roy, Mac and Jimmy left.

On the return journey, they passed the devastated phone box and stopped a couple of yards further on. A policeman was on duty by the box.

'Let's go and see what we can find out,' said Mac, 'only this time, I get my rank back.'

Roy grinned at that. 'You can have seniority too,' he said as they climbed out of the car and approached the constable. 'Afternoon, Constable, I'm Inspector Macdonald, this is Inspector Spalding and DC Finch.'

Because Roy was in uniform, the constable didn't question their identities but threw up a salute. 'Afternoon, Sir.'

'Were there any witnesses to this incident?' said Mac.

'I don't know anything about that, Sir, I'm only here to keep everybody away,' replied the constable, 'although I believe the post office people reported it, Sir, so they might know something. Mr and Mrs Willmot they be.'

Mac thanked the young constable and the three men crossed the road to the post office. The bell above the door announced their arrival and the man behind the anti-theft glass looked up and smiled.

Mac smiled back. 'Mr Willmot, I presume,' he said, extending a friendly hand. 'I'm Inspector Macdonald.' He waved at the other two in turn. 'Inspector Spalding and DC Finch. I understand you reported the explosion?'

'That's correct Inspector, but I've already told you everything I know,' Mr Willmot replied.

'Not to us, I'm afraid. You see, we're from the Lincoln Constabulary and we too are very interested in the man who was blown up,' said Mac.

'Oh, I see,' said the old gentleman, 'is he dead?'

"Fraid so, Sir, he didn't last very long,' said Mac. 'Can you tell us what you actually saw?'

'Well, as I told the other inspector, a grey-haired lady came out of the phone box just a couple of minutes before the man went in, then boom, fair shook the building it did.'

'Yes, I see, Sir, but did you see anything before that?' Mac persisted.

'I can't say I did, no, I can't say I did.'

Mac's heart dropped. 'Did the man drive up to the box in a van, a blue van, stop for a minute and then drive away?'

The old man held his chin in a thoughtful pose, then shook his head. 'No, no blue van to my knowledge. The only thing that stopped there for a minute was a car, but only for a few seconds, then he drove off. Well, more like a bat out of hell, I'd say, ruddy noise he made.'

Mac's heart quickened at that. 'Did you say noise, like a sports car?'

'Oh, a sports car all right, only bigger, more special like. I can't bring the name to mind, but I can tell you who's got one like it, Prince Cha—'

'Was it an Ashdown Marsden?' Mac interrupted.

'Good Lord, yes! How did you know, Inspector?'

Mac rounded on Roy and Jimmy, his eyes gleaming. 'Bingo!'

He faced the old man again. 'Can you tell me which way he came from?'

'Oh yes, he came from Norwich way, oh, and there's something else too, he parked in the hidden lay-by.'

'How do you know that?'

'That's easy, Inspector, the road runs straight for four miles or so, and being quiet round these parts, you can hear a car engine gradually disappearing if he sticks to the road. But very often, lovers park there for a kiss and a cuddle and you can hear the engine change tune as they pull in, if you know what I mean. This bloke did it with a flourish, you know, fancy gear changing as he slowed down.'

Mac smiled at the old man gratefully. 'Mr Willmot, you have been more help than you can possibly imagine, thank you very much indeed.'

'You're more than welcome, Inspector, any time,' the old man smiled.

The three policemen took their leave and made their way back to the car.

'You thinking what I'm thinking, Guv?' Jimmy said as they settled in their seats.

'You can bet your three stripes I am,' said Mac.

'What three stripes, Guv?'

'The three I'll give you across your brow with my pet truncheon if

216

you come up with any more ideas in a strange police station,' Mac replied with some sarcasm.

'Guv, if you want to hide something from a thief, you stick it under his nose. The trouble is, he'll find it eventually,' said Jimmy.

Mac dwelt on that for a few seconds. 'You're right, of course, after all, chloroform on a folded handkerchief, a parked van, he would have arrived at the same conclusion, I suppose.'

'I rest my case,' said Jimmy, smugly.

Mac grinned at Roy. 'I get his cheek all the time, especially when he knows he's right.'

'Why don't you chop him off at the knees?' Roy suggested.

'Apparently somebody already has, but we didn't know that, not for ages. We thought he was standing in a hole,' Mac said gleefully.

'Give over, Guv, I am five foot nine, you know,' Jimmy protested mildly. 'I made it by half an inch.'

'And I for one am very glad that you did, old son, but don't let it go to your head, will you,' said Mac. 'Anyway, we're straying away from the point.'

'And the point is?' Roy queried.

Mac rubbed his chin with his thumb and forefinger. 'Well, try this for size. We know that Grant is off his rocker, but we also know that he's very shrewd, very cunning. First of all, he poses as William Brent. Why? To throw us off the scent while the real Brent takes off in the Ashdown Marsden for an unknown destination. Then, when we're out of the way, he gets in touch with the Earl, and tells him exactly what he wants.

'Now, unless I miss my guess, the hire van was also parked in the garage, it's plenty big enough for two vehicles. As soon as we're out of sight, Grant takes the opportunity to hit the road, but to where? Well, I think I know why, if I don't know where, and that is to plant the bomb, which brings me back to the Ashdown Marsden and that list. Put yourself in Grant's place: what would you do if you knew that the law was on your tail? You'd get rid of them if you wanted to move Alison to another hiding place.'

'Guv, something's puzzling me: why didn't he take her earlier?' said Jimmy.

'Two reasons: first, he had to get everything ready at the second hiding place. Second, he didn't expect us so early, and I wouldn't mind betting that put a dent in his ego,' said Mac.

'I'll go along with that, Guv, but where does this Brent fit in?'

'I think that Grant was using Brent as his pawn. After he hatched his plot to kidnap Alison, Brent became essential to the plot as the fall guy, to do all the dirty work. He gets Brent to hire the van, to transport her to the Old Manse; he also gets Brent to take her in the boot of the Ashdown Marsden to wherever she is now, gets him back to the phone booth and then - boom! At least, that's how I read it,' said Mac.

'Dead men tell no tales, eh,' said Roy.

'That's right, dead men don't, but that list does, unless I'm very much mistaken. You see, Grant wanted Brent out of the way, so he gives him a list of instructions, mixes in a little bit of praise for his "good friend's" qualities, and how he, Brent, was essential to the success of the plot. Brent, his ego boosted, goes eagerly along with the plot, probably following the instructions exactly, especially as regards time. Grant was banking on this because he wanted to make sure that he blew up the right man.'

'Go on, Guv, I'm all ears,' said Jimmy.

'Well, picture it in your mind. Brent takes the roadster and a short while later, Grant follows in the hire van, complete with wig and women's clothes. He times his arrival at the hidden lay-by so that he can don his disguise as a woman. He then makes his way to the phone box, plants his bomb inside and emerges just as Brent arrives.' Mac paused. 'Grant then makes his way back to the van, changes back into his own clothes and takes off in the roadster, leaving the hire van behind, complete with Brent's fingerprints.'

'You keep saying Brent, Mac, don't you mean Brentford?' Roy was puzzled.

'WB - Walter Brentford, William Brent, actor. It's the same bloke. Robert Andrew Penton-Fairfax is also an actor, but we're getting away from the point, which is that it's now perfectly obvious to me that the list holds the vital clue, or clues, as to Alison's whereabouts.'

'In the light of your theory, Mac, it must do, so let's get to it,' said Roy, producing a copy of the list.

'Just before he died, Brent managed to gasp out two words, "Alabama Roy". What do we make of that?' said Mac.

'He could have been trying to say something else, Guv, after all, he'd been blown up so he wouldn't have had full control of his speech,' said Jimmy.

'Precisely, Jimmy, so what exactly was he trying to say?'

'Search me, Guv.'

'I'll tell you something else,' said Mac, 'the Ashdown came in from the general direction of Norwich, so I'll bet my last quid that Alison's hidden somewhere in that region.

'So what happens now?' said Roy.

'First things first. We drive to Lincoln to brief our actress for when Grant puts his Swiss call through. Also, I want to phone Jan and give her the contents of this list. If anyone can make sense of it, she can.'

An hour or so later, Jimmy pulled into the police station at Lincoln. All three disembarked and went inside to Roy's office.

'Can I get a private line without anyone eavesdropping?' Mac asked Roy.

'You can if I'm by the switchboard,' said Roy, 'give me a couple of minutes and I'll buzz you.' He disappeared through the door and two minutes later, the desk phone rang and Mac answered.

'Mac, when you hear a click followed by a continual buzz, dial your number, OK.'

'Thanks, Roy.'

Two minutes later, Mac was speaking to Jan. 'Hello luv, it's me.'

'Who's me then?'

Mac closed his eyes and smiled to himself as he recognised all the signs of one of Jan's send-ups.

'Mac, your husband.'

'Husband, Mac. Ah yes, I seem to remember. Yes, it's all coming back to me now, you're a policeman, aren't you?' Jan replied vaguely.

Mac grinned to himself: better play along, I suppose.

'Course you remember, I'm five feet twelve and a half with a leg on each corner and a penchant for belting Scottish females with convenient memories.'

'I can remember your penchant, but I've never seen your convenient memory,' Jan replied sweetly.

Mac sighed. 'Jan, luv, serious now, OK.'

Jan chuckled. 'OK sweetie.'

Mac read out the contents of the list and Jan wrote them down. She read them back to him to double check. He also told her about 'Alabama Roy' and William Brent.

'See what you can come up with, luv, and phone this number,' he gave her the number. 'I'll phone you back, to stop any eavesdropping, OK?'

'OK, sweetie, leave it to me, what are you going to do now?'

'I'm off to chat up an actress,' Mac replied, mischievously.

'Ooh! Bully for you, lover boy, I hope you get the part you're after,' said Jan with mock peevishness.

'I already have,' Mac chuckled, 'it's alongside a certain Scottish twit with a delightful Scottish accent, who has yet to be tied to the railway lines, you zany character you.'

Jan's voice tinkled with laughter down the phone. 'I love you too, you dozy great flatfoot. Now, what are you really going to do?'

'Set up a Swiss bank at Lincoln's main telephone exchange, that's where the actress comes in; she's an amateur by the name of Joan Caldwell, Jean Calder on stage. She works as an operator at the exchange, which is a massive stroke of luck for us.'

'Do I take it that you're going to bamboozle our liberty-taker into thinking he's rich all of a sudden?'

'Kerect, pudd'n chop, and with a bit of luck, we may put him off balance. He may just be complacent enough to give us a lead as to you-know-who's whereabouts.'

'I do hope so, sweetie. How much time have you got left?'

'Noon, day after tomorrow. Trouble is, he could phone Zurich at any time between now and then, so I want our actress friend to be script perfect by then.'

'OK, flatfoot, I wont keep you. Oh, by the way, I was going to take in lodgers, but I won't bother now that you're still in circulation,' Jan chuckled.

'All right you, I've got the message,' Mac grinned to himself. 'The quicker we wrap this up the quicker I can get home. Jan?'

'Yes, luv?'

'Don't ever change, OK? Bye now.'

Two minutes later, Roy returned and put his thumb up. 'OK, Mac.'

'Thanks, Roy, all arranged, Jan'll be in touch wherever I am.'

'Why don't you go get your Chief to give Jan one of those walkie talkies, Mac, it would save time and be a lot safer,' Roy suggested. Mac nodded his agreement and picked up his walkie talkie. A few minutes later, one was on its way to Jan.

'Let's go and chat up an actress,' said Mac.

'Pardon?' said Roy, raising an eyebrow.

'It's a long story,' Mac smiled, 'let's just get to the telephone exchange.'

Mac and his team, plus Roy, reached the exchange at 7.15 pm, Mac having phoned ahead to the head supervisor that they were on their way. The supervisor introduced herself as Sally Prentice and she took the five men on a tour of the complex.

'We pride ourselves in the knowledge that we can connect anyone, anywhere in the world rapidly, just as long as they have a phone handy,' she told them with pride.

'Struth,' said Jimmy, 'does that mean my mother-in-law can yak my head of at a moment's notice?'

'Only if you pick up your receiver,' Sally chuckled pleasantly.

'Thank gawd for that,' said Jimmy.

Mac grinned at Roy. 'Now we have two comedians.'

He addressed Sally. 'Now then, Sally - may I call you Sally?' She nodded. 'Please don't take offence, but we're only interested in one particular section, but it's for a special reason, so at this point, I must take you into my confidence. I must also ask you please, Sally, not to take this any further. We're trying to trap a very cunning villain and we need your help, plus the help of a very talented actress who, we've been reliably informed, works for you.'

Sally positively beamed. 'Ask away, Inspector, I, that is we, are at your disposal. Please, follow me and I'll introduce you to Mrs Caldwell. I take it you've never met.'

'No, we haven't had that pleasure,' Mac smiled.

Sally led the way through bank after bank of whirring, clicking electronic wizardry, finally coming to a halt behind an auburn-haired woman sitting at a switchboard and busily talking to someone through her headphone. Seconds later, she had made her caller's connection and turned to face Sally, who had tapped her on the shoulder as soon as she had finished. She flashed a dazzling smile at Mac and company, showing near perfect white teeth.

'Joan, this is Inspector Macdonald,' said Sally.

'Good evening, Inspector, I've been expecting you,' Joan greeted them in a lovely, cultured voice. 'It seems that my overrated talents are required,' she said modestly.

Mac took an instant liking to her, as did Roy and the others, Jimmy Finch most of all. He could not take his eyes off her and the feeling was mutual.

'Mrs Caldwell—'

'Please, Inspector, call me Miss or better still, Joan,' she interrupted. 'It's a long story,' she said hurriedly as she saw the puzzled look in Mac's eyes. She took a swift look at Jimmy's face. He had got the message.

'Right then Joan, if we can have some privacy, we'll get straight to it,' said Mac.

'I suppose we could use the rest room, couldn't we Sally?' Joan asked politely.

'Most certainly.'

'You must come too, Sally, we'll need your expert advice,' said Mac.

Sally beamed again and led the way to the rest room. They took their seats round a large table in the centre of the room. Sally ordered tea and biscuits and they got down to business.

'Now, exactly do you want me to do, Inspector?' Joan asked.

'I want you to speak English with a Swiss accent,' said Mac, 'can you do that?'

Joan's eyes widened. 'English, with a Swiss accent? I don't know, I've never tried, I'm not even sure what it sounds like.'

'There's one way to find out,' said Jimmy.

'How?'

'Phone Switzerland,' said Jimmy simply.

Joan smiled gratefully at his moonstruck face. 'Brilliant idea, Mr erm ...'

'Finch, Jimmy Finch, at your service, ma'am.' He beamed happily.

'Thank you, Mr, er, Jimmy, what a splendid idea. We can phone their main switchboard complex and record the voice, then all I need is about ten minutes' practice.'

'I can do that for you if you want to brief Joan, Inspector,' Sally volunteered.

'Would you please, Sally?' That would be a big help, and when you come back, I'll tell you your little part.'

'I'm on my way,' said Sally and she was gone.

Mac fished in his pocket for a piece of paper and handed it to Joan. 'Don't lose it please because you'll need it. Now listen carefully because we've got to get this right when the time comes, or the consequences may be dire. I can't tell you any more than that; I wish I could but I daren't. All I can tell you is that we've got to trick a madman into believing that he's just had two million pounds deposited into his secret account in a Swiss bank.'

Joan took a deep breath. 'You mean everything hinges on me, on my performance?'

Mac nodded.

'I may not be good enough, Inspector, I wouldn't want to let you down,' said Joan anxiously.

'You'll be just fine and dandy,' Jimmy encouraged her, trying to instil her with confidence. 'I just know you will.'

Joan flashed Jimmy a grateful smile. 'Do I get a script, Inspector?'

'Erm, sort of, what we'll do is ask you questions, somewhat similar to what he may ask, and you simply answer. If you get it wrong or it can be improved upon, we'll put it right between us, OK.'

'I'll do my best, Inspector, I should be able to get into the part fairly quickly - it's what I was trained for, that, plus awkward customers on the phone!'

There was a knock on the door and a young lad came in pushing a tea trolley laden with tea, biscuits, sandwiches and cakes.

'Compliments of the canteen, Sir,' said the young lad. 'Tuck in, there's more if you want it.'

'Thank you very much indeed, that's just what we could do with, son,' said Mac gratefully, realising just how hungry he was.

For the next five minutes or so, conversation was cut to a minimum as the hungry men tucked in.

Sally came back at last, carrying a tape recorder. 'Here you are, Inspector, I phoned my opposite number in Switzerland and told her that I needed her accent, speaking English for a stage part. She was most happy to oblige and spoke for five minutes, reading from anything that came to hand. She wished me well in my role and I hadn't the heart to tell her differently.'

'Excellent,' Mac smiled at her, 'thank you, you really are most efficient.' Sally blushed, and Mac turned his attention to Joan. 'Here you are, young lady, go and find yourself a nice quiet spot to practise.'

'May I have a listen first please?'

'Most certainly,' said Mac, switching the tape recorder on.

Everyone listened to the heavily accented voice as they looked at the intense concentration on Joan's face. After a couple of minutes she began to relax and nodded imperceptibly. She switched off the machine and stood up. 'Give me ten minutes, Inspector, fifteen at the most, I should have it by then.'

She picked up the tape recorder and left the room, giving Jimmy a quick glance. He gave her a reassuring smile.

Mac had noticed the rapport between the two and was slightly concerned because he knew Jimmy's marital history. In spite of his jokey reference to his mother-in-law, Jimmy had recently suffered a very dirty divorce. He was the innocent party and had been very badly hurt.

'Either I'm going to lose a son or gain a daughter,' he mused. Still, it was none of his business. He shrugged his shoulders and turned to Sally..

'Sally, do you know The Old Manse by the park?'

'I can't say I do, but I know the park.'

'Can you tell me which section of the switchboard a phone call from the park area will come through to?' said Mac. 'It's imperative we intercept that call when it comes in.'

'This call you're expecting is the man calling Switzerland, right?' Mac nodded.

'And you want to intercept and transfer it to our switchboard, away from the satellite?'

'Absolutely correct, Sally.'

'Then we'll need an engineer,' said Sally.

Mac groaned inwardly. 'Why do we need an engineer?'

'To trip the satellite relay so that he can wire the call direct to our board,' said Sally simply.

'You mean, without the relay, he can't phone overseas?' said Mac.

'That's right, Inspector.'

'Well, why can't we trip the relay now and make sure?'

'Because there are literally dozens of them handling overseas calls, mainly from businessmen, to trip them all would cause chaos on the switchboard.

Mac groaned again. 'All right, I accept that, so what do we do?'

'Well, luckily, all the relays for the satellite lines are housed in one console, and each relay is for a designated area. An engineer can see any relay at work and know immediately which area the call is coming from.'

'Then what?'

'To keep it simple, the engineer has on headphones connected to what he calls his box of tricks, or snooper box. A couple of wires with crocodile clips on the ends run from this box. As soon as the caller starts to dial, the relay begins to the operator and as overseas calls have a fairly long number, the engineer has time to clip on his crocodile clips and listen in,' said Sally.

'But that'll be too late!' said Mac in alarm. 'By the time the caller has started speaking, it will be to Switzerland and that's precisely what we're trying to avoid.'

'That's true,' Sally frowned, 'unless he checks for numbers, and that may be rather difficult.'

'How do you mean?'

'Well, you may or may not remember the old-fashioned relay system I'll explain it to you simply. A finger or stylus used to move up and down a set of contacts, nought to nine, picking out whatever number you dialled, simply by obeying a seat of impulses sent out by the caller's phone. An experienced engineer could tell you what number was being dialled, just by observing where the stylus stopped.'

'And the new system?'

'Micro chip, and very much smaller, I'm afraid. Everything happens inside a little box now instead of a big relay, all very compact and more efficient than the old Strowger system.'

Mac furrowed his brow, then he had an idea. 'Didn't you say that each relay covered a certain area, Sally?'

'I did, yes.'

'Then all we have to do is keep an eye on one certain relay.'

'Erm, not quite, Inspector. Sometimes two or more use the same overseas line at the same time - though not very often, I might add - so a 'change over' system is built in. Let me explain. If two or more people are trying to use the same line at the same time, the calls are automatically transferred to another stand-by line. The delay is around half a minute only.'

'That delay could come in handy,' said Mac thoughtfully. 'Now what can you do about picking out the numbers as they come through?'

Sally closed her eyes and thought for a moment. 'I wonder,' she murmured. Suddenly she snapped her fingers. 'The box of tricks!'

'Pardon?'

'When the new system was installed, a digital display was designed to make sure that everything did what it should whenever a caller dialled,' said Sally. 'We tried all sorts of ways to trick the system to see if it would dial the wrong number, and once or twice we won, but it only served to show us where the faults lay and they were quickly rectified.' said Sally. 'It should do the trick, but it takes about ten to fifteen minutes to install.'

'Have you still got this box of tricks?'

'Now that, I do not know. It may be gone by now, but if it isn't, it's in the spares stores gathering dust. The system here is so good, you see, the box of tricks is hardly ever needed, unless of course there's a major breakdown at an outside source, such as a junction box being hit by a car, or struck by lightning.'

'Sally, if you can find this box, can you get it installed without causing too much fuss?'

'I don't see why not, if it helps to catch a madman.'

'Will you lay it on with as little fuss as possible, and while you're doing that, we can coach Joan.'

'What happens if the call comes through and the engineer hasn't quite finished his looping in?'

Mac cursed inwardly, he had completely overlooked that all too real possibility. He smiled wryly at Sally. 'Thanks, but it was a temporary mental aberration, Sally, I'm not normally given to these memory lapses believe me. Anyway, I have very good reason to believe that he won't call for some time yet. Nevertheless, thank for reminding me. Now, please give me a call when the engineer has everything rigged - assuming, of course, that you can find your box of tricks.'

'If we don't have it here, Inspector, don't worry, we'll find one somewhere. In any case, I can let you know within a few minutes,' said Sally. As she turned to the door, she spoke over her shoulder. 'If I'm not back in five minutes, you'll know that I've found one.'

'Thank you,' said Mac as he sat down, realizing just how weary he really was.

Jimmy had noticed too. 'Why don't you get your head down, Guv, for half an hour? We can help Joan, if only to give her some practice on the accent. You can take over afterwards.'

'I second that,' said Bob, 'after all, it's no good trying to do two things at once is it, trying to learn the accent and a script.'

'Go ahead Mac,' said Roy, 'the lads are right, you have to keep an edge on this creep, and you did have, as you so beautifully put it, a mental aberration.'

'Don't worry, lads, I haven't run out of steam just yet, the adrenaline will flow when it's needed,' said Mac testily.

Joan came back at that moment, and Mac was glad of the welcome distraction.

'Ah, you're back, how did it go?' he gave her a big smile.

'Quite vell, thank you,' she replied, 'in fect, very vell, I think.'

Mac's eyes widened, and his jaw dropped slightly: the accent was impeccable.

''Strewth, who just walked in, Greta Garbo?' said Bob.

'Sounded more like that other one to me, you know erm ...' said Jimmy, snapping his fingers as if trying to remember.

'Anita Ekberg? said Terry, joining in the spoof.

'No, no, the other one,' Jimmy persisted.

'Ursula Andress?' said Terry.

'Ah, I've got it!' said Jimmy triumphantly. 'Paul Robson.'

Joan blushed in embarrassment and took a half-hearted swing at Jimmy's wickedly grinning face. He hurriedly ducked as the others burst out laughing.

'Only kidding, luv, only kidding!' he yelped. 'You were terrific, honest, I mean that, just great.'

Mac positively beamed, his exhaustion temporarily forgotten. 'That's the truest thing he ever said in his miserable life, Joan. I think we're halfway home, yes, I think our friend is going to swallow the bait hook, line and sinker.'

'Thank you, Inspector,' said Joan, 'I hope I can justify your faith in me.'

'We think you'll do just fine,' said Roy, 'so why don't we all sit down and try an actual conversation.'

For the next half hour of so, Mac and the others plied her with the sort of questions that Grant was likely to ask her. When Mac called for a rest, Joan tentatively asked how they rated her performance.

'Why don't you judge for yourself,' said Jimmy, grinning from ear to ear. 'I've been taping your performance while you weren't looking.'

'You haven't!'

'I have.'

'You sneak!'

'Don't care,' Jimmy grinned wickedly.

'All right you two,' Mac smiled, 'you'll be fighting next. Push the button, Jimmy, and let's see if the lady has won an Oscar.'

Jimmy pressed the rewind button. All eyes were on the tape recorder - all, that is, except Jimmy's and Joan's. They had eyes only for each other.

Everyone listened intently to the end of the recording. For two seconds there was silence, then sudden, spontaneous applause from the men seated at the table, with Jimmy clapping more enthusiastically than the rest.

'Excellent, excellent!' Mac enthused.

'I can honestly say that you would have fooled me one hundred per cent, I really mean that,' said Roy sincerely.

'Fantastic,' Bob Saunders agreed.

'Beautiful, first class, well done,' said Terry.

'Thank you, gentlemen, you really are most kind,' Joan smiled, then she looked at Jimmy, her brow raised slightly in question.

'Now that,' said Jimmy emphatically, 'has got to be the best Paul Robson I've ever heard.'

Joan smiled at him, knowing full well what he meant this time.

Just then Sally popped her head round the door. 'All rigged up, Inspector, ready when you are.'

'You found the box of tricks then, Sally? Good girl. Come on, you lot, let's see what we have so we can work on a plan of action.'

They all trooped out behind Sally, who led them to another room. The engineer was standing by his equipment and Sally introduced him as Bill Williams.

A table had been placed by the console of relays, with various wires running down to a large box which had been placed on the table. Every few seconds or so, sounds came from the console

228

and numbers flashed up in orderly rows in the box's visual display.

'I see you've made the connections then, Mr Williams, any problems?' said Mac.

'A couple, Inspector, but that was human error rather than the fault of the machine. It's OK now though,' the engineer replied.

'Good man, now, can you show me how this little lot works?'

'Certainly.' Williams pointed to the console. 'There are forty eight relays in there, numbered one to forty eight, and here,' he pointed to the box on the table, 'we have twelve digital read-out liquid crystal strips, each can take up to twenty numbers. Now, the first number tells us which relay is being checked. The next three numbers tell us where the call is coming from - by that I mean the district. There'll be a two digit space, then the next four digits show where the call is going to, the country that is, followed by the actual district and phone number.'

'Yes, I see, so if a call was being put through to Switzerland, how quickly could you check it?'

'Well, if I was looking for a call to Switzerland, first I would look up the code in this book,' said Mr Williams.

'It is,' said Mac, 'a call to Switzerland, I mean.'

'Well, that simplifies things. So I look in the overseas code book.'

He opened a small suitcase, took out an official-looking book and flipped through the pages until he found what he wanted. 'There we are, Inspector, the code for Switzerland.'

Mac took out his notebook and opened it. 'Will you write this number down, Mr Williams, because this is the call I must intercept before it's completed. I can't emphasise enough the importance of this interception. Now, Mr Williams, can you intercept this call and transfer it to the switchboard here before the dialling has finished?'

'Yes, it's possible, I think I can, but I'd have to wait until the last digit had been dialled to be certain that it was the right number.'

'That's cutting it fine, but never mind. Now, assuming we have the right number, then what happens?'

'I loop into the call, which puts it through to the switchboard and then trip the relay, otherwise, the call would go overseas as well.'

'Couldn't you trip the relay first?' said Mac hopefully.

'No, if I did that, it would sever the connection, break the link.'

'I see, so how would you loop in?'

'Well, to make absolutely sure, rather than wire into a local relay, which could be complicated, I can bypass the relay and connect directly to a switchboard line. Our little box of tricks here can act as the overseas one,' said Mr Williams. 'Now all you have to tell me is, which part of the switchboard do you want?'

Mac looked at Joan. 'Joan?'

'Oh, my section please, I'm used to it.'

'Right, give me five minutes to run a trace and loop in, then we're all set,' said Mr Williams.

'OK fine. If you and Joan get together on this, I have one or two things to do, so when you have things sorted out between you, I'll be in the rest room with my lads and Roy.'

'Leave it with us, Inspector, Joan and I can sort this out. She can show me where she sits and I'll run a trace. It won't take all that long.'

'Thanks, Mr Williams. OK lads, follow me, lots to do.'

Back in the rest room, Mac waited for everyone to settle down. 'Right lads, let's get organised. First things first. Smithy has been on watch at The Old Manse for hours and he doesn't have a walkie talkie. I want one of you to relieve him. Anyone like to volunteer?'

'I'll go if you like, Guv,' said Bob, 'anything special you want me to do?'

'Yes, one in particular. Jimmy, that gadget of yours, the one you used to pick up our chap's phone call, do you mind if Bob borrows it?'

'Be my guest, Guv,' said Jimmy, 'I'll show him the controls.'

'Thanks, Jimmy,' said Mac. 'Bob, I want to know the very second that Grant starts to dial, use your walkie talkie. It doesn't matter if it's a false alarm, we'll be listening out constantly this end, with our eyes glued to the box of tricks. Take him some food and drink from the canteen. He can get his head down for a bit while you keep watch, OK?

'Right Roy,' continued Mac, 'the relays and Joan's switchboard are a good forty yards apart and out of sight of one another, so we'll have to have walkie talkies at both sites. We can take turns at it, Terry, Jimmy, you and me. Four pairs of sharp eyes shouldn't miss anything.'

'Good idea. Tell you the truth, I'm looking forward to hearing this bloke's voice, which reminds me, we'll need spare headphones.'

'Good thinking, Roy, but I don't think that'll be a problem so let's have another look at that list.'

Mac spread the list flat on the table. 'This A.R. looks like a venue of some sort and A is more than likely Alison. Now, Brent or Brentford is instructed to reach his destination at 10am and he left here at ... let me see, about eight o'clock.'

'That would be about right for Norwich, which is where you said she'd be,' Roy agreed, 'but why are the times so tight?'

'Grant made him stick to the times stated so that he would sure to be in the phone box at exactly 2 o'clock,' said Mac.

'Of course, stupid me, that does make sense,' Roy grimaced.

'I'll give you a buzz, Guv, just as soon as I find the sarge,' said Bob.

'OK, Bob, brief him on what's happened so far, and what's going to happen. If he has any questions, tell him to give me a buzz on the walkie talkie, oh, and just in case anyone does drop in on our frequency, use very guarded language. Do not under any circumstances refer to anyone by name, OK?'

'Understood, Guv, I'm on my way.'

'Right,' said Mac, 'let's get back to this little lot. It says, "Park the car in the garage marked one", which tells me there could be a row of them on the premises. Now ... "Use the same route that we used in the good old days"... Well, they're actors, so this could be a theatre. He also mentions Tilly lamps, so if it is a theatre, it's probably closed down. Do you know any theatres that have closed down, Roy?'

'Can't say I do,' said Roy, 'but maybe Joan can help.'

'I'll go and ask her right now,' said Mac, making a bee-line for the door.

He found Joan sitting at the switchboard, concentrating on the lights. Just as he arrived, a light came on and Joan plugged in. 'Hello, Bill, I can hear you fine ... right, isolate this one, fine ... yes, I'll mark it ... thank you, Bill.'

She smiled at Mac. 'Almost ready, Inspector, oh, by the way, don't forget the time difference between here and Switzerland.'

'Don't worry, we'll be on constant watch anyway. Oh, while I think about it, when our chap phones, he'll be expecting a receptionist, so you'll be a switchboard operator and a bank executive as well.'

'I'm quite looking forward to it really, but one thing puzzles me, Inspector, why did you choose a woman?'

'Why not, Joan? For one thing, quite a few women have made it to the top in banking. And we reckon it'll appeal to our man's ego to try and impress a woman with his new-found wealth.'

'Well, that might make my part easier,' Joan smiled broadly.

'It just might. Now, can you tell me of any theatres or cinemas that have closed in Norwich recently? It could be very important.'

Joan thought for a minute, then slowly shook her head. 'Not off hand, Inspector, no. I'm only an amateur with the local repertory company, and we rent an old converted cinema here in Lincoln. I'm not widely travelled, I'm afraid. I'm sorry, I just don't know.'

'How could I find out at this time of night, it's very nearly eight o'clock?'

'Try the theatrical agencies, that is, if there's anyone working now.'

Mac wrinkled his nose. 'Still, I can always look through the yellow pages.'

'Or *The Theatrical Review*,' Joan suggested. 'They advertise in the back pages, ten per cent and all that.'

'Good idea, how can I get hold of one?'

'I have some in my locker, Inspector, they publish once a month, and I have quite a few back numbers.' She got to her feet, 'I'll go and get them for you if you like.'

'Would you please? Thanks, I'll be in the rest room.'

Back in the rest room, Mac explained to Roy what had happened. 'I think I'll give Jan a buzz to see if she has any ideas.'

The walkie talkie crackled into life as he spoke. 'Inspector Macdonald please, this is Jan.'

Mac looked at Roy in mild surprise. 'Now that's what I call timing. He pressed the speak button. 'Jan, I was about to call you.'

'Hello sweetie,' she began, and Mac had the grace to blush, grinning sheepishly, conscious of the smirks on the faces of his colleagues.

'Jan,' he interrupted hastily, 'be careful what you say, there are five or six of these things, all on the same waveband.'

Jan chuckled. 'I wasn't going to say anything to embarrass you,' she said coyly.

'It's what you don't say that's embarrassing, you she-devil.' Mac tried to keep his voice low enough for her ears only.

Jan's tinkling laugh came over the airwaves. 'I've got something for you.'

'There you go again,' said Mac in exasperation, 'you're still at it.'

'What did I say luv?'

'It's not what you say, it's the way you say it, you ... you Scottish Siren, you,' said Mac, half forgetting that Terry, Jimmy and Roy were still listening.

'Mary had a little lamb, she kept it in a bucket, and every time the lamb got out, the bulldog tried to—'

'Jan!' Mac exploded.

'—put it back,' Jan finished.

'What are you trying to do to me?' Mac groaned, trying not to burst out laughing.

The sound of muffled laughter behind him made Mac whip round, his face stern; but his eyes gave him away. Roy's head was bowed, one hand across his brow, shoulders shaking as he tried to suppress the laughter that was erupting from his body like a volcano. Mac shifted his gaze to Terry and Jimmy, who both looked as if butter wouldn't melt in their mouths. Jimmy was concentrating on something on the ceiling, while Terry was trying to outstare his toe cap. Mac shifted his gaze to all three in turn, nodding his head knowingly. Slowly, he raised the walkie talkie to his ear again, still looking from one to the other. 'All right, Jan, just what have you got for me?'

At that, Roy, who couldn't contain himself any longer, spun on his heel and made a rapid exit from the room. 'I must go to the toilet,' he said in a quavering voice. Strangely, Jimmy and Terry also felt the need to go, and all three rapidly departed, shutting the door behind them.

.As soon as they were outside, they all howled with laughter. Inside, Mac, in spite of himself, laughed too. 'OK, what did you come up with, luv?' he asked Jan once he'd composed himself again.

'I've studied your list. This A.R. is obviously a venue of some kind, but the thing that stands out, the clue if you like, is the phrase, "at the A-R". It's like "at the race track" or "at the cinema" or - and I think this one takes the prize - "at the theatre", get it?'

'Yes, I think I do, anything else?'

'This chap in hospital, you said that he said something like "Alabama Roy". Let's look at it properly, from his point of view. From what you've told me, his injuries were pretty severe and one of the most damaging was a massive blow to the back of the head. Now, if I'd had a smack like that, I'd be pretty well inarticulate, don't you agree? So anything I tried to say would probably come out different from what it should be.'

'That's what we thought ... and?'

'Well, luv, this chap in the hospital and the grouse filcher, they're both actors, and it says in the list "Using the route that we used in the good old days". Now that tells me the place is, or was, a theatre.'

'We came more or less to the sa—'

'Let me finish, luv. So, armed with this information, I did a bit of checking on theatres in the Norwich area and lo and behold, I found one that had closed recently.'

Mac's pulse raced as he heard this. 'Don't keep me in suspense, luv, tell me the name, because that's where Alison is, I'm sure of it.'

'Alabama Roy.'

'What?'

'Or, with the full use of your facial muscles, Alhambra Royal.'

'That's it, Jan,' said Mac excitedly, 'that's got to be the place! And that's exactly where I'm going now. Thanks a bundle, my love, must go. By the way, Jan, I love you and I don't care who's listening.'

'I'm listening sweetie, and that's enough. Now away wi' ye, go rescue our damsel in distress, over and out.' The set went dead then started up again. 'I love you too, pea brain.' Click.

Mac chuckled at that. 'Women,' he thought to himself, 'they just have to have the last word, bless 'em.'

The three men trooped warily back into the rest room, waiting for the eruption. Roy got his ha'p'orth in first. 'That's a rare woman you have there, Mac, she sounds like a lot of fun, even if it is at your expense.'

Mac had the good grace to grin at him. 'I wouldn't be without her, even though she runs me ragged sometimes. She has one hell of a brain, very shrewd.' He then repeated his conversation with Jan, and although they had caught most of it on their own sets, they listened with avid interest.

'Phew, we've got to get to the Alhambra just as soon as we possibly can then, otherwise ...' Roy began.

'Whoa, hold your horses, we just can't desert the place. At least myself and one other has to stay here just to listen in, and help Joan along too. Grant may try a few red herrings to trip her if he gets suspicious - going on his form, he'll probably do just that. Don't forget, Smithy or Bob will be listening on Jimmy's gadget to see if Grant picks up his phone, and a presence here is our edge over him.'

'Mm, sticky, what do you suggest?' said Roy.

Mac though for a few seconds. 'Well, I don't think our friend will phone Switzerland tonight, the odds are against it, because it takes time to put the wheels in motion to shift two million pounds from one country to another. I'll take bets on Grant having checked them out, that's why he gave us the forty-eight hour time limit. I tell you what, Roy, you and Terry hold the fort here, I'll take Jimmy with me to Norwich. I'll brief Smithy and Bob by walkie talkie on the way, OK?'

'Sounds fine to me, Mac, it's about the only thing we can do with our scant membership.'

'Right, let's not waste time, skates on, Jimmy, we've a fair way to go.'

A few minutes later, Mac and Jimmy were racing towards Norwich, taking the route past The Old Manse.

Mac switched to 'speak' on the walkie talkie. 'Smithy, Bob, do you read me, over?'

'Guv? This is Bob Saunders, I think something's up!'

'How do you mean?'

'Well, I've tried to locate the sarge with my beeper, but he's nowhere to be seen at The Old Manse.'

'What! But ...'

'Hang on, Guv, there's more. I thought at first he'd gone to the phone box at the edge of town, you know the one, to get in touch with you, Guv, him not having a walkie talkie. Well, to cut it short, he wasn't there, but I started to receive a faint beep on my beeper, just as you called actually.'

'Are you still at the phone box?'

'Yes, Guv.'

'Stay there, we'll be with you in a few minutes. Out.'

Mac spoke rapidly. 'Clog it, Jimmy, Smithy may be in trouble.'

'Fasten your seat belt, Guv. We're about to go through the sound barrier.'

Some minutes and four scorched tyres later, they reached the phone box and came to a screeching halt. Mac was the first out of the car. He raced to Bob Saunders who was listening intently to his beeper. 'Hear anything?'

'I think I can hear his voice, but it could be my batteries are a bit duff. Try yours, Guv.' Mac and Jimmy switched on their sets with the same negative results.

'Guv, I hate to be the pessimist,' said Jimmy, 'but it could be that Smithy's batteries are low, which means he could have been trying to reach us for some time.'

'Which means he may be injured or stuck somewhere, is that what you're saying, Jimmy?'

''Fraid so, Guv.'

Mac frowned and paced up and down once or twice. Suddenly he snapped his fingers. 'Bob, you couldn't hear him beep at The Old Manse, but you could here, so we're going in the right direction if we carry on towards Norwich, right?'

'Let's go and get him before his batteries run out,' said Jimmy, who was already making for the car.

They drove rapidly for about half a mile, checking with their beepers. As they got louder, Mac thought he heard Smithy's voice.

'Stop the car Jimmy, I can't hear anything above the noise of the engine.'

Jimmy stopped the car and cut the engine. Mac got out and pressed the speak button on the tiny handset. 'Smithy, can you hear me?'

A very faint voice answered. 'Help me, somebody, I'm trapped in the car.'

'My God,' said Mac, 'where are you Smithy, have you any idea?'

'It's a bit hazy, but I think I'm about a mile out of town, towards Norwich. I'm upside down in a ditch. I can't get the door open and my foot's trapped. I can't hold on much longer, my head hurts and—!' The beeping stopped.

'Smithy, Smithy, talk to me,' Mac shouted at the handset.

'It's no good Guv, he's fainted by the sound of it,' said Jimmy, biting his bottom lip. 'He said a mile didn't he? Well, he must be close by so let's drive on a bit further, Guv, eh.'

They drove slowly for a few minutes, scanning from left to right. Suddenly Mac spotted something. 'There's the start of a ditch on the left, drive as close as you can, Jimmy.'

'Guv, there it is, look where the turf's ripped up!' Jimmy shouted excitedly. 'And there's broken glass.'

They halted at the injured turf and Mac was first out of the car, dashing to the edge of the ditch. 'He's here, come on you chaps, let's get him out.'

'Shouldn't we call an ambulance, Guv?'

'No, not yet anyway. If he's badly injured, then that's different. Look, let's get him out first and then we'll know. Don't get me wrong, you blokes - we don't want to blow it at this stage in the game, but if Smithy needs an ambulance, he'll get one.'

They extracted the big man from the wreck after Jimmy smashed the rear window. He and Bob crawled in and while Bob took Smithy's considerable weight, Jimmy managed to slide the driver's seat back to free the trapped foot, then he undid the seat belt. Between them, they got Smithy out without causing him any more damage, getting him up the steep bank with Mac's help.

Smithy was beginning to revive by this time and, with the help of a little hot tea from Bob's flask, he was soon complaining about his sore foot.

'Are you all right, old son, anything broken?' Mac asked with great concern. 'Do you need an ambulance?'

'No, Guv, I don't think so, just shook up a bit, that's all. Me foot hurts though, but nothing broke, I don't think,' Smithy replied shakily.

'Can you stand up do you think, Sarge?' said Jimmy.

'Help me up and we'll soon find out.'

They helped him to his feet and supported him as he tried his weight on the bruised foot. Smithy winced. It held his weight but was too painful to stand on for long.

But Smithy had something else on his mind. 'Help me to a seat of some sort so I can clear my brain, I've got something urgent to tell you, Guv!'

CHAPTER THIRTY-TWO
GRANT'S HAND IS FORCED

Grant drove rapidly away from the hidden lay-by. He had to get back before he was missed. He arrived back at The Old Manse at about 4.30 pm and quickly parked the roadster in the garage at the back of the house.

Once indoors, he ran upstairs to the top floor and, going from room to room, he carefully peered through the windows, looking for any sign of a policeman on the street side and the park side. Finally, satisfied that he was not being observed, Grant made his way down to the lounge and poured himself a drink. He took it to his favourite armchair and, once seated, inserted a cigarette into a slim, elegant holder, lit it, and took a long satisfactory drag before exhaling the blue smoke luxuriously.

He cast his mind back to the events of the past week: how he had impersonated Alison at the hospital and at Hamilcourt with no one the wiser. How he had gone upstairs as Alison, then come down as himself, with no one realising that Alison was already missing and, in the space of two hours, had been swiftly transported in the hire van to this very house. Then, under the very noses of the police from not one but two constabularies, Alison had been spirited away again.

The police obviously knew by now who was responsible for her abduction but were powerless to act against Grant because, at the moment, everything was purely circumstantial. No one apart from Brent had seen the abduction and the good lady certainly wasn't here ... The police even thought that he was Brent, because he had carefully avoided being photographed for years when this present kidnap plan was being formulated. He had even instructed Brent to destroy all known and any subsequent film stills - in any case, it had been many moons since he had been asked for one personally.

Grant congratulated himself on how cleverly he had manipulated the police, Brent, Alison and Robin. Yes, he knew that Robin had fingered him to the police, it was inevitable, but it would make no difference to the outcome: his expert manipulation of everyone concerned would see to that. Nobody could, or would even dare try to make a move against him because of Alison's safety and Grant would make sure that they did not find her until he was ready.

Tomorrow he would phone Switzerland, not once but twice, a few hours apart. This was necessary to be certain that the money really was deposited, because whoever was on his tail was a darn slight more intelligent than Grant had given him credit for. So be it, he would have to be a little more careful in future.

Grant's reverie was interrupted by the sound of the front door knocker. He frowned and stood up. Opening the door, he was mildly surprised to see the paper boy. The boy visibly cringed in Grant's presence.

'Well, what can I do for you?' Grant growled. 'Why don't you drop the paper through the letter box like you usually do?'

'I'm-I'm- Please, I have to c-collect your money or I can't l-leave you a paper, Mr Baker says so,' the boy stammered, 'you're three weeks in arrears.'

Grant almost exploded at the effrontery of the stupid man, but then he thought better of it. 'Oh, I'm sorry son, I'd completely forgotten all about it. Come in, lad and I'll go and get you some money,' he smiled.

The paper boy relaxed and gently exhaled the breath he had been holding unconsciously, waiting for the explosion. He managed a tentative smile and followed Grant into the house, halting just inside the door. Grant disappeared from sight to return a minute later with a five pound note.

'Here you are, son,' he said, holding out the fiver.

The lad took it and offered Grant the early evening paper. Grant unfolded it to look at the headlines while waiting for his change. He scanned the front page from top to bottom quickly, then his eyes moved to the stop press. Suddenly, his heart missed a beat as the little block of news leaped out of the page at him.

'MAN BLOWN UP IN MYSTERY PHONE BOX EXPLOSION. POLICE SAY VICTIM STILL ALIVE THOUGH UNCONSCIOUS. FULL STORY, LATE EDITION.'

The shock almost put Grant out of gear, but he quickly recovered his composure and his brain began to work rapidly.

'Excuse me, Mister.'

Grant came back to earth at the sound of the lad's voice.

'Er what?'

'I haven't any change,' said the boy nervously.

Grant was thinking hard, he had to get away from here quickly to remove Alison. Although he had looked carefully for policemen and found none, it did not mean that there wasn't one watching, even now. He made a quick decision.

'No change?' he said with false joviality. 'That won't do, will it? I tell you what, sonny, you do me a favour and I'll give you a quid to go with the change out of the fiver.'

'Cor, thanks, Mister, what do you want me to do?'

'My phone is out of order, so will you phone a taxi for me at a phone box?'

The lad frowned as if trying to think. 'The only phone I know of that hasn't been vandalised is the phone in the launderette,' he said. 'Will I be allowed to use it, Mister?'

'Of course you can use it, it's a public pay phone isn't it?' Grant smiled at him.

'Well, you don't put money in, you pay the man in the cubicle and he puts it in a box.'

'Just show him the money and he'll let you use it, he probably overcharges and pockets half of the money anyway,' said Grant with a knowing wink at the young lad.

The boy smiled. 'In that case, I'll go right now, Mister, it's only a hundred yards from here,' he indicated to his right.

Grant gave him a number to ring and the lad wrote it down in his grubby little note book with a well chewed stub of pencil.

'Off you go son and tell him that I want one as soon as possible at this address.' He felt in his pocket and pulled out a pound coin. 'Here you are, son, as I promised. He gave the boy the coin, 'As quickly as possible now.'

The boy took the money and with a cry of thanks, headed for the launderette. Grant watched him go, then shut the front door. Best to do it this way, they might have a tap on his phone by now. It was the usual thing for the police to do in exceptional cases, and was this not an exceptional case? From now on, any phoning would have to be done from public places other than his own phone, they couldn't tap them all and while Alison was still missing, he could move about fairly freely without fear of arrest.

But in the unlikely event of his being arrested, he had thought about that too. He had deposited letters, sealed with wax, at three different venues, to be given to the press if he didn't phone the holders to destroy them at or before a certain date. The holders were a solicitor, a bank manager and a vicar.

If he was arrested, he would threaten the police and whoever else was involved with these letters, without disclosing their whereabouts, although he would tell them the contents. But it wouldn't come to that; he had them by the short and curlies and they damn well knew it.

The unexpected knowledge of Brent surviving the blast was just a small hiccup and didn't matter a great deal. Even if it was laid at his door, the police still couldn't arrest for the sake of Alison's safety. If they did arrest him, the contents of the letter would soon be front page news. He could picture the headlines:

'COUNTESS OF WESTMINSTER KIDNAPPED, POLICE KEEP SILENT'

They would probably be followed by something about her not yet being found, bumbling incompetence by police and Home Office etc. Who knows, even the government might come tumbling down, but that was wishful thinking.

By the time the taxi had arrived, Grant had already made his plans.

CHAPTER THIRTY-THREE
THE DECOY

'What's this important information, Smithy?' Mac asked. 'Well, I watched the house like you said. I couldn't see whether Grant was in or not, well, not until he came to the door for his paper. I settled down to watch after that, looking through a privet hedge. Not even the owners of the house knew I was there. Well, anyway, Guv, after about ten minutes or so, a taxi drove up, and Grant invited the driver inside. He was inside for about twenty minutes, which I thought was strange, seeing as how it's his living, and time's time and all that.'

'Yes, yes, get to the point Smithy,' Mac prompted impatiently.

'Well, the driver comes out eventually, at least, I thought it was the driver at the time. Even now, I'm not sure.'

'How do you mean?'

'Well, he came out again on his own, looked up and down the street, got into his taxi and drove off towards Norwich, so I thinks to myself, why call a taxi, keep the driver for twenty minutes, then send him away again empty-handed?'

'The crafty swine swopped places with the taxi driver,' said Mac, eyes gleaming. 'The question is, why?'

'That's what I thought, Guv, so I was about to take the bull by the horns and go and knock on his door, but I got saved the trouble.'

'How so?'

'The front door opened and the taxi driver, or his exact double, walked out onto the pavement and stood there for a couple of minutes, just looking up and down, so straight off, I came from behind the hedge as though I lived there - the taxi driver wouldn't know me - and collected my car from round the corner and took off after the taxi. I went about a mile before I spotted it, parked by the side of the road it was, so I stopped my car well back from him.

'I got out and opened my bonnet as if I'd got engine trouble. I reckon I was there about ten minutes, then I heard his engine start up and he began to move away. By the time I got me bonnet shut and me engine started, he was well on his way. I went after him like a bat out of hell and was just catching up nicely when this car coming in the opposite direction suddenly swerved at me. His headlights were on full beam as well as a couple of them spot-lamps on his bumper. I know it was broad daylight, Guv, but all those lights were in my eyes, blinding me. Course, I just instinctively snatched the wheel to the left to avoid a collision, and the next thing I know, I'm upside down in the ditch.'

Mac didn't speak for a minute, he frowned and stroked his chin with his hand, deep in thought. At last he spoke. 'You know what I think, the taxi was a red herring, a decoy. The second man you saw on the doorstep was Grant, wearing one of his disguises.'

'What the hell for, what's he up to now?' said Jimmy.

'I'm not sure, old son, but I think it's got something to do with that empty theatre, and if it is, it could be he's got the wind up for some reason or other. Alison could be in danger if she's there so I think we'd better motor. Are you OK, Smithy?'

'Don't mind me, Guv, I'm feeling better by the minute, but I'm puzzled. How do you know Grant's gone to the theatre, and what theatre are you on about?'

'Long story, Smithy, I'll tell you as we go along. To answer your first question though, try this for size. For some reason or other, Grant gets the wind up back at the house and comes up with the taxi idea to fool you.'

'But he'd have used the phone, Guv, and I'd have heard him wouldn't I?' said Smithy.

'Not if he tipped that paper boy to phone for him from somewhere else,' Mac replied. 'Anyway, somehow or other, he got the taxi driver to act as a decoy and stop where he stopped. This gave Grant the opportunity to get out the Ashdown Marsden to get in front of you, using the back lanes. He probably told the taxi driver to move when he saw four flashing lights. After he ditched you, he probably turned the car round and headed back to Norwich.'

'Cor blimey, Guv, now that you come to mention it, I think I did hear that engine again, even though I was upside down. Cripes, it's all coming back to me now, he was going like a bat out of Hell.'

'And that,' said Mac, now firmly convinced, 'is the clincher. Come on you blokes, let's go and find the Alhambra Royal, it's bound to be in a prominent position.'

Just over an hour and ten minutes later, they arrived in Norwich and after a few enquiries, they located the theatre. 'Park out of sight Jimmy, and we'll do a bit of gumshoeing,' said Mac. Jimmy pulled round the first corner he came to and cut the engine.

'You stay here, Smithy,' Mac ordered, 'you may be a handicap with that foot of yours.'

'Guv,' Smithy growled, 'no disrespects but like it or not, I'm coming. I owe this bloke one, so I've suddenly gone deaf and I didn't hear you say that.'

Mac should have blown his top but did not. 'Didn't say what?' he said, affecting an air of innocence.

'Who's red hot?' said Jimmy.

'Search me, I'm an innocent bystander myself, and I don't interfere with lovers' quarrels, dearie,' said Bob, patting his hair into place in a camp fashion.

Mac shook his head slowly and let out a deep sigh. 'Mutiny yet. If I'd got a yardarm handy, I'd swing the lot of you.'

'Sorry, Guv,' said Smithy, 'but I can block a door off and I don't need my foot for that.'

'OK, I'll let you win this one, so let's get to it eh! Better bring your torches, I think we're going to need them.'

They approached the now defunct theatre from the front and Mac motioned to his big sergeant to guard the front entrance. In spite of a slight limp, Smithy moved swiftly to the glass doors and tried to open them. He couldn't.

Mac acknowledged that he had seen this and motioned Smithy to join them again. The four men moved past the theatre until they found a narrow entrance with a sign bearing the legend 'car park, theatre staff and guests only'. Mac cautiously led the way in, four pairs of eyes darting everywhere, missing nothing. They approached the end of the building and Mac peered round the corner, keeping flat to the wall. He breathed a triumphant 'Ah!'

'Found something, Guv?' Jimmy whispered.

'Anyone got a pair of binoculars?' Mac whispered back.

'Here you are, Guv, I've got me pocket ones,' said Bob, passing them forward.

Mac took them and adjusted them to his eyes. 'Bingo, lads, garages one to seven.' Deep in thought, he handed the binoculars back to Bob Saunders.

'Jimmy, now we can use your talents as a shadow. Go and do a bit of pathfinding, find a way in without breaking in, then give us the nod, OK.'

'Right, Guv,' Jimmy said with relish, 'give us a second to take me shoes off.' They were off in a trice and Jimmy waited for the usual comments. When none were forthcoming, he looked round the faces of his friends. 'Well, nobody complaining then?'

Mac merely grinned. 'Get on with it, Jimmy, if our friend is in there, he'll take one whiff of those and probably come out at a gallop with his hands up, or one hand up at any rate - the other'll be holding his nose.'

Jimmy took his leave with a parting shot. 'I'll remember you lot in my won't.'

'You mean in your will,' said Bob.

'No, I mean I won't,' Jimmy replied, and was gone.

Three or four minutes passed and Mac peeped around the corner. Jimmy was on his way back and when he saw Mac, he signalled him to come on. Mac, Bob and Smithy swiftly followed Jimmy, who led them to a back entrance, stopping outside.

'This is the rear entrance to the dressing rooms, they're in a passage way that lead to a set of steps. I think they go up onto the stage. I haven't looked in the dressing rooms Guv, not without backup,' Jimmy whispered.

'Good lad,' Mac whispered back, 'did you hear anything?'

'Not a bleeding dickie bird, Guv.'

'OK, lads, let us proceed with infinite caution. I suggest we lose our shoes and carry them with us,' said Mac, and proceeded to do just that.

It was Jimmy's turn to take the mickey. 'Have I got time to make out me will, Guv?' he grinned. Mac just smiled and motioned Jimmy ahead and they moved in single file, silently behind him. There was just enough light inside for them to see as Jimmy silently pointed out to them the dressing rooms, four on each side of the passage way and Mac signalled them to take a door each. Swiftly and as silently as possible, they each opened a door and checked inside. Finding nothing, they repeated the exercise on the opposite side of the passageway. Again, nothing.

'Let's go and look up there,' Mac whispered, pointing to the steps. The four men, Mac in the lead, climbed the steps halfway up, and they made it to the top without incident. At the top, it opened out into what could only be stage wings. There were ropes, pulleys, handles, and a hole bank of switches. The shone their torches all around them; still nothing. Mac motioned with his torch towards the stage and they moved slowly forward in single file until they reached the point where the wings ended and the stage began. Mac stopped and listened, trying to accustom his eyes to the gloom. Gradually, he could make out a bare stage with sunken footlights at the front. Mac decided to use his torch, rapidly scanning everywhere, gradually moving forward, the others following suit.

'Two of you, Jimmy, Bob, go and search the seats down there and up in the gallery,' Mac ordered in a low voice, and they departed in different directions.

Mac and Smithy wandered around the stage, looking for anything that would give them a clue. 'Guv, I can smell petrol,' said Smithy, from somewhere behind a curtain.

'Petrol?' Mac said in alarm. A kind of panic welled up inside him as he suddenly had visions of a booby trap, and throwing caution to the winds, he shouted out, 'Stand still everybody, the whole place may be a booby trap, Smithy can smell petrol.'

'It's only a faint whiff, Guv,' said Smithy. 'Hang on a bit, ah, it's here on the floor, come and take a look.'

Mac couldn't smell petrol and crossed to where Smithy was stooping down, shining his torch on the floor.

'Here you are, Guv, something has been standing here by the look of that ring.' He rubbed his finger into it and smelled it, and Mac did the same. It was undoubtedly petrol.

'Who the hell would want to use petrol in here, unless they wanted to torch the place?' Smithy said, puzzled.

A little bell jangled in Mac's head. 'Who indeed, Smithy? How about a man filling tilly lamps, especially if he's in a hurry, or it could have a tiny leak, which is probably more likely.'

'Well that certainly fits, Guv, no electricity and this is still wet,' said Smithy, indicating the floor. 'And somebody's been here recently too.'

Mac stood up and walked rapidly to the centre of the stage.

'Panic over, lads,' he shouted, 'somebody has definitely been here, and within the last hour or so, I'd say. Carry on your search and don't miss a trick. Look everywhere, alcoves, closets, broom cupboards and toilets, everywhere, then bring your lights over here.'

'Right, Guv.'

Mac returned to Smithy. 'We could do with some extra light. Let's see if we can find something, anything at all. Maybe our chap's left his Tilly lamps, if it was him, that is,' said Mac.

They scouted around and their search took them back to the wings.

'I can smell petrol again, Guv,' said Smithy, sniffing the air like a bloodhound.

'So can I now,' said Mac, 'let's take a look round. Look, there's some wickerwork stage baskets or whatever they're called, let's try there.'

As they approached, the smell of petrol got stronger. Both men shone their torches all around them and at the back of the baskets, finding nothing. Smithy suddenly bent forward and took a sniff at one of the baskets.

'There's a strong whiff here, Guv, it's probably inside,' he said and he made a move to open the lid.

'Hold it Smithy,' said Mac suddenly, 'it may be a booby trap, he's a crafty soul is our actor friend, so gently does it, old son.'

Very carefully, Mac searched all around the lid for any sign of wires, cords, anything that could act as a trigger. Finding nothing, he said ruefully, 'Oh well, here goes' and reached forward with a slightly trembling hand to lift the lid.

Suddenly, a hand shot forward and gripped his wrist in a vice-like grip and Smithy growled, 'No you don't, Guv, you're too valuable to lose. If there is a booby trap, I think I know what it is.'

'Steady on, Smithy, that's my drinking arm,' Mac protested.

'Sorry, Guv, no harm intended, but as I said, I've seen a petrol trap before and this just might be the same.'

'Explain, me old son.'

'Well, look at the lid for a start, it lifts up and down while the rest stands still. I know I've just stated the obvious Guv, but let me explain. First, you take a matchbox, open it and take a match out, shut the box then force the match in between the bottom of the drawer and the outer cover so that it's held firmly. Then you tape the box, or in this case because of the weave, you could tie it under the lid with the match head on, two or three would be better, facing the front, get it, Guv?

'Now with your lid shut, the match would be out of sight. Now, in front of the match head or heads, you stick a piece of sandpaper, or get the sanded strip off your matchbox, you can tape it on or, using the wickerwork, tie it on. All you have to do then is lift the lid, pull the matches out further than you need, put your petrol soaked rags or other goodies inside. Now comes the tricky bit. As you close the lid, you put your finger in the staple here and pull until the basket bows outwards, lower the lid gently and then gradually ease the basket back into shape. As it straightens out, the sandpaper touches the match heads and gradually pushes them back into the box, or tries to. See what I mean, Guv?'

'God, I do see what you mean, it would just catch fire.'

'Don't you believe it, Guv, smell that petrol through the cracks? That's over saturation, that is. And another thing: when you lift the lid, you cause a draft and the bloody thing is lit before the lid is halfway up. Your natural instinct is to let go of the lid, and when that happens, the downward pressure as the lid drops forces the flames towards the bloke who opened it, and if he's bending down, Guv, well ...'

Mac took all this in and shook his head at the depths to which some people could sink without feeling, without the slightest pang of conscience, even revelling in the knowledge that they had hurt, maimed or killed.

Suddenly, an incredible idea came into his head. Could it be that Alison was in the trunk? 'Let's take a closer look, Smithy, Alison could be in there.'

'Shine your torch with mine, Guv, we'll soon see.'

Both men bent down very close to the lid and began a minute search. Very gently, they poked and probed, gently scratching at anything that looked foreign to the basket.

'You know, Guv, if you use very fine cotton after the fire has started, the cotton burns almost instantaneously, releasing both the box and the sandpaper strip and they just fall down, leaving hardly a trace of the cotton, if any at all. Now if this was a torch job the arson examiners wouldn't be able to prove a darned thing because the matchbox and sandpaper would be lying willy nilly in the bottom of the basket - if there was any basket left, that is, and if there were any matchbox and sandpaper either. If anyone wanted to torch this place for the insurance, Guv, this is the way to get away with it, especially if he could get a dupe to open the basket late at night. He could pay the burglar to rifle the place, telling him to open the baskets because that was where the valuable stuff was kept. Burglar lifts lid, lid strikes match, match ignites petrol and hey presto, one dead burglar, one burnt-out basket and no evidence. Course, if they had us on the job, they wouldn't get away with—' He stopped suddenly.

'Aha, the crafty swine, here we are, Guv, here it is, or one of them. He's poked the cotton out of sight.'

'Phew old son, that was close, now what do we do?'

'Well, first of all, you stand back while I reverse the process, that is, if you want it open, Guv.'

'If it is booby trapped, I'll stake my life that Grant was here, and so was Alison. What's more, she may still be here, maybe in that basket, so let's see, shall we?'

'Stand back then, Guv, and let the dog see the rabbit,' said Smithy as he pulled at the staple until the front of the basket bowed outwards about half an inch or so. Then very slowly he lifted the lid so that if the matches were touching the sandpaper, there would not be enough friction to ignite the heads. As the lid lifted clear, Mac moved forward and shone his torch. 'The diabolical maniac,' he breathed as the potentially lethal match heads came into view.

Smithy opened the lid fully and rested it safely backwards, breathing a sigh of relief as he did so. Alison was not in the basket.

'Guv,' he said quietly, 'look at this.' He pointed to a small sandbag now resting on the lid, and a round rubber bulb-like object, lying in the bottom of the basket. One end of a rubber pipe was attached to the bulb and the other end sloped upwards with the end wedged into the wickerwork in such a way that it could not be detected from the outside without close inspection.

'See that sandbag, Guv, that cotton would have burned through or snapped when the lid banged down. It would have dropped onto that old motor horn bulb, which is probably an old theatre prop. The bulb, I have no doubt, is filled with petrol and as soon as the sandbag hit it, the pressure would squirt the petrol out of the pipe over anyone standing in front of the basket.'

'Yes, I get the picture. If I'd opened that basket, I would now be a human torch,' said Mac, shuddering at the thought. He patted his big sergeant's arm gratefully. 'Thanks, old son, you saved my life, I owe you one.'

'Aw, cobblers, Guv, you'd have done the same for me.'

Jimmy and Bob arrived on the scene at that point. 'Cripes, is that petrol I can smell? said Bob, moving closer.

'Don't strike a bloody match, for Gawd's sake!' Smithy warned, pointing to the wicker basket. He explained at length what they had found.

'Bloody hell,' Jimmy exclaimed, 'why can't we go and pick this bloody sadist up, Guv?'

'Not enough evidence, Jimmy,' Mac replied regretfully. 'What we have is purely circumstantial if you look at it carefully enough and anyway, if we did finger his collar, what would happen to Alison? He'll swear black's blue that he hasn't touched her and although we're ninety-nine per cent certain that he's got her somewhere, we can't really prove it. We also have to think about the forty-eight hour time limit, less than that now, and what happens to her at the end of it if he's in custody. Also, what happens to us, or rather me, if we blow it. No, Jimmy, we grin and bear it to the bitter end, whatever the outcome.'

'I suppose you're right,' said Jimmy, 'erm, we can't find anything out there, Guv, so what happens now?'

Mac addressed Smithy. 'Leave that lid open for the time being until I think this one out. Meanwhile, let's get back onto the stage, with four torches going, we should be able to see a bit better and find a clue of some sort.'

'What are we looking for, Guv, anything in particular?'

'Something, anything that doesn't look right for a place that's been closed for some months,' said Mac.

Once on stage, they used their combined lights to fairly good effect as they inched forward, eyes glued to the floor. 'There isn't enough dust to show any recent footprints,' Mac muttered as they searched.

They reached halfway across the stage and Bob suddenly stopped dead. He stooped down and shone his torch on something that he had spotted. 'Guv, look at this, they look like fresh screw or nail holes to me, look, there's a tiny bit of fresh sawdust and scratches.'

As the other three added their torch beams, Mac said, 'By your left foot Jimmy, is that a ring, petrol maybe?'

Jimmy shone his torch directly at the ring and touched it with his finger. He brought it up to his nose and sniffed. 'Yep, that's petrol all right, and still damp too.'

'There're four sets of fresh screw holes, look,' said Bob, 'and what's more, this a trap door.'

'Trap door, four sets of fresh screw holes,' Mac mused to himself, stroking his chin. 'Now something could have been fastened there, something that had to be immobile for some reason.'

'Such as, Guv?' Smithy asked.

'Dunno yet,' Mac replied, 'let's take a look down below, we may come up with an answer. The trouble with Grant is, he's so damn cunning. He could be leaving false trails. Look what he left us to find. That wicker basket for instance, an obvious smell of petrol to lead us to it, but what for? He knows that if it went off and hurt somebody, namely one of us, how would we explain our presence here without giving the game away? He knows that we daren't do that. By the same token, if someone did get hurt, he knows it would slow us down, not by a lot, mind you, but that's extra time for him. He knows we can't touch him while he's got Alison, she's his ace card and he knows it. She's the pivot pin: whoever controls her controls the game, for want of a better choice of words.'

Underneath the stage, using their torches in unison, the four men examined everywhere and everything but were hampered by the lack of blanketing light.

'Guv?'

'Yes Jimmy?'

'This is a proper theatre, isn't it?'

'As far as I know, why?'

'Well, I may be wrong, but don't these places have emergency generators, you know, like hospitals do?'

'My God, of course they do! At least most of them do. Well done, old son, let's hope you're right. The question is, if there is a generator, where the devil is it?'

'I'll look on the main switchboard, Guv, if there's a switch marked "emergency lighting", we can trace it back to the source through the wiring.'

'Get to it then, Jimmy. Bob, you're the mechanic, go with him in case you do find it and it needs attention,' said Mac.

After the two men had gone on their search, Mac and Smithy continued the search for anything that looked like a clue. They worked in silence for a couple of minutes, but Mac's mind was turning over.

'You know something, Smithy, this bloke is nerveless, devious and as crafty as a car load of monkeys. Talk about clever - how on earth did he know we were going to show up here? Assuming Alison was here, of course, I mean, his timing is immaculate.'

'He must have had wind of us coming, Guv,' said Smithy.

'Yes but how? We didn't know ourselves until an hour or so ago and we didn't put it out on the walkie talkies.'

Mac stopped as he thought of something. 'Now that's not quite right, Smithy, I did talk to Jan about it, come to think of it.'

'He could have been listening in, Guv.'

'He could have, but somehow I have my doubts. That wavelength is tight and I mean tight enough to have to have the controls locked, because the tiniest knock could blank us out. No, it has to be something else, old son, but what? Brent only got himself blown up at two o'clock. He was in hospital within half an hour and dead within three quarters ...'

'That could be it, Guv, he could have phoned the hospital and found out that Brent was still in one piece and—'

'—not quite dead,' Mac interrupted. 'And he talked, only two words mind you, but it was enough, because he knew what it meant. Anyway, we're here, and he knows that we're here so it makes no difference for the moment. Oh, and while I think about it ...' He reached into his pocket and pulled out his beeper. He pressed the button and spoke.

'Bob, Jimmy, find anything?'

'Yep, there's a genny, Guv, we found the switch and we're tracing the wiring back. From what I can see, it's out the back somewhere.'

'That's what I'm calling about. If you do find it can still be used, make sure all the outside lights are off before you start it up, we don't want to advertise our presence here, do we?'

'Leave it with us, Guv, no sweat.'

Mac pocketed his beeper. 'Stroke of luck for us, by the sound of it, I hope Bob can get it going.'

'You know Bob, he could give an engine the kiss of life if it came straight off the scrap heap.'

'That's true, old son, and if he ever gets fed up with police work, which I doubt, we could dispense with half of the police mechanics.'

Mac flashed his torch around and spotted the wire cage around the lifting machinery. 'That looks interesting, wonder what it's for,' he mused. 'I dare say we'll find out soon enough if we can have some light.'

Mac's beeper sounded and he fished it out of his pocket.

'Guv, we've found the genny, it's a diesel and in good nick, by the look of it. Bob's having a dekko now.'

'Where is it, Jimmy?'

'It's in a brick building by the garages, Guv. There's a diesel in the tank and spare fuel by the look of it. Hang on, Bob's testing the compression with the crank handle, yep, he's nodding OK, and he's going to wind it up. Here we go then, keep your fingers crossed.'

Seconds later, they felt rather than heard a *thump thump thump* that settled down to a barely audible hum.

'Guv, it's working a treat. I'm coming in now to throw the main emergency switch.' Jimmy sounded elated.

'Good work, lads, I'll find our wall switches unless the lights down here are worked from up there,' said Mac.

The lights on the top of the stairs came on as Mac was looking and Jimmy appeared at the top. 'They're here, Guv' and he switched them on down below. Mac blinked as almost total blackness was suddenly illuminated by a dozen or so lights.

'Ah, that's better, good work, Jimmy. Now maybe we can get somewhere, so let's all start on the stage and pick that over first.

As they reached the stage, Bob came in through the wings. 'The generator's on, Guv, it'll run steady until the tank's empty. It's governed to put out 240 volts, so it doesn't require anyone in attendance.'

'Great, now we can work the stage in a straight line, and with this amount of light, we shouldn't miss much. Now, before we start, I want you blokes to imagine that you are Grant, or Penton-Fairfax, to give him his real name. If you had a hostage and you brought her here, where would you put her? Bear in mind that you've put her life on the line, with the deadline at noon the day after tomorrow, using some sort of device that's timed to dispose of her. Now, it could be an explosive device like a time bomb; after all, he left one in the phone box. Now, I'm inclined to think he would use a bomb again, operated by a simple mechanism such as an alarm clock, but he could dream up anything. Don't you forget the lethal job he performed with the wicker basket. This is a theatre, probably plenty of props to give you a few ideas.

'And there's another thing to bear in mind: if Alison was here and set up for the kill, pardon the expression, then it must follow that whatever device he rigged up, it was fairly easy to dismantle and take with him to wherever he's put Alison now.'

'So what you want, Guv, is for us to be as devious, crafty and as diabolically dirty as that bastard Grant?' said Jimmy.

'Exactly.'

'Some would say us coppers are like that anyway,' said Jimmy.

'That's only true for a tiny minority of us, thank God, and I hope only a tiny minority of the public think we are too. It's bad enough having to battle it out with villains without having the worry of adverse public opinion,' Mac observed wryly. 'But let's get on, time's awastin', as they say. Right, let's form a straight line across the stage, starting from the way I think he came in.'

They spent the next ten minutes examining the stage surface, missing nothing. Ring marks similar to the ones Smithy had found were detectable, but only just. The holes in the trap door were clearly evident and obviously recent additions. They stopped looking when they reached the far side.

'Right, so much for that, what have we got?'

'Well, someone's been here for certain,' said Jimmy, 'those petrol rings are fresh, not many hours old, I'd say.'

'That ties in with the note, it mentions tilly lamps,' Mac agreed, 'they must be around here somewhere, unless he's taken them with him. OK, lads, let's take a look below again.'

He led the way below the stage and once again, four pairs of eyes looked everywhere as they descended the steps. At the bottom, Mac took a couple of steps forward and surveyed the scene, the other three men ranged alongside him.

The floor of the stage, which was now the ceiling, was very high, about twelve to fourteen feet. There were various trap doors, two of which had mobile staircases still in place. One had a spiral helter skelter type chute and two more had various fittings fastened either side of the trap door for reasons beyond Mac's comprehension. But the one that interested him was the biggest trap door in the centre of the stage. He walked over to it and studied the machinery that operated it. His eyes took in the big wooden handle on the manual machinery, noting also the four cranking positions, two on either side of the machinery. His eyes wandered to and from both pieces of machinery, a frown on his brow. He called over his shoulder.

'Bob, how does this work?'

Bob Saunders studied the machinery for a few minutes, bending, probing, examining and finally uttering a satisfied grunt. He stood up, smiling in triumph. 'Cracked it, Guv.' He pointed to the first piece of machinery. 'That works from electricity when it's going up, and an adjustable band brake on the way down.'

He pointed to a graduated crescent shaped plate and pointer. 'That's used according to the amount of weight on the trap door above. This machine is manual and is obviously used in case of a fault in the other one. You see this wooden handle, Guv, well that releases the band brake and allows the trap door to fall. You pull the handle back for that, see the connecting rods here? When you let the handle go and as soon as the trap door reaches here, the safety catch trips to operate the brake bands, and, I imagine, well I'm almost certain, that the handle snaps forward and that's why there's a heavy wire mesh guard around it. This bit here is the hydraulic damping system with a built-in adjustable governor, depending how fast you want to fall or need to fall.'

'Very lucid, old son, but something puzzles me: why four handles and why this secondary machinery when we have an emergency generator?'

'Well, in answer to your first question, Guv, once the trap door has dropped it has to be returned as quickly as possible to eliminate accidents, you know, people falling through the hole. So it has to be highly geared for a rapid return, how can I put it?' He snapped his fingers together. 'If you put two gears together, one very small and one very large ... Er, are you following me, Guv?'

Mac nodded. 'Carry on.'

'Well if you use the small cog as a driver, the big one turns very slowly, but if you reverse the process and use the big one as a driver, the small one really whizzes round but it needs a hell of a lot of muscle especially if it has to lift a body back up again - four handles, four strong men.'

'Got it, but why not let the generator do the job instead?'

'This is 400 plus volts, Guv, the lighting is only 240 volts.'

'Enough said,' Mac nodded, 'now, let's get this straight, if that handle is pulled, the trap drops, right?'

'Right, Guv.'

'And that half moon plate is adjustable according to the weight on the trap door, that's what you said?'

'I did, Guv.'

Mac grinned impishly, slowly turned and caught Jimmy's eye. 'How heavy are you, Jimmy?'

Jimmy's mouth dropped open in shocked surprise and he spluttered. 'Fourteen and a half tons, and I've got two wooden legs, with woodworm in one and death watch beetle in the other. What's more, I haven't got a bleedin' parachute.'

Mac and the others grinned from ear to ear. 'Go and find a sandbag before I change my mind,' Mac chortled and Jimmy shot off to do just that. He located a pile over by the wall, picked one up after a struggle, and carried it back.

'Ah, good lad,' said Mac, 'how heavy d'you think it is?'

'Oh, about as heavy as a bag of cement, feels like it anyway. Want me to put it on the trap door, Guv?'

'Yes please, give him a hand, Bob, then come and work this little lot.'

The two men struggled up the stairs and returned a few minutes later, panting from their exertions.

'How heavy is that cement, anybody know?' said Mac.

'A good eight stone, I'd say,' Bob suggested, 'you agree Jimmy?'

'Give or take a couple of pounds,' Jimmy nodded.

'Good, set the gauge, or whatever you call it, Bob, and give me a demonstration.'

Bob bent down and straightened up again almost immediately.

'That was quick,' said Mac.

'It's already set on eight stone, Guv, or near enough. It's on a hundred and twelve pounds.'

Mac raised his eyebrows. 'I thought it might be. Unless I miss my guess, that's the weight of your average female. How heavy would you say Alison was, or still is, I hope?'

'Eight, eight and a half I should think, according to the newspapers,' said Smithy. 'Are you thinking the same as me Guv?'

Mac nodded slowly. 'Do your stuff, Bob, stand back lads, just in case.'

Bob stepped around the back of he wooden handle and with a 'here we go' snatched it back to its full extent before letting it go.

The trap door appeared to drop like a stone until it was over halfway down. The wooden handle snapped back with an almighty 'thwack', as the trap slowing mechanism was tripped and the trap door slowed rapidly down through a sliding scale of negative velocity and coming to a gentle halt which surprised all that witnessed it. The time lapse between the wooden handle coming to a rest and the chair coming to a rest was about seven tenths of a second.

Mac whistled in admiration. 'Phew, now that's what I call a clever piece of machinery. How's your stomach feel, Jimmy?'

'Where me heart is, and me heart's in me mouth thanks, Guv,' Jimmy replied with a sickly grin.

'Never mind, old son, some other time, eh?' Mac grinned back at him.

He then turned his attention to the trap door and the machinery. He backed off a few paces and his face became a study of intense concentration. He looked up at the hole in the stage vacated by the trap door, then down at the machinery that operated the lift electrically and finally at the big wooden handle. He studied for a good five minutes, wagging his finger negatively in the air when someone was about to speak. Suddenly, he snapped his fingers, his eyes gleaming.

'Cracked it, Guv?' Smithy asked tenuously.

'Maybe, maybe not, let's put it through the mangle.' He pointed his finger at the trap door. 'Come on you lot, fresh nail or screw holes, what does that suggest?'

'Something was fastened to it, we're more or less agreed on that, Guv,' said Bob.

'Yes but what, and why this particular door?' Mac persisted.

Jimmy snapped his fingers. 'Blood hell, a hangman's drop!'

'That's what I thought at first when I saw that dirty great handle, but then that trap slows to a stop instead of smashing into the bottom, so if he'd intended a hanging, he would have to measure the exact amount of rope,' said Mac, getting into his stride.

'Unless he intended a slow strangulation, using the victim's own weight, Guv,' said Bob soberly.

'No no no, old son, I had thought about it, but it's not his style, is it? Just think about it for a minute. We know that he likes springing surprises, so if he put a rope around someone's neck, they'd know what was coming, wouldn't they? No, I think he had something else up his sleeve ... but what?'

Bob shook his head. 'I still say a slow strangulation, Guv, it's dead obvious the way the trap drops.'

'This bloke isn't obvious, he's devious, Bob, always coming up with the unexpected. If we're going to catch him and recover Alison within the next thirty-six hours or so, we've got to think like him and what's more, out-think him.' He smacked his fist into his palm.

'You keep looking at that handle, Guv, any particular reason?' said Bob.

'Yes, I have an idea in my head that won't go away. Look, try this for size. Grant fixes a chair to the top of that trap, then he fastens Alison to the chair, we'll say with rope. Now, there's no electricity to operate the lights unless he uses the generator, hence the Tilly lamps. He also doesn't want to raise the rap door, he wants to lower it.' Mac was tapping the wooden handle as he spoke. 'Which brings us to the question, how did he intend to operate the handle when he was many miles from here? Well, I think I can guess: with a piece of rope and some sort of timed release, using one of his clocks.'

'Bloody hell, Guv, it's beginning to make sense,' said Jimmy.

'Right, so let's take a look, shall we,' said Mac briskly. 'First, let's take the amount of poundage required to pull that handle back. What's your guess, Bob?'

Bob curled his mouth down at the corners as he tried to work it out, trying to picture a similar situation. 'Oh, erm, a good hefty pull, say, erm, similar to starting an outboard motor, erm, maybe just a little bit harder than that.'

'How about a sandbag to make sure,' said Mac smiling.

Bob took him up quickly. 'Certainly, a sandbag would do it, but that would hold the handle back and bugger the machinery up.'

'Maybe, but hold hard a minute, take a look here.' He pointed to the end of the wire guard. 'See that?'

'See what, Guv?'

'Don't touch the guard, lads. See that twine wrapped around it there? Look at the knot, it's tight, so tight, that unless you have very good finger nails, you have to cut it if you want to remove the evidence.'

'Evidence, Guv?'

Mac nodded. 'Jimmy, have you got your roll of sticky tape with you?'

'Never without it, Guv.'

'Stretch a strip along here,' said Mac, pointing to the edge of the guard. 'Go along the whole length, over the twine too, and see what dust you can pick up.'

Jimmy pulled out his tape and picked the end free. He pulled out a foot of it, spinning it on his thumb and forefinger, and handed the end to Bob. 'Hold that mate, while I get a length unwound.' Then, having got more than he needed, he bit it off with his teeth. 'Stretch it gently, mate, and I'll follow you down.'

As the two men gently laid the tape along the guard, Mac ran his finger along it, pressing it down firmly. Jimmy then peeled the tape off again, keeping it taut as they turned it over.

'Take a look, Guv,' he invited.

Mac started at Bob's end and sure enough, the dust that had collected on the guard was now stuck firmly to the tape, like a negative image, with the exception of a patch an inch or so in length, exactly where the twine was positioned.

Mac nodded in quiet satisfaction. 'I thought so, Grant fixed this twine and probably cut it in a hurry. The question is, what the Hell was it for?'

He studied the situation for a few minutes, various ideas going through his mind. He looked up towards the underside of the stage, turned around on his heel and walked forwards as he spotted the catwalk. He studied it for a minute.

'Jimmy?'

'Yes, Guv?'

Get up on that catwalk and look for signs of recent visitors, I've got a feeling the answer I'm looking for might be up there.'

'OK, Guv, said Jimmy and he made his way to the cat ladder and climbed to the top. 'Plenty of light up here.'

'Describe what you see, old son, from the catfloor upwards.'

'It's a boardwalk, Guv,' said Jimmy. 'Hang on a bit, I've got an idea.' He stepped backward down the cat ladder until his eyes were dead level with the boardwalk.

'What the devil are you up to now?' Mac was curious.

'Well, you know how you can see a shine on a Tarmac road, especially when you're in a dip? Well, I may be able to do the same here Guv, to see if the dust had been disturbed,' said Jimmy.

'And can you?'

'Gimme a sec, Guv, I've got to get me eyes dead level,' Jimmy replied as he manoeuvred himself into position. After a few seconds he let out a satisfied 'Aha! Thought so, it sticks out like a sore thumb, I can actually see a patch as if somebody's walked about a bit.'

Jimmy paused and lifted his head, trying to pinpoint the spot, but he could not. 'Guv, I lose sight of it when I lift my head, can you come up?'

'Coming,' Mac replied and climbed the cat ladder.

Jimmy climbed up to let him up, then climbed down again. 'Hang on let me get me eye back in,' he said, positioning himself again. 'Right, Guv, go forward.'

Mac moved forward and Jimmy guided him steadily. 'Bit more, Guv, go on, bit more, not quite ... bit more ..., stop, half a step, that's it Guv, you're smack in the middle.'

Mac stood stock still and noted his position before speaking to Jimmy. 'Nice one, old son, that's one for the book, what made you think of that?'

'Something glinted as my eyes were level with the boards and the idea just came to me.'

'Glinted, where?' Mac was more than curious.

'The back of you somewhere, Guv, hang on and I'll see if I can pinpoint it again,' said Jimmy, as he levelled his eyes with the boards again. He failed to see it the first time so he bobbed his head up and down as if he had just climbed the cat ladder. A glint caught his eye then he lost it again. He persisted with the head bobbing until he saw it and held it in his gaze. 'Got it, but if I move my head, I'll lose sight of it. Put your finger down, Guv, and I'll try to guide you.'

Mac bent down and with his forefinger dead straight, he began to point.

'That's no good, Guv, got a pencil?' Mac had, and produced it.

'Right,' Jimmy resumed, 'hold the pencil upright with the flat end downwards, that's it ... now move it away from you, and stop when I say.'

Mac moved the pencil slowly until Jimmy said, 'Stop, that's it, Guv, you've just blocked the light. Now mark the spot and take your pencil about a foot away from me and we'll do the same again.'

Mac did this until Jimmy called a halt. 'Stop there, Guv, you're now directly behind it. Mark that and the shiny bit is somewhere along a straight line between the marks.'

Mac looked closely and Jimmy joined him, but could see nothing.

'Whatever it is, Jimmy, I can't see it,' said Mac, exasperated.

'Mind if I use me tape, Guv?'

'Good idea, tear a strip off.'

Jimmy tore off an adequate strip of sticky tape and very gently stretched it over the two marks Mac had made. 'Run your finger over it Guv while I hold it in position,' Jimmy suggested. Mac did this and Jimmy gently eased the tape off the floor, turning it over. He turned around until the tape was fully illuminated. He then gently twisted the tape to and fro until a glint among the dirt and grit caught his eye. 'See it Guv?'

'I do, old son,' said Mac, as he pulled out a folding magnifying glass. He studied the object for some seconds. 'Well bless my cotton socks, it's a tiny piece of copper wire and what's more, not so long ago, it was inside a plastic cover. It's brand new.' He handed the magnifying glass to Jimmy, 'Take a look.'

Mac held the tape at one end while Jimmy studied the quarter millimetre long piece of copper wire.

'Know what I think, Guv? This bloke stripped a piece of wire to make a good connection. This bit broke away and fell on the floor in such a way that it caught the light, which is lucky for us and unlucky for the bloke who did it. You know, Guv, the odds against us finding this tiny piece of copper wire must be millions to one against.'

'Of course, and if it's true what you say, then Grant could have been assembling one of his precious bombs or—' Mac stopped in mid-sentence and stepped to the rail of the catwalk. He studied the position of the big wooden handle below and ten feet in front of him. He then gradually arched his eyes upwards until he spotted what he half hoped he would find. 'Aha! I thought as much,' he breathed to himself.

'What is it, Guv?' Jimmy ventured.

Mac didn't answer, he strode rapidly down the catwalk and descended the ladder. He made his way directly under where he descended the cat ladder. He made his way directly under where he had been standing and let his eyes travel down. Suddenly, he strode forward as he spotted something on the wall. He let out a cry of elation.

'There it is, by George!'

'Tell us then, Guv.' Bob Saunders was puzzled. 'Don't keep us on tenterhooks.'

'That bastard was going to use a sandbag or something heavy, look here.' Mac pointed to a single wheel pulley hanging by a rope from a staple that was fixed in the wall. 'That's an old pulley, but that,' he pointed to the staple, 'is a recent addition to the wall, you can see the fresh brick where bits have broken away when it was knocked in.' His eyes dropped down, 'and what's more,' he pointed to a distinct ring on the floor, 'that's where he stood a Tilly lamp.'

Mac bent down and picked up the pulley. He walked backwards stretching the rope to its full length. He then looked up and pointed. 'See that pulley up there? He was going to use that and this, plus a long length of rope, to operate the handle and, unless I miss my guess, he was going to operate it from the catwalk up there, using an explosive device to motivate it. He was also going to fix a sandbag on the end of the rope.'

'But that sandbag would hold the handle back, Guv, and I don't think the trap door would work properly,' Bob insisted.

'It would if the sandbag was rigged in such a way, it would part company with the rope when its job was done, enabling the handle to snap back into place as it was meant to,' said Mac.

'But does it matter if the handle snaps back? I mean, would this bloke be bothered whether it did or not, after it had done its job?' said Smithy.

'I think he did want it to snap back to do another job, and I think that is where the twine comes in,' Mac replied. 'But what it was for is something we have to think about.'

'What happens now, Guv? It's more or less a racing certainty that Grant's been here with all this evidence knocking about, but he's certainly not here now, so where is he?' Smithy ventured to ask.

'That, old son, is the burning question, but more to the point, where has he moved Alison to?'

'He could have taken her back to the Manse, I mean, after all, we've been there once, Guv, so I expect he wouldn't think we'd go back there again, what with us looking right mugs the last time,' said Jimmy.

'He's cute, Jimmy, but I don't think he's that cute. No, he's always got an ace up his sleeve, he caters for all eventualities, and you can bet your sweet life that he's catered for this one,' said Mac. 'He's like a chess player, he loves a challenge. We're the chess pieces, with Alison a mere pawn. What we have to do is try to figure out his next move, try to out-manoeuvre him, and this bloke is a master.'

'It's getting on for midnight, Guv, so what's our next move?' said Smithy, stifling a yawn.

'Get back to the switchboard, I think. There isn't a lot we can do tonight so I suggest that we leave everything the way that we found it, just in case Grant does come back; that way, we may throw him a bit if he can see nothing has been disturbed. He may even think that we missed out on this one and it will do his ego a power of good, enough to make him slip up and lead us to Alison, but then, we can all dream I suppose,' said Mac, ruefully.

'What about that wicker basket, Guv? That thing is positively lethal,' said Smithy, somewhat concerned.

'I've thought about that, old son, soak the matches with water and dampen the sandpaper too. A damp match has never worked

263

for me, or anyone else for that matter.' Mac smiled at his big sergeant. 'I used to do that to my grandad's matches. I used to spit on my finger and touch each match head and in ten minutes, Bob's your uncle. It was ages before he cottoned on to me.'

'What happened then, Guv?' Bob was all ears.

'He blew his stack of course and threatened me with all sorts,' Mac recalled with some nostalgia. 'I tried to wriggle out of it though when I offered to dry them out again.'

'And did you?'

'You haven't heard the half of it yet,' said Mac, 'I put the box in the hearth in front of the coal fire to dry out and shut the door to stop the heat from escaping - I was full of brilliant ideas at that age, but I digress. After about five minutes, I pushed the box closer because I thought they weren't drying out quick enough. Grandad had dropped off in his old armchair, by the way.

'Anyway, as I was saying, I was getting impatient and kept inching the box closer until all of a sudden ... woosh! The whole bloody lot went up, startling me so much that I took a swipe at them and they landed, believe it or not, on top of the cat. The cat, as you can imagine, took one flying leap out of the way, clawing his way up Grandad's leg in his haste to escape. The room by this time was full of acrid sulphur fumes and smoke. Grandad woke with a yell that brought Mum running in. She took one look and screamed blue bloody murder and Grandad must have thought he was in Hades. Oh boy, oh boy!' Mac howled at the memory.

By this time, the rest of them were howling with laughter too. 'Haw haw haw! I can picture it I can!' Jimmy spluttered. 'Go on, Guv, what happened then?'

'Well, with Mum screaming, Grandad bawling, the cat screeching and me thinking I'd set the damned house on fire, I scarpered sharpish, yelling blue bloody murder, and hid in the garden shed until things died down a bit. Pandemonium reigned in our house for about ten minutes.'

'I wish I'd been there, Guv, better than going to the pictures,' Jimmy guffawed. 'Coo, I bet your mum made your arse sting.'

'That she did, Jimmy, but I'll tell you one thing, I never played with matches again, no Sir, I didn't,' said Mac with a grin.

Smithy wiped his damp eyes 'I didn't think butter would melt in your mouth, Guv. I'll go and see to those matches before you can get to 'em, you're dangerous, you are.'

Mac laughed at that little joke. 'OK, Smithy, we're all coming up now. I've seen enough to satisfy me for the time being.'

Ten minutes later, everything was left as they had found it . The generator was stopped and Mac with his faithful team emerged from the car park entrance.

Once inside the car, Mac contacted Roy and Terry, telling them of their findings at the theatre. 'Anything happening at your end yet?'

'Not yet, Mac,' Roy replied, 'everything's ready though, but I'd rather you were back here to handle it when Grant picks up the phone.'

'We're on our way now, Roy, so see you in an hour or so.'

'OK Mac, over and out.'

'OK Jimmy, let's motor,' said Mac.

Less than fifty years away, a shadowy figure watched them go. As he listened to the sound of the engine die away into the distance, he slipped a cigarette into a slender holder. He stood and smoked it until the glowing end almost reached the filter, before discarding it by blowing through the holder. The man watched the glowing ember arc through the air until it hit the ground many years away, exploding into hundreds of tiny sparks. He then turned on his heel and melted into the shadows.

Five minutes later, a grey metallic roadster gently growled its way from a side road into the main road. It headed towards the theatre, using the lowest possible engine revolutions. There were no flashing road signals as it gently turned into the now deserted theatre car park and disappeared from sight around the back.

CHAPTER THIRTY-FOUR
THE STAGE IS SET

Mac and his men arrived back at the telephone exchange in the early hours of the morning and Mac immediately sought out Roy and Terry.

'Any developments this end,' he asked Roy, 'any snags?'

'None that we can see,' Roy replied, 'we've checked everything at least twice. The only thing we haven't done is phone in from the outside.' He politely stifled a yawn which Mac did not fail to notice.

'Roy, I'm not trying to get rid of you but why don't you go home, get a good night's kip and I'll see you bright and early in the - correction - this morning. Your wife will be taking in lodgers like Jan has threatened to,' Mac grinned.

'Thanks for the offer but if you don't mind, I want to stay to the bitter end, whatever the outcome. I want to see this bloke caught and if I can have a hand in it, sleep can wait.'

'Come on, Roy, for this bloke, everyone has to be on his toes so sleep is essential. We're all going to get some rest one way or another, so if you're staying, we can sleep in pairs on a rota. Anyway, thanks for the offer, old son, you're more than welcome, and it'll ease the load a bit.'

'Aren't we forgetting something?'

'What's that?'

'Joan, what about Joan? She has to sleep sometime too. She's been on the go more or less since nine o'clock this morning, sorry, yesterday morning and it's now,' Roy looked at his watch, '2 am.'

Mac smacked the palm of his hand to his brow. 'Blast, I completely forgot about poor old Joan. Look, what about the supervisor, Sally whatsername?'

'Prentice.'

'She sounds capable enough to do the job if we brief her the same as we did Joan. If she's agreeable, she and Joan can spell one another,' Mac suggested.

266

'She went home a few hours ago,' said Roy. 'Do you want me to sound her out? She left her telephone number, just in case.'

'Thanks, you do that then and I'll go and see how things are going with Joan,' said Mac.

'Look, Mac, something's puzzling me.'

'Oh? Spit it out, old son.'

'Why are we going through all this rigmarole, you know, fooling Grant into really thinking that he's phoning Zurich?'

'A couple of reasons really, Roy. Firstly, it takes quite a while to transfer a massive sum of money from one country to another, incurring a lot of complicated red tape to unravel. Then there's another thing, certain Zurich banks are noted for their varying degrees of co-operation with the police, not because of the criminals who may or may not be depositing large sums of money, but because of the money itself. Two million quid of other people's money, invested properly, brings in a lot of profit for the bank. That's a large part of their income. Do you know how much a million pounds would earn you in interest in this country, Roy?'

'No, I don't.'

'Two hundred and forty pounds a day, old son. So you can begin to imagine just how much profit a bank needs to earn to be able to pay that much interest.' Mac smiled at the look of surprise on Roy's face. 'However, there are a couple of banks over in Zurich who, with no questions asked, take your money, which they invest of course, and they preserve your anonymity if you don't expect interest on your deposit in return.'

'Well, I'll be buggered,' Roy declared, 'now that, I didn't know.'

'Ah you see, Grant did. How? I don't know, unless he flew over to find out because they don't discuss this sort of think over the phone. It has to be one to one, man to man, no witnesses, you see, no comeback. The point is, this particular bank is at the bottom end of the co-operation scale and so Sir Donald and the Earl are going to have their work cut out, not only to get the money transferred in less than forty-eight hours, but—'

'Hang about a bit, Mac,' Roy interrupted, 'surely it doesn't take that long to shift money from one country to another?'

'I thought you might say that,' Mac countered. 'But you're talking about crooks and crooked money and I'm talking about an honourable man trying to do in less that forty-eight hours what normally takes, well, who knows, weeks maybe. Don't forget, Operation Grouse is hush hush, and the poor old Earl is more or less on his own.'

Understanding dawned on Roy's face. 'It's beginning to make sense now; this chap Grant is backing his horse both ways. If the money isn't there because of these snags, when he phones that bank to find out if it's there, they're naturally going to tell him no.'

'That's it exactly, and if this bank which normally handles transactions of this sort has to tell him no, then Grant is going to know that, either the Earl has been unable to meet the deadline or, if it has been deposited within the deadline, either the Earl has more international pull that Grant first thought—'

'—or we're in on it somewhere,' Roy finished for him.

'Exactly old son, so we hedge our bets too you see and keep Grant sweet to allay any suspicions he might have.'

'But what if he phones the real bank again a bit later on, and they tell him no after Joan has told him yes?'

'If he does that before my Chief and the Earl have the bank sewn up right, it's goodbye Alison,' Mac replied frankly. 'But we have to cater for that contingency as well so, when Grant phones, we'll tape the conversation and I'll give my Chief a transcript so they can more or less repeat it if Grant phones again from another part of the country,' Mac replied.

'But what happens if he phones through another exchange, for his first call I mean?' Roy seemed concerned.

'If he did that, we'd be sunk, old son. I'm banking on him not knowing that we overheard his telephone conversation with the Earl. I'm also banking on him keeping close by Alison. He knows that we're on to him and that he's holding Alison, but then again, this egotistical maniac likes walking a knife edge. It's hard to explain, Roy, but this bloke likes an audience in this case, us. You see, he knows we cannot, dare not, broadcast Alison's disappearance, making us his captive audience. Look at it this way. To Grant this whole thing is a play, only on a bigger stage. He's the star and the director. We're the bit players, the puppets in his evil hands and does he love pulling our strings. Have you noticed how he's always one step ahead of us? No, you wouldn't really, you came into this thing late. Look how he turned things around when he called you in, for example: suddenly we were burglars. And how the devil did he know that we were going to the Alhambra Royal? Anyway, to get back to your original question, I don't think Grant will phone from another part of the country because I have a gut feeling that Alison isn't too far away and he's going to stick around to make sure we don't find her before he's ready.'

'He's a complex character, Mac, and no mistake,' Roy mused.

'He's all of that, Roy. Anyway, I'm hoping Sir Donald can get this bank to help, money or no money, just in case Grant does use another exchange, heaven forbid, so if you can go and chat Sally up, I'll get in touch with my boss. By the way, where's Jimmy?'

'I'll give you three guesses, and you'll be right the first time,' Roy replied, grinning.

Realisation dawned on Mac's face and he nodded knowingly. 'Stupid of me to ask really, he's certainly gone on our Joanie, hasn't he?'

'I think you'll find the feeling's mutual, Mac, hope it keeps fine for the pair of them.'

'Me too, old son, me too,' said Mac. 'Now go and win Sally over while I do my stuff.'

Roy moved away and Mac made for the rest room. After a few steps he stopped and turned around. 'Smithy, Terry, Bob, go and find Jimmy, that shouldn't be hard,' he smiled wryly, 'and sort out two hourly sleeping arrangements in pairs. Put Inspector Spalding and me together. Smithy, you and whoever sleep first, you could do with it after your experience. Oh, and find out if there are any showering facilities or even laundry facilities, I feel a bit scruffy myself.' He rubbed his fingers round his chin. 'I could do with a good scrape too.'

'OK, Guv, leave it with me,' said Smithy.

In the rest room Mac phoned a very sleepy sounding Chief Constable. 'Oh hello Mac, I'd just got my head down for ten minutes, anything to report?'

Mac recounted the recent events, finishing with the tiny clue of freshly scraped copper wire.

'Well done, Mac, from what you tell me your middle name should be Sherlock,' Sir Donald congratulated him.

'It was really quiet simple, Sir,' said Mac modestly, 'it just fell into place really when I put all the clues together, although the twine bothers me. I still can't see what it was to be used for, but enough of that for the moment, Sir. How did you get on with the bank?'

'Sticky, Mac, decidedly sticky, he certainly knows how to pick 'em, doesn't he, our feather plucking friend? They don't want to know.'

'You mean they won't co-operate at all, Sir?'

'Not exactly, Mac.' The Chief paused for a second. 'How can I put it, they're just being difficult. You see, we're talking about trapping a villain and all they can see is a potential profit loss - ostensibly, that is. But of course, they don't want to admit to being that sort of bank, you know, the sort of bank—'

'—that aids and abets criminals for profit,' Mac finished for him.

'That's it exactly, so in the ... err ... traditions of the police force, we're looking at ways to use that to our advantage.'

'And how do you propose to do that, Sir? Time's getting short. Our chap may have sussed out our little telephone exchange ploy and use a different exchange. He may even try to trip us up by using our one first, and another for a double check later. He's a crafty old sod, Sir, and I wouldn't put it past him.'

'Yes, I know,' said the chief, 'I had thought of that, so I got in touch with the Chief of Police in Berne, Hans Elwies. I've met him before at an Interpol convention and we got on quite well. Anyway, the gist of it is, I explained everything to him, leaving out who had been kidnapped, of course, and he agreed to co-operate.'

'Good for you, Sir, and what did you come up with?'

'Mac, least said, soonest mended, no names, no pack drill. Let it suffice to say that Hans Elwies knows this particular bank very well. He knows how they operate so he's going to compromise them somehow or other. He won't tell me how, but in his own words, he's going to make them an offer that can't refuse.'

'Sounds like he's been watching The Godfather, Sir.'

The Chief chuckled. 'That's precisely what I said and he said that was where he got the idea from, although what it is I just don't know.'

'As long as it works, I won't ask either, Sir.'

'There's something else Mac,' the Chief said quietly. 'The Earl is being asked all sorts of questions as to why he's trying to transfer that amount of money out of the country so quickly. He just says that he's transferring funds for a rainy day, that sort of thing. He's doing his best to play it down but things got a bit sticky with a couple of people, so I shut them up with the Official Secrets Act, telling them it was of vital national importance and that the Earl was only acting as an intermediary because his title gave him more pull. So now the people concerned are doing their damnedest to speed up the process, but keeping the Earl out of it. The snag is, that very fact could slow the process down, hence the use of Hans Elwies.'

'I see your problem, Sir, let's hope that Mr Elwies comes up with the goods.'

'He says it's going to take two to three hours, maybe longer, so I'm getting my head down, Mac, and if you take my advice, you'll do the same.'

'I'm getting a sleep rota laid on, Sir. Please give me a buzz as soon as you know anything. If Mr Elwies does come up trumps before our chap phones, we can dispense with our phoney bank at Lincoln exchange. If he doesn't, Sir, we'll do our best to fool him and give you the gist of the conversation to pass on to Zurich, just in case they do co-operate and our chap does phone again. Bye for now, Sir.'

Mac toyed with the idea of calling Jan but discarded it when he looked at his watch. Dear Jan, by now she would have bathed the children, dressed them in clean night clothes and put them to bed. She would then check that the house was secured against intruders before retiring to bed herself. She would be sound asleep by now, Mac thought to himself smiling.

But he was wrong. The walkie talkie suddenly came to life, bringing him back to earth with a start. 'Scots twit calling pea brain.' It was Jan's voice, very low and very soft, almost a whisper. Then the set went dead.

Mac almost panicked as the set went dead. The he realised Jan's intention. Her voice was meant for him only. Only he and she knew who 'Scots twit' and 'pea brain' were.

He smiled and spoke into the walkie talkie. 'Why aren't you asleep, you conniving lump of Scots womanhood?'

'Just wondered if you're OK, sweetie, I haven't heard from you for hours,' Jan chuckled softly. 'Did you find anything at the Alhambra Royal?'

Mac chuckled. 'I thought you might be a little bit curious, so pin back your ears, bane of my life..'

Mac related everything from start to finish, omitting nothing. He told Jan his own conclusions and mentioned his puzzlement over the small piece of twine tied around the guard.

Jan was silent for a few seconds. 'Sweetie, describe everything to me so that I can sketch it out on paper. Use the position of the trap door as the central point, give me the size and distance of the pulleys, the size of the machinery, distances and heights as near as you can remember, especially the position of that twine. I won't promise you anything, but I may get a fresh slant on things, see it from buggerlug's point of view.'

Mac chuckled at Jan's description of Grant. 'I'll bet his ears are burning, luv, that's a great name for him,' he chuckled.

Jan's laughter tinkled in his ear. 'I'll bet he has a better name for you.'

'Oh, why?'

'Because you, pea brain, have upset his little plans by discovering about the Alhambra Royal and he's not going to be very pleased with you, is he?'

'Yes, luv, but I don't see...'

'Look,' Jan interrupted, 'he knows that you almost found Alison once. He also knows that you can probably do the same again and he can't afford that, so if I were him, I know what I'd do.'

'And what would you do?'

'I'd simply bring the date forward, you know, the deadline for depositing the money in Switzerland. That way, I'd be out of the country just that much quicker,' Jan said brightly.

'You wouldn't, I mean he wouldn't, he couldn't ... could he?'

'Why not?'

'Because even he knows the difficulties of moving large sums of money from one country to another,' Mac replied.

'Yes, but he also knows the pulling power of a belted Earl, pea brain, especially one whose wife's life is at stake, and don't ask me to repeat that little mouthful again.'

'Mmmm,' Mac mused to himself, Jan's little quip going right over his head as the implications of her observations sank in.

'Still in the land of the living, sweetie?' Jan queried.

'It's a whole new ball game now isn't it, luv?' said Mac quietly. 'It's all up to Hans Elwies now.'

'Don't worry, sweetie, nobody gets to be a Police Chief by being a dumbo, so put your money on him bringing home the goods,' Jan said reassuringly. 'Go and get some sleep, I want you in good physical condition when you do eventually come home.'

'Now that sounds promising, good physical condition. I wonder why?'

'Well, the vacuum cleaner's broke, as is the washing machine, oh, and the tumble dryer wants looking at. The roof's leaking and ...'

'Hold it, hold it, hold it,' Mac chuckled, 'you certainly know how to turn a man on, don't you, you, you ...'

Jan's laughter tinkled again. 'I love you too, you great lump, so go and get some sleep, you've got to be on your mettle to beat this Johnnie come lately.'

'I love you, Jan. I will get some sleep and don't worry, we'll catch him, but we have to find Alison first, make sure that she's safe before we make a move. Night, luv, see you soon.'

'Night, night, pea brain, over and out.' Mac's set went dead.

He sat silently for several minutes, smiling at Jan's banter and wishing that all this was finished so he could go home to his beloved wife and children. His thoughts were interrupted by a knock on the door. It opened and Smithy pooped his head round.

'OK to come in, Guv?'

'Certainly, Smithy,' Mac smiled at his big sergeant, 'sorted anything out?'

'I asked about washing facilities and apparently they're all through there, Guv.' Smithy pointed to a door on the other side of the rest room. 'Baths, showers and disposable razors plus fold up cot beds in here.' He indicated the one wall.

Mac walked over to where Smithy was pointing and pulled at a folded handle. As he did so, a cot bed came into view complete with mattress, pillow and blanket. As he lowered the cot, two legs swung down automatically as gravity took over and steadied the cot beautifully as they met the floor. It looked very inviting.

'Now that's handy,' said Mac delightedly, 'I feel tired already. Only joking, Smithy, who have you picked as your partner?'

'Bob Saunders feels a bit peeked so he's with me. Jimmy and

Terry can climb in when we've warmed the fleas up a bit,' Smithy grinned.

'Don't forget, they'll be well fed by then,' Mac smiled wryly.

Smithy's face dropped a bit at that. 'Cor, I never gave it a thought, Guv,' he grinned ruefully.

'Well they might be hungry again when it's my turn,' Mac observed cheerfully, 'so get yourselves organised. Me, I'm going to get spruced up. We'll take it in turns to do that and for once, I'm pulling rank.'

'Thought you might, Guv, I didn't think you were going to grow a beard.'

'If Sir Donald wants me on the walkie talkie while I'm in there,' Mac pointed to the direction of the washrooms, 'get me immediately, it's dead important. I'll tell you about it later so pass it on to the others.'

And Mac disappeared through the other door to freshen up.

It was seven o'clock in the morning when Mac was aroused from his fitful sleep by his big sergeant.

'Guv, wake up Guv, the Chief wants you urgently.'

'Chief, what ...?' Mac's brain was fuddled but within seconds, he was as wide awake as a tired man can be as Smithy handed him his walkie talkie. 'Macdonald, Sir, sorry, I was asleep.'

'Sorry to wake you, Mac, but I've just heard from Mr Elwies.'

Mac's adrenaline flowed then and he was suddenly fully alert. 'Go on, Sir,' said Mac, fingers crossed.

'He did it, don't ask me how, but he did it, by George!' The Chief sounded elated. 'And not a moment too soon either.'

'Why's that, Sir?'

'Because our chap has phoned the Earl and brought the deadline forward to noon today.'

'Oh blast,' Mac groaned, 'that's exactly what Jan predicted he would do.'

'And that's not all.' The Chief was hardly listening to Mac. 'He told the Earl that he was so angry at our interference, he was going to give us only ten minutes to get to Alison before, as he put it, "she expired". The Earl was so shocked by this that he offered to give him another million pounds to ensure Alison's safety proper, but our chap refused. He said something about having to hide her at a safer place because of, as he put it, "those meddlesome policemen".'

'My God, Sir, we have only five hours to find her,' said Mac, horrified, 'and I must admit that I haven't a clue where he or Alison are.'

The Chief groaned. 'Now what the hell do we do?' Worry was reflected in his voice.

Mac thought for a while.

'Mac?'

'Hang on, Sir, I'm trying to think,' said Mac, who by now was off the cot bed and pacing up and down. Suddenly he snapped his fingers.

'Sir?'

'Go on, Mac, I'm listening.'

'We'll take our chap's call here, that is, if he stays local, and that'll give us some idea roughly where he is. Inspector Spalding can have his squad cars on the look-out for his roadster and they can shadow him, relaying his position at all times and maybe, just maybe, somehow he'll give the game away as to Alison's whereabouts.'

'You're clutching at straws, Mac, because he's not going to give you the satisfaction of showing himself or his car, is he?'

'With all due respect, Sir, he has to use the phone and what's more, if he intends to flee the country, he has to move to some airfield or other. He hasn't phoned to confirm that the money has been deposited yet and if I have anything to do with it, I'll try to delay him so that he as so little time to the deadline, he will have to use a fast car. A taxi won't be quick enough and they can be unreliably late, so I'm banking on him having to use the Ashdown Marsden.' Mac was trying to convey the hope in his voice that belied the sick feeling in his stomach.

There was a long silence that seemed to drag on interminably. Finally, the Chief Constable spoke. 'Do you think he's gone back to The Old Manse?'

'I doubt it, Sir, he'll hide up somewhere else so that he can move about unobserved, after all, he can't afford to be followed. To be on the safe side, I'll send Finch with his gadget to pick him up on his own phone, but I'll lay odds he's not at the house.'

Mac heard the sigh over the phone. 'Mac, I'm asking you and the lads to perform miracles or I've got to break silence over this one and involve every copper from Land's End to John o'Groats and frankly, I think it's going to be the latter. I'm sorry, Mac, but Alison's life is at stake here and five hours from now, it won't matter a damn, will it? We'll have failed and bang will go the credibility of you, me, the Home Office, and any other body the press can grab a field day out of.'

'Hold on a minute, Sir, don't say die yet. Five hours is a long time when there are seven sets of brains, and I'm including Jan, pitted against one, even though he does hold the advantage for the moment. Don't forget, Sir, Jan pointed us to the theatre in the first place and what's more, she's working on a theory right now. I have a lot of faith in her, Sir, and much as I hate to admit it, she has an instinct for spotting things that other people miss, so please, hang on, Sir, we're not in the Bloody Tower yet.'

There was a few seconds silence then the Chief came to a decision. 'You're right, of course Mac, go to it then, you haven't done too badly up to now. As a matter of fact, come to think of it, you've done very well in a very short time. Look, I'll take the bump if you fail, no need for us all to go down the drain. I'm coming up to retirement so what's a couple of years anyway?'

'That's very big of you, Sir, but I'm afraid that won't sit very well with the lads and I can't allow that to happen either, it's too much for one man to bear...'

'All right, all right,' the Chief managed a grateful chuckle, 'I might have know you bloody heroes would stick your oars in. Thank you.'

'Forget it, Sir,' said Mac, determination in his voice, 'we're not finished yet, we have a fish out there waiting to be hooked and we're going to think up some very special bait. So if you don't mind, time is short and I'd like to get on with it, Sir.'

'Right Mac, I won't detain you any longer, good luck, over and out.'

The set went dead and Mac looked at it for a moment, his head in a whirl. He had just put his own head on the chopping block alongside that of his Chief in a moment of chivalrous madness, knowing that the odds of finding Alison and catching Grant were stacked against him. 'You bloody great thumping idiot,' he thought to himself, 'now you've done it, haven't you?'

He was suddenly conscious of the others looking at him silently, expectantly. Mac came down to earth with a bump. 'You blokes heard all that?'

'We most certainly did.' It was Roy who spoke. 'And without wasting any more time, I'm going to do my bit right now. If this bloke gets past my men, he's going to have to crawl underneath the pavements to do it.'

'How many unmarked cars have you got? It's no good using official police cars against this mad bastard,' said Mac.

'Yes, I realise that, old sport, so they'll have to beg borrow or steal or use their own. Don't worry, Mac, I'll sort something out,' Roy assured him.

'Whoa, slow down a bit, old son, we mustn't be panicked into doing something rash. No disrespects, Roy, but we have to plan this properly,' Mac said calmly.

Roy took a deep breath, nodded slowly and exhaled. 'You're right Mac, what do you suggest?'

'A change-over of cars if he gets spotted. Let me explain. Grant has an Ashdown Marsden, special edition, more at home on a racing circuit than our roads and he's going to be hard to catch once he breaks cover, so I suggest that all your cars be in such a position so that as one car has to turn off or drop out if he thinks he's been rumbled, another one can take up the tail. Now then, as soon as Grant is spotted, his position and direction must be radioed to all cars, enabling them to take up a suitable position to maintain contact with our quarry.'

'That seems sound Mac, but where will he break to?'

'Now that,' said Mac, 'is the burning question, and I'm plumping for an airstrip somewhere, probably a private one and not too far away either. I can't see him making for a regular airport, can you?'

'You said that he probably flew over to Zurich, Mac, and that suggests a private charter plane to me as well, rather than a regular flight,' Roy agreed.

'What makes you think that, Roy?'

'Speed for one thing. It cuts out the delay of waiting for a regular flight, plus his name wouldn't be on a passenger list in case anyone back-tracked in an investigation.'

'Now that's what I call cooking with gas,' Mac grinned in approval. 'Together, we'll out-think him yet.'

'I hope so, Mac. Look, I'd better check out any private charter firms in and around Lincolnshire to see of any of them flew a passenger to Switzerland. When do you think he went?'

Mac furrowed his brow in thought. 'Let me see, it would have to be before he doubled for Alison at the hospital, before the Glorious Twelfth. Yes, before he went to stay with Alison. I'd say around the tenth or before - say a week before. I shouldn't imagine many people could charter a private plane to Switzerland. After all, if they have that sort of money to throw away, they could *buy* a plane.'

'Leave it with me, Mac, I'll set the cars up first and get a few people on to checking out the private boys. I'm off back to the station, I can work better from there. I'll be in touch just as soon as, OK Mac?'

When Roy had gone, Mac turned to Jimmy. 'Jimmy, take your gadget with you and a tool box and overalls. Go and talk your way into the house opposite The Old Manse. Tell them what you like, but get in and you must, and keep out of sight. If Grant picks that phone up, I want to know immediately, but more importantly, we'll have him spotted. You can pick up some work clothes from here and ask to borrow one of their repair vans. Nick one if necessary and I'll square it afterwards. Now go quickly, he could phone at any time now.'

Jimmy was gone in a flash and Mac turned to Smithy, Terry and Bob. 'Right, let's get out to where it's at, lads.' And without waiting for any reply, he was on his feet and making rapidly for the exit. At the switchboard, Joan and Sally were chatting happily together. Both were wearing headphones, keeping one ear open for Grant.

'Ah, Sally,' Mac smiled at her, 'sorry to drag you out of bed but we had to have a stand-in just in case Joan keeled over and I couldn't think of anyone better qualified.'

'Flattery will get you everywhere, Inspector,' Sally smiled back, 'anyway, strange as it may seem to you, I like it here. Job satisfaction and all that.'

Mac nodded at Joan. 'How are you feeling, when did you sleep last?'

'Don't worry about me, Inspector, I practise Yoga when I get low. It relaxes me when I get overwrought or tired and I feel absolutely fine, thank you. You should try it sometimes, it really is very beneficial, clears your brain, relaxes and retones the body generally. I use it when I'm doing a difficult part.'

'You're a real treasure,' Mac marvelled, 'maybe I'll do that one day when this little lot's over. Which reminds me, the chap we're after has brought his deadline forward as regards the deposit in Zurich to noon today - four and a half hours from now. We want to delay him for a couple of hours and we want him to call back at least once to verify that his money is there. 'What we're trying to do, Joan, is pinpoint his position. Do you think that you can handle it?'

'I'll have to, Inspector, or I'm no actress. It won't be the first time I've had to ad-lib while someone's trying to remember their lines. As we say during rehearsals, it'll be all right on the night.' She gave Mac a reassuring smile.

Mac nodded. 'I believe you, but I'll be listening in anyway. I think between us we should be able to bamboozle him for a while.' He crossed his fingers and added, 'I fervently hope so anyway.'

He turned to Terry and Bob. 'You two stay with the engineer by the satellite relays and get him to remind you what to look for on the 'box of tricks' if and when 'chappie' phones in. Just as soon as you're sure it's him, buzz me on the walkie talkie the moment that the engineer intercepts and transfers the call to Joan's line, OK?'

'OK, Guv.'

'Keep on your toes, we have just over four hours to go,' Mac warned, 'don't for God's sake blow it, don't miss anything, we may have one chance only at our chap, so at least one of you keep your eye on the digits on that box of tricks at all times, is that nice and clear?'

Terry and Bob nodded and went to their posts. Mac put his walkie talkie to his ear and switched to 'transmit'. 'Everybody talk to me - Roy, Jim, Jan, Sir Donald, acknowledge please.' They did.

For the next half hour or so, Mac co-ordinated plans with Roy regarding strategic car placings should Grant be forced to break cover. Jimmy had managed to talk his way into the house opposite The Old Manse. After knocking on the door and being confronted by an elderly lady and gentleman, Jimmy had earmarked them as a couple of old-fashioned romantics who always looked forward to happy endings. Not having the heart to disappoint them, he told they that he wanted to keep surveillance on a 'Mr Big' who might or might not be hiding in The Old Manse. The old couple were tickled pink at the prospect of being part of an intrigue, and could barely conceal their excitement.

As the minutes ticked by back at the telephone exchange, the tension mounted as everyone waited for something, anything, to happen. Mac was beginning to feel the strain more than most. He actually jumped as Roy's voice erupted from the walkie talkie.

'Mac?'

'Listening.'

'I've traced the charter firm that our chap hired and what's more ... You won't believe this, Mac, you really won't.'

'Won't believe what?'

'He's hired him again. Same plane, same pilot, same place.'

'You're right Roy, I don't believe it. Nobody could be that stupid, it's too obvious ... But then again, you never know...'

'The crafty bastard, it could be a ploy. Nevertheless, he's got to fly from somewhere and this field is as good as any, I suppose.'

'Something smells here, Roy, let me dwell on it for a bit,' Mac said thoughtfully. 'Have you anything laid on, tail wise I mean?'

'Would you believe a total of twenty-eight assorted vehicles, manned mostly by volunteers? said Roy proudly.

'How the Hell did you manage that in such a short space of time?' Mac voiced his admiration. 'Bribe 'em with a pay cut?'

Roy chuckled. 'Nope, just mentioned that we were looking for a madman, that's all it took to spur these chaps here to more or less shanghai the rest of our motley crew from wherever they happened to be. They're all on hand radios, by the way, standard frequency. I've told them your name and rank and they will listen out for your word of command.'

'Good show, old son, tell them my code name is Earhole from now on, time is short, very short.'

'OK, anything happening your end yet, Mac?'

'Nothing, old son, no phone call, nothing. Our chap certainly knows how to put a body on tenterhooks. All we can do is wait, hope and pray.' Mac sighed with exasperation and muttered to himself: 'Come on, you bastard, make a move.'

CHAPTER THIRTY-FIVE
GRANT PHONES SWITZERLAND

Jimmy had installed himself in the upstairs front bedroom of the Watson residence. Jack and Alice Watson, whose house it was, could scarcely contain themselves at the prospect of being in on a major 'bust', and Jimmy was hard pressed to keep them away from the window. A compromise was reached when Jimmy promised to call them if anyone approached who needed to be identified.

Jimmy had been sitting in the window for about twenty minutes when suddenly the front door of The Old Manse opened. He sat bolt upright with expectancy as a figure emerged. He relaxed slightly as the figure took the form of a woman wearing a turban, with a couple of rollers showing at the front. There was a cigarette drooping from her lips and she was carrying a mop and bucket. She was obviously a cleaning lady but Jimmy took no chances. He called out over his shoulder and through the open door, the prearranged signal.

'Stranger in sight.'

Old Jack Watson came into the bedroom at a gallop and crouched down beside Jimmy, his rheumy old eyes wide with excitement. Jimmy pointed towards the cleaning lady and old Mr Watson squinted his eyes, trying to identify her. 'Oh, that be Olive, Olive Jones, she clean there once or twice a week.'

'You sure, Mr Watson?'

'Sure as I can be from this distance, Mr Finch, hang on.' He half turned and called out, 'Alice, gerrin 'ere, gal, and tell us who this'n is.'

Alice materialised as if from nowhere and hurried to her husband's side. She peered out of the window at the woman, mopping the doorstep, across the road. 'That be Olive Jones, the cleaning lady. She do one or two of the big houses around the park, she do, what she be doing here today though I dunno, she be a day early.'

Jimmy became suddenly alert. 'A day early, did you say?' His eyes locked onto the figure across the way who was now polishing the brasswork on the big heavy door. 'Has she ever done that before, been a day early, I mean?'

'Oh yes, once or twice, though why I dunno,' Mrs Watson replied. 'Could be that she has other arrangements sometimes. She do have her own key, that I do know, Mr Finch. I don't like her myself, always got that cigarette dangling from her mouth, disgusting habit that, I reckon.'

Old Jack grinned. 'Makes me smoke a pipe she do,' he nodded in the direction of his wife, 'always maintains the baccy's too far from me mouth to hurt any. I don't argue none.' His eyes twinkled.

'You fought for your beer and baccy in the Great War, so I reckon you've earned it.' She turned to Jimmy. 'He's got medals for bravery under fire you know...'

'Urmph. Mr Finch has got more important things to attend to than listen to idle chit chat, Alice luv, why don't you make us all a nice cup of tea,' Old Jack intervened, obviously embarrassed by the sudden limelight.

'I made the last one so it's your turn, my lad, and bring some of those chocolate digestives with you. Put 'em all on the silver tray.'

There was a twinkle in her eye as old Jack opened his mouth to grumble but shut it again. Jimmy smiled at the pair of them and as old Jack left to make the tea, curiosity got the better of him. 'Just how did he win his medal, Mrs Watson?'

'Mmm what? Oh, he rescued an officer from no man's land, he'd been hit by machine gunfire. Then he charged single-handed and blew up the machine gun post with hand grenades. He was badly wounded too, they nearly lost him, but three months later, my Jack was back up the front line where he wanted to be, bless him.'

'Erm, what medal did he win, Mrs Watson?' Jimmy asked the question as nonchalantly as possible.

'What? Oh, the Victoria Cross, but Jack doesn't like me talking about it. He says I embarrass him and he was only doing his duty.'

Jimmy shook his head slowly in wonderment. He couldn't for the life of him picture this old man, well into his nineties, doing the things his wife had described. Jimmy shook his head again and resumed his watch on the big house opposite.

The walkie talkie came to life and Mac's voice said, 'Jimmy, talk to me, anything yet?'

Jimmy pressed the speak button. 'Hello Guv, I'm under cover. Nice old couple. Got me a great view of The Old Manse, no sign of our friend though, only the cleaning lady. She calls twice a week apparently and has her own latch key.'

'Cleaning lady?'

'That's right, Guv, as a matter of fact, she's just finished and she's putting her coat on. I can see her through the open door. Now she's outside, locking the door. She's away up the road, Guv, towards the town centre.'

'Going home, I expect, to get her feet up, wish I could do the same. Any movement inside the Manse? Chimney smoke, lights, any sign of our chap at all, Jimmy?'

'Absolutely none that I can see, Guv, and you're wrong about the cleaner, she's just popped into the launderette. Got someone's washing in, I suppose. Blimey, what some folks do to make a living!'

'Jimmy, shush.' Mac's voice was urgent. 'Something's happening at this end.'

Jimmy heard Terry's voice reading out numbers, his voice getting more excited as the numbers began to correspond to the numbers on his piece of paper and then ... 'Loop in quick, Guv, it's Joan's call now.'

Jimmy knew that what he was listening to could only be the activity caused by Grant phoning in through the exchange relays to Switzerland. What Jimmy didn't know was where Grant was phoning from: certainly not from the Manse or he would have picked up Grant's call - assuming Grant hadn't found the bug in the phone. Jimmy doubted that: the bug was tiny and looked like part of the design anyway.

Meanwhile, at the telephone exchange, Joan licked her lips and swallowed hard as she waited for her light to come on. Long seconds passed before it finally did. Even so, she gave a start when the red light suddenly came alive. She reached for one of the extension leads and plugged it into the relevant socket. Mac switched on the tape recorder at the same time.

'Grand Bank of Switzerland, welcome, please, how may I help

you?' Joan began in a superb imitation of the recorded voice that Sally had acquired earlier.

'Good morning, my dear,' came the clear precise tone of the practised thespian Andrew Grant. 'Why did you speak English when you addressed me? I could have been Dutch, or even Chinese.'

The quiet menace of Grant's voice could not be disguised and Joan visibly shuddered. Mac spotted this and mouthed the words. 'Don't panic, he's trying you out.'

Joan nodded and took a deep breath. 'Did I surprise you, Sir? I'm so sorry but your call came through the part of my switchboard that deals only with the British Isles, so I naturally answered in English.' She bit her lip and looked at Mac, who was nodding and smiling his approval.

'I see, well that makes sense I suppose,' Grant grudgingly acceded. My name is Penton-Fairfax, Robert Andrew Penton-Fairfax, and I would very much like to check my account, if you please.'

'I'm sorry, Sir, I can't do that. I operate the switchboard only. I shall have to put you through to the Chief of Accounts, one moment please.'

Inspiration came to Mac in a flash and he rapidly signalled to Joan to hand him the headset. She hesitated, then understood. 'Putting you through now, Sir,' she said into the mouthpiece. She quickly removed the headset and handed it to Mac who donned it rapidly.

'Accounts, Lars Svenson, how may I help you?' said Mac, trying to imitate the accent used by Joan.

'That accent of yours, Mr Lars Svenson, has a decidedly Scottish twang,' said Grant, highly suspicious.

Mac thought quickly. 'Ha ha ha, and so would yours if you spent your formative years in Stirlingshire,' he chuckled. 'My mother is a Scot, you see, and clever enough to marry a rich Zurich merchant.' Mac chuckled again. 'Now, Sir, how can I be of assistance.'

Grant seemed to accept the explanation but there was still some doubt left, and Mac heard it in his voice as he spoke. 'Yes, my name is Robert Andrew Penton-Fairfax, and I'm hoping for some pleasant news concerning my account.'

'I see, and what is your account number, Mr Fairfax?'

'Penton-Fairfax,' Grant reminded him haughtily.

'Just part of the check, Sir, just part of the check.'

'Check, what check, dammit?'

'You could be anyone, Sir, for all we know. And now, what is your account number please?'

Grant controlled his anger and in a trembling voice said, 'AG account number 787423 England.'

Mac repeated the account number back to Grant and said, 'Very good Mr Penton-Fairfax, that seems to check out with what I have here. Now, Sir, if you will replace your phone, I will call you back directly.'

'What the devil for?' Grant practically exploded.

'Mr Penton-Fairfax,' Mac replied evenly, 'I have a lot of information in front of me, including your address and telephone number. I now propose to phone that number and I fully expect you to answer it.'

'And if I don't answer the phone, what then?'

'Then as far as this bank is concerned, you are not who you say you are, Sir,' Mac replied, now thoroughly enjoying himself.

'But Mr Svenson, I am not phoning from home. I am calling you from my friend's home. I really am Robert Andrew Penton-Fairfax.' Grant sounded exasperated.

'Mr Penton-Fairfax, that, I am afraid, will not suffice. I suggest you phone me again, from your home this time. Goodbye.'

'No wait,' Grant almost screamed down the phone, 'no wait,' he repeated in a calmer voice. 'I'm only about a hundred yards from home, give me five minutes and then call me, I'm er, ha ha ha, out exercising my dogs actually.' He tried to inject a little humour into his voice. 'Just give me five minutes then. Goodbye.'

Mac signalled Joan to break the connection. She did so rapidly.

'Before you kick me in the kneecaps for taking your job, Joan, let me explain.'

'No need, Inspector, I'm sure you had a perfectly sound reason,' Joan smiled sweetly.

'The best actually. You see, the man you and I have just been chatting to is missing, and I suddenly realised that this is one way of finding him.'

He lifted his walkie talkie and pressed the speak button. 'Jimmy, talk to me.'

'Jimmy, Guv.'

'Can't explain right now but look for Grant arriving back at the double, I think I've forced his hand.'

'Right, Guv, I'm looking now ... hang on, the cleaning lady's on her way back, in a bit of a hurry too, by the look of her.'

Mac could have crowed with delight. 'That's Grant, Jimmy, it's got to be.'

Jimmy's mouth dropped as he spotted something. 'Guv, I think you're right. She, or he is taking bloody great long strides, not like a woman's run at all. I've just remembered something else too, she, or he was polishing the door brasses left handed.'

Mac was delighted. 'Jimmy, I'm going to phone him in a couple of minutes and if he answers, you'll hear him on your gadget. Did you hear that, Roy?' Mac continued in the same breath.

'Loud and clear Mac, well done, I'll pass on the info to my lads so they can be ready if he's home.' Roy was obviously delighted.

Joan flashed Mac a delightful smile. 'Your little gamble paid off then, Inspector, a flash of genius I'd say and I'm not at all piqued.'

Mac had the good grace to blush slightly. 'Thanks for the compliment, Joan, will you phone The Old Manse for me?'

'What's his number, Inspector?'

'Bloody hell, I haven't the faintest idea,' said Mac, 'it never occurred to me to find out.'

Joan was already thumbing through the directory, stopping at the 'Ps'.

'Ah, here it is Inspector,' she said and, using a pencil, she began to dial.

A breathless voice answered in Mac's ear. 'Penton-Fairfax here, Mr Lars Svenson, I presume?'

Mac could have kissed the phone, it was Grant after all. 'Ah, Mr Pento-Fairfax, it was you all the time. I am very sorry, but we have to do these things to protect your investment, and our own reputation.'

'That's understandable,' said Grant, generously. 'Now, Mr Svenson, will you confirm that my account has swollen somewhat.'

'Yes, I can confirm that your account has "swollen somewhat", as you put it.'

'How much?'

'You want me to tell you over the phone, Sir?'

'I do.'

'Ah well, so be it. The exact amount subject to final transactionary signatures is ... two million pounds exactly.' Mac tried to sound convincing. 'And there is also a proviso, which I do not fully understand as yet.' Mac's brain was turning over wildly for anything that would delay Grant, anything that would make him slip up and lead them to Alison.

'Proviso, what damned proviso?' Grant sounded alarmed.

'As I said, Sir, I do not fully understand it myself, all I can tell you at this point is that, and I quote: "Withhold or delay final transaction until the last possible moment—".' Mac suddenly stopped dead.

'Well, go on, what the hell have you stopped for? You were saying something about delaying the final transaction,' Grant barked.

Mac held the silence for a few seconds longer.

'Well,' Grant challenged, 'I'm waiting.'

Mac sighed deliberately and spoke in a sheepish, subdued voice.

'I'm extremely sorry, Mr Penton-Fairfax. I should not have disclosed that information to you, it was for my eyes only, apparently.'

'Was it, by George, was it indeed? And pray tell me, why have you got to delay the final transaction?' Grant demanded.

'Please, Sir, I shouldn't have disclosed—'

'But you're too damned late, you *have* disclosed haven't you, and now I demand to know why you are supposed to delay the final transaction. Or do I take my business elsewhere?' Grant threatened emptily.

Mac smiled at that. Grant was rattled but he was still holding the ace card. Mustn't overdo it, or Alison's life could really be on the line. Grant had got to be made to expose Alison's whereabouts before the deadline and this could be the moment when her fate was decided, one way or another.

'Oh very well, Mr Penton-Fairfax, if you must know, further instructions were to be received to the effect that a certain commodity was to be delivered before the final transaction.'

'And where was the final instruction to come from, or rather from whom?' Grant asked cautiously.

'The Earl of Westminster, no less,' Mac replied.

There was no reply from Grant for several long seconds and Mac knew that he was weighing up the pros and cons. He decided to let him stew for a bit longer.

'Sir, Mr Penton-Fairfax, are you still there?'

'Yes, I'm still here.'

'Does that make any sense to you, Sir? Mac asked innocently.

'Oh yes, I was a little confused at first, but I fully understand now, erm, thank you for reminding me, Mr Svenson.'

'My pleasure, Mr Penton-Fairfax, glad to be of help to you, Sir,' Mac replied, not quite knowing what to say or do next to delay Grant. Time was getting short and Alison's whereabouts was still a mystery to everyone except Grant.

'I shall be calling you again, Mr Svenson, I have to get thing moving at my end. Careless of me to forget. Thank you for your timely reminder.' Grant did his best to dismiss the whole thing off-handedly. 'I'll be in touch shortly, Mr Svenson. Thank you and goodbye.'

'My pleasure, Mr Penton-Fairfax, I shall be looking forward to hearing from you again, Sir. Goodbye.'

The line went dead and Mac made a grab for his walkie talkie. 'Jimmy?'

'Listening, Guv.'

'It's him all right, so whatever happens, don't lose him, don't let him out of your sight. He may put two and two together and realise he's just blown his cover. On the other hand, he may just be a little concerned over our phone call; he must realise he's been conned.'

'I'm all ears and eyes, Guv, and what's more I've got plenty of help here.'

'Help?'

'Mr and Mrs Watson Guv, they've been watching The Old Manse like a couple of hawks since they heard you say that there was something happening,' Jimmy enlightened him.

'They're not a hindrance then, Jimmy,' Mac chuckled.

'Far from it, Guv, bless 'em,' Jimmy chortled back.

'Good, now if Grant phones again or leaves the building, I want to know immediately, right Jimmy?'

'Right Guv, over and out.'

Mac immediately contacted the Chief Constable. 'You there, Sir Donald?'

'I'm all ears this end, Mac.'

'Did you listen in, Sir?'

'Yes, I heard the whole thing, what are you plans now?'

'I've taped the whole conversation, Sir - Grant's, Joan's and mine. I'm going to have it played to you rather than give you a transcript, so if you can retape it your end, you can then pass it on to the real bank in Zurich, just in case Grant does try to bypass us and use another exchange. But the most important thing right now, Sir, is to inform the Earl of the latest developments.'

'Good, very good so far,' the Chief agreed.

'Sir, I've just thought of something.'

'Go on!'

'Wouldn't it be better for the Zurich bank to transfer the phone call back to this exchange, always assuming it can be done of course. That way, there shouldn't be any foul up.'

'I don't see why not, Mac, but you can find out more about that where you are, I think. Nevertheless, I'll lay it on at Zurich. Now make arrangements for that tape to be played so that I can get on with it.'

'Right, Sir, I'll get Sally Prentice on to it. She's the Chief Supervisor and she's been a big help to me up to now, she can do the tape and the reverse call from Zurich for me, if it can be done, that is.'

'I won't waste time, Mac, get on with it, less than two hours left to the deadline. Good luck, over and out.'

'Roy?'

'Listening, Mac.'

'Grant's home, Jimmy Finch is on stakeout at this very minute, keeping an eye on The Old Manse. If anything moves, he'll give you a shout. Get that, Jimmy?'

'Loud and clear, Guv.'

'I have to stay here at the exchange for a while longer, just in case Grant phones again.'

'Mac?' It was Jan's voice and it sounded urgent.

'Jan, what's up?'

'I've been doing a bit of analysis of our grouse-plucking friend with the help of our pet computer. I've fed everything into it about him, you know, habits, behaviour patterns, traits etc; I won't go into details, luv, but in short, I've been trying to find Alison.'

Mac's heart began to race at that. Jan wouldn't build his hopes up without reason. He swallowed hard. 'And?' he asked as calmly as his voice would allow.

'I think I know where she is,' Jan said quietly, 'at least, the computer is ninety five per cent certain and I'm inclined to agree.'

Mac could scarcely bring himself to ask the next question. He couldn't trust his voice to remain calm. He took a deep breath. 'Where, Jan?'

'She's back at the Alhambra Royal.'

'Wh ... that's incredible ... how?'

'Time factor, sweetie, you caught him short. He wouldn't have had time to set up anywhere else, would he?'

'My God, you're right, he wouldn't, would he? Come to think of it, it's the only place to take her—'

'Mac ... Mac, listen to me,' Jan interrupted him, 'time isn't on your side. Get on the road now and I'll be in touch. I have a few things to do this end regarding that twine you found on the wire guard. Now get yourselves organised and I'll be in touch if and when I come up with something, OK sweetie? Out.'

Mac opened his mouth to respond but changed his mind. It was always best not to interrupt Jan's flow when she was analysing. She always worked best alone.

He barked into his walkie talkie. 'Did everyone hear that?' Everyone acknowledged. 'OK, everybody, keep your ears glued to your walkie talkies and be ready to act at a moment's notice. Jimmy, don't lose Grant now and you deal directly with Inspector Spalding if he breaks cover.'

'OK, Guv.'

'I hear you, Jimmy,' said Roy, 'now for Gawd's sake, Mac, get moving, you have to cover an hour and forty minutes' ground in an hour and a half. Get going and we'll cover this end.'

'How on earth am I going to be able to cover the ground before the deadline, Roy?' Mac groaned.

A very gentle and cultured voice answered him and Mac jumped in surprise. 'If you can make you way to Potter's Farm, Inspector Macdonald, Mr Cuncliffe and I will expedite your arrival before the deadline, be assured.'

'Sir, your Lordship, how ...?'

'Never mind that now, Inspector,' said the Earl, 'time is of the essence so please make your way here as soon as possible.'

'Yes, Sir, I'm on my way. Potter's Farm, you said?'

'It's a mile due west of where you are, just follow the main trunk road out of Lincoln,' the Earl instructed, 'please hurry,'

Within a few minutes, Mac and Smithy were on their way, Mac having left hurried instructions with Jason, Terry and Bob. The walkie talkie came to life as Smithy bombed towards Potter's Farm.

'Inspector?'

'Sir?'

'To satiate your undoubted curiosity as to how I acquired this walkie talkie would take some time,' said the Earl. 'It occurred to me that you might at some stage require the services of a decent helicopter, plus pilot, of course, so I pulled rank so to speak and ... well, let's say that things fell nicely into place.'

'I for one am very glad you did, Sir,' said Mac.

'Do you have misgivings, Inspector, about my presence, I mean? Please don't, I have no intention of interfering in the execution of your duty. However, it's only fair to warn you that if this villain and I ever come face to face, protocol and decorum will probably cease to exist for the length of time that it will take me to dispose of this ... this verminous creature. I shall exact dire payment for the hurt he has caused my dear wife.'

The venom in the Earl's voice made Mac shudder and prompted him to reprimand His Lordship. 'Sir, I must warn you against the use of any physical violence, especially a gentleman of your standing. You cannot, you must not take the law into your own hands. Please, let common sense prevail, let justice take its course, be seen to be done, Sir.'

'Mr Macdonald, if that poor excuse for a man has hurt my wife in any way or even ki—' the Earl stumbled over the word '—killed her, I *shall* exact my revenge. There can be no justice without revenge,' he said quietly.

Just as quietly Mac replied, 'Also, Sir, there can be no revenge without justice.'

The airwaves crackled for long seconds before the Earl spoke again. 'Forgive me, Inspector, I will try to maintain self control but please, make certain that you get to him first, I can't promise self restraint, he does have my wife and if she's hurt ...'

'Erm, may I suggest you dispense with the mace, Sir, after all, we don't want murder added to the issue.'

'How the devil did you know about the mace?'

'Just a lucky guess, Sir.'

'Quite so, Inspector, but have you given any thought to how we punish the man? Assuming of course that my wife is rescued unharmed and this man is incarcerated. We must consider the ethics and the indignities of a public trial and the distress that will cause my wife, let alone myself.'

Mac though about it for some seconds. 'Quite frankly, Sir, no, I haven't, but one thing I know for certain, if I catch him, I hold on to him. That, after all, Sir, is my job.'

'I can see you approaching, Inspector, at least, I think it's your car, would you mind flashing your headlights please.' Smithy obliged. 'Ah yes, thank you, two hundred yards, turn left through the first farm gate, you can probably see me waving.' Mac acknowledged and a few minutes later, the four men were airborne, heading rapidly for Norwich and the empty theatre. Empty that is except for one solitary resident, unconscious and tied to a chair that was once again screwed firmly to the central trap door.

Roger Cuncliffe motioned everyone to put on headsets, waiting until they were suitably adorned before he spoke. 'Where exactly are we heading, Inspector?'

'The Alhambra Royal in Norwich.'

'Can I land there, do you think?'

'There's a car park at the back, I don't know whether it's big enough though. How big are your rotors?'

'Thirty six foot diameter, old boy, and then I must allow for a little jinking, you know, prop wash off the walls and surrounding buildings if any. A whirlwind of my own making, if you like, so I need at least seventy feet to be safe. I'm good, but not that good, old boy,' Roger grinned amiably.

'Now you have me there old son, I just don't know,' Mac shrugged his shoulders regretfully.

'Then we shall have to play it by ear, old sport,' Roger grinned again, and got on with the business of flying the helicopter. Hardly another word was spoken until they reached their destination. Roger circled one or twice, sizing up the situation.

'Just about sixty feet I'd say, bit risky old boy, but I'll try it if you like?'

Mac looked at his watch, ten minutes to noon, very little time left. He made up his mind suddenly for all of them. 'Go for it,' he said through gritted teeth.

Roger simply nodded, and said, 'Sit absolutely still, whatever happens, OK chaps?'

Everyone nodded, held their breath, and marvelled at Cuncliffe's superb display of aerial dexterity and skill as he fought to land the helicopter through the worst buffeting they had ever felt in their lives. The downwash of the big rotors was forced outward to the surrounding buildings which, in their turn, bounced the wash back towards the big rotors, causing opposing pressures. The helicopter bounced up and down like a yo-yo on a very short string. There were periods of absolute stability but they were very short and Roger was going to have to cash in on one of these periods to land safely.

'Hang on, you lot!' he yelled. 'I have to bide my time. When we do land, it'll be with a bigger bump than usual so don't be surprised, just sit tight, OK?' Seconds later the helicopter was down and Roger cut the engine.

'Well you got it down, how do you get out again?' Mac was intrigued at the thought.

'Easy, old boy, if you think about it. I was trying to land against an upward pressure, so that same pressure will literally chuck the chopper back into the air again, see?'

'Yes, I can now that you've explained it, thank you,' said Mac.

The four men had been making their way towards the back of the theatre during this conversation and now Mac signalled for silence. He spoke quietly into his walkie talkie. 'Bob? Mac, where's the genny?'

'Oh, hello, Guv, it's by the garages, big green door.'

Mac made his way to the door and opened it wide. 'I'm looking at it, Bob, run me through start up, will you please?'

'Right, Guv, firstly, make sure the "pull to stop" is pushed back in on the panel.'

'Right, that's back in. Next?'

'On the left hand side, you'll see a row of six big buttons, these are decompressors or valve lifters to relieve the cylinder pressure while you crank. Push all six in as far as they will go. They won't go until you turn the release rod to the right, the one with the six fingers on it, see it, Guv?'

'I see it, right, six buttons knocked home, now what?'

'Set the hand throttle to "run" and crank like hell. As soon as you get up a good old speed on the fly wheel, knock the valve lifter release bar to the left, and all six buttons should fly back out.'

'OK, here we go.' Mac cranked as fast as he could, then hit the valve lifter release bar. The engine caught, and after an initial thump-thump-thump, settled down to a steady run. 'Running, Bob, now what?'

'Leave it running, Guv, and don't alter the throttle setting.'

Suddenly, urgency entered Bob's voice. 'There's something going on here Guv, it's him again I think.' The set just went dead.

Mac had already left instructions in case Grant phoned again and did not bother to acknowledge Bob Saunders. He led the way into the theatre, looking at his watch as he did so. 'Five minutes to twelve, get as many lights on as you can, just as soon as we get to that emergency switch. Oh, and Sir,' Mac addressed the Earl, 'if the Lady Alison is here, do not, I beg you, do not attempt to free her from whatever situation she may be in.'

'Why?'

'Because she may be booby trapped, Sir. I'm sorry.' Mac felt terrible, having to say it.

'Oh my God, please don't say that.' The anguish in the Earl's voice was heartbreaking and Mac's heart went out to him but...

Mac reached the emergency switch and threw it. A single light came on above a bank of switches. He turned them all on. He ran through the wings towards the stage, closely followed by Smithy, Roger and the Earl, and as they burst through onto the stage, the sight that confronted them brought a moan from the Earl. For there, in the middle of the stage, was the pitiful and unconscious figure of a woman, gagged and bound securely to a chair.

It was Alison.

As the Earl made a move to go to her, Mac gently but firmly blocked his way.

'Sir, please remember what I said.'

'Yes, I'm sorry, but the deadline, Inspector ...'

'Yes, Sir, I know, now gently please, forward, but stay behind me.'

Mac moved forward as quickly as he dared. 'Keep your eyes peeled for booby traps, wires and things.'

He stopped in front of the still figure of Alison, looking hard for anything other than restraining bonds. The Earl's voice came over his shoulder. 'Is she...?'

'She's still alive, Sir.'

'Thank God!'

'Sir, we have less than two minutes to noon. If there is a booby trap, it's got to be below. Please, touch nothing and listen for my shout. Do you understand, Sir?'

The Earl hesitated then nodded and Mac shot off below the stage, hitting the light switches as he went down the steps two at a time. A quick glance all the way round confirmed his previous deductions as to the operation of the trap door. The rope was in place with the sandbag on the end, tied back to the catwalk and probably a home-made bomb on the catwalk, to set the whole thing in motion. Mac ran to the guard, his eyes searching, searching ... yes, there it was. A new piece of twine was now in place. One end was tied tightly in the original place, running across the guard in front of the big wooden handle and through the other side of the guard. Mac followed it through a series of pulleys until he could see where it ended.

Mac literally jumped as Jan's voice suddenly came through the walkie talkie. 'Mac, the twine is a trigger, gun or crossbow.'

Mac saw the crossbows, two of them, at exactly the same time as Jan spoke, and his jaw dropped in horror. In two seconds flat, the whole diabolical scheme fell into place. He glanced at his watch. There was less than half a minute to go. He screamed at the top of his voice. 'Release her, cut the ropes, for God's sake, get her out of that chair.'

His anguished, urgent shout produced a sudden burst of violent activity above his head and he looked at his watch again. The second hand was approaching zero hour. It went past, plus one, plus two, plus three.

Mac glanced fearfully at the big wooden handle and made a sudden decision. He would hold it, or try to, against the weight of the sandbag, if it was freed by an explosive device. He moved forward rapidly to grab the handle, just a split second too late as the device detonated.

Mac watched the sandbag fall as if mesmerised. The rope went taught and whipped the big wooden handle back. Mac whipped his head round and up, to see the big trap door open and the chair descend. As it parted company with the stage floor, the sight that met his eyes would be forever imprinted on his mind.

Standing straddled across the gaping hole was the Earl, holding on to his beloved Alison by her arms, using only the strength of his own arms and hands. He saw Smithy and Roger swiftly moving in to help.

Just as the chair came to a halt, the big wooden handle shot forward with an almighty *thwack*, releasing the deadly bolts. Mac watched in fascination as they buried themselves in the back of the chair where less than a second ago, Alison had been tied.

He realised that he was holding his breath and exhaled volubly. He found his voice. 'Is she all right, Sir?'

'Heaven bless her, Inspector, yes,' came the emotional reply through the hole in the stage.

'I'm coming up, please do nothing until I get there, Sir.' Mac's request was also an order. He rapidly climbed the stairs to the stage, to be confronted by a wonderful, heart-rending sight.

The Earl was kneeling on the stage, holding his beloved Alison like a tiny baby, tears of happiness trickling slowly down his face. Her bonds were already lying on the stage.

Smithy spoke apologetically. 'I took the ropes off, Guv, I checked for booby traps before I did.' Mac just nodded.

'She's deeply unconscious, Inspector,' said the Earl softly. 'May I take her now?'

Mac felt her pulse. It was weak but steady. He turned to Roger Cuncliffe. 'Have you got oxygen in the chopper?'

'Yes, and blankets.'

'How long will it take you to fly to Westminster if you have enough fuel?'

'Inspector, I like the cut of your jib,' said Roger, fully understanding what Mac was implying, 'don't worry, I'll have these two lovebirds back before she's missed, in no time at all. I'll radio ahead when I get airborne and lay on all the care that Alison requires.'

He and Mac helped the Earl to his feet, and Mac watched, as two old friends, one with a precious bundle, made for the wings. He raised his walkie talkie and pressed the speak button.

'Sir Donald, come in please.'

'Go ahead, Mac.'

'We've got her, Sir, unconscious but alive ...'

Mac was nearly deafened by the spontaneous shouts of glee from the rest of the team over the airwaves, Jan included.

'Mac, I cannot describe how I feel at this very moment, however can I thank you?'

'Don't thank me, Sir, Jan pinpointed her.'

'No I didn't, the computer did,' Jan interrupted, 'and don't forget, buggerlugs is still on the loose.'

'Yes I know, Jan, but he's secondary now that Lady Alison is safe. Now we can concentrate one hundred per cent on netting him without any fear of reprisals against her,' said Mac.

'Mac,' Jan persisted, 'don't underestimate him. As soon as he knows that Alison is free, he'll go spare. You'll have punctured his ego and he'll probably try again. In short, my love, he won't give in. You've got to finger his collar, and I mean pretty damned quick.'

CHAPTER THIRTY-SIX
GRANT SPOTS THE 'PHONE CON'

Andrew Grant was suspicious. Something was not quite right. The phone call to Zurich seemed somehow, for want of a better word, unreal. That Lars Svenson fellow had seemed odd, to say the least. Admittedly, on the surface he seemed real enough, he knew the phone number of the Manse, but that meant nothing at all, anyone could find that out.

Grant paced up and down, trying to pinpoint what it was that told him something was amiss. Finally, he shook his head and picked up the phone. He dialled Robin's number and was informed by the butler, Jenkins, that His Lordship was not available and no, His Lordship had left no messages. No, he did not know where His Lordship was or when he would be back.

Grant slowly replaced the handset, totally confused. This didn't sit right at all somehow. Of course Robin would be away from Hamilcourt, trying his hardest to transfer funds overseas, but surely he would leave some way to be contacted in an emergency ... unless he knew something that he shouldn't know ... couldn't know ... could he?'

Grant sat down slowly in his chair, his brow furrowed in deep thought. He tried to think where he had gone wrong. Admittedly this policeman was a little sharper than he had first thought but hadn't he, Grant, managed to stay at least one jump ahead all the way through? So, the inspector had forced his hand a bit, but that didn't explain why the Earl had made himself unavailable, unless of course he knew where Alison was. But then if he did, The Old Manse would be swarming with blue uniforms by now and he would be under arrest and so that was out of the que—

Grant suddenly sat bolt upright. The thing that had been bugging him suddenly hit him right between the eyes. How could he have been so stupid, so blind? It was so obvious that he had almost missed it. His telephone call to Switzerland hadn't been to Switzerland at all. It had all been faked.

Grant couldn't help but congratulate himself on his own cleverness. Oh yes, it had been cleverly done, but people really would have to get up very early in the morning to catch Robert Andrew Penton-Fairfax, alias Andrew Grant, actor extraordinaire, master of disguise. Not many people knew that a telephone call from one country to another, using a satellite, is totally different from a local call. A satellite call is weak when first received, so it has to be boosted before it is passed on to the recipient. Also, a fair amount of static has to be removed and this necessitated a fairly complex and expensive machine to do the job properly, to ensure that the recipient received a clear and lucid message ... and that meant a delay of three quarters of a second per caller, one and a half seconds in all.

There had been no such delay.

Grant smiled to himself, congratulating himself on his own brilliance because he had spotted something that a man of lesser intellect would have missed.

Something else was also bothering him. There was usually a policeman watching the house from some vantage point, but Grant had failed to spot one anywhere. He climbed the stairs to the top floor and looked out of the window overlooking the park. He looked long and hard for a few minutes before making his way to the front of the house. Approaching the front window with caution, not getting too close, he searched as far up and down the street as possible. Nothing out of the ordinary.

The telephone van across the street caught his eye, it had been there for quite a while. Curiosity made him left his eyes upwards to the telephone wires and suddenly he stiffened.

The telephone wires ran parallel with the houses and only two in the whole row boasted telephones, but not in the house opposite, or the ones either side of it.

Grant frowned and stared hard at the offending van, then a movement in an upstairs window caught his eye. He stared hard but could hardly make out what it was. He crossed quickly to an old-fashioned wardrobe and removed a pair of binoculars that were hanging on brass hook. He went back to the window and focused them quickly. Gradually, the faces of two old people came into view. They were looking at him, or rather, in his direction. Grant frowned and lowered the binoculars to the ground floor window until another face came into view, a face that seemed very familiar to him. He studied it for a few moments until recognition dawned. It was that copper, the one blessed with the Shanghai squitters, to coin an old acting phrase.

It was DC Finch, and he was talking animatedly into a king-size walkie talkie.

Grant quickly read the situation for what it was, and knew that he had been spotted. He was puzzled. Too many coincidences were manifesting themselves for his liking and the damnable inspector was always just one step behind, no matter what he did, or where he went. But how?

Grant racked his brain and cast his mind back, step by step. The further he went back, the more he frowned. He paced up and down, trying to think clearly, then paused as a germ of an idea came to him. Suddenly the truth hit him, right between the eyes.

'Of course, you bloody idiot,' he admonished himself, 'he didn't want the loo, he wanted ...'

He practically rang to the telephone, quickly unscrewing both the earpiece and mouthpiece until he found the tiny, solitary bug placed there by Jimmy. Grant stared at it with mixed feelings, he head nodding slowly as the little pieces of the jigsaw, came together.

'So that's how you kept up with me, Inspector,' Grant murmured. 'Very very good, but no more ... no more. Now you work in the dark.'

Grant thought for a moment then he smiled to himself. 'You, my little bug,' he thought silently, 'are going to pave the way for my escape completely unobserved by that shower across the way. So firstly, my tiny little friend, I will replace you oh so ver-ry ver-ry gently.'

With the bug safely stowed once more inside the mouthpiece and the handset lying in its cradle, Grant paced up and down, deep in thought. He snapped his fingers and walked over to an old-fashioned chest of drawers. Opening the top one, he took out an ancient battery driven tape recorder and a small microphone. He plugged in the microphone as he walked back to his chair.

Five minutes later, he was satisfied with the result. He stood up and walked over to the telephone, lifted the handset and placed it on the table, then placed the tape recorder on the table by the handset. Satisfied with the arrangement, he dialled a number, bending down to listen for a reply. There was a rapid response and a voice answered. As it did so, Grant switched on the tape recorder and stepped back smiling. Swiftly he crossed to the window and focused the binoculars onto Jimmy and, sure enough, his hunch proved right. In one hand, Jimmy held the walkie talkie and in the other, a smaller machine that could only be the recorder of the phone bug. Jimmy was talking nineteen to the dozen into the walkie talkie, no doubt reporting that Grant was dialling.

A few minutes later, Grant was sitting in his car, having swapped his Olive Jones disguise for a more fetching one of a blonde model, and departed from The Old Manse by the back door and through the park. Jimmy was too busy listening in amazement to the messages going out on Grant's phone and being picked up on his gadget.

Andrew had parked the Ashdown Marsden on the other side of the park in a pub car park, alongside the regulars who, with the landlord's kind permission, parked off the road during non opening hours. He had also changed the number plates and added a couple of 'go faster' stripes to alter the roadster's appearance.

Grant sat very still in the car and sized up the situation. It was perfectly obvious to him now that the opposition was determined that he was not going to be blessed with two million pounds. They had even engineered a fake phone call to allay his suspicions. Whoever was responsible for that little ruse was indeed a clever boy and clever little boys usually went to the top of the class. One thing was certain, whoever the brainy chap was, he would never be stuck in a rut for ideas. His intellect was certainly on a par with Grant's own. That bloody copper!

A little warning bell jangled inside Grant's head. If this clever chap had sussed out Alison's hiding place once, he could most certainly do it again and that was not on. He must get to Alison before they did.

The more Grant thought about the situation, the darker his mood became. Black hate began to dominate him as he thought of how he had been thwarted at every turn by that damned police inspector.

He looked at his watch impatiently; the tape recording he had made should have brought quicker results than this. Suddenly, he cocked an ear and smiled as he picked up the sound of a siren.

Just one at first, then two, then three until they merged with one another and it was impossible to distinguish one for the other.

Grant smiled to himself as he imagined police cars chasing all over the place. Handy things, these bomb hoaxes, especially if there were half a dozen of them.

Grant grinned insanely as he started the engine. He selected first gear, let in the clutch and rapidly headed for Norwich and the Alahambra Royal, keeping a weather eye open for police cars. He passed two or three unmarked cars but the crews, unaware of Grant's special skills, were not looking for an Ashdown Marsden driven by a stunning blonde.

Overhead, a helicopter flew in the same direction and Grant glanced at it as it rapidly drew ahead. He ignored it at first until the warning bell jangled yet again. His head jerked upwards again ... could it be? Robin Devereaux had used a chopper to fly from Scotland and furthermore, he was unavailable right now. Strange that the helicopter was heading in the general direction of Norwich.

As realisation began to dawn and things began to slip into place, suddenly Grant knew for certain where the helicopter was heading. It was heading for Norwich and the Alhambra Royal.

He glanced at the helicopter which by now was just a speck in the sky. There was hatred in his eyes as he realised where Robin was ... he was in that accursed helicopter and what was more, he was going to rescue Alison.

Black rage almost consumed Grant and he all but lost control of the car. He quickly recovered and stabbed his foot hard on the throttle: he had to get to the theatre before Robin did.

Grant now accepted that, thanks to the bloody inspector, he would remain relatively poor. There was no two million pounds in his bank account, there never would be and that fact made the bloody copper the second person on the list to die.

Alison was the first.

Grant came down to earth rapidly as he realised that the helicopter would get to the theatre long before he could by road. He cursed violently and pushed the throttle pedal to the floor. The great-hearted engine responded, and the gleaming car leaped forward, the speedometer registering over a hundred miles per hour.

After a long, hair-raising drive, Grant reached the edge of the city. He checked the dashboard clock, it said twelve noon. He cursed as he drove towards the centre of Norwich and the Alhambra theatre. Maybe, just maybe, there was something he could do. Hopefully, Robin and company were just too late to save Alison, in which case they would know that they were dealing with a man who kept his word.

At eight minutes past twelve, Grant parked his car directly outside the theatre, ready if need be for a quick getaway. He cut the ignition and, after rapidly glancing all around for any sign of the police, he stepped out on to the pavement.

A whining sound came to his ears from the direction of the Alhambra car park entrance. Puzzled, he turned his head to listen. A motor coughed into life, a fairly large familiar motor: a helicopter motor. Grant threw caution to the winds and ran towards the car park entrance, hitching high the hem of his dress. The motor was now emitting a healthy roar as Grant hared down the driveway and he knew that the helicopter was about to take to the air. He ran faster, not quite knowing what he would see.

He skidded to a halt at the end of the driveway, half blinded by the dust disturbed by the rotors. He rubbed his eyes to clear them and squinted in the direction of the helicopter. Robin was sitting down, holding Alison like a baby. He was just reaching for the door to shut it when he spotted Grant, who had by now discarded his blonde wig. They spotted each other at the same time.

Baleful glare met baleful glare. Malevolence matched malevolence. Two hearts, each filled with murder, each wishing only to harm the other.

Slowly, Robin eased his precious burden onto a seat. Police inspector or no police inspector, this beast of a man had hurt Alison, tried to take her beautiful life and he, her husband, was about to administer justice. He would strangle this poor excuse for a man with his bare hands. Revenge was indeed right.

Grant watched Robin lay down his burden and he knew that he was coming to him. Good, he would kill him first, and then his precious Alison, and just for good measure, he would kill the pilot.

Roger Cuncliffe had turned to inform Robin that he was ready to take off. He watched as Robin placed Alison gently on the seat.

It was then that he saw Grant slowly advancing towards them and read the situation exactly right. He also saw that the passenger door was wide open. Quickly, he reached above his head, grabbing at a steel cable bound in leather at the centre. He pulled down hard. The cable was attached to a special cantilever arrangement, designed to enable the pilot to shut the door without having to leave his seat, and as Roger pulled downwards, the door slammed shut before Robin could do anything to stop it. Robin turned to protest, but Roger was already twisting hard on the throttle, watching the revolutions climb. Even as Robin tried to open the door, Roger flung the helicopter into the air, gaining height rapidly.

Robin looked out of the window for some minutes before finally turning to look at Roger. There were tears in his eyes as he mouthed the words 'thank you'. Roger merely nodded, then he pointed to the walkie talkie and indicated the theatre below. Robin understood and picked up the walkie talkie. He switched to 'on'. 'Inspector Macdonald?'

'Sir?'

'Our man is in the car park, please apprehend him as quickly as you can.'

Mac spluttered. 'He's what? I'm on my way, Sir.' The set went dead. A few minutes later, it crackled back into life.

'Macdonald calling helicopter.'

'He's gone, hasn't he, Inspector?'

'How did you know Sir?' Mac asked quietly.

'Because it's Alison he wants, Alison and myself, I saw it in his eyes before we took off.' Robin's voice was flat, unemotional.

Mac remained silent for a few seconds. 'You were that close to each other, Sir?'

It was Robin's turn to remain silent for a few seconds before he answered. 'Close, but not close enough, Inspector. I wanted to kill that scum, but I was prevented from doing so.'

'Prevented, Sir ... I see.'

'Do you, Inspector?'

Mac could only guess at what drama had been enacted in the theatre car park and though it best to let sleeping dogs lie. He pursued the subject no further. 'Sir, may I suggest you take your good lady home before she's missed. Once she's home, that will scotch any rumours that Grant may spread about.'

'Yes, yes Inspector, my heartfelt thanks to you and your dedicated team of stalwarts, what would I have done without you?'

Embarrassed, Mac replied. 'Come now, Sir, if we weren't available, someone else would have been.'

'Not with the same results,' Robin said quietly. 'We thank you, Alison and I, from the bottom of our hearts. I will heed your advice, Mr Macdonald, and I'll never forget you, what you did for us. I'll never be able to repay you, over and out.' The set went dead.

Mac was silent for some minutes, dwelling on Robin's last words. At last he spoke to his sergeant. 'That's that then, Smithy, for the time being.'

'For the time being, how do you mean, Guv?'

Mac sighed, 'I've got a feeling that this bloke is going to be very hard to catch, don't ask me why, I just know, I can feel it.'

'Come on, Guv, we could have picked him up at least twice,' said Smithy.

'Oh yes, that's true, but Alison was around then, so he couldn't go too far away, could he? Besides, his disguises are so good, he can practically metamorphose.'

'Meta who?'

'Never mind, Smithy,' Mac grinned and switched on his walkie talkie.

'Everybody, all back to Lincoln Central and we'll sort something out from there.

Hours later, back at Lincoln Central, Mac and his colleagues were gathered in a smoke-filled room, elated at the timely rescue of Alison. Disappointed at losing Grant.

Mac was explaining to Roy: 'It was a close run thing, especially when we couldn't find any booby traps on her body, or anywhere, and time was nearly up.'

'I'll bet.'

'And when that booby trapped sandbag fell, I didn't know whether to have a shit, shave, shampoo or a haircut. Honestly, it was all over in seconds, well, about two I'd say. And when that bloody trap door fell, I didn't know what to expect so you can imagine my feelings when I saw the Earl straddling the hole. He was holding Alison in the air just with the strength of his arms alone.'

'How heavy is she, Mac?'

'Oh, eight, eight and a half stone, I reckon, but the Earl is a powerfully built bloke remember, and with a love as powerful as his, he would have found the strength even if he'd been dying and only had one arm,' said Mac with great conviction.

'Well, she's safe now,' said Roy, 'and woe betide anyone who tries to get near her, let alone kidnap her.'

'Amen to that,' Mac agreed.

'So what happens now, Mac, about this Grant chap or rather, Penton-Fairfax?'

'Well, now that the unofficial bit's over, we can go nationwide after him because of the telephone box incident. We'll probably leave that to Mike Graham in Norwich.'

Roy sighed. 'Pity really, me knowing what I know about this bloke, I'd love to take to take it on but I'm in the wrong manor.' He sighed again and shrugged his shoulders regretfully.

'And pigs might fly, old son. Who are you trying to kid? I can't see an invisible boundary stopping you from putting you oar in,' said Mac with a cheerful grin.

Roy grinned back and said nothing and Mac did not pursue the point. He switched his attention to Bob Saunders instead. 'What happened at the exchange after we started the emergency lighting, Bob, you know, when you said something was happening?'

'Oh that, believe it or not, Guv, that was a genuine caller to the same bank. You should have seen the rigmarole that we went through to reconnect him to Switzerland,' Bob grinned.

'That was a cute move of Grant's, setting up those bomb hoaxes, I mean,' said Jimmy. 'The tape was still running when we got there.'

'It cleared the way for him though, didn't it?' said Smithy. 'A right cunning bleeder, that one.'

'And still is, Smithy,' Mac agreed, 'all the more reason to catch him before he can do any more damage.'

'Erm, Guv?' said Jimmy. 'Can I, er, have a word with you in, er, private, it won't take a sec.'

Mac smiled to himself; he knew what the request would be before Jimmy asked it. 'Certainly Jimmy,' he said with a straight face, 'let's go in here.' He indicated a door and motioned Jimmy through it.

'Guv?' Jimmy was clearly embarrassed.

'Yes, Jimmy, you may stay a couple of days,' Mac answered the unasked question, smiling broadly.

Jimmy's mouth dropped open. 'How did you know that I was going to ask you that, Guv?'

'That's a stupid question, old son, you look positively lost without Joan,' Mac laughed. 'But seriously Jimmy, you've been hurt once, you know.'

'So has Joan, Guv, but honestly, my life has suddenly ... suddenly, Jimmy struggled for the right words.

'She's like the sun coming up in midwinter, isn't she?'

'That's it exactly, Guv, we feel as if we've known each other all our lives.'

'And you want to spend a couple of days "sick leave" up here, is that it?'

'That's it, Guv, just to sort ourselves out, like. It's a hell of a long way to one another's houses, if you know what I mean.'

Mac folded is arms and furrowed his brow. 'I'd hate to lose you old son, but ...'

'Oh don't worry, Guv, she wants to move down to our end. You erm, don't think she can get a job on the police switchboard or something do you,- Guv?' Jimmy asked hopefully.

'Jimmy, if she can go out of her way to help the police, I'm darned sure we can do something for her, OK, so go and have your couple of days and leave the rest to me.'

CHAPTER THIRTY-SEVEN
LETTER NUMBER THREE

Many weeks went by, with no sign of Grant anywhere. He had vanished without a trace. Slender leads petered out and his track grew cold. Meanwhile, other things had happened, and all for the better. Well, almost all.

While she was tending her sick mother, Tommy Smith's wife had found out that she was pregnant. Smithy was overjoyed and couldn't get home quick enough at the end of each shift. His mother-in-law came to stay with them eventually, an arrangement that suited Smithy right down to the ground because he and she got on famously.

Jimmy and Joan married quickly and in due course settled down in a police house. Joan was inducted as a civilian telephone operator for the police force, and was liked by all who came into contact with her.

The crippled boy, Benjy Cartwright, came to the attention of the Earl and Countess of Westminster, and through them, Roger Cuncliffe. Roger took to Benjy on sight and rapidly took him under his wing. Visits to spine specialists proved that Benjy's condition could be improved dramatically, but it would take about three years of painful surgery. Benjy himself was over the moon because he spent almost as much time in the air as he did on the ground.

Robin and Alison were practically inseparable after their ordeal. Robin promised to swap his hunting gun for a camera and actually began to really notice the wildlife and beautiful countryside all around him, much to his wife's gratification.

Because of the secrecy of Operation Grouse, there were no knighthoods, no medals, no mention anywhere in the national press, no garden party at Buckingham Palace. The only mention the team got, including Mac, was in the Police Gazette when DCs Finch, Saunders and Sanderson were promoted to Detective Sergeants. Detective Sergeant Smith, Thomas was promoted to Detective Inspector, and Detective Inspector Macdonald, John, was promoted to Chief Inspector. All for services above and beyond the call of duty.

As the weeks went by, everything settled back to a more or less normal routine. There was still no trace, no sign, not the slightest inkling of Robert Andrew Penton-Fairfax, alias Andrew Grant, actor extraordinaire, master of disguise, abductor of the aristocracy, madman, genius *manqué*.

No trace, that is, until one fine morning ...

The Prime Minister, Henry Beddows, was sitting at his desk, attending to the affairs of State as he had been doing for the last hundred years or so. He finished reading the last document of the morning with a sigh of relief, and signed it with a flourish, then sat back in his comfortable chair and pulled out his watch. He leaned forward and pressed the intercom button. 'John?'

'Prime Minister?'

'Bring the tea tray and my mail please.'

The door opened within a minute and John Deeman entered, bearing a big silver tray, complete with teapot, two cups with saucers, milk jug and sugar bowl. Under his arm he carried a bundle of mail wrapped in elastic bands, which he put into the 'in' tray.

'Anything special this morning, John?'

'Yes, I believe so, Henry,' John replied quietly, reaching into his coat pocket.

Something in the tone of John's voice made him pause in the act of filling his pipe. He looked at the letter John Deeman was holding, and a feeling of dread came over him.

'Oh my God,' he whispered, 'not another one of those ...?'

John did not answer, he just held out the letter until the PM plucked up enough courage to take it, which he did with trembling hands. Slowly he brought it into focus, reading the address very steadily:

TO THE PRIME MINISTER
NUMBER TEN DOWNING STREET

Deliberately and with great precision, Henry Beddows slit open the envelope and extracted, with the same slow deliberation, a folded sheet of paper. He opened it and read the contents right to the end, closing his eyes after he had done so. Slowly, he lowered the letter until his hands were resting on the desk. He was visibly trembling.

John Deeman spoke quietly, gently. 'Henry?'

The PM slowly opened his eyes and looked at his friend of many years standing. Finally, he spoke.

'It's him again, John.'

John swallowed hard. 'What does he want this time?'

The PM rose to his feet, turned, and leaving the letter on his desk, walked slowly to the window.

'I just do not believe this man, John, I cannot believe the audacity of this - this maniac.' He gestured to the letter on the desk, unable to bring himself to speak further.

John Deeman picked up the letter with trembling hands and read it through, shock and horror registering on his face with every word. They seemed to leap out from the paper, as the implication of what he was reading struck home.

'My God,' he breathed, 'my God, he's really set his sights high this time. He's going right to the top.'

He let his eyes drop down to the letter again. Nine words leaped out of the page and seemed to burn into his eyes and through to his brain.

'*I fully intend to abduct Her Majesty the Queen.*'